Blood Infernal

Blood Infernal

The Order of the Sanguines Series

James Rollins
and Rebecca Cantrell

An Imprint of HarperCollinsPublishers

BLOOD INFERNAL. Copyright © 2015 by James Czajkowski and Rebecca Cantrell. All rights reserved. Printed in the United States of America. No part of this book may be used or reproduced in any manner whatsoever without written permission except in the case of brief quotations embodied in critical articles and reviews. For information address HarperCollins Publishers, 195 Broadway, New York, NY 10007.

HarperCollins books may be purchased for educational, business, or sales promotional use. For information, please e-mail the Special Markets Department at SPsales@harpercollins.com.

FIRST HARPERLUXE EDITION

HarperLuxe™ is a trademark of HarperCollins Publishers

Library of Congress Cataloging-in-Publication Data is available upon request.

ISBN: 978-0-06-239892-5

15 ID/RRD 10 9 8 7 6 5 4 3 2 1

James

To Rebecca, for joining me on this journey

Rebecca

To my husband and son

"How are thou fallen from heaven, O Lucifer, son of the morning! how are thou cut down to the ground, which didst weaken the nations!"

—Isaiah 14:12

Summer, 1606
Prague, Bohemia

At last, it is almost done . . .

Inside his hidden lab, the English alchemist known as John Dee stood before a giant bell made of flawless glass. It rose tall enough for a man to stand upright within its inner chamber. The wondrous work had been fashioned by an esteemed glassmaker on the far-away island of Murano, near Venice. It had taken a team of artisans over a year, using massive bellows, and a technique known only to a handful of masters, to spin and blow a colossal pearl of molten glass into this sculpture of perfection. Afterward, it had taken five additional months to transport the precious bell from its island birthplace to the cold court of Holy Emperor Rudolf II in the far north. Upon its arrival, the emperor had ordered a secret alchemist's laboratory to be built around it, surrounded by additional workshops that extended far beneath the streets of Prague.

That had been ten long years ago . . .

The bell now stood atop a round iron pedestal in the corner of the main laboratory. The pedestal's edges had long since gone red with rust. Near the bottom half of the bell stood a round door, also of glass, fastened on the outside with strong bars and sealed so that air could neither enter nor escape.

John Dee shuddered where he stood. Although he was relieved by the coming completion of his task, he dreaded it, too. He had grown to hate the infernal device, knowing the horrific purpose behind its forging. Of late, he avoided the bell as much as he could. For days he would putter around in his lab, his long tunic stained with chemicals, his white beard nearly dipping into his flasks, his rheumy eyes averted from the bell's dusty glass surface.

But now my mission is nearly complete.

Turning, he stepped to the fireplace and reached to its mantel. With gnarled fingers, he worked the elaborate catches to open a small chamber carved into the marble. Only he and the emperor knew of the tiny chamber's existence.

As he reached inside, a frantic knocking arose behind him. He turned back to the bell, to the creature that had been imprisoned inside it. The beast had been captured by men loyal to the emperor, dragged here only hours ago.

I must work quickly.

The ungodly beast beat against the inside of the bell, as if it sensed what was to come. Even with its preternatural strength, it could not break free. Older and far stronger creatures had tried and failed.

Over the past years, John had caged many such beasts inside that glass cell.

So many . . .

Though he knew he was safe, his feeble heart still raced, the animal part of him sensing the danger in a way that his logical mind could not gainsay.

He let out a shaky breath, reached into the secret chamber of the mantel, and drew out an object wrapped in oilcloth. The prize was tied with a scarlet cord and encased inside a wax shell. Careful not to crack the waxy covering, John carried the bundle to the draped window, clutching it close against his chest. Even through the cloth and wax, a dreadful coldness emanated from the object and numbed his fingers and ribs.

He opened the thick curtains a crack, allowing in a shaft of morning sunlight. With trembling hands, he placed the package in the pool of light that fell atop his stone desk and positioned himself on the other side of the bundle so that not the smallest shadow fell upon the object's surface. He drew a sharp flensing knife from his belt and cut through the wax and the scarlet cord. With great care, he parted the oilcloth as flakes of white tallow broke off and fell to his desk.

Early-morning Czech sunlight shone on what lay revealed inside the cocoon of wax and cloth: a beautiful gemstone, as large as his palm, glowing an emerald green.

But this was no *emerald*.

"A diamond," he whispered to the silent room.

The chamber had gone quiet again as the creature inside the bell quailed away from what shone upon his desk. The beast's eyes darted around as light reflected from the gem and formed shimmering emerald veins across the plaster walls.

John ignored the prisoner's fear and instead stared into the heart of the diamond at an inky darkness roiling inside. It flowed like a mix of smoke and oil, a living thing, as trapped inside the diamond as surely as the creature was inside the bell.

Thank God for that.

He touched the icy gem with one finger. According to legend, the stone had been quarried from a mine deep in the Far East. Like all great stones, this one was said to carry a curse. Men had killed to possess it, dying soon after it came into their hands. Smaller diamonds mined from that same vein graced the crowns of faraway rulers, but this one had not been put to such vain use.

Carefully, he lifted the green diamond. Decades had passed since he'd had it hollowed out. Two jewelers had lost their eyesight using tiny diamond-tipped drills to create the empty space inside the stone's luxuriant green heart. A sliver of bone so thin it was almost translucent stoppered the small opening—a bone fetched from a Jerusalem tomb over a thousand years before—the last intact piece of Jesus Christ.

Or so it was claimed.

John coughed. The metallic taste of blood filled his mouth, and he spat into a wooden bucket he kept near his desk. The disease that ate him from within left him little peace these days. He struggled for breath, wondering if this time the breath would fail to come. His lungs wheezed in his chest like a broken bellows.

A muffled knock against the door startled him, and the stone slipped between his fingers and fell to the wooden floor. He lunged toward the precious green object with a cry.

The stone landed on the floor, but it did not break.

Pain lanced from John's heart into his left arm. He fell against the desk's stout leg. A beaker of yellow liquid crashed to the floor and spread across the boards. Smoke rose from the edge of a bearskin rug laid out on the floor.

"Master Dee!" A young voice sounded from the other side of the door. "Are you hurt?"

The lock clicked, and the door swung open.

"Stay—" John gasped with effort. "—away, Vaclav."

But the young man had already rushed inside, coming to his master's aid. He lifted John from the floor. "Are you ill?"

John's disease was beyond the skill of even the most powerful alchemists in Emperor Rudolf's court to heal. He struggled for breath, letting the boy hold him upright until at last his coughing quieted. But the sharp pain in his chest did not lessen as it usually did.

The young apprentice touched John's sweaty brow with gentle fingers. "You have not slept this last night. Your bed was untouched when I arrived this morning. I came up to check—" Vaclav's voice broke off as he glanced toward the glass bell—and discovered the creature imprisoned inside. It was a sight never intended for his young, innocent eyes.

A gasp escaped Vaclav's lips, a mix of surprise and horror.

She stared in turn back toward the boy, a hunger in her gaze as she placed a palm against the glass. A single fingernail scratched at the surface. She had not fed for days.

Vaclav's gaze took in the woman's naked body. Wavy blond hair fell past her round shoulders, tumbled across bare breasts. She could almost be considered beautiful. But in the faint light from the curtains, the thick glass gave her snow-white skin a green cast, as if she had already begun to decay.

Vaclav turned to John for some explanation. "Master?"

His young apprentice had come into his service as a clever little boy of eight. John had watched him grow into a young man with a bright future ahead of him, skilled at mixing potions and distilling oils.

John loved him like one of his own sons.

Still, he did not hesitate as he lifted the sharp flensing knife and slashed the boy across his throat.

Vaclav grabbed at his wound, his eyes pinned to John's by disbelief and betrayal. Blood flowed between his fingers and spattered onto the floor. He sank to his knees, both hands seeking to catch his life's blood.

The creature in the bell hurled her body against the sides with such force that the heavy iron pedestal rocked.

Do you smell the blood? Is that what excites you so?

John bent to gather up the fallen green stone. He held it up to the sunlight to check the seal. Darkness rolled inside, as if seeking a crack, but there was no exit. He made the sign of the cross and whispered a prayer of thanks. The diamond remained intact.

John placed the stone back in the sunlight and knelt next to Vaclav. He stroked curly hair back from the young man's face.

Vaclav's pale lips moved, and his throat gurgled.

"Forgive me," John whispered.

The young man's lips formed a single word.

Why?

John could never explain it to the boy, never atone for his murder. He cupped his apprentice's cheek. "I would that you had not seen this. That you had lived a long life of study. But that was not God's will."

Vaclav's bloodstained fingers fell from his throat. His brown eyes turned glassy with death. With two fingers, John closed the boy's warm eyelids.

John bowed his head and muttered a quick prayer for Vaclav's soul. He had been an innocent, and he rested in a better place now. Still, it was a tragic waste.

The thing in the glass bell, the monster that had once been human, met his eyes. Her gaze flickered to Vaclav's body, then back to John's face. She must have read the anguish there because, for the first time since she had been delivered to him, she smiled, baring long white fangs in clear delight at his misfortune.

John struggled to his feet. The pain in his heart had not lessened. He must finish his task quickly.

He stumbled across the room, closed the door that Vaclav had left open, and locked it. The only other key to this room rested on the floor in a pool of Vaclav's cooling blood. John would not be disturbed again.

He returned to his duty, running a finger along the glass pipe that ran from the bell toward his desk. He examined its length for any new flaws or chinks, taking his time.

I am too close for any mistakes.

At its end, the pipe narrowed to a tiny opening, barely larger than a sewing needle, the work of a craftsman at the height of his powers. John drew the thick curtains apart until a ray of morning sunlight fell on the small end of the glass pipe.

The pain grew in his chest, locking his left arm to his side. He needed his strength now, but it was rapidly fading.

With his shaking right hand, he picked up the stone. It glittered in the sunlight, beautiful and deadly. He clamped his lips against the dizziness and used a tiny set of silver tongs to pull the bone sliver from one end of the stone.

His knees shook, but he gritted his teeth. Now that the sliver had been removed, he must keep the stone bathed in sunlight. Even a momentary shadow would allow the smoky darkness inside to escape into the larger world.

That must not happen . . . at least, not yet.

The blackness flattened and ran up the sides of its small prison, reaching for the tiny opening, but it stopped, plainly fearful of venturing into the light. The evil inside must somehow sense that unfiltered sunlight held the power to destroy it. Its only refuge remained inside the diamond's verdant heart.

Slowly, and with great care, John settled the small hole carved out of the diamond over the open end of the glass pipe. Sunlight covered them both.

He retrieved a flickering candle that rested on the stained desk and raised it above the diamond, letting wax drip over the gem and glass pipe, ensuring an airtight seal between them. Only then did he close the curtain and allow darkness to fall over the green gem.

Candlelight illuminated the dark mass still moving inside the heart of the diamond. It swirled around, creeping up the sides to the opening. He held his breath, watching it flow along the edge. It seemed to probe his seal, and only after discovering no opening into the laboratory did the darkness flow up along the glass pipe. It followed the pipe's length and continued its inexorable course to where the pipe ended—at the glass bell and the woman inside.

John shook his grizzled head. Though she had once been human, she was no longer a *woman*. He must not allow himself to view her as such. She had quieted and stood still in the center of the bell. Her luminous blue eyes studied him.

Her skin glowed white as alabaster, her hair like spun gold; both had a watery green cast through the thick glass. Even so, she was the most beautiful creature he had ever seen. She placed one palm against the glass. Candlelight flickered across lovely long fingers.

He crossed the room and placed his palm over hers. The glass was cold against his skin. Even without the pain and encroaching weakness, he had always known that she would be his last. She was the six hundred sixty-sixth creature to stand in that coffin. Her death would complete his task.

Her lips formed a single word, the same as Vaclav. *Why?*

He could no more explain it to her than he could to his dead apprentice.

Her eyes went to the blackness that slid ever closer to her prison.

Like the others, she lifted her hand up toward the foul mist as it swept into her glass cell. Her lips moved silently, her face rapturous.

In the early years he had always felt shame at watching this private dark communion, but those feelings had long since left him. He leaned against the glass, trying to get as close as he could. Even the pain in his chest vanished as he watched.

Inside the bell, the black smoke coalesced along the top of the inner cell, forming a mist of tiny droplets that rained down upon the cell's lone occupant. The moisture flowed along her white fingers and her upstretched arms. She threw her head back and screamed. He did not need to hear her cry to recognize her posture of ecstasy. She rose up on her toes, breasts thrust out, quivering as the droplets caressed her body, touching every part of her.

She shuddered one final time, and then collapsed against the side of the bell, her body slumping to the bottom, now lifeless.

The mist hovered over her form, waiting.

It is done.

John pushed away from the bell. He stepped around Vaclav's corpse and hurried to the window. He yanked the curtains fully open, wide enough to allow the morning sunlight to kiss the side of the bell. The girl's cursed corpse burst into flame inside, adding her foul smoke to the waiting haze.

The black mist—now stoked incrementally stronger by the girl's essence—fled from the sunlight, retreating toward the only dark path left open to it: the glass pipe leading back to the diamond. Using a handheld silver mirror, he reflected sunlight along the pipe, chasing and herding the foul blackness back into the emerald heart of the gemstone, to its only place of refuge in this sunlit world.

Once it was again fully entrapped, John carefully broke the wax seal, freeing the diamond from the pipe. He kept the tiny opening always in the light as he carried it to a pentagram he had drawn on the floor long ago. He set the stone in the middle, still in the sunlight.

So close now . . .

Carefully, John drew a circle of salt around the pentagram. As he did so, he chanted prayers. His life was nearly spent, but at last, he would achieve his life's dream.

To open a portal to the angelic world.

More than six hundred times, he had drawn this same circle, more than six hundred times he had chanted the same prayers. But in his heart, he knew this time would be different. He recalled the verse from Revelation: *Here is wisdom. Let him that hath understanding count the number of the beast: for it is the number of a man; and his number is six hundred three score and six.*

"Six hundred and sixty-six," he repeated.

That was the number of creatures he had imprisoned in the bell, the number of smoky essences he had collected upon their flaming deaths into this one diamond. It had taken a decade to find so many, to imprison them, and to gather together the evil essence that animated these damned creatures. Now those same energies would open the portal to the angelic world.

He covered his face with his hands, trembling bodily. He had so many questions for the angels. Not since the times chronicled by the Book of Enoch had angels come to man without the command of God. Not since then had men benefited from their wisdom.

But I will bring their light to earth and share it with all of mankind.

He moved to the fireplace and lit a long taper. He carried it around the circle, igniting five candles placed at the corners of the pentagram. The yellow flames looked weak and insubstantial in the sunlight, guttering in the draft from the window.

At last, he closed the curtains, and darkness cloaked the room.

He hurried back and knelt at the edge of the circle.

From the gemstone, inky smoke flowed from the tiny opening, moving tentatively, perhaps sensing the larger world still glowed with the new day. Then it seemed to grow bolder, rushing toward John, as if to claim him, to make him pay for its long imprisonment. But the circle of salt held it at bay.

Ignoring the threat, John's voice hissed against the crackling fire as he recited words in the Enochian language, a language long thought lost to mankind. "I command thee, Master of Darkness, to show me the light that is the opposite of your shadows."

Within the circle, the black cloud quivered once, twice, expanding and contracting like a living heart. With each beat, it grew larger than before.

John clasped his hands in front of him. "Protect me, oh Lord, as I look upon the glory thou hast wrought."

The darkness coalesced into an oval large enough for a man to step through.

Whispered words brushed John's ear.

"COME TO ME . . ."

The voice rose from out of the portal.

"SERVE ME . . ."

John picked up an unlit candle from beside his knee and lit it from one on the corner of the pentagram. He held the flame aloft, calling again upon the protection of God.

A new noise reached him as if something shifted on the far side of the portal, accompanied by a heavy *chinking* sound, the clang of metal on metal.

Words returned, worming into his mind. "OF ALL MORTALS, I HAVE FOUND THOU ALONE WORTHY."

John rose and took a step toward the circle, but his foot brushed Vaclav's outstretched hand. He stopped, suddenly sensing how unworthy he was to look upon such glory.

I have killed an innocent.

His silent confession was heard.

"GREATNESS HAS ITS PRICE," he was assured. "FEW ARE PREPARED TO PAY IT. THOU ART UNLIKE THE OTHERS, JOHN DEE."

He trembled at these new words, especially the last two.

My name is known, spoken by an angel.

He teetered between pride and fear, the room spinning drunkenly. The candle fell from his fingers. Still lit, it rolled into the circle, then through the portal to cast its light on what lay hidden on the other side.

He gaped at a figure of incredible majesty seated atop a shining ebony throne. Candlelight glinted off eyes of black oil in a face of stern beauty, each plane seemingly sculpted from onyx. Atop that beautiful countenance rested a broken crown of silver, its surface tarnished black, jagged edges looking like horns. From beyond wide shoulders rose mighty wings, whose feathers were as dark and glossy as a raven's. They curved high, sheltering the naked form within their embrace.

The figure shifted forward, disturbing the tarnished silver chains that encased his flawless form, securing him to his throne.

John knew upon whom he stared.

"Thou art no angel," he whispered.

"I AM . . . AND HAVE ALWAYS BEEN." Though that smooth voice filled his head, the figure's lips did not move. "THY WORDS HAVE SUMMONED ME. WHAT ELSE COULD I BE?"

Doubt fluttered in John's chest, accompanied by a growing pain. He had been wrong. Darkness had not summoned light—it had called to darkness instead.

As he stared in horror, a link of the chain shattered from the figure's form. Fresh silver shone brightly from the fractured edge. The creature was breaking free.

The sight cut through John's trance. He fell away from the circle and stumbled toward the window. He must not let this creature of darkness enter this world.

"HALT . . ."

That single syllable of command stabbed a fiery lance of pain through his head. He could not think, he could barely move, but he forced himself onward. With hands like claws, he grabbed the thick curtain and pulled with all his feeble strength.

The velvet tore.

Sunlight flooded the room, shining onto the bell, the desk, the circle, and, finally, the portal of darkness. A piercing scream rose behind him, filling his skull to bursting.

It was too much.

But it was enough.

As John Dee slumped to the ground, his last sight was darkness again fleeing the sunlight, retreating to its place of refuge in the gem. He offered one final prayer to the world as he left it.

May no one ever find that cursed stone . . .

At noon, soldiers shattered the laboratory door with a battering ram. The men fell to their knees in the hall as the emperor himself swept past them.

"Lift not your faces from the ground," he ordered.

The soldiers obeyed without question.

Emperor Rudolf II walked past their prostrate forms and into the room, taking in the pentagram, the puddles of wax, and the two dead bodies upon the floor—the alchemist and his young apprentice.

Rudolf knew what their deaths meant.

John Dee had failed him.

Not sparing the corpses a second glance, Rudolf stepped into the mystical circle and retrieved his precious diamond from the center. A black mass quivered hatefully inside its leaf-green heart. Cold fury emanated from the stone and clawed at Rudolf's mind, but it could do no worse. Whatever else he had done, Dee had contained the evil.

Keeping the bright stone in the sunlight, Rudolf stoppered the opening with the sliver of bone that lay abandoned on the corner of the desk, translucent as a snowflake but still so very powerful. He lit a candle and sealed the bone to the diamond using drips of tallow that burned his fingers.

Once done, he sat in the battered chair. With careful movements, he covered the luminous green stone and the darkness that it held with fresh oilcloth. Afterward, he tied the wrapping and lowered the bundle into a cauldron of warm tallow that Dee kept always near the fireplace. Rudolf submerged the bundle to make certain that wax sealed each bit.

He glanced at the men in the hall. They lay as ordered, their faces pressed into the floor. Satisfied that he was unwatched, he opened the secret compartment in the fireplace mantel and tucked the foul object inside. Using the Enochian language, he whispered a quick prayer of protection before closing the secret door.

For now, the evil was hidden.

Weariness dragged at his limbs. It had been long since he had enjoyed a real rest, and he would find none this day either. With a sigh, he fell again into the wooden chair beside Dee's desk and picked up a scrap of parchment from an untidy pile. He dipped a quill into a silver inkwell and began to write in the Enochian alphabet. Few had been taught the language's secrets.

When finished, the emperor folded the paper twice, sealed it with black wax, and pressed the seal on his ring into the hot liquid. A trusted man would ride out within the hour to deliver it.

The emperor sought help.

He needed the counsel of the only one who had delved as deeply as Dee into the world of light and dark angels. He stared at the bodies on the floor, praying she could undo the damage wrought here.

He lifted his hastily written note. Sunlight shone against the black letters of her famous name.

Countess Elisabeta Bathory de Ecsed

First

*For Jesus said unto him, "Come out of the man,
thou unclean spirit!"*
*And he asked him, "What is thy name?" And he
answered, saying, "My name is Legion: for we
are many."*

—Mark 5:8–9

1

Don't get caught.

That warning kept every muscle tense as Dr. Erin
Granger crouched behind a card catalog in the center of
the Vatican Apostolic Library's reading room. Elaborate
frescoes decorated the white surface of the arched ceiling
that hung far above her head. Shelves of the rarest books
in the world stretched on either side of her. The library
contained over seventy-five thousand manuscripts and
over a million books. Ordinarily, as an archaeologist,
this was exactly the kind of place she would have loved
to while away hours and days, but it had recently become
more of a prison than a place of discovery.

Today I must escape it.

She was not alone in this plot. Her accomplice was Father Christian. He stood on one side of her, in plain sight, silently urging her to hurry with furtive waves of his hand. He appeared to be a young priest, tall with dark brown hair and the sharpest of green eyes, his cheekbones defined, his skin flawless. He could be easily mistaken for a youth in his late twenties, but he was decades older than that. He was once a monster, a former *strigoi*, a creature who had survived on human blood. But long ago he had joined the Catholic Order of the Sanguines and taken a vow to live eternally on the blood of Christ. He was a Sanguinist now, and one of the few that Erin trusted implicitly.

So she took him at his word concerning this stranger beside her.

The young nun, Sister Margaret, hid next to Erin behind the counter. She breathed heavily, struggling to wiggle out of her dark habit, her wimple already on the floor between them. From the perspiration on the woman's brow, she was human. Erin swore she could hear the nun's frantic heartbeat. It was likely a match to her own.

"Here," Margaret said, shaking loose her long blond hair, catching Erin's gaze with dark amber eyes. Sister Margaret was about Erin's size and coloring, and that made her essential to their plan.

Erin pulled Margaret's habit over her head. Black serge scraped against her cheeks. The cloth smelled freshly laundered. She shrugged the garment across her body and smoothed it over her hips as best she could while still crouched. Margaret helped position her abandoned white wimple over Erin's head, adjusting it around her cheeks to cover her blond hair, tucking away a few errant strands.

Once finished, the nun sat back on her heels, appraising Erin's disguise with critical eyes.

"What do you think?" Christian asked from a corner of his mouth, leaning an arm on the card catalog to further hide their actions.

Margaret nodded, satisfied. Erin now looked like an ordinary nun, practically anonymous in Vatican City, where only tourists and priests outnumbered the sisters in their habits.

To finish the subterfuge, Margaret slipped a black cord that held a large silver cross over Erin's head and handed her a silver ring. Erin slipped the warm circle onto her ring finger, realizing that she'd never worn a band there before.

Thirty-two years old and never married.

She knew how her father, long dead, would have been horrified at such a prospect for his daughter. He had preached ardently that it was a woman's highest duty to create babies that served God. Of course, he would have been equally mortified to know that she'd attended a secular school, gotten a PhD in archaeology, and had spent the past ten years proving that much of the history recorded in the Bible was entirely without miraculous origins. If he hadn't already shunned her for fleeing the religious compound as a teenager, he would have damned her now. But she had made peace with that.

A few months ago, she had been offered a glimpse into the secret history of the world, a world not explained by the books she had studied in school or the science that was the bedrock of her own personal faith. She had met her first Sanguinist—living proof that monsters existed and that devotion in the church could tame them.

Still, a large part of her remained the same skeptic, still questioning everything. While she might have accepted the existence of *strigoi*, it was only after she had met one, saw its ferocity, and examined its sharp teeth. She trusted only what she could verify herself, which was why she had insisted on this plan to begin with.

Margaret pulled her own blond hair back into a ponytail like Erin usually wore. Beneath her habit, the nun had already been wearing an old pair of Erin's jeans and one of her white cotton shirts. From a distance, she could pass for Erin.

Or at least I hope so.

They both turned to Christian for his final approval. He gave a thumbs-up, then leaned down to whisper in Erin's ear.

"Erin, the danger ahead is real. Where you are about to trespass is forbidden. If you are caught . . ."

"I know," she said.

He handed her a folded map and a key. She attempted to take them, but Christian held firm.

"I'm willing to go with you," he said, his eyes bright with concern. "Just say the word."

"But you can't," she countered. "You know that."

Erin glanced over to Margaret. For this subterfuge to work, Christian had to stay in the library. He had been assigned as Erin's bodyguard. And rightfully so. Of late, the number of *strigoi* attacks across the breadth of Rome was escalating. Something had stirred the monsters up. And not just here. Reports from around the globe indicated a shift in that balance between the light and the dark.

But what was causing it?

She had her suspicions but she wanted confirmation before sharing them, and this trespass today might gain her the answers she needed.

"Be careful," Christian finally said, releasing the map and key. He then took Margaret's hand and helped her stand. It was hoped that everyone would assume that the blonde beside Christian was Erin, keeping her absence undetected.

"Your blood," Erin whispered. She would need that final item as much as she would the key.

Christian gave a small nod and slipped her a stoppered glass vial containing a few milliliters of his own black blood. She added the cold vial to her other pocket next to a small flashlight.

Christian touched his pectoral cross and whispered, "Go get 'em, tiger."

Then he ushered Sister Margaret out from behind the card catalog toward the table where Erin had left her backpack and notebook. She stared at the backpack, hating to leave it behind. Inside, sealed in a special case, was a tome more precious than all the multitudes of ancient volumes secured in the Vatican's secret archives.

It held the Blood Gospel.

The book of prophecies had been written by Christ, inscribed in His holy blood. Only a few pages of that book had revealed themselves. She pictured those fiery lines scribing to life across those ancient blank pages. They were stanzas of cryptic prophecies. Some had already been deciphered; others still remained a mystery yet to be solved. But even more intriguing were the hundreds of blank pages that had still not revealed their hidden contents. It was rumored that those lost secrets might contain all the knowledge of the universe, of God, of the meaning of existence, and what lay beyond.

Erin found her mouth going dry even now at the thought of leaving behind such a font of knowledge. Pride also prickled through her, knowing such knowledge was meant for her. Back in the deserts of Egypt, the book had been bound to her. Its words could only be read if she held the book in her hands. So, up until this moment, she had carried it everywhere, never letting it out of her sight.

But now she must.

Nuns didn't carry backpacks, so for her disguise to work, she would have to leave the precious tome in Christian's capable care.

And the sooner I get this done, the sooner I can be back.

That knowledge drove her to her feet. She had a lot of ground to cover, and if she didn't return by evening when the library closed, they would all be caught. Pushing that thought out of her head, she kept her back bowed so that no one could see her face. She took a deep breath and stepped out from behind the catalog into the quiet murmur of the library.

No one seemed to pay her any special notice as she walked slowly toward the front door. She willed herself to remain calm. Sanguinists had senses so acute that they could hear a human heartbeat. They might wonder why a nun walking through the tranquil library had a galloping heartbeat.

She passed rows of shelves and scholars seated at polished wooden tables next to stacks of books. Many of these scholars had waited years to come to this place. They were bent reverently over their tasks, as devout as any priest. She had once been no different from them—until she'd discovered an alternate, deeper vein of history. Well-known texts and familiar paths no longer contented her.

That was just as well. Such ordinary scholarly ways were no longer open to her. She had recently been dismissed from her post at Stanford University following the death of a student on a dig in Israel. She knew that she should be preparing for her future, worrying about her long-term career, but none of that mattered. If she and the others didn't succeed, no one would have a future to worry about.

She pushed open the heavy library door and stepped out into a bright Italian afternoon. The spring sunshine felt good against her face, but she didn't have time to linger and enjoy it. She quickened her pace, hurrying through the Holy City toward St. Peter's Basilica. Tourists were all around, consulting maps and pointing.

They slowed her down, but eventually she reached the grand and imposing basilica. The building symbolized papal power, and no one looking upon it could fail to recognize its strength and grandeur. Even knowing its stern purpose, the beauty of its façade and its massive domes always filled her with awe.

She made straight for the giant doors and passed unchallenged between marble columns so tall that they spanned two floors. As she strode through the atrium and into the nave of the massive basilica itself, she cast a glance at Michelangelo's *Pietà* on her right, a sorrowful sculpture of Mary cradling her son's dead body. It served as a reminder and quickened Erin's steps.

Many more mothers will be mourning their lost children if I fail.

Still, she had no idea *what* she was doing. For the past two months she had scoured the Vatican Library, searching for the truth behind the Blood Gospel's last prophecy: *Together, the trio must face their final quest. The shackles of Lucifer have been loosened, and his Chalice remains lost. It will take the light of all three to forge the Chalice anew and banish him again to his eternal darkness.*

The skeptical part of her—that part that still struggled with the truth about *strigoi* and angels and miracles unfolding before her eyes—wondered if the task was even possible.

To reforge some ancient chalice before Lucifer broke free of Hell?

It sounded more like an ancient myth than an act to be performed in modern times.

But she was a member of the prophetic trio referenced in the Blood Gospel. The three individuals consisted of the *Knight of Christ*, the *Warrior of Man*, and the *Woman of Learning*. And as that learned woman, it was Erin's supposed duty to discover the truth behind those cryptic words.

The other two members of the trio awaited her solution, keeping busy with their own tasks while she worked at the Vatican libraries, trying to find answers. Neither of them was in Rome at the moment, and she missed them both, wanting them by her side, if only as a sounding board for her multitude of theories.

Of course, it was more than that with Sergeant Jordan Stone—the Warrior of Man. In the few short months since they had first met, she had fallen for the tough and handsome soldier, with his piercing blue eyes, his easygoing humor, and his steadfast sense of duty. He could make her laugh in the most stressful moments, had saved her life countless other times.

So what was there not to love?

I don't love that you're not here.

It was a selfish thought, but it was also true.

During the last few weeks, he had begun to drift away from her and everything else. At first she thought that he might be upset because he had been taken away from his regular job with the army and assigned to the Sanguinists against his will. But lately she'd begun to suspect that his remoteness came from something deeper, and that she was losing him.

Doubts plagued her.

Maybe he doesn't want the same kind of relationship that I do . . .

Maybe I'm not the right woman for him . . .

She hated even to think about that.

The third member of the trio, Father Rhun Korza, was even more problematic. The Knight of Christ was a Sanguinist. She had come to respect his strong moral code, his incredible fighting skills, and his dedication to the Church, but she also feared him. Shortly after they had met, he had drunk her blood in a moment of dire need, almost killing her in the dark tunnels under Rome. Even now, walking through St. Peter's, she could easily recall his sharp teeth piercing her throat, the strange ecstasy of that moment, sealing forever the act as both erotic and disturbing. The memory frightened and fascinated her in equal measure.

So for now, the two remained close colleagues, though a wariness stood between them, as if both knew that the line that had been crossed in those tunnels could never be fully erased.

Maybe that's why Rhun vanished out of Rome these past months.

She sighed, again wishing the two men were here, but knowing the task before her was hers alone. And it was a tall order. If the trio must reforge something called *Lucifer's Chalice*, she must discover some clue as to the nature of that prophetic cup. She had searched the Vatican's archives: from its subterranean crypts moldering with age to shelves high up in the *Torre dei Venti*, the Tower of Winds, whose very steps Galileo himself had once tread. But for all of her study, so far she had come up empty-handed. There was only one last library left for her to explore, a collection forbidden to anyone with a beating heart.

The *Bibliotheca dei Sanguines*.

The Sanguinist Order's private library.

But first I must get there.

The library was buried far below St. Peter's, in tunnels restricted to the Sanguinist Order, to those *strigoi* who had vowed to serve the Church, who had forsaken the consumption of human blood to survive only on the blood of Christ—or more precisely, on *wine* transubstantiated by blessing and prayer into that holy essence.

She stepped more briskly across the vast basilica, noting that extra Swiss Guards had been stationed here. The entire city-state was on heightened alert because of the surge of *strigoi* attacks. Even with her nose buried deep in books, she had heard stories that the monsters involved in these murders were somehow stronger, quicker, and harder to kill.

But why?

It was another mystery, one whose solution might be found in that secret library.

Over the past few months, she had read thousands of dusty papyrus scrolls, ancient parchments, and carved clay tablets. The texts were recorded in many languages, written by many hands, but none of them had the information she needed.

That is, until two days ago . . .

In the Tower of Winds, she had discovered an old map concealed between the pages of a copy of the Book of Enoch. She had sought out that ancient Jewish text—a book purported to have been written by the great-grandfather of Noah—because the work dealt with fallen angels and their hybrid offspring, known as the Nephilim. It was Lucifer who had led those fallen angels during the war of Heaven. In the end, he was cast down for challenging God's divine plan for mankind.

But upon opening that ancient volume in the Tower of Winds, a map had fallen free. It had been drawn in strong black ink on a piece of yellowed paper and annotated by a flowery medieval hand and showed another library in Vatican City, one older than any of the others.

It was the first she had heard of this secret library.

From the map, it appeared this collection was hidden within the Sanctuary, the warren of tunnels and rooms below St. Peter's where some Sanguinists made their home. In those ancient tunnels Sanguinists flocked to spend untold years of their immortal lives in quiet contemplation and prayer, removed from the cares of the bright world hundreds of feet above. Some had lived in those halls for centuries, sustained by mere sips of sacramental wine. Every day priests delivered wine to their still forms, holding silver cups to their pale lips. They sought only peace, and access to their tunnels was carefully controlled.

According to the map in her pocket, the Sanctuary held the oldest archives in the Vatican. She had privately consulted Christian about this place, learning that most of the documents hidden there had been written by Sanguinist immortals who had lived through the events of the ancient world. Some had known Christ himself. Others had been old even before those times, converted to the order after hundreds of years of savagery as feral *strigoi*.

Though the Sanctuary was forbidden to humans, Erin had been down there once before, accompanied by Rhun and Jordan. The trio had brought the Blood Gospel into the Sanguinists' innermost sanctum, to receive the blessing of the founder of the Order of the Sanguines, a figure known as the Risen One. But she had learned then that he had a name more significant to Biblical history.

Lazarus.

He had been the first *strigoi* whom Christ had commanded into service.

Upon learning of this library, Erin confronted the current head of the order in Rome, Cardinal Bernard. She had sought permission to enter that library to continue her line of research, but she had been soundly rebuffed. The cardinal had been firm that no human had ever been allowed to cross its threshold. He also assured her that the library only contained information about the order itself, nothing that would help with the quest.

Erin hadn't been surprised by the cardinal's reaction. Bernard treated knowledge as a powerful treasure to be locked away.

She had tried playing her trump card. "The Blood Gospel itself anointed me as the Woman of Learning," she had reminded Bernard, quoting the recent prophecy revealed in the desert. *"The Woman of Learning is now bound to the book and none may part it from her."*

Still, he refused to bend. "I have read deeply and widely from this library. No one in the Sanctuary ever walked with Lucifer and his fallen angels. The stories of his fall were written long after it happened. So there remains no firsthand account of how or where Lucifer fell, where he is imprisoned, or how the shackles that bound him in eternal darkness were forged or could be remade. It would be a waste of time to search that library, even if it weren't forbidden."

As she had glared into his hard brown eyes, she realized he would not break those age-old rules. It meant she had to find her own path down there.

She stared across the last few yards of the basilica, toward a statue of St. Thomas—the apostle who doubted everything until presented with proof. She smiled softly through her nervousness.

There's an apostle after my own heart.

She continued toward the statue. Below its toes lay a small door. It was normally unguarded, but as she rounded toward it, she discovered a Swiss Guardsman standing before the threshold, half hidden within the door's alcove. She clenched her teeth and moved to the side, out of direct sight. She knew who was to blame for this new addition.

Damn you, Bernard.

The cardinal must have posted a guard after their earlier heated conversation, suspecting she might attempt to sneak below on her own.

She searched for a solution—and discovered it within the grasp of a girl a few steps away. The child appeared to be eight or nine, bored, dragging her feet across the ornate marble tiles. She rolled a bright green tennis ball between her palms. Her parents ambled several yards ahead of her, talking animatedly.

Moving quickly, Erin fell into step with the girl. "Hello."

The girl glanced up, her blue eyes narrowing in suspicion. Freckles ran across her nose, and her red hair was braided in two pigtails.

"Hello," the girl said reluctantly in English, as if she knew that she had to answer nuns.

"Could I borrow your ball?"

The girl pulled the tennis ball protectively behind her back.

Okay, new tactic.

Erin lifted a hand, revealing a five-euro note in her fingers. "Then maybe I could buy it?"

The child's eyes widened, staring hard at the temptation—then thrust the fuzzy ball toward her, making the trade, while surreptitiously staring at her parents' backs.

With the deal done, Erin waited until the child had moved off, joining her mother and father. She then tossed the ball underhand in a long arc across the nave toward a tight knot of people several yards past from the posted guardsman. The ball pegged a short man in a gray overcoat on the back of the head.

He yelled sharply, cursing in Italian, causing a commotion that echoed through the vast space. As she had hoped, the Swiss Guardsman moved off to investigate.

Erin used the distraction to hurry forward and fit the key Christian had given her into the door lock. At least the hinges proved to be well oiled as she pulled the way open. Once through, she closed the door behind her and locked it by feel, her heart hammering.

She placed her palm against the door, worry rising inside her. *How am I going to get back out without being caught?*

But she knew it was too late for second-guessing.

Only one path lay open to her.

She clicked on her flashlight and took stock of her surroundings. A long tunnel stretched in front of her. The rounded ceiling looked about nine feet tall, and the walls curved in. Next to the door a dusty oak table held beeswax candles and matches. She took a few of each but didn't light them. They'd be good backups to have in case the battery failed in her flashlight.

She pulled the map out of her pocket. On the back, Christian had drawn a schematic of the tunnels that led down to the Sanctuary itself. Knowing there was no turning back, she gathered her heavy skirt in one hand and set off. She had at least a mile to cover before she reached the Sanctuary gate.

Her light bounced up and down as she hurried, its narrow beam moving ahead of her, revealing mouths of secondary tunnels. She counted them under her breath.

One wrong turn, and I could be lost down in this maze for days.

The fear made her move faster as she descended narrow staircases and traversed the maze of tunnels. The tiny vial of Christian's blood bumped against her thigh, reminding her that the price for knowledge was sometimes blood. It was a message that had been drilled into her as a child, made acutely real when her father discovered a book hidden under her mattress. Her father's rough voice echoed in her ears, drawing her into the past.

"What happened to Eve when she ate from the tree of knowledge?" her father asked, towering over the nine-year-old version of herself, his powerful farmer's hands clenched into threatening fists at his sides.

She wasn't sure if she was supposed to answer his question and decided to stay silent. He was always angrier over things she said than when she kept her mouth shut.

The book—The Farmer's Almanac—lay open on the well-swept floorboards, lamplight shining on its creamy pages. Until today, she'd only ever read the Bible, because her father said that it contained all the knowledge that she would ever need.

But within the pages of the almanac, she had discovered new knowledge: when to plant seeds, when to harvest crops, the dates of the phases of the moon. It had even contained a few jokes, which proved her downfall. She had laughed too loudly and had been caught, sitting cross-legged under her desk reading.

"What happened to Eve?" he had pressed her, his voice low and dangerous.

She decided to try to protect herself with Biblical quotes, keeping her manner timid. " 'And the eyes of them both were opened, and they knew that they were naked.' "

"What was their punishment?" her father continued.

"'Unto the woman he said, I will greatly multiply thy sorrow and thy conception.'"

"And that is the lesson you will learn by my hand."

Her father forced her to choose a willow switch and ordered her to kneel in front of him. Obedient, she dropped to her mother's clean floor and lifted her dress over her head. Her mother had sewn it for her, and she didn't want it to get dirty. She folded it carefully and placed it on the floor next to her. Then she gripped her cold knees and waited for the blows to come.

He always let her wait a long time for the first one, as if he knew that the anticipation of the pain was almost as bad as the blow itself. Goose bumps rose up on her back. Out of the corner of her eye she saw the almanac, and she wasn't sorry.

The first blow cracked across her skin, and she bit her lips to keep from crying out. If she did, he would add more blows. He switched her bare back until blood ran down and soaked into her underwear. Later she would have to clean the bright red spatters off the walls and floor. But first she had to endure the lashes, waiting until her father decided that she'd shed enough blood.

Erin shuddered at the memory, the dark tunnels somehow making it more real. Her back twinged even now, as if remembering the old pain and the lesson learned.

The price of knowledge was blood and pain.

Even before her back had healed, she had returned to her father's office and read the rest of the almanac in secret. One section contained a weather forecast. For a year she'd tracked it to see if the authors knew what the weather would do, and they were often wrong. And she realized that things in books could be *wrong.*

Even the Bible.

Back then, the fear of punishment hadn't stopped her.

And it won't stop me now.

Her feet pounded the stone, carrying her along until at last she reached the door to the Sanctuary. It was not the main entrance into their territory, but a rarely used back door, one that opened not far from their library. This gateway looked like a blank wall with a small alcove that held a stone basin, not unlike a small bowl or cup.

She knew what she must do.

The secret gate could only be opened by the blood of a Sanguinist.

She reached to her pocket and retrieved Christian's glass vial. She studied the black blood roiling inside. Sanguinist blood was thicker and darker than any human's. It could move with a will of its own, flowing through veins without the need of a beating heart. That was about all she knew about the essence that sustained both the Sanguinists and the *strigoi*, but she suddenly wanted to know more, to tease out the secrets of that blood.

But not now.

She emptied the vial's dark contents into the stone basin, while speaking words in Latin. "For this is the Chalice of My Blood, of the new and everlasting Testament."

The blood swirled within the cup, stirring on its own, proving its unnatural state.

She held her breath. *Would the gate reject Christian's blood?*

The answer came as the dark pool seeped into the stone, vanishing away, leaving no trace.

She let out a sigh, whispering the final words, "*Mysterium fidei.*"

She took a step back from the sealed wall, her heart pounding in her throat. Surely any Sanguinists nearby would hear that telltale beat and know she was standing at their threshold.

Stone ground heavily on stone, slowly opening a passage before her.

She took a step toward that waiting darkness, remembering her father's painful lesson. *The price of knowledge was blood and pain.*

So be it.

2

Why am I always stuck underground?

Sergeant Jordan Stone dragged himself forward with his elbows through the cramped tunnel. Rock pressed tightly on him from all sides, and the only way to move forward was to wriggle like a worm. As he struggled, dirt sifted into his hair and fell into his eyes.

At least I'm still moving.

He pushed forward another few inches.

A heavily accented voice called from the tunnel ahead, encouraging him. "You're almost through!"

That would be Baako. He pictured the tall Sanguinist who hailed from somewhere in Africa. Last week, when

Jordan had inquired about his exact country of origin, Baako had been vague, saying only, *Like many nations in Africa, the one I come from has borne many names, and likely will bear many more.*

It was a typical Sanguinist answer: dramatic and basically useless.

Jordan stared ahead. He could vaguely make out a dull glow, a promise that this damned tunnel did indeed reach an inner cavern. He fought toward that light.

Earlier today, Baako had climbed down this recently discovered tunnel, returning with the news that the shaft led straight to the sibyl's temple. A horrific battle had been fought in that cavern a few months back, when an innocent boy had been used as a sacrificial lamb in an attempt to open a gate to Hell. The effort had failed, and afterward a giant earthquake had sealed the place up.

As he crawled, another voice in a lilting Indian accent urged him from behind, poking fun at him. "Maybe you shouldn't have had such a big breakfast."

He glanced back toward Sophia, making out her lithe shadowy form. Unlike the dour Baako, this particular Sanguinist always seemed on the verge of laughter, a perpetual shadow of a smile on her lips, her dark eyes shining with amusement. He usually appreciated her good humor.

Not now.

He rubbed dust from his stinging eyes.

"At least, I still *eat* breakfast," he called back to her.

Jordan gritted his teeth and continued onward, wanting to see for himself what remained of that temple in the aftermath of the battle. Following the quake, the Vatican had cordoned off this entire volcanic mountain. The church could not let anyone find the bodies below, especially those of the *strigoi* and their dead Sanguinist brothers and sisters.

A typical cover-your-ass operation.

And as the Vatican was his new employer after the army reassigned him here, he found himself a part of that cleanup detail. But he wasn't complaining. It meant more time with Erin.

Still, while that should have thrilled him, something nagged at the corners of his mind, a dark shadow that dampened his emotions. It wasn't that he didn't still love her. He did. She was as brilliant and sexy and funny as ever, but those qualities seemed to matter less to him every day.

Everything seemed to matter less.

She clearly sensed it, too. He found her staring quizzically at him, often with a pained expression. Whenever she brought it up, he brushed her concerns away, dismissing them with some joke or a smile that never reached his heart.

What the hell is wrong with me?

He didn't know, so he did what he always did best: he put one foot in front of the other. He kept working, keeping himself distracted. Everything would get sorted out in the end.

Or at least, I hope it will.

And if nothing else, working here offered him some space from Erin, allowing him to try to find that center that he seemed to have lost. Not that he had found himself with much free time. Over the past week, they had been moving bodies from the mountain's outermost tunnels, letting the *strigoi* remains burn away under the Italian sun, and securing the bodies of the Sanguinists for proper burial. Jordan's background with the Army had been in forensic investigations. It was a skill set much suited to the task at hand.

Especially when this tunnel was discovered.

Nobody remembered seeing this mystery passageway before, and from the freshly excavated appearance of the surrounding walls, it looked to have been dug recently.

A fact that presented an interesting dilemma: was the tunnel formed by someone digging *down* into that inner temple cavern or someone clawing their way *out* from below?

Neither prospect was a good one, but Jordan had come down to investigate.

As last, he spilled painfully out of the tunnel and sprawled onto a rough stone floor. Baako helped him up, pulling him to his feet as effortlessly as if lifting a small child instead of a six-and-a-half-foot-tall soldier.

A small lamp on the cavern floor offered some illumination, but Jordan flicked on his helmet light as Sophia climbed out of the tunnel, rolling gracefully to her feet, looking barely disheveled.

"Show-off," he scolded, brushing dust from his clothes.

That perpetual ghost of a smile grew wider. She combed her short-cropped black hair from her wide brown cheeks as she searched. With her sharp unnatural gaze, she didn't need the lamp or his helmet light to take in the room.

Jordan envied such night-vision. Stretching a kink out of his neck, he began his own search. As he drew in a deep breath, the smell of sulfur filled his nostrils, but it wasn't as intense as when he was last down here, during the battle, when a wide crack in the floor had been fuming with smoke and fiery brimstone.

Still, a new odor underlay the sulfur.

The familiar reek of the dead.

Jordan noted the corpses of several *strigoi* scattered to his right, their bodies broken and burned, their flesh cracked and split. A part of him wanted to turn and run, a natural instinct when faced with such a slaughterhouse of horror, but he had a duty here. Leaning hard on his background to settle himself, he took out a video camera and filmed the room. He took his time, making sure that he captured each body, more out of force of habit than anything else. He had worked as a crime scene investigator as part of the Army's Joint Expeditionary Forensic Facility in Afghanistan, and he had learned to be thorough.

He moved deeper into the cavern, filming the stone altar, trying not to remember the young boy, Tommy, who had been chained there, his lifeblood dripping to the floor. The boy's angelic blood was the catalyst to open a gateway to the underworld, and in the end, it was the same boy's bravery that was instrumental in closing it.

Tommy had left his mark on Jordan, too, healing him with a touch of his palm. Jordan could still feel that imprint, and it seemed to burn brighter with every passing day.

"Well," Baako said, drawing him back to the present, "what do you think?"

Jordan lowered his camera. "It . . . it's definitely *changed* since we were last here."

"How so?" Sophia asked, joining them.

Jordan pointed to a pile of dead rats in the far corner. "They're new."

Baako crossed over, picked up one of the tiny bodies, and sniffed at it. The action made Jordan cringe.

"Interesting," Baako said.

"How's that *interesting*?" Jordan asked.

"It's been drained of blood."

Sophia took the rat, examined it herself, and confirmed the same. "Baako is right."

The small Indian woman offered the dead body to Jordan.

"I'll take your word for it," he said. "But if you're right, that means something was down here, feeding on those rats."

Which could only mean one thing . . .

Jordan dropped his hand to the machine pistol holstered at his side. It was a Heckler & Koch MP7. The gun was compact and powerful, capable of firing 950 rounds a minute. It had always been his go-to weapon, only now the magazine was loaded with silver rounds. He also checked the silver-plated KA-BAR dagger strapped to his ankle.

"One of the *strigoi* must have survived the attack," Sophia said.

Baako glanced to the tunnel. "It must have fed on the rats until it was strong enough to dig its way out."

"Maybe it wasn't a *strigoi*," Jordan said, his heart thudding in his throat as a sudden realization rose. "Help me search the bodies."

Sophia cast him a quizzical look, but the two Sanguinists obeyed. One by one, they examined the faces of the dead.

"He's not here," Jordan said.

Baako frowned. "Who's not here?"

Jordan pictured the boyish face of his former friend, someone whom he had trusted wholeheartedly, only to have that confidence betrayed in this cavern.

"Brother Leopold," Jordan mumbled to the darkness. He stepped to a spot on the floor, where blood still stained the rock. "Rhun stabbed Leopold right here. This is where he fell."

His body was gone.

Baako swung an arm to encompass the room. "I already checked the space. The earthquake collapsed all the other passages."

Jordan shone his light toward the narrow tunnel. "So he made his own."

Jordan closed his eyes, again seeing Rhun giving Leopold his last rites, Leopold's blood spilling into a huge pool under his body. With such a mortal wound, how had Leopold managed to survive, let alone find the strength to dig himself out? There couldn't have been enough sustenance in that pile of rats.

The same question must have been on Sophia's mind. "The tunnel is at least a hundred feet long," she said. "I'm not sure even a healthy Sanguinist could claw through that much dirt and stone."

Baako knelt beside the bloodstain on the stone floor, taking in its expanse. "Much blood was spilled. This brother should be dead."

Jordan nodded, coming to the same assessment. "Which means there's something we've missed."

He returned to the tunnel, studied the cavern, then began to slowly walk in a grid pattern across the room, looking for anything that could explain what had happened. They moved bodies, checking beneath them. Jordan even dropped to his hands and knees and examined the old crack in the floor by the altar, discovering a thin gold line where it had sealed.

Sophia squatted next to him and passed her brown hand over the entire length of the crack. "It looks closed."

"That's good news, at least." Jordan straightened, cracking his head on the bottom edge of the altar, and knocking his helmet askew.

"Careful there, soldier," Sophia said, hiding a small smile.

Jordan reseated his helmet. As he did so, his headlamp glinted off two pieces of what looked like glass, green as a broken bottle of beer, resting in the shadow of the altar.

Hmm . . .

He slipped on a pair of latex gloves and picked up one of the two pieces. "Looks like some sort of crystal."

He held it higher. In the lamplight, rainbows of light reflected from the broken surfaces. He examined the shattered edge, then returned the piece next to the other one. The two pieces looked as if they'd once been a single stone, about the size of a goose egg, now broken in two. He fitted the halves together, noting that the stone appeared to be hollowed out inside, like an egg.

Baako stared over his shoulder. "Have you seen it before? Maybe during the battle?"

"Not that I recall, but a lot was going on." Jordan rolled the object to examine it from every angle. "But look at this."

His gloved fingertip hovered over lines imbedded in the crystalline surface. They formed a symbol.

He glanced to Sophia. "Have you ever seen anything like this?"

"Not me."

Baako merely shrugged. "Looks somewhat like a cup."

Jordan realized he was right, but maybe it didn't just represent a *cup*. "Maybe it's a chalice."

Sophia cocked a skeptical eyebrow toward him. "As in Lucifer's Chalice."

This time he shrugged. "It's at least worth investigating."

And I know a certain gal who would be very intrigued by it.

With his phone, Jordan snapped several pictures of the stone and symbol, planning on emailing them to Erin as soon as he had a signal.

"I should crawl back outside and send this to—"

A scraping sound drew all their attentions back to the tunnel. A dark figure snaked out of the darkness and into the light. Jordan barely registered the fangs—before it launched straight at him.

3

A pang of regret flared through Rhun's silent heart. He sat on his heels at the base of a tall dune and listened to the soft hiss of grains sliding down the Egyptian slopes. It filled him with a sense of profound peace to be here, alone, doing God's work.

But even that purity was marred by a darkness at the edges of his senses. He turned slowly toward it, drawn by a compass submerged deep in his immortal blood. As he bent over, searching for the source, sunlight glinted off the silver cross hanging from his neck. His black robe brushed the sand as his palm skated across the hot surface of the desert, skimming over the fine grains. His questing fingertips sensed a seed of malevolence below the surface.

Like a crow hunting a buried worm, Rhun cocked his head, narrowing his focus to one point in the sand. Once he was sure, he pulled a small spade from his pack and began to dig.

Weeks ago, he had arrived with a team of Sanguinists tasked with accomplishing this very duty. But the pieces of evil unearthed here had threatened to master the others, to consume them fully. In the end, he had forced them to abandon the dig site and head back to Rome.

It seemed Rhun alone was capable of withstanding the evil buried here.

But what does that say of my own soul?

He poured each shovelful of burning sand through a sieve, like a child at the beach. But this was not work for children. The sieve caught neither shells nor rocks.

Instead, it captured teardrop-shaped bits of stone, black as obsidian.

The blood of Lucifer.

Over two millennia ago, a battle had been fought in these sands between Lucifer and the archangel Michael over the young Christ child. Lucifer had been wounded, and his blood fell to the sand. Each drop had burned with an unholy fire, melting through the tiny grains to form these corrupted bits of glass. Time had long since buried them, and now it was Rhun's duty to bring them back to the light again.

A single black drop appeared, resting in the bottom of the sieve.

He picked the drop up and held it a moment in his cupped palm. It burned against his bare skin, but it did not seek to corrupt him, as it did the other Sanguinists. Unlike them, he saw no scenes of bloodshed and terror, or lust and temptation. Prayers filled his mind instead.

Opening a leather pouch at his side, he dropped the black pebble inside. It tapped against two others, all that he had found this day. The drops were smaller now, and harder to find. His task was almost complete.

He sighed, staring across the empty sand.

I could stay . . . make this desert my home.

A cask of sanctified wine waited for him back at his camp. He needed nothing else. Bernard had sent word that he was to increase his efforts, that he was needed back in Rome. So, reluctantly, he had, although he did not wish for this assignment to end.

For the first time in centuries, he felt at peace. A few months ago, he had redeemed his greatest sin when he had restored his former lover's lost soul, changing her from *strigoi* back to a human woman. Of course, Elisabeta—or *Elizabeth,* as she preferred to be called now—had not thanked him for it, cursing him instead for returning her mortality, but he did not need her gratitude. He sought only redemption, and he had found it centuries after he had given up any hope.

As he straightened, forgoing his search, a distant mewling reached his ear. He tried to ignore it as he carefully tied the leather pouch and packed away his tools. But the sound persisted, plaintive and full of pain.

Just some desert creature . . .

He climbed toward his camp, but the sound pursued him, scratching at his ears, shredding his sense of solace. It was high-pitched, like the screech of a house cat. Irritation grew inside him—along with a trickle of curiosity.

What was wrong with it?

He reached his small camp and plotted how to break down his tent and clear out his gear to leave no trace of his trespass here.

Still, none of his thoughts lessened the ache of that cry in his ears. It was like hearing the scratching of a dry branch against a bedroom window's glass. The more one tried to ignore it and return to slumber, the louder it became.

He had at best one more night alone in the desert. If he didn't do something about that mewling, he would never enjoy his last moments of peace.

He stared in the direction of the crying, took one step, then another toward its source. Before he knew it, he was running across the sun-washed sand, flying over the dunes. As he drew closer, the sound grew louder, drawing him inexplicably onward. A part of him recognized something unnatural about this hunt, how it drew him, but he sped faster anyway.

At last, he spotted the source in the distance. The mewling rose from an acacia bush that cast a faraway shadow. The desert tree must have found an underground water source, its tough roots fighting for survival in this dry land. The thorny trunk listed to one side, a testament to the relentless winds.

Long before he reached the tree, a noxious smell struck him. Even upwind, the scent was familiar, marking the presence of a beast corrupted by the blood of a *strigoi* into something monstrous.

A *blasphemare*.

Was it that corrupted blood that had drawn him so inextricably across the desert? Had its evil impinged upon his already sharpened senses—senses honed from weeks of mining the sands for those malevolent drops? He slowed enough to pull his blades from their wrist sheaths. Sunlight flashed off the silver knives, ancient *karambits*, each curved like a leopard's claw. He would need such claws to fight what lay ahead. By now, he could identify the scent of his prey: a *blasphemare* lion.

He circled the tree from a distance. His eyes searched the shadows until he spotted a mound of tawny fur, mostly hidden beneath the bower. In her natural form, the lioness must have been stunning. Even as a tainted creature, her magnificence was undeniable. The corruption had filled her form with thick muscle, while her fur grew thick as velvet. Even her massive head, resting between her paws, revealed an intelligent face.

Still, sickness throbbed in each weary beat of her heart.

As he drew closer to her, he noted black blood crusted on her shoulder. It appeared a wide swath of fur had been burned away across her flanks.

He could guess the origin of this corrupted lioness— and her injuries. He pictured the hordes of *blasphemare* that had accompanied Judas's army during the battle fought here last winter. There had been jackals, hyenas, and a handful of lions. Rhun had believed that such beasts had been driven off or killed, along with the *strigoi* forces, at the end of that war, when a holy angelic fire had swept across these sands.

Afterward, a Sanguinist team had been sent forth to hunt down any straggling survivors, but clearly this beast must have escaped the fire and the hunters.

Even wounded, she had survived.

She raised her golden muzzle and snarled in his direction. Her eyes glowed crimson out of the shadows, their true color stolen by the *strigoi* blood that had corrupted her. But even this effort seemed to sap her remaining strength. Her head sank back again to her paws. She had not long to live.

Should I end her suffering or wait for her to die?

He moved forward, closing the distance, still unsure. But before he could decide, she pounced out of the shadows and into the burning sunlight. The move caught him off guard. He managed to roll to the side, but sharp claws raked his left arm.

He spun to face her again as his blood dripped onto the hot sand.

She lowered into a wary crouch. The skin on her muzzle wrinkled back into a hiss. The sound chilled even his cold heart. She was a powerful foe, but she could not spend much time away from the tree's shadow. She was still *blasphemare*, and she would weaken quickly in the direct sunlight.

He moved to place himself between her and the safety of the tree.

The threat agitated her, setting her tail to swishing in savage arcs. She bunched her hind legs and leaped. Yellow teeth aimed for his neck.

Rhun met the challenge this time, jumping toward her in turn, a plan in mind. He spun to the side at the last second, dragging his silver knife across her burned shoulder. He landed in a roll, turning to keep her in sight.

Blood flowed heavily out of the laceration, pouring forth like pitch, thick and black. It was a mortal wound. He backed away, giving her the leeway to retreat into the shadows and die in peace.

Instead, an unearthly yowl burst from deep in her chest—and she was upon him again, ignoring the safety of the shadows to attack him in full sunlight.

Caught off guard by this surprising assault, Rhun moved too slowly. Her teeth closed on his left wrist, grinding together, trying to crush his bones. His blade fell from his fingers.

Twisting in her grip, he slashed down with his other hand—sinking that blade into her eye.

She screamed in agony, loosening her jaws on his damaged wrist. He pulled his arm free, digging his heels into the sand and pushing away from her. He cradled his damaged wrist against his chest, girding for another charge.

But his blade had struck true, and she collapsed on the sand. Her one good eye looked into his. The crimson glow faded to a deep golden brown before she closed her eye for the last time.

The curse had left her in the end, as it always did.

Rhun whispered, "*Dominus vobiscum.*"

With yet another trace of corruption removed from these sands, Rhun began to turn away—when once again a plaintive mewling reached his ears.

He stopped and turned back, cocking his head. He heard the soft skitter of another heartbeat. A small shadow sidled out from the shadows, moving toward the dead lioness.

A cub.

Its fur was snowy and pure.

Rhun stared in shock. The lioness must have been pregnant, giving the last of her life to give birth, a mother's final sacrifice. He now understood why she hadn't retreated to the shadows when given the opportunity. The lioness had been fighting him in her final moments to protect her offspring, to drive him away from her cub.

The infant nosed the lifeless bulk of its mother. Dread filled Rhun. If the cub had been born of her tainted womb and had fed on her corrupted blood, then it was surely *blasphemare* as well.

I will have to destroy it, too.

He collected the blade that had dropped into the sand.

The cub nudged its mother's head, trying to get her to rise. It mewled as if it knew it was orphaned and abandoned.

As he edged toward the creature, Rhun studied it cautiously. While it scarcely reached his knee, even such small *blasphemare* could be dangerous. Closer now, he noted its snowy coat bore grayish rosettes, mostly dotting its round forehead. The cub must have been born after the battle, making it no more than twelve weeks old.

If Rhun had not stumbled upon the cub, it would have died an agonizing death under the sun or starved to death in the shadows.

It would be a kindness to take its life.

His grip tightened on his *karambit.*

Sensing his approach for the first time, the young cub looked up at him, it eyes shining in the sunlight. It sank back on its haunches, revealing it was a male. The cub leaned his head back and meowed loudly, clearly demanding something from him.

Those small eyes found his again.

He knew what the cub wanted, what all young creatures craved: love and care.

Sensing no threat, Rhun lowered his arm with a sigh. He slipped the knife back into its wrist sheath and stepped closer, dropping to one knee.

"Come to me, little one."

Rhun beckoned, then reached slowly as the cub approached on splayed paws, comically outsized for his body. As soon as Rhun touched the warm fur, a rumbling rose from the small form. A soft head butted against Rhun's open palm, then brittle whiskers rubbed his cold skin.

Rhun scratched under the cub's chin, which stoked that purr louder.

He stared up at the searing sun, noting that the cub seemed oblivious, unharmed by light.

Strange.

Rhun carefully lifted the animal to his nose and drew in the cub's scent: milk, acacia leaves, and the musky scent of a baby lion.

No hint of a *blasphemare's* corruption.

Moist eyes stared up at him. The irises were a caramel brown, rimmed with a thin line of gold.

Ordinary eyes.

He sat down as he pondered this mystery. The cat climbed into his lap, while he absently stroked the velvety chin with his uninjured hand. Purring, the cub rested his muzzle on Rhun's knee, sniffing a bit, and licking at some blood that had soaked into his trousers from his injured wrist.

"No," he scolded, pushing the tiny head away and starting to stand.

Sunlight flashed off the silver flask strapped to Rhun's leg. The cub pounced at it, hooking a claw around the strap that secured the wine flask in place and chewing at the leather.

"Enough."

While the cub was clearly only playing, Rhun pushed the stubborn animal off his leg and straightened the flask. He realized he had not drunk a drop of wine since yesterday. Perhaps that weakness had softened his heart against the creature. He should fortify himself before he made any decision.

I must act from a place of strength, not sentiment.

To that end, Rhun unfastened the flask and lifted the wine toward his lips, but before he could take a sip, the lion cub rose on his hind legs and knocked the bottle out of Rhun's fingers.

The flask fell into the sand, the holy wine spilling forth.

The lion bent and lapped from that red font. While the cub was surely dehydrated, looking for any liquid to quench his thirst, Rhun still stiffened in fear. If the cub had even a drop of *blasphemare* blood, the holiness in the wine would burn the creature to ash.

He tugged the cub away. The cat glanced back at him, wine staining his snowy muzzle. Rhun wiped the droplets away with the back of his hand. The cub appeared unharmed. Rhun looked closer. For a brief instant, he would have sworn those small eyes shone with a pure golden shine.

The cub butted his head against Rhun's knee again, and when the small creature stared up at him again, the eyes had returned to that caramel brown.

Rhun rubbed his own eyes, blaming the brief illusion on a trick of the desert sunlight.

Still, the fact remained that the cub had moved in the sunlight and consumed sacramental wine without any ill effect, proving the young cat was no *blasphemare*. Perhaps the holy fire had spared the cub because the animal was an innocent in his mother's womb. Perhaps it also explained why the lioness had lived through the blast, weakened but strong enough to bring forth this new life.

If God spared this innocent life, how can I abandon it now?

With the decision made, Rhun gathered the cub up in his tunic and headed back toward his camp. While it was forbidden for a Sanguinist to possess a *blasphemare* creature, no edict forbade them from owning ordinary pets. Yet, as he crossed the desert with the warm cub purring against his chest, Rhun knew one firm certainty.

This was no *ordinary* creature.

4

Words from Dante's *Inferno* filled Erin's head as she passed through the Sanguinist gate to enter the order's private Sanctuary: *Abandon hope, all ye who enter here.* According to Dante, that warning had been inscribed above the entrance to Hell.

And it would be fitting enough here, too.

The antechamber beyond the gate was lined by torches made of bundled rushes, placed at regular intervals along the walls. Though smoky, they illuminated a long hall, lit brightly enough that she clicked off her flashlight.

She set off along its length, noting that the walls had no elaborate frescoes as could be found in St. Peter's

Basilica. The order's Sanctuary was known to be simple, almost austere. Beyond the smoke, the air smelled of wine and incense, not unlike a church.

At the end of the hall, a large circular chamber opened, equally unadorned.

But it didn't mean the room was *empty*.

Smooth niches had been carved into the bare walls. Some spaces held what appeared to be exquisite white statues, with hands folded in prayer, eyes closed, faces either downcast or lifted toward the ceiling. But these statues could *move*, they were in fact ancient Sanguinists, those who had sunk deeply into meditation and contemplation.

They were known as the Cloistered Ones.

The gateway she and Christian had chosen to use to enter the Sanctuary opened into their inner sanctum. She had picked this doorway because the Sanguinist library lay within the Cloistered Ones' meditative wing—which made sense as the proximity of such a storehouse of knowledge would be useful for reflection and study.

Erin stepped to the threshold of the large room and stopped. Surely the Cloistered Ones must have sensed the gateway opening nearby or heard her frantic heartbeat, but none of the figures stirred.

At least not yet.

She waited another moment. Christian had told her to give these ancient Sanguinists time to adjust to her presence, to see what they decided. If they wanted to keep her out of their domain, they would.

She stared across the space to a distant archway. According to the map, it marked the entrance to the library. Almost without realizing it, she moved toward it. She stepped slowly—not to be quiet, but out of respect to those around her.

Her gaze swept the walls, waiting for an arm to raise, a hoarse voice to call out. She noted several of the still figures wore clothing and robes from orders that no longer existed in the world above. She imagined those ancient times, trying to picture these quiet, contemplative forms as former warriors for the Church.

All of these Cloistered Ones were once as alive as Rhun.

Rhun had been headed to one of these niches, ready to turn his back upon the outer world, but then he had been summoned by prophecy to seek out the Blood Gospel, joining her and Jordan on this ongoing quest to stop a coming apocalypse. But at times, she saw the world-weariness in that dark priest, the weight of the bloodshed and horrors he had experienced.

She had begun to understand his haunted look. Lately she woke all too often with a scream clenched in her throat. The horrors she had endured played in a never-ending loop in her dreams: soldiers torn to pieces by savage creatures . . . the clear silver eyes of a woman Erin had shot to save Rhun's life . . . *strigoi* children dying in the snow . . . a bright young boy falling on a sword.

Too much had been sacrificed to this quest.

And it was far from over.

She stared at the unmoving statues.

Rhun, is this the peace you truly seek or do you just want to hide down here? Would I hide down here if I could, lost in study and peace?

Sighing softly, she continued across the wide room. None of the Cloistered Ones acknowledged her passage. At last, she reached the archway that led into the pitch-dark library. Her fingers touched her flashlight, but then moved to the beeswax candle she had pocketed earlier. She lit the wick from one of the neighboring torches, then stepped across the threshold into the library.

As she held the candle aloft, the flickering glow illuminated a hexagonal space, lined by shelves of books and cubbyholes for scrolls. There were no chairs to sit in, no reading lights, nothing that hinted at human needs. Walking by candlelight made her feel as if she had traveled back in time.

She smiled at the thought and consulted her map. To her left, a smaller archway led to another room. The medieval mapmaker had noted that this room contained the Sanguinists' most ancient texts. If there was any knowledge of Lucifer's fall and imprisonment in Hell, that's where she should begin her search.

She headed there and found another hexagonal room. She pictured the layout of this library, imagining it sprawling out with similar rooms, like the comb of a beehive, only the treasure here was not a flow of golden honey, but an ancient font of knowledge. This room was similar to the first, but here there were more scrolls than books. One wall even held a dusty shelf of copper and clay tablets, hinting at the older nature to this particular collection.

But it wasn't the presence of such rare artifacts that drew her to a stop.

A figure, covered in a film of dust, stood in the center of the room, but like the Cloistered Ones, this was no statue. Though his back was to her, she knew who stood there. She had once looked into his eyes, black as olives, and had heard his deep voice. In the past, the few words spoken by those ashen lips had changed everything. Here was the founder of the Sanguinist order, a man who had once counted the holiest of the holy among his friends, the one who had died and had risen again at the hand of Christ himself.

Lazarus.

She bowed her head, not sure what else to do. She stood for what seemed an interminable time, her heart pounding in her ears.

Still, he remained motionless, his eyes closed.

Finally, with no word spoken against her trespass, she took a deep shuddering breath and stepped past his still form. She didn't know what else to do. She had come here with a specific goal in mind, and as long as no one stopped her, she would continue on the course she had started.

But where to start?

She searched the shelves and cubbies. It would take years to translate and read all that could be found here. Lost and overwhelmed, she turned to the room's sole occupant, its makeshift librarian. Her candlelight reflected off his open dark eyes.

"Lazarus," she whispered. Even his name sounded far too loud for the space, but she pressed on. "I am here to find—"

"I know." Dust fell from his lips with those few words. "I have been waiting."

An arm rose smoothly, shedding more motes into the air. A single long finger pointed to a clay tablet that rested near the edge of a shelf. She moved over to it, glancing down. It was no larger than a deck of cards, terracotta in color. Lines of script covered its surface.

Erin carefully picked it up and examined it, recognizing the writing as Aramaic, a language she knew well. She skimmed the first few lines. It recounted a familiar story: the arrival of a serpent in the Garden of Eden and its confrontation with Eve.

"From the Book of Genesis," she mumbled to herself.

According to most interpretations, that serpent was Lucifer, come to tempt Eve. But this account seemed to refer to the snake as just another animal in the garden, only craftier than the others.

She brought her candle closer to the most significant descriptor of that snake, phonetically speaking it aloud. *"Chok-maw."*

The word could be interpreted as wise or crafty, or even clever or sly.

Erin continued to translate the tablet, finding the story written here much like the account in the King James Bible. Again Eve refused to eat of the fruit, saying that God had warned her that she would die if she disobeyed. But the serpent argued that Eve wouldn't die, but instead she would gain knowledge—knowledge of good and evil.

Erin let out a small breath, realizing that in this story, the serpent was actually more truthful than God. In the end Adam and Eve hadn't *died* after consuming the fruit, but as the snake foretold, they had gained knowledge.

She pushed this detail aside as insignificant, especially upon reading the next line. It was wholly new. She translated aloud, the candle trembling in her hand.

"*'And the serpent said unto the woman: Swear a vow that ye shall take the fruit and share it with me.'*"

Erin read the passage twice more to make sure she hadn't mistranslated it, then continued on. In the next line, Eve swore a pact that she would give the snake the fruit. After that, the story continued along the same path as the Bible: Eve eats the fruit, shares it with Adam, and they are cursed and banished.

Her father's words echoed in her head.

The price of knowledge is blood and pain.

Erin read the entire tablet again.

So in the end, it seemed Eve had broken her promise to the serpent, failing to share the fruit.

Erin pondered this altered story. What did the serpent want with such knowledge in the first place? In all the other Biblical stories, animals didn't care about knowledge. Did this expanded story further support that the serpent in the garden was indeed Lucifer in disguise?

She shook her head, trying to make sense, to discern some significance. She looked over at Lazarus, hoping for some elaboration.

His eyes only stared back at her.

Before she could question him, a sound echoed to her, coming from beyond the library, the heavy grating of stone.

She stared in that direction.

Someone must be opening the nearby Sanguinist gate.

She checked her wristwatch. Christian had warned her that a sect of Sanguinist priests tended to the Cloistered Ones, bringing them wine to sip. But he hadn't known their schedule or how often they came down here. She had counted on a little luck to get her by.

And that just ran out.

As soon as those priests got closer, they would hear her heartbeat, blowing her cover. She prayed Bernard wouldn't be too hard on Christian and Sister Margaret.

She returned the tablet to its shelf, but as she turned around, ready to face the consequences of her trespass, Lazarus leaned forward—and blew out her candle. Startled, she stumbled backward. The library sank into darkness, illuminated only by the faraway torches in the main chamber.

Lazarus placed a cold hand on her arm, his fingers tightening as if to urge her to stay quiet. He guided her forward so she could peer into the chamber of the Cloistered Ones.

The ancient Sanguinists stirred. Fabric rustled, and dust fell from their old clothing.

At her side, Lazarus began to sing. It was a hymn in Hebrew. The Cloistered Ones in the chambers outside took up the chant, too. The fear in Erin fell away, caught in the rise and fall of their voices, as steady as waves against a shore. Wonder welled through her.

Figures appeared on the far side. A clutch of black-cloaked Sanguinist priests entered the chamber, carrying flagons of wine and silver cups. They stared at the Cloistered Ones, mouths agape. Apparently such singing wasn't a common occurrence.

Lazarus's fingers lifted from her shoulder, but not before a final squeeze of reassurance. She understood. Lazarus and the others were protecting her. Their song would drown out her heartbeat.

Erin stood stock-still, hoping that their ruse worked.

The young priests went about their duty, offering cups to lips, but those same lips only continued singing, ignoring the wine. The Sanguinists exchanged worried glances, clearly puzzled. They tried again, but with no better outcome.

The rich powerful voices only soared louder.

Eventually the small group of priests relented, retreating back down the entry hall and away. Erin listened as that distant doorway ground closed—only then did the singing stop.

Lazarus walked her to the torch-lit chamber as the Cloistered Ones went quiet and still again. He motioned toward the exit.

Erin turned to him. "But I didn't learn anything," she protested. "I don't know how to find Lucifer, let alone how to reforge his shackles."

Lazarus spoke, his voice deep but distant, as if he were talking to himself rather than to her. "When Lucifer stands before you, your heart will guide you on your path. You must fulfill the covenant."

"How am I supposed to find him?" Erin asked. "And what covenant are you talking about? The prophecy in the Blood Gospel?"

"You know all that you can know," he said, his voice drifting farther away. "The way will be revealed, and you will follow it."

Erin wanted to shake better answers from him, even took a step back in his direction. Questions chased through her head, but she voiced the most important one aloud.

"Will we succeed?" she asked.

Lazarus closed his eyes and did not answer.

5

March 17, 5:21 P.M. CET
Rome, Italy

I must break free . . .

Leopold's consciousness drowned in a sea of dark smoke. As a Sanguinist, he'd grown used to pain—the ever-present burning of his silver cross against his chest, the searing of sacramental wine down his throat—but those pains were trivial compared to his current agony.

Bound within a dark well of smoke, he was lost, senseless to the world around him. Even the awareness of his own limbs had been stripped from him by this black pall.

Who knew the lack of pain, of any sensation, could be the worst torture of all?

But even more monstrous were those moments when the darkness would recede, and he would find himself looking out his own eyes again. Too often, they revealed horror and bloodshed, but even those brief respites from eternal darkness were welcome. In those moments, he tried to draw as much life back into himself as he could before he was drowned again by the demon that possessed his body. But as much as he struggled to hold on, it never lasted. In the end, such hopes proved crueler than any torment.

Better to simply let go, to allow the flame of myself to be extinguished into this nothingness, to add my smoke to the multitude that have come before me.

And he knew there were others before him. Occasionally wisps of smoke would brush through him, carrying with them snatches of another's life: a flash of a lover's face, the sting of a lash, the laughter of a child running through clover.

Is that all my life will become? Scraps in the wind?

As he pictured that wind, the darkness shredded around him, as if torn apart by a gale. He found a naked woman pressed under him on a bed. A streak of scarlet ran down her neck and between her breasts, coating a golden locket that hung there. Her eyes, as green as oak leaves, met his. They were wide with fear and pain, and they begged him to let her go.

Gasping, he forced his gaze away, to the sumptuous room. Heavy silver curtains had been drawn across the windows to keep out the sunlight, but he sensed that they would soon be opened. With the eternal clock of a Sanguinist, he knew sunset was less than an hour away.

Other bodies lay broken on the cold marble floor to either side of the bed, naked and unmoving.

He counted nine.

The demon inside me must be hungry.

But it wasn't just the demon.

A half dozen *strigoi* shared the chamber, some slumbering and slated, others still feasting on the dead. The intoxicating scent of blood lingered in the air, enticing Leopold to partake in this slaughter. But he also sensed his belly was full.

Perhaps that is why I have broken free, even for this brief moment.

He intended to take advantage of it.

He pushed higher off the woman, though one hand still clutched her arm. She shrank away, her heart fluttering like a wounded bird. The demon had fed too deeply upon her. He could not save her, but perhaps he could release her to die in peace. Summoning all his concentration, he forced one finger, then another to let go, willing his hand to obey.

Sweat sprang up on his brow from the effort, but he succeeded, freeing her arm. Unable to speak, he nodded to tell her that she should go.

Trembling, she looked down at her arm, then back at him.

Candlelight flickered against green eyes, and reminded him of another flash of emerald. *The green diamond.* Impotent hate flashed through him. Just to think of that stone numbed his body, making it even more difficult to move.

By my own hand, I doomed myself—and so many others.

He had been ordered to break that foul gemstone by a master who he had believed could return Christ to this world. But upon shattering that stone, he had unleashed a demon instead. He remembered that icy blackness flowing out of the heart of the shattered diamond, invading his body, bringing with it other voices, snatches of other lives. He was quickly lost, deafened by that cacophony—but one name rose above the others.

Legion.

That was the name of the darkness that had suffocated him, of the demon that had consumed him.

Since then, he had drifted in and out of awareness.

But for how long?

He could not tell. All he knew for sure was that the demon seemed to be gathering others to its side, building an army of *strigoi*.

With a great effort, Leopold lifted his hand before his own face as the woman dragged herself away, tangling in the bedsheets. He ignored her as shock rang through him. His normally pale white hand was as black as ink. He turned his head, discovering a mirror on the wall.

In its reflection, he was naked, a sculpture in ebony.

Leopold screamed, but no sound came from his lips.

The woman fell from the bed, stirring up one of the slumbering *strigoi*. The monster hissed, spitting blood. As it reared up, Leopold spotted a black palm print in the middle of its bare chest, like a brand or tattoo, only that blackness reeked of corruption and malevolence, far worse than even the stench of the *strigoi* who bore it.

Worst of all . . . that oily darkness was a match to the hue of his new skin.

But that was not all.

Leopold reached his arm out, splaying his fingers, realizing a new horror.

That mark on the beast is the same shape and size as my hand.

The demon must have marked this monster as his own, perhaps enslaving it as surely as it had Leopold.

The *strigoi* grabbed the woman, twisted her around, and ripped out her throat.

Before Leopold could react, darkness again welled up, dragging him back into that smoky sea, taking with it the sight of the ravaged woman. For once, he didn't resist, happy to let the horrors of that room vanish. But as he drowned into nothingness, he let go of any hope of escape.

A new desire filled him.

I must find a way to atone for my sins . . .

But along with that goal came a nagging question, one that might prove important: *Why was I allowed to break free for so long just now? What drew away that demon's attention?*

5:25 P.M.

Cumae, Italy

Damn, this bastard's fast . . .

Jordan brought up his machine pistol and fired three bursts toward the attacker who had climbed out of the tunnel. His rounds spattered against the rock wall of the cavern temple, finding no target.

Missed again . . .

From its fangs, it was plainly a *strigoi*, but he had never seen one move like that. The creature was there, and a split second later the monster was across the room, as if it had teleported the distance.

Baako and Sophia had Jordan's back, literally. The three of them stood in a circle, shoulder to shoulder. Baako carried a long African sword, while Sophia wielded a pair of curved knives.

The *strigoi* hissed from behind the room's altar. A long laceration bled across his chest. It was a wound Baako had inflicted as the beast first charged at them, saving Jordan's life in the process.

Unfortunately, it was the only successful strike his team had inflicted.

"It's trying to wear us down before the kill," Sophia said.

"Then time for a new strategy." Jordan pointed his gun, but as his finger pulled on the trigger, he shifted his aim to the side and fired into emptiness, anticipating that the *strigoi* would move again.

It did—right into his line of fire.

A scream pierced the roar of his weapon. The *strigoi* flew backward, blood spraying the walls.

Lucky shot, but I'm taking that point on the scoreboard.

The *strigoi* spun away, vanishing again into a blur. Jordan searched, swinging his weapon, but then, from out of nowhere, cold hands snatched Jordan off his feet and hurled him toward the wall. Still in midair, he drew the dagger from his ankle sheath, preparing to fight.

Unfortunately, the beast had armed itself, too—not only grabbing Jordan, but also Baako's sword. As they hit the wall together, his attacker shoved the stolen blade through Jordan's stomach.

He gasped, falling to his knees.

Baako and Sophia came instantly to his aid. With an arcing blow, Sophia severed the *strigoi's* sword arm. She drove her second blade into its stomach and ripped the monster from groin to neck.

Cold black blood spurted across Jordan's face.

He stared down at the blade still impaled through him.

Little late, guys.

5:28 P.M.
Rome, Italy

Pain shredded the darkness around Leopold, casting him back into the world, back in to that blood-soaked room. He clutched his belly, expecting to feel rent flesh and spilling guts. Instead, his fingers discovered smooth skin and a round intact belly, still full of blood from the demon's last feeding.

Leopold rubbed his naked abdomen, still feeling a ghost of that pain.

He saw the same blood-soaked abattoir as before—but he also saw into another chamber overlapping this one: a dark cavern with an altar in the middle.

I know that place.

It was the sibyl's temple, hidden at the heart of a volcanic mountain in Cumae, the same place where Leopold had loosed the demon Legion into this world.

But how am I seeing this vision?

It was as if he were viewing the scene through another's eyes. As he watched, clawed hands rose up and clutched a belly pouring forth with oily black blood, while loops of viscera tumbled forth.

But it wasn't just *sight* he shared with this other—he also *felt* that pain.

Then that distant form collapsed on its side. It had to be a *strigoi*, likely a member of Legion's army, perhaps one that the demon had enslaved. Leopold pictured the black brand on the chest of the *strigoi* here.

Did that mark serve as some sort of psychic link? Would it end as this beast died?

Black smoke billowed around him, preparing to drag him away. Yet, he still saw into that cavern temple, the link still intact as the *strigoi* faded. Even while dying, the beast searched the cavern, as if looking for some way to save itself.

Instead, its gaze fell upon the altar, focusing upon two pieces of an emerald stone.

The green diamond.

Is that what you were sent to fetch?

Somewhere deep inside Leopold's possessed soul, he sensed that longing from Legion. Leopold vaguely remembered tunneling out of that temple, his limbs impossibly strengthened by the demon that possessed him, but the monster had also been frantic to escape that mountain, to be free of that prison of volcanic rock. After centuries of being locked away inside that gemstone, it plainly could not stand to be trapped a moment longer, and in its haste, it forgot to take the stone with it.

But why does it need that stone?

The diamond shone brightly atop the altar, as if to mock Legion's failure. But the *strigoi's* eyes had begun to glaze, fogging the view. There was little life left. That gaze shifted to movement nearby, a scuffling of legs. Those limbs parted enough to reveal a man kneeling on the rock, a blade through his belly.

Through that link, Leopold looked into the man's blue eyes.

Recognition rang through him.

Jordan . . .

With that thought, Legion stirred to life again, rising from the ashes of the *strigoi* who was dying in that cavern. Darkness swelled up inside Leopold. Within that tide, he felt the demon's attention swing toward him. He could feel it picking through his memories. He tried his best to bottle up his knowledge.

About Jordan, about the others.

But he failed.

As he fell into nothingness, he felt his own lips move, heard his own voice, but it was not Leopold, but Legion, who spoke Jordan's other name, his truer name.

"The Warrior of Man . . ."

Dear Lord, what have I done?

Leopold fled away, down the only path still open to him for a few breaths more, down that fading link.

5:31 P.M.

Cumae, Italy

Sprawled in a pool of his own blood, Jordan stared up at the cavern roof. Baako kept his large hands pressed onto Jordan's wound, while Sophia tossed aside the long blade. Jordan had barely felt the impaled sword being yanked free. A strange numbness kept his belly cold, making the bloody pool under him feel hot.

Baako knelt over him, offering a reassuring smile. "We'll get you stabilized and back to Rome in no time."

"You're . . . a bad liar," Jordan grunted.

He would never survive being dragged up that tunnel with his stomach sliced open. He doubted if he'd even make it across the room.

Knowing this, a vision of Erin's face shimmered in his head, her brown eyes laughing, a smile on her lips. Other memories overlapped: a lock of wet blond hair falling across her cheek, her bathrobe falling open, revealing her warm body.

I don't want to die in a hole, away from you.

For that matter, he didn't want to die at all.

He wished Erin were here right now, holding his hand, telling him it would be all right, even if it wouldn't. He wanted to see her one more time, tell her that he loved her, and make her feel it. He knew she was afraid of love, believing it would melt away like snow, that it couldn't last.

And now I'm proving it to her.

He clutched Baako's iron-strong arm. "Tell Erin . . . I'll always love her."

Baako kept pressure on his wound. "You can tell her yourself."

"And my family . . ."

They would need to know, too. His mother would be devastated, his sisters and brothers would mourn him, and his nieces and nephews would barely remember him in a few years.

Should've called my mother more often.

Because whatever malaise of emotions that had afflicted him of late extended beyond Erin to his family, too. He'd cut himself off from them all.

He clenched his teeth, not wanting to die, if only to make amends to everyone. But the spreading pool of warm blood told him that his wounded body didn't care about his future plans of babies and kids and sitting in rocking chairs on a porch, watching the corn grow.

He turned his head, as Sophia checked on his attacker.

At least, I don't look as bad as that guy.

The *strigoi* didn't have long to live, either. Strangely, the creature's eyes stared directly at him. Those cold bloodless lips moved, as if speaking.

Sophia leaned closer, one eyebrow arching high. "What was that?"

The *strigoi* drew in a deeper, shuddering breath and, in an accent that Jordan knew well, it spoke. "Jordan, *mein Freund* . . . I'm sorry."

Sophia pulled her hand back from the creature's body. Jordan was equally shocked.

Leopold.

But how?

The *strigoi* shuddered and went still.

Sophia sat back and shook her head. The beast was dead, taking with it any further explanation.

Jordan struggled to understand, but the world faded as he bled away the last of his life. He felt himself falling away, the room receding, but instead of into darkness, it was into brilliance that he plummeted. He wanted to raise his hand against it, especially as it grew brighter, burning into him. He screwed his eyelids closed, but it didn't help.

He had felt such a burning light only once before, when he'd been struck by lightning as a teenager. He had survived the bolt, but it had left its mark, burning in a fractal pattern of scar tissue across his shoulder and upper chest. Those strange vinelike designs were called Lichtenberg figures, or sometimes, lightning flowers.

Now ribbons of liquid fire radiated along those scars, filling them completely—then stretching even farther. Tendrils of heat grew outward, rooting into his stomach, where a searing agony exploded. The fire writhed in his gut like a living thing.

Is this what death truly felt like?

But he didn't feel himself weakening. Instead, he felt inexplicably *stronger.*

He took another breath, then another.

Slowly the room slipped back into focus. Nothing seemed to have changed. He still lay in a pool of his own cooling blood. Baako continued to press hard against his wound.

Jordan met the African's concerned gaze and pushed at his hands. "I think I'm okay."

Better than okay.

Baako shifted his palms and glanced at the spot where the sword had impaled Jordan. Strong fingers wiped the residual blood away.

A low whistle escaped Baako.

Sophia joined him. "What is it?"

Baako glanced up at her. "It's stopped bleeding. I swear the wound even looks smaller."

Sophia examined him, too. Only her expression grew more worried than relieved. "You should be dead," she said baldly, gesturing to the spread of blood. "You received a mortal wound. I've seen many over the past centuries."

Jordan pushed up into a seated position. "People have counted me out before. I even died once. No, make that *twice.* But who's keeping track?"

Baako sighed. "You *healed,* just as the book said you would."

Sophia quoted from the Blood Gospel. " *'The Warrior of Man is likewise bound to the angels to whom he owes his mortal life.'* "

Baako clapped him on the shoulder. "It seems those angels are still watching over you."

Or they're not done with me yet.

Sophia returned her attention to the dead *strigoi.* "It knew your name."

Jordan was glad for the distraction, remembering the last words spoken from those dying lips.

Jordan, mein Freund . . . *I'm sorry.*

"That voice," he said. "I swear it was Brother Leopold's."

"If you're right," Sophia said, "that is one miracle that can wait. We should get you to the medics at camp."

Jordan fingered open his shirt. The wound was now just a sticky scab. He wagered even that would be gone in a few hours. Still, he pictured that sword piercing through him, which raised another mystery.

"Have you guys ever seen a *strigoi* move like that?"

Baako looked to Sophia, as if she had more experience.

"Never," she answered.

"It was not just fast," Baako said. "But strong, too."

Sophia moved to the dead creature's side, rolled it to its back, and began to strip away its clothes. Three bullet holes decorated the corpse's center mass. Jordan was pretty impressed that he'd hit the creature at all. As Sophia peeled the shirt away, Jordan sucked in a surprised breath.

Emblazoned on the *strigoi's* pale chest was the imprint of a black hand. Jordan had seen one like it once before—burned on the neck of the now dead

Bathory Darabont. Her mark had bound her to her former master, branding her as one of his own.

The presence of it here now meant only one thing.

"Someone sent this creature down here."

5:28 P.M.
Rome, Italy

I am Legion . . .

He stood before a silvered mirror, drawing himself fully back into his vessel to center himself after his sojourn to that dread cavern. In that reflection, he saw an unremarkable body: weak limbs, sunken chest, soft belly. But his mark graced this one's form, painting his skin as dark as the void between stars. Eyes as blackened as dead suns stared back out of that mirror.

He let those eyes close and searched the shadows that made up his true essence. Six hundred and sixty-six spirits. He let those tendrils run through his awareness, reading what still remained, looking for answers. He caught glimpses of a common pain from the past, of a glass prison, of a white-bearded figure staring inward with disgust.

But from such pain came his birth.

I am many . . . I am plural . . . I am Legion.

Within those swirls of darkness that made up his being, a single flame glowed, flickering in those endless shadows. He drew closer to that fire, reading the smoke that came from it as the spirit that sustained it slowly smothered.

He knew that one's name, the vessel that he possessed.

Leopold.

It was from the smoke of that weakening flame that Legion had learned the ways of this present world. He had rifled through those memories, those experiences, to ready himself for the war to come. He had built an army, enslaving others with merely a touch of his hand. He let the strength of his darkness flow into them. With each touch, his eyes and ears in this world multiplied, allowing his awareness to grow ever larger across the land.

He had one purpose.

He pictured a being of immensely dark angelic power, seated on a black throne.

Centuries ago, those six-hundred-and-sixty-six spirits had been woven by that black angel, securing Legion inside that gemstone. He was left there as a harbinger for what was to come, a dark seed waiting to take root in this new world and spread.

When he was finally freed from the gem, he attached himself to the creature who broke that stone. *Leopold.* Legion rooted himself deep into his new vessel, attaching himself to Leopold, taking possession, the two becoming one. The vessel was the pot from which he could grow into this world, spreading his branches far and wide, claiming others, branding them, enslaving them. And while his foothold in this world depended on Leopold living, he could still travel along those branches and control them from afar.

His duty was to open the way for his master's return, to ready this world for its purification, when the vermin known as mankind would be purged out of this earthly garden. The dark angel had promised Legion this paradise, but before he could be awarded this prize, he must first complete his task.

And now he knew there were forces aligned against him.

That he also learned from the flickering flame inside him.

Legion did not fully understand that threat, but he recognized that his vessel fought to keep certain scraps hidden from him. Moments ago, he felt that flame of Leopold's spirit flare brighter with shock, saw it shudder in the darkness, drawing his attention. From that smoke, he learned a name, put a face to it.

The Warrior of Man.

But not just that name. Others slipped free, too, as memories burned away to smoke.

The Knight of Christ.

The Woman of Learning.

Whispers of prophecy rose with that smoke, along with an image of a book written by the very Son of God. He studied that flame now, trying to learn more.

Who else stands in my way?

6

Talk about an exercise in futility . . .

With gritted teeth, Tommy shinnied up another couple of inches on the knotted rope that hung from the center of the gymnasium. Below his toes, his class-mates yelled either words of encouragement or insults. He couldn't really tell which from up there, especially past the pounding of his heart and gasping of his breath.

Not that it would matter anyway.

He had always hated gym, even before his cancer diagnosis. Uncoordinated and not particularly fast on his feet, he was usually picked last for most sports. He also quickly discovered that he would rather stay away from any ball than jump after it.

I mean what's the point?

Only one activity truly interested him: climbing. He was actually good at it, and he liked the simplicity of it. It was all about him and the rope. Whenever he climbed, his worries and fears faded away.

Or at least most of them.

He clamped his knees on the rope and tugged up higher. Sweat trickled down his back. The weather was always warm in Santa Barbara, and almost always sunny. He liked that. After spending time in Russia and aboard an icebreaker in the Arctic, he never wanted to be that cold again.

Of course, after being frozen solid in an ice sculpture of an angel, anyone would appreciate the Southern California sunshine.

He stared up toward that sunshine now, where it flowed through a row of windows at the top of the gymnasium.

Almost there . . .

In another two yards, he should be able to touch the wire cages that protected the lights that hung from the ceiling. Touching the dusty wires was a badge of honor in the ninth-grade class, and he intended to reach them.

He stopped for a moment, readying himself for the last bit of the ascent. Lately, he got out of breath so easily. It was worrisome. Half a year ago, he had been touched by an angel . . . literally. Angelic blood had flowed through him, curing him of his cancer, strengthening him, even making him temporarily immortal. But that was gone, burned away in the sands of Egypt.

He was just an ordinary boy again.

And I plan to stay that way.

He hung for a moment, staring upward and taking a deep breath.

I can do this.

A sharper shout reached him from below. "That's far enough! Come back down!"

That would be Martin Altman, Tommy's only friend at the new school. He'd lost his old friends when he had moved in with his aunt and uncle. After Tommy's parents had died, they were his only blood relatives.

He pushed that thought away before dark memories overwhelmed him. Glancing between his toes, he saw Martin staring up at him. His friend was tall and lanky, with long arms and legs. Martin was always ready with a corny joke, and laughter came easily out of him.

Of course, Martin's parents hadn't died in his arms.

Tommy felt a flare of anger at his friend, but he knew it came from a place of petty jealousy, so he stamped it back down. Still, the rope slipped between his sweaty palms. He clutched tighter.

Maybe Martin's right.

A wave of dizziness further convinced him. He started back down, but everything grew steadily fuzzier. He struggled to hold on as he descended more rapidly, sliding now, burning his palms.

Whatever you do, don't let—

Then he was falling. He stared up at the sunshine flowing through the windows above, remembering another time he had plummeted through the air. Then, he had been immortal.

Not so lucky today.

He slammed into the pile of mats at the base of the rope. Air burst from his chest. He gasped, trying to refill his lungs, but they refused to cooperate.

"Move!" shouted Mr. Lessing, the gym teacher.

Everything went gray—then he found his breath again. He heaved in great gulps of air, sounding like a hoarse seal.

His classmates stared down at him. Some were laughing, others looked concerned, especially Martin.

Mr. Lessing pushed through them. "You're okay," he said. "Just got the wind knocked out of you."

Tommy fought to slow his breath. He wanted to sink through the floor. Especially when he spotted Lisa

Ballantine's face among the others. He liked her, and now he'd made a fool of himself.

He tried to sit up, tweaking a spike of pain up his bruised back.

"Go slow," Mr. Lessing said, helping him to his feet, which only made Tommy's face heat up even more.

Still, the room tilted a little, and he clutched the gym teacher's arm. This day couldn't get any worse.

Martin pointed to Tommy's left hand. "Is that a rope burn?"

Tommy looked down. His palms certainly were red, but Martin pointed to a dark mark on the inside of his wrist.

"Let me see that," Mr. Lessing said.

Tommy shook free and stumbled away, covering the blemish with his other hand. "Just a rope burn. Like Martin said."

"Okay, then everyone clear out," Mr. Lessing ordered. "Showers. Double time."

Tommy hurried away. He was still light-headed, but it wasn't from the fall. He kept the lesion covered. He didn't want anyone else to know, especially not his aunt and uncle. He would keep it secret for as long as he could. While he didn't understand what was happening, he knew one thing for sure.

No chemotherapy this time around.

He rubbed the spot on his wrist with his thumb, as if trying to erase it away, because he knew he was out of miracles.

His cancer was truly back.

Fear and despair welled through him. He wished he could speak to his mother or father, but that was impossible. Still, there was one person he could call, one person he could trust with his secret.

Another immortal who, like him, had lost her immortality.

She'll know what to do.

6:25 P.M. CET
Venice, Italy

Standing in the middle of the convent's garden, Elizabeth Bathory adjusted her broad-brimmed straw hat to cover her face, to shade her eyes from the low-hanging spring sun. To protect her skin, she always wore a hat when she worked outside, even here in the tiny herb garden inside the walled courtyard that served as her prison.

She had been taught centuries ago that those of royal blood should never have skin the same hue as the peasants who worked the fields. Back then she had her own gardens at C˘achtice Castle, where she had grown medicinal plants, studying the arts of healing, plying cures out of a flower's petals or a stubborn root. Even then, she had not gone outside with her clippers and baskets without some manner of shade.

Though this small herb garden paled next to her former fields, she appreciated her time among the convent's fragrant collage of thyme, chives, basil, and parsley. She had spent the past afternoon clearing out old, woody growths of rosemary to fill in those new spaces with lavender and mint. Their homely scents drifted up into the warm air.

If she closed her eyes, she could imagine that it was a summer day back at her castle, that her children would soon run out to meet her. She would pass them her gathered herbs and walk with them through the grounds, hearing their stories of the day.

But that world had ended four hundred years ago.

Her children were dead; her castle in ruins. Even her name was whispered as a curse. All because she had been made into an accursed *strigoi*.

She pictured Rhun Korza's face, remembering him atop her, the taste of her own blood on his lips. In that moment of weakness and desire, her life had been forever changed. After her initial shock at her transformation into a *strigoi*, she had come to embrace that damned existence, to appreciate all it offered. But even that had been stripped from her this past winter—stolen away by the same hand that had given it.

Now she was simply human again.

Weak, mortal, and trapped.

Curse you, Rhun.

She bent down and savagely clipped a branch of rosemary and tossed it to the flagstone path. Marie, an elderly nun, worked the gardens with her, sweeping the path behind her with a handmade broom. Marie was a wrinkled-up apricot of a woman, eighty if she was a day, with blue eyes filmed with age. She treated Elizabeth with a kind condescension, as if the nun expected her to grow out of her troublesome behavior. If only she knew that Elizabeth had lived more centuries than this old woman would ever see.

But Marie knew nothing of Elizabeth's past, not even her full name.

None at the convent was given this knowledge.

A twinge in one knee caused Elizabeth to shift her weight to the other, recognizing the pain for what it was.

Aging.

I've had one curse replaced with another.

Out of the corner of her eye she spotted Berndt Niedermann crossing the courtyard on his way to the dining hall for dinner. The elegant German lodged in one of the convent's guest rooms. He was dressed in what passed in this era for formal: pressed trousers and a well-tailored blue jacket. He raised a hand in greeting.

She ignored him.

Familiarity was not yet called for.

At least for the moment.

Instead, she stretched a kink from her back, glancing everywhere but in Berndt's direction. The Venetian convent was not without its charm. In the past, the convent had been a grand house with a stately entrance overlooking a wide canal. Tall columns flanked a stout oaken door that led to the dock. She had spent many hours staring out her room's window, watching life travel by on the canals. Venice had no cars or horses— only boats and people on foot. It was a curious anachronism, a city largely unchanged from her own past.

Over the last week, she had chatted with the German lodger on occasion. Berndt was an author visiting Venice to research a book, which seemed to entail walking around the stone streets and eating fine food and drinking expensive wine. If she had been allowed to accompany him for one day, she could have shown him so much more, filled him with the history of this flooded city, but that was never to be.

She was always under the watchful eye of Sister Abigail, a Sanguinist who made it clear that Elizabeth must never leave the convent grounds. To keep her life—mortal as it was now—Elizabeth had to remain a prisoner within its stately walls.

Cardinal Bernard had been clear on that point. She was imprisoned here to atone for her past crimes.

Still, this German might prove useful. To that end, she had read his books, discussed them with the author over wine, careful to praise them when she could. Even these brief conversations were not private. She was only allowed to speak to guests while closely supervised, usually by Marie or Abigail, that gray-haired battle-ax of a Sanguinist.

Still, Elizabeth found gaps in their supervision, especially lately. As the months of her imprisonment ticked away, the others had begun to let their guard down.

Two nights ago, she had been able to slip into Berndt's room while he was out. Among his private belongings, she had discovered a key to his rented canal boat. Rashly, she had stolen it, hoping he would think he had misplaced it.

So far, no alarm had been raised.

Good.

She wiped her forehead with a handkerchief as a small boy in a blue messenger cap appeared at the other end of the courtyard. The child moved in the careless modern way that she had seen Tommy use, as if children today were not in control of their limbs, allowing them to flop uselessly when they moved. Even at a younger age than this boy, her long dead son Paul would never have traipsed so artlessly.

Marie hobbled over to greet the messenger, while Elizabeth strained to overhear their conversation. Her Italian was passable now, as she'd had little to do beyond work in the garden and study. She studied far into the night. Everything she learned was a weapon that she would one day wield against her captors.

A honeybee lit on her hand, and she lifted it to her face.

"Be careful," warned a voice behind her, startling her. That would never have happened when she was a *strigoi*. Then she had been able to pick out a heartbeat from fields away.

She turned to discover Berndt standing there. He must have circled the courtyard to approach her so discreetly. He stood close enough that she could smell his musky aftershave.

She glanced down to the bee. "I should be fearful of this small creature?"

"Many people are allergic to bees," Berndt explained. "If it were to sting *me*, it might even kill me."

Elizabeth lifted an eyebrow. Modern man was so weak. No one perished from bee stings in her time. Or perhaps many had, and one simply had not known.

"We cannot allow such a thing to happen." She moved her hand away from Berndt and blew on the bee to make it fly.

As she did so, a figure stepped out of the shadows of the courtyard wall and headed toward them.

Sister Abigail, of course.

Her Sanguinist minder looked like a harmless old British nun—her limbs thin and weak, her blue eyes faded with age. As she reached them, she tucked in a wisp of gray hair that had escaped the side of her wimple.

"Good evening, Herr Niedermann," Abigail greeted him. "Dinner is soon to be served. If you'll head to the hall, I'm sure—"

Berndt interrupted her. "Perhaps Elizabeth would care to join me."

Abigail grabbed Elizabeth's arm with a grip that would leave a bruise. She did not resist. Bruises might engender sympathy from Berndt in the right circumstances.

"I'm afraid that Elizabeth cannot go with you," Abigail said in an irritated tone that brooked no argument.

"Of course I may, Sister," Elizabeth said. "I'm not a prisoner, am I?"

Abigail's square face flushed hotly.

"Then it's settled," Berndt said. "And perhaps afterward we could go for a short boat ride?"

Elizabeth forced herself not to react, fearing Abigail would hear the sudden spike of her heartbeat. *Would the missing key be noted?*

"Elizabeth has been ill," Abigail said, clearly struggling for any explanation to keep Elizabeth within the convent's walls. "She mustn't overtire herself."

"Perhaps the sea air will do me good," Elizabeth said with a smile.

"I can't allow it," Abigail countered. "Your . . . your father would be very mad. You certainly don't want me to call Bernard, do you?"

Elizabeth gave up toying with the woman, as much as it delighted her. She certainly didn't want Cardinal Bernard's attention drawn this way.

"That's unfortunate," Berndt said. "Especially as I must leave tomorrow."

Elizabeth looked sharply toward him. "I thought you were staying another week."

He smiled at her concern, clearly mistaking it for affection. "I'm afraid business calls me back to Frankfurt earlier that I was expecting."

That presented a problem. If she intended to use his boat to make her escape, it would have to be this night.

She thought quickly, knowing this was still her best chance—not just of escape, but so much more.

She had grander plans, to be more than just free.

While Elizabeth could walk under the sun again, she had lost so much more. As a mortal human, she could no longer hear the softest sounds, smell the faintest wisps of scent, or witness the glowing colors of the night. It was as if she had been wrapped in a thick blanket.

She hated it.

She wanted her *strigoi* senses back, to feel that unnatural strength flowing through her limbs again, but most of all, she desired to be immortal—to be unfettered not just from these convent's walls, but from the march of years.

I will let nothing stop me.

Before she could move, the cell phone hidden in the pocket of her skirts vibrated.

Only one person had that number.

Tommy.

She moved back from the German. "Thank you, Berndt, but Sister Abigail is correct." She gave him a quick curtsy, realizing too late that no one did such things anymore. "I am feeling a touch faint from working the gardens. Perhaps I should take my meal in my room after all."

Abigail's lips tightened into a hard line. "I think that is wise."

"A shame," he said, disappointment ringing in his voice.

Abigail took her by the arm, the nun's fingers even tighter now, and led her to her room. "You are to stay here," she commanded once they reached her small cell. "I will bring your dinner to you."

Abigail locked the door behind her. Elizabeth waited until her footsteps faded, then crossed to the barred window. Alone now, she retrieved the telephone and returned the call.

When she heard Tommy, she immediately knew something was wrong. Tears frosted his voice.

"My cancer's back," he said. "I don't know what to do, who to tell."

She gripped the phone harder, as if she could reach through the ethers to a boy she had grown to love as much as her own son. "Explain what has happened."

She knew Tommy's history, knew that he had been sick before an infusion of angelic blood had cured him, granting him immortality. Now he was an ordinary mortal, like her—afflicted as he had been before. Though she had heard him use the word *cancer*, she never truly comprehended the nature of his sickness.

Wanting to understand more, she pressed him. "Tell me of this cancer."

"It's a disease that eats you up from inside." His words grew soft, forlorn, and lost. "It's in my skin and bones."

Her heart ached for the boy. She wanted to comfort him, as she often did with her own son. "Surely doctors can cure you of this affliction in this modern age."

There was a long pause, then a tired sigh. "Not my cancer. I spent years in chemotherapy, throwing up all the time. I lost my hair. Even my bones hurt. The doctors couldn't stop it."

She leaned against the cold plaster wall and studied the dark waters of the canal outside her window. "Can you not try this chemotherapy again?"

"I won't." He sounded firm, more like a man. "I should have died back then. I think I'm supposed to. I won't go through that misery again."

"What about your aunt and uncle? What do they say you should do?"

"I haven't told them, and I'm not going to. They would make me go through those medical procedures again, and it won't help. I know it. This is how things are supposed to be."

Anger built inside her, hearing the defeat in his voice.

You may not wish to fight, but I will.

"Listen," he said, "no one can save me. I just called to talk, to get this off my chest . . . with someone I can trust."

His honesty touched her. He, alone in the world, trusted her. And he alone was the only one whom she trusted in return. Determination grew inside her. Her own son had died because she had failed to protect him. She would not let that happen to this boy.

He talked for a few minutes more, mostly about his dead parents. As he did, a new purpose grew in her heart.

I will break free of these walls . . . and I will save you.

7

March 17, 6:38 P.M. CET
Vatican City

Out of the frying pan, and into the fire . . .

After safely escaping the Sanguinist library undetected, Erin had met up with Christian and Sister
Margaret before being summoned to Cardinal
Bernard's offices in the Apostolic Palace. She followed
a black-robed priest down a long paneled hall, passing through the papal apartments on her way to the
Sanguinists' private wing.

She wondered why this sudden summons.

Has Bernard learned about my trespass?

She tried to keep the tension out of her stride. She
had already attempted to question the priest ahead of

her. His name was Father Gregory. He was Bernard's new assistant, but the man remained close-mouthed, an attribute necessary for anyone serving the cardinal.

She studied this newly recruited priest. He had milky white skin, thick dark eyebrows, and collar-length black hair. Unlike the cardinal's previous assistant, he wasn't human—he was a Sanguinist. He looked to be in his early thirties, but he could be centuries older than that.

They reached Bernard's office door, and Father Gregory opened it for her. "Here we are, Dr. Granger."

She noted the Irish lilt to his words. "Thank you, Father."

He followed her inside, slipping free an old-fashioned watch fob on a chain and glancing down at it. "We're a touch early, I'm afraid. The cardinal should be here momentarily."

Erin suspected this was some ploy of Bernard's, to leave her waiting as a petty show of superiority. The cardinal still bristled that the Blood Gospel had been bound to her.

Father Gregory pulled out a chair for her before the cardinal's wide mahogany desk. She placed her backpack next to her seat.

As she waited, she took in the room, always finding new surprises. Ancient leather-bound volumes filled floor-to-ceiling bookcases, an antique jeweled globe from the sixteenth century gleamed on the desk, and a sword from the time of the Crusades hung above the door.

Cardinal Bernard had wielded that very sword to take Jerusalem from the Saracens a thousand years before, and she had personally witnessed his skill with it a few months back. While he seemed to prefer to work behind the scenes, he remained a fierce warrior.

Something to keep in mind.

"You must be worn out after your long day of study," Father Gregory said, returning to the door. "I'll fetch you some coffee while you wait."

As soon as he closed the door, she crossed around to the other side of the cardinal's desk. She studied the papers strewn across the surface, reading rapidly through them. A few months ago she would have balked at invading the cardinal's privacy, but she had seen enough people die to preserve Bernard's secrets.

Knowledge was power, and she would not let him hoard it.

The topmost sheet was written in Latin. She skimmed the words, translating as she went. It seemed two *strigoi* had attacked a nightclub in Rome, killing thirty-four people. Such open attacks were unusual, almost unheard of in modern times. Over the passing centuries, even the *strigoi* had learned to conceal themselves and hide the bodies of their prey.

But apparently that wasn't true any longer.

She read through the private report on the massacre and discovered an even more disturbing detail. Among the dead was a trio of Sanguinists. She swallowed at the seeming impossibility of that.

Two strigoi *had killed three trained Sanguinists?*

She moved the sheet aside and read the next report, this one in English. It described a similar attack on a military base outside of London, twenty-seven armed soldiers killed at their evening mess hall.

Erin shuffled through the remainder of the pages. They documented strange and ferocious attacks across Italy, Austria, and Germany. She became so lost in the horrors of these accounts that she barely noted the office door swinging open.

She raised her head.

Cardinal Bernard entered, dressed in the scarlet robes of his station. With his white hair and calm demeanor, he could easily be mistaken for someone's kindly grandfather.

He sighed, nodding to his desk. "I see you've read my intelligence reports."

She didn't bother trying to deny her actions. "They're light on specifics. Have you learned anything more about these attackers?"

"No," he said as they exchanged places. He took his desk chair, and she returned to her seat. "We know their tactics are savage, undisciplined, and unpredictable."

"How about witnesses?"

"So far, they've left no survivors. But from this latest attack, at the discotheque, we were able to obtain surveillance footage."

Erin sat straighter.

"It is quite gruesome," he warned, tilting his computer monitor toward her.

She leaned forward. "Show me."

He opened a file, and soon grainy footage showed a handful of dancers moving around on a dark floor. Lights strobed, and though the footage had no audio, she could imagine the heavy bass beat of that music.

"Watch these two," Bernard said, pointing.

He indicated two men, both dressed in dark clothing, at the edge of the screen. They moved slowly out onto the dance floor. One had white skin, one black. She squinted closer, studying the dark figure. The video quality was too poor to pick out features, but it seemed as if his skin drank in the light. His face looked unnatural somehow, more like a mask than human skin.

As if the dancers sensed the hunters in their midst, the small crowd parted, keeping a ragged circle of free space around the two creatures. They were right to be wary. A moment later, the two *strigoi* lashed out, moving so quickly that their images blurred on the screen. She had never seen *strigoi* move at such speeds.

In less than ten seconds, only the two *strigoi* remained standing. Broken and bloody bodies lay at their feet. Each figure picked up a wounded woman from the floor, slung her over his shoulder, and disappeared out of the frame.

Erin shuddered to think what lay in wait for those poor girls.

The cardinal tapped a key, and the image froze.

Erin swallowed hard, thinking of the pain and fear those people must have felt in their final moments. None of them had stood a chance.

"Are the police looking for these killers?" she asked.

The cardinal moved his monitor back around. "They are searching, but they don't understand what they're hunting."

"What do you mean?"

"The police were never allowed to see this footage. As you know, we cannot allow proof of the existence of *strigoi* to be revealed to the world at large."

She sat back in her chair. "Then how can the people protect themselves?"

"We have sent additional teams out. They patrol the city night and day. We'll find this pair of killers and destroy them. That is our sacred duty."

Erin wondered how many innocent lives would be claimed before that happened. "Those *strigoi* were fast, like nothing I've seen before."

The cardinal grimaced. "And they aren't the only ones. We have similar reports globally. For some reason, the *strigoi* have begun to change, to grow more powerful."

"So I've heard, but why is this happening? Why now?"

"I don't know for sure, but I fear that it is related to the prophecy."

She bunched her brows, guessing what he was referring to. "That Lucifer's shackles have somehow loosened."

"And because of that, more evil is entering our world. A fundamental balance has begun to shift, giving additional strength to evil creatures, while sapping holy forces at the same time."

She stared harder at the cardinal, sizing him up. "Do you feel weaker?"

He clenched one hand atop his desk. "Here, on these blessed grounds, I do not. But we have lost eighteen Sanguinists in the field over the past twelve weeks."

Eighteen? The order had already begun fading in numbers over the past decades, much like the Catholic priesthood. The Sanguinists could not afford to lose more foot soldiers, especially if a war was coming.

"Do the attacks have any geographic pattern?" she asked. "Perhaps if we knew where all of this started, it could offer us a clue to stopping it."

His eyes narrowed, studying her. "Dr. Granger, as usual, you always seem to hit the nail on the head."

She sat straighter. "You figured something out."

"We've been meticulously recording dates and locations of these attacks."

"To build a database," she said. "Smart."

He nodded acknowledgment of her compliment and tilted his monitor toward her again. He quickly brought into view a map of Europe. Small red dots bloomed, marking attack sites. She balked at the sheer number, but she kept her focus.

"If you extrapolate backward," Bernard said, demonstrating on the map, "it appears these attacks have been expanding outward from a single location."

He zoomed into the epicenter of the attacks.

She read the name written there, feeling the blood sink into the pit of her gut. "Cumae . . . that's where the sibyl's temple is located."

And where Jordan is working.

She stared over at Bernard. "Have you heard anything from Jordan and his team? Did they learn anything?"

The cardinal sank heavily into his seat. "That was the other reason I summoned you. I thought you should hear it from me first. There was an attack—"

He was interrupted as Father Gregory arrived with a silver coffee service. Erin glanced back, a light-headed panic rushing through her. Gregory must have heard the frantic flutter of her heartbeat and froze at the door.

Erin turned back to Bernard. "Is Jordan okay?"

Bernard motioned to Father Gregory. "Leave the coffee on the table over there. That will be all."

Erin didn't bother waiting for Bernard's assistant to leave. Her days of waiting until the Sanguinists got around to telling her things were over.

"What happened?" she blurted out, leaning aggressively forward.

Bernard held up a palm, plainly urging her to calm down. "Do not fear, Jordan and his team are unharmed."

Erin settled back. She let out a shaky breath, but she also sensed that the cardinal was holding something back. But with her most important concern addressed, she waited until Father Gregory left to confront Bernard.

"What aren't you telling me?" she asked.

"This morning, Jordan's team discovered a new tunnel, one that looked recently excavated. It appears something may have dug its way out of that buried temple."

"*Something?* What does that mean?"

"We don't know. But we do know that Brother Leopold's body is missing from that temple."

She took this all in. During the battle in that temple last winter, Leopold had been killed by Rhun . . . or at least, it sure looked that way. But if his body was now missing, that meant either he was still alive or someone had taken his body.

She returned again to a worry closer to her heart. "You said there was an attack."

"A *strigoi* ambushed Jordan and his team down in that temple."

She stood up and crossed to the coffee service, too anxious to keep sitting. She poured herself a cup, reminding herself that Jordan was fine.

Still . . .

Warming her palms on the cup, she faced Bernard. "Was this attacker one of these super *strigoi*?"

"It appears so. The good news is that the others are bringing the *strigoi's* body back to Rome for study. We may learn something from the remains."

"When?" she asked sharply, anxious to see Jordan, to make sure that he was safe.

"They should be here in the next hour. But they also found something else in the chamber, something they didn't want to discuss over the phone. In fact, Jordan said that he wanted you to see it first." The cardinal looked peeved that someone was withholding information from him. "He believed you might recognize it, because, as he adamantly insisted, you are the Woman of Learning."

She took a sip of the coffee, allowing the heat to warm away the residual chill of her panic. She appreciated Jordan's confidence, but she hoped it wasn't misplaced. With no idea what he was bringing back from Cumae, she pondered the mystery of Leopold's missing body and returned to Bernard's cryptic assertion.

Something dug its way out of that temple.

7:02 P.M.
Rome, Italy

Legion sidled along the edge of a tall wall in the heart of Rome. He kept the barrier's shadow over his form. Though the sun had sunk below the horizon, the surrounding streets still glowed with twilight. He preferred darker places to prowl. As an extra precaution, he pulled the hood of his coat farther over his head, knowing one certainty.

No one can look upon my bare face and not recognize my glory.

Yet, so much more remained *unknown*.

And that must end.

His vessel, the one called Leopold, has proven valuable. From that flickering flame that still glowed in the darkness inside his being, Legion had learned more about this prophecy and those who stood against him in his duty.

The words of that divination rang through him with each step.

Together, the trio must face their final quest. The shackles of Lucifer have been loosened, and his Chalice remains lost. It will take the light of all three to forge the Chalice anew and banish him again to his eternal darkness.

He pictured the face of the one known as the Warrior of Man, fixing that image of his blue eyes and hard planes of his face. The Warrior exuded all that masculinity represented, a true figure of a man.

As he continued along that tall wall, a large vehicle rushed past on the road beside him, stirring up trash, belching out foul fumes. From Leopold's memories, he knew this was called a bus. But he retreated to his own memories. As a fallen one, he had spent endless years walking this garden of a world, well before man had trampled through it. Where once wild things grew, mankind had clad the land with artificial stone. Where once clear streams trickled under blue skies, now there was filth—both in the water and in the air.

Even from the beginning, he had known man was unfit to inherit this paradise. During the war of the heavens, where he had joined others against God's plan for man, he had hoped to claim this garden for himself. But in the end, he and the others lost that battle and were cast down, and now mankind had proven, as he had envisioned, to be a blight in this garden, a weed that needed to be rooted out and burned.

I will take this paradise back.

He would let nothing stop him.

Not even prophecy.

To that end, he must learn more about this trio, enough to stop them. He ran his shadowy fingertips along the wall next to him, feeling the burn of holiness in those stones. This barrier separated Rome from Vatican City. He prowled its length for one determined purpose.

He had learned from Leopold the names of the remaining two members of the trio: the Woman of Learning and the Knight of Christ. They were likely nearby, hiding in this bastion of godliness. He pulled his fingers from the wall and stared down at his palm, swirling the darkness across his skin.

If he laid his hand upon one of the trio, he could possess them in an instant.

With a single touch, I can end this prophecy's threat.

The first step toward that goal approached him now. He had hoped to find such a one haunting the edges of this holy city. The figure walked toward him on the sidewalk, looking like any other pedestrian. But with the sharpened senses, Legion registered one significant difference.

No heart thudded in this one's chest.

He was a *Sanguinist,* a word learned from Leopold. This servant of God registered Legion's own unnatural state a moment too late. Legion grasped the man's bared forearm with his black fingers. His prey fell to his knees as Legion burned away his will, pushed his shadows into this one's heart.

You will be my eyes and ears in that holy city.

Legion stared up at the wall. With this slave he could learn where his enemy was hiding, and end this threat.

I will not fail again.

7:15 P.M.
Vatican City

As she waited for Jordan's return, Erin studied the map on Bernard's computer monitor, noting the outward spread of the attack from Cumae.

"It's like a plague," she mumbled.

The cardinal glanced up from the reports he had been reviewing. "What was that?"

She pointed to the screen. "What if we consider the pattern of these strange *strigoi* attacks more like a disease, a pathogen that is spreading far and wide?"

"How does that help us?"

"Perhaps instead of trying to find a way to thwart these attacks, we should concentrate our efforts on finding Patient Zero. If we can find him—"

A short rap on the door cut her off.

"Come in," Bernard called out, straightening the crimson skullcap of his station. The cardinal was vainer than he would ever admit.

She turned as the door swung wide and Father Gregory stepped inside, but he was only holding the way open for others. She caught sight of the first visitor and was out of her seat and halfway across the room before she realized it.

Jordan caught her in his arms and lifted her off her feet. She hugged him back, hard. Once he let her down, she leaned back, keeping her hands on his shoulders, while taking him all in.

Despite the cardinal's prior reassurance, a knot of concern for his well-being had remained. But he did indeed look fine. In fact, he looked terrific, his tanned skin practically glowing with health.

She lifted on her toes, inviting a kiss. He leaned down and gave her a peck on the cheek. His lips burned, as if he were feverish. She settled back to her heels, a hand rising to touch her cheek.

A peck on the cheek?

Such a tepid sign of affection was out of character, and it felt like a rejection.

She studied his clear blue eyes and reached up to run a hand through his shock of short blond hair, wanting to ask him what was going on. He didn't react to her touch. She laid the back of her hand against his forehead. His skin was burning hot.

"Do you have a fever?"

"Not at all. I feel great." He stepped back and jerked his thumb toward his companion behind him. "Probably just overheated from chasing after this guy."

It was Christian, but from the young Sanguinist's expression, he was equally concerned. Jordan was definitely not telling her something.

Before she could press the issue, Christian entered the room. He was dressed casually in worn black jeans and dark blue windbreaker, beneath which showed a priest's shirt and collar. He nodded to Bernard.

"Sophia and Baako are bringing the *strigoi's* body to the pope's surgery."

Erin let go of her worry about Jordan's continuing estrangement and focused on the mystery he and the others had delivered to their doorstep. If they could discover the source of this *strigoi's* unusual strength and speed, then maybe they could devise a way to short-circuit it in the future.

But apparently that would wait.

Christian pulled a khaki rag from his jacket pocket. He glanced guiltily toward Jordan. "Sophia asked me to show this to Erin."

Erin caught her breath as she recognized the scrap. It was a piece of Jordan's shirt—only it was caked in dry blood, with a clear slash through the middle. She looked anxiously at Jordan.

He grinned back. "Nothing to worry about. I just got nicked during the battle."

"Nicked?" She sensed he was holding back. "Show me."

Jordan lifted his palms. "I swear . . . there's nothing to see."

"Jordan . . ." A warning tone frosted her voice.

"Fine." He reached a hand and lifted up his T-shirt. A set of six-pack abs came into view.

Definitely nothing wrong with them.

She ran a finger across his unusually warm skin, noting the thin line of a scar. That was new. Without taking her hand from Jordan's belly, she looked back at the bloody shirt that Christian held. The cut in the front of the shirt matched the scar.

"Just a nick or not," she said, "this shouldn't have healed so quickly."

Bernard came around to examine Jordan, too.

"According to Sophia and Baako," Christian explained, "Jordan spontaneously healed, suffering no ill effects."

No ill effects?

His skin blazed under her fingertips. He would barely meet her eyes. She remembered another time when he had burned so hotly. It was when he was healed by Tommy's angelic blood. Was this evidence of the prophecy concerning the Warrior of Man? The words echoed in her head: *The Warrior of Man is likewise bound to the angels to whom he owes his mortal life.*

Jordan tugged his shirt back down, glancing at Erin. "I didn't want you to worry. I was going to tell you when we were alone."

Were you?

She hated that she doubted him, but she did.

"I figured we had a more important detail to address first," Jordan continued.

He pulled something out of his camouflage pants and held it up for all to see. Its sharp edges flashed in the candlelight. It looked like two pieces of a broken green egg.

"We found this near the altar down in the sibyl's temple," Jordan explained.

He crossed the room and put the pieces down on the cardinal's desk. They gathered around it. Its facets cast rainbows across their faces, brighter than she'd ever seen—yellows like sunshine, greens like the sun on the grass, blues like a summer sky. The pieces certainly weren't made of ordinary glass.

"What kind of stone is it?" she asked.

"Diamond, I think," said Christian, as he leaned closer. "A green diamond, more precisely. Exceedingly rare."

Transfixed by its beauty, Erin gazed at the stone. The crystal cast dappled reflections around the desktop. Those glowing emerald teardrops reminded her of tiny leaves, dancing in a summer wind.

Jordan nudged the two pieces together. "We found it already broken into these two halves, but at one time, it must have been a single gemstone. And look at this . . ."

He rolled the stone over to reveal a symbol etched into the crystal.

Erin leaned closer, traced it with her index finger. It looked as if the design had been melted into the stone.

"Strange, isn't it?" Jordan said, noting her attention. "It's like the symbol was always part of the diamond, not carved in afterward."

Erin frowned. "I've heard of flaws and inclusions in gems, but it's hard to believe that such a precise emblem formed naturally."

Christian nodded. "I agree."

She straightened. "Besides, I've seen this symbol before."

A small part of her enjoyed their shocked expressions.

"Where?" Bernard asked.

She pointed to the cardinal's bookshelf. "Right here."

Proving it, she stepped over and took down a small leather-bound tome. She herself had delivered this depraved book to the cardinal, picking it up from the snow in Stockholm after Elizabeth Bathory had dropped it. It was the Blood Countess's personal diary, a record of her atrocities and macabre experiments.

Erin stepped back to the desk and opened the book's brittle cover. It was centuries old. Still, she swore she could smell the scent of blood wafting forth from its pages. She flipped past drawings of medicinal plants until she reached Bathory's later experiments, those that held detailed drawings of human and *strigoi* anatomy. Her eyes were drawn to the neatly written notes of horrific tests performed on living women and *strigoi*, grisly acts that must have caused terrible suffering and death.

She hurried past them.

At the end of the book, Erin found what she sought. Scrawled as if in great haste on the last page was a symbol.

It matched the one on the stone exactly.

"What does it mean?" Bernard asked.

"We'll have to ask the woman who wrote it," Erin said.

Jordan groaned. "Something tells me she's not going to be that cooperative, especially after what Rhun did to her. She's not exactly the forgiving type."

"Still," Erin said, "Rhun might be the only one who could convince her."

Jordan sighed. "In other words, it's time to put the band back together again."

He didn't look happy, but Erin felt a flicker of relief at the thought of them all together again, the trio of prophecy reunited.

She pictured Rhun's ashen face, his haunted dark eyes, and turned to Bernard.

"So where exactly is our missing Knight of Christ?"

8

One last duty, and I'll be free to return to Rome.

Though in truth, Rhun was not in any particular hurry. After returning from Egypt, he had stopped first at the pope's summer residence in the rural countryside of Castel Gandolfo. With the pontiff rarely visiting, the residence was run like a country estate. The pace was slow and deliberate, changing only with the seasons.

Rhun stood at a window and stared across the spring fields and down to the moonlit waters of Lake Albano. He did not realize how much he had missed the sight of water after his months in the desert. He drew in a deep breath filled with the scent of water, green things, and fish.

Then a sharp pain flared in his heel, drawing his attention back to the stone floor and the mischievous lion cub chewing on the back of his shoe. The snowy-white cub was lying flat on the floor, his paws stretched in front of him like the sphinx. Except a sphinx normally didn't have its head tilted to the side, its teeth embedded in leather.

"Enough of that, my friend." Rhun shook the determined cub off his foot.

The young lion had tolerated the journey from Egypt. Before the flight to Italy, the cub had devoured a huge breakfast of milk and meat, then slept curled up for hours in the crate.

Apparently you're hungry again . . . for shoe leather.

A knock on the door caused them both to look in that direction. Rhun hurried over, hoping it was the person he had privately asked to meet him in this remote corner of the papal residence. He opened the door to discover a chubby priest, with gray hair shaved into a friar's tonsure. His head barely reached Rhun's shoulder.

"Friar Patrick, thank you for coming."

The fellow Sanguinist ignored Rhun's formal manner and pushed into the room. He clasped both of

Rhun's hands in his cold ones. "When they said you had come to see me, I did not believe it. It has been so many years."

Rhun smiled at his enthusiasm. "Friar Patrick, you shame me. Has it been so long?"

The man scrunched his face in thought. "I believe the last time we spoke, man had just set foot on the moon. I know you were here recently, but you came and went so quickly." He scolded him with the wag of a finger. "You should have stopped by."

Rhun nodded. He had been busy at the time, dealing with the threat of a traitor in the order, but he didn't bother trying to explain. Luckily, Friar Patrick's attention was quickly diverted to the castle's other guest.

"Oh my!" Patrick dropped to a knee and reached for the cub, his fingers fondling those soft ears. "This certainly makes up for your long absence. It's been ages since I've seen such a magnificent beast."

The friar had long cared for the pope's menagerie, from the days when it had consisted of horses, cattle, pigeons, and falcons. In spite of his small stature and well-padded frame, he could harness a team of horses faster than anyone. Over a century ago, Rhun had worked alongside him in the stables. No one had a better kinship with God's creatures than Patrick.

"This little one looks hungry," Patrick said, proving that natural affinity now.

"And I just fed him a huge meal not long ago."

The old friar chuckled. "That's because he's a growing lad." Patrick stood and motioned to the door. "Come. Follow me. I already have a cozy place picked out for him. After you sent word about your charming companion, I made sure everything was ready."

With the cub loping happily behind them, Patrick led Rhun out of the room, down a set of stairs, and outside to the papal grounds. He marched them across the back acres to where an old set of stables stood.

As soon as Rhun stepped inside, the smell of horse, leather, and hay took him back a hundred years. The strong slow heartbeats of the horses surrounded him like music. Only a few beasts lived in the stable now, nowhere near as many as in times past, when every journey required something with four legs.

The horses whickered at the sight of Patrick, who deftly produced a lump of sugar from his pocket for each, stroking one nose after another as he bustled past the stalls.

Rhun picked up the curious lion cub to keep him from darting into the stalls.

Finally, Patrick reached the door to his office and ushered them inside. Pictures of horses lined the walls—both photographs and pencil drawings. Rhun recognized a horse from his own day, a champion that Patrick had bred.

The friar followed his gaze. "You remember Holy Fire, don't you? What a champion, that one was. I swear he fell from his mother's womb and landed sure on his feet."

Patrick ignored his cluttered desk and stepped to a small refrigerator. From inside, he pulled out a metal milk jug and took a large ceramic bowl down from a shelf, then filled the basin to the brim.

As soon as he placed it on the floor, the cub dove straight for the bowl, half-burying his muzzle as he lapped. A loud purr filled the room.

For an odd moment, Rhun felt himself pulled out of his body. He found himself staring down into a white pool in front of his nose, felt icy milk sliding down his throat. Then he snapped back into his own body, stumbling back a step in surprise.

Patrick gave him a pinched look of concern. "Rhun?"

Rhun shook his head, collecting himself, not sure what had happened. He stared at the cub, then back to Patrick, ready to dismiss the event as nothing more than exhaustion. For now, he had more practical concerns to address.

"Thank you for agreeing to watch him. I know the cub will be a burden, but I appreciate you keeping him for as long as you can."

"I'm happy to do so, but I can't keep a lion forever, not around horses. Eventually, he'll need to be given to a zoo, some place with the space to care for him properly." He stared up at Rhun and patted the cub's side. "While he's a charmer, I'll give you that, it's not like you to bring home strays. What's so unique about this little fellow?"

Rhun was not ready to explain about the cub's *blasphemare* origins, so he danced around the subject. "He was abandoned. I found him next to the body of his dead mother."

"Many creatures are alone, yet you don't drag them to my stable."

"He's . . . different, maybe special."

Patrick waited for more of an explanation, but when it didn't come, he clapped his hands to his thighs and stood up. "I can give him a few weeks. But just in case, I'll start making inquiries about a permanent home for him."

"Thank you, Patrick."

The phone rang on his desk. The friar frowned at it. "Sounds like someone else needs my attention."

As Patrick answered the call, Rhun bent down to give the cub's nape a quick ruffle, then headed toward the door, but as he exited the office, Patrick called back to him.

"It seems I'm mistaken, Rhun. It seems someone needs *your* attention."

Rhun stepped back into the office.

Patrick lowered the phone's receiver. "That was the cardinal's office. It seems His Eminence wants you to head immediately to Venice."

"Venice?"

"Cardinal Bernard will meet you there himself."

Rhun felt a shiver of unease, guessing the source behind this summons. Elisabeta had been sent to Venice after events in Egypt. There she was watched over and guarded at a convent, a prisoner of its walls.

What has Elisabeta done now?

Rhun recalibrated his plans. With the lion dropped off, he had intended on heading straight to Rome, to deliver the satchel of black stones, those drops of Lucifer's blood mined from the Egyptian sands. But this sudden change required securing the stones first. He didn't want such malevolence anywhere near Elisabeta.

He stepped to the friar's desk. Patrick must have read his expression. "What else do you need me to do, my son?"

Rhun removed the leather bag from his pocket and placed it on the desktop. The friar recoiled, sensing the evil. "Can you secure this in the cardinal's safe here at the castle? No one must touch what's inside."

Patrick eyed the satchel with distaste, but he nodded. "You come with many curious possessions, Rhun."

Rhun clasped the friar's hand. "You've relieved me of two burdens today, my old friend. I appreciate it."

With the matter settled, he headed out, but he felt little relief. He did not know what to expect in Venice. He knew only one thing for certain.

Elisabeta would not welcome his visit.

Second

The Jews therefore strove among themselves,
saying, How can this man give us his flesh to
eat?

Then Jesus said unto them, Verily, verily, I say
unto you, Except ye eat the flesh of the Son
of man, and drink his blood, ye have no life in
you.

Whoso eateth my flesh, and drinketh my blood,
hath eternal life; and I will raise him up at the
last day.

—John 6:52–54

9

As the helicopter swept over the Adriatic Sea, Jordan checked his watch. They'd made good time getting here from Rome. Ahead, the city of Venice glowed against the black backdrop of its lagoon, like some jeweled crown abandoned in the Italian waters.

Aboard the aircraft, he and Erin were accompanied by a trio of Sanguinists. Up front, Christian crouched over the controls, while Sophia and Bernard shared the back cabin with them. The addition of the cardinal on the trip had surprised Jordan.

Guess Bernard got tired of sitting around Rome.

Still, the cardinal and the others were skilled warriors. Jordan certainly didn't mind the extra muscle, especially after the attack in that underground temple. Even now his belly burned, a fire stoked by some miraculous healing ability. The same heat coursed through the old scar tissue that twined across his shoulder and upper torso from the lightning bolt that had struck him as a teenager.

Erin leaned against that shoulder now. He held her fingers. Every so often during the flight, she had cast him a worried glance. He couldn't blame her, even Sophia and Baako were spooked by his near death.

The helicopter gave a strong jolt, drawing Jordan's attention out the window as the city of Venice came into view. Christian swung the aircraft into a turn, tilting for a better view.

"Right below us," Christian radioed back through the set of headphones they all shared, "is St. Mark's Square. That red-and-white tower is the Campanile and that building that looks like a gothic wedding cake is the Doge's Palace. Next to it is St. Mark's Basilica. The order has its own domain below those sacred grounds, much like at St. Peters. That's where we'll spend the night after we question Elizabeth Bathory about that symbol."

Erin squeezed Jordan's hand, leaning over him, taking it all in. "Venice has stood like this for close to a thousand years," she said. "Imagine that . . ."

He smiled at her enthusiasm, but he had to force it a bit. He still felt strangely disconnected. And it wasn't just his dampened reaction to the woman he loved. Today he had missed both lunch and dinner, and he still wasn't hungry. And even when he did force himself to eat, the food tasted bland. He ate more out of duty than any true desire.

He rubbed his thumb along the new scar on his belly.

Something has definitely changed.

And while he should be bothered by it, even scared, instead he felt a deep calm, as if whatever was happening was meant to be. He couldn't put it into words, so mostly avoided talking about it, even with Erin, but it somehow felt *right*.

Like he was becoming better and stronger.

As Jordan pondered this mystery, Christian flew them away from St. Mark's Square and landed the aircraft on top of a nearby luxury hotel. As the chopper powered down, Jordan did a quick weapons check: sidearm, machine pistol, and dagger. He glanced around at the others, waiting for Christian to give them the all clear so they could climb out.

Erin looked excited, but he also noted the shadows under her eyes. For an ordinary civilian, she had been through too much in too short a time. She had never really had time to recover, to internalize all that had transpired over the past year.

From the pilot's seat, Christian waved them permission to exit, but Sophia held them back, plainly wanting to leave first. During the flight here, the small-framed Indian woman had sat with her eyes half-closed, radiating a sense of peace. Whether that stillness came from her faith or an unnatural ability to remain unmoving, Jordan wasn't sure. Now she opened the door and flowed out to the helipad with a surprising grace.

Bernard followed her, showing no less poise. As the cardinal stepped free, a gust of wind billowed open his dark coat, revealing the crimson garb of his station beneath. His gaze swept the rooftop for any threats. Though Bernard had spent the trip here in prayer, with his gloved fingers folded piously on his lap, he didn't look any more settled now.

Then again, the target of this cross-country trip, Elizabeth Bathory, would likely prove a challenge to them all. Especially for the cardinal, who had a long and bloody history with the woman. The two of them had an enmity that spanned centuries.

Christian came around, ducking under the chopper's slowing blades, to offer a hand to Erin as she exited. The fading rotor wash blew Erin's blond hair into a gauzy halo as she glanced back to Jordan. Her amber eyes glowed under the stars, her cheeks were flushed, and her lips were slightly parted as if waiting to be kissed.

For a moment, her beauty cut through that burning fog that filled him.

I do love you, Erin.

That will never change, he silently swore—but deep inside, he wondered if he could keep that promise.

8:54 P.M.

In her room at the convent, Elizabeth lay fully clothed atop her hard bed and watched the play of city lights that reflected off the canal and dappled her ceiling. Her thoughts were half a world away, with Tommy.

She touched the phone hidden in the pocket of her skirt. As soon as she was free, she would figure out how to help him. Her own children had been stolen from her. She would not let that happen to Tommy. No one took what was hers.

She turned her head toward the window, to where she had hidden the stolen key to Berndt's boat in a small hole in the stucco. For the moment, she must simply wait, try to keep her breathing even, her heartbeat slow. She could not let the handful of Sanguinist nuns who mingled with their mortal sisters here at the convent sense her anxiety, to suspect her plot to escape these walls this very night.

The convent imposed a midnight curfew on its guests, and as usual, Abigail would keep a post at the front desk until the convent's gates were barred shut. After that, the old nun would retire to her room at the back of the house. But Elizabeth could not count on her sleeping. Elizabeth remembered how the night always poured energy into her *strigoi* body, demanded that she go outside and feel moonlight and starlight on her skin. The Sanguinists must have a similar experience, no matter how much they tried to control their pleasures with prayer.

A door slammed closed down the corridor.

Another tourist returning to bed.

As it was spring, the convent's guest quarters were full, which was a good thing. With so many beating hearts in this wing, Abigail would find it difficult to pick out the rhythm of Elizabeth's among so many. Those extra heartbeats might be enough to allow her to escape.

And I must escape.

She reviewed her plan in her head: remove the boat key from the window, creep down the carpeted corridor carrying her shoes, unbar the iron gate at the side of the convent, and circle the house to Berndt's boat. From there, she would cast off the lines, let the current drift her some distance before starting the craft's engine, and be on her way to freedom.

Her plans after that were troublesomely vague.

Before she fell among the Sanguinists last winter, she had buried a great stash of money and gold outside of Rome, a treasure she had gathered from the bodies and homes of those she had preyed upon after waking up in this era after centuries of sleep in a sarcophagus full of holy wine.

Rhun had trapped her in that stone coffin as surely as he had her imprisoned here.

One hand rose to touch her room's wall, determined to let nothing stop her from reaching Tommy before it was too late for the boy. Once free, she would find a *strigoi* and persuade it to turn her—then she would bring that same gift to Tommy's bedside.

Then you will live . . . and be forever at my side.

Her ears pricked up at the sound of footsteps in the corridor. A large party approached, too many to be a family of tourists.

Had the nuns somehow grown wise to her plans?

She sat up in bed as hard knuckles rapped firmly on her door.

"Countess," a male voice called out with an Italian accent.

She immediately recognized the barely veiled authority in that voice. It set her jaw to aching. *Cardinal Bernard.*

"Are you awake?" he asked through the stout door.

She toyed with the idea of pretending to be asleep, but she didn't see the point—and she was curious about this unexpected visit.

"I am," she whispered, knowing he would hear it with his acute senses.

She rose to receive them. Her skirts rustled against the cold tile floor as she unlatched the door. As usual, the cardinal was bedecked in scarlet, a vanity that amused her. Bernard must always let everyone know of his elevated status.

Behind his shoulder, Abigail scowled at her. She ignored the nun and nodded to Bernard's other companions, most she knew well: Erin Granger, Jordan Stone, and a young Sanguinist named Christian. She noted someone conspicuously absent from this entourage.

Rhun was not part of their ranks.

Was he too ashamed to show himself?

Anger flared through her, but she merely pressed her lips more tightly together. She dared not show agitation. "It is late for a visit."

"My apologies for disturbing you at such an unseemly hour, Countess." The cardinal spoke with an oily diplomatic smoothness. "We have a matter that we wish to discuss with you."

She kept her face passive, knowing that whatever had brought this group to her door must be something urgent. She also sensed her chances of escaping this night were vanishing.

"I would be happy to talk to you in the morning," she said. "I was preparing myself to retire."

Sister Abigail reached across and hauled Elizabeth bodily into the corridor, not bothering to hide her unnatural strength. "They mean now."

Jordan placed a restraining hand on the nun's arm. "I think we can do this without any roughness."

"And this is a matter of some discretion," Bernard said, waving Abigail off.

A muscle twitched under the nun's eye. "As you wish. I have other matters to attend to, so I will leave Lady Elizabeth in your charge."

Abigail released Elizabeth, turned on her heel, and stalked off.

Elizabeth enjoyed watching her leave.

"Would you like to talk in my bedchamber?" She gestured back at her cell, allowing a vein of irritation to show. "Though it is quite cramped."

Bernard stepped closer, while glancing down the corridor. "We'll be taking you to our chapels below St. Mark's Basilica, where we might speak in private."

"I see," she said.

The cardinal reached to her arm, as if to escort her by the hand, but instead, he dropped a cold metal shackle around her wrist and fastened the other end to his own.

"Shackles?" she asked. "One of your strength cannot control a small, helpless mortal woman such as me?"

Jordan grinned. "Mortal or not, I'm guessing there's nothing *helpless* about you."

"Perhaps you are right." She tilted her head and smiled at him.

He was a handsome man—a strong jaw, a square face, and a hint of wheat-colored stubble across his chin and cheeks. A heat emanated from him, an internal fire that she might enjoy warming herself beside.

Erin took his hand, asserting ownership of her man. Some things did not change with the passage of centuries.

"Lead me to my fate, Sergeant Stone," Elizabeth said.

As a group, they paraded through the convent and out the main gates. She caught sight of Berndt's boat and felt a twinge of irritation, but she allowed it to fade away.

While she wouldn't be taking her boat ride to freedom this night, perhaps a more interesting opportunity had arisen.

9:02 P.M.

Erin trailed behind the Sanguinists as they wended through the alleys and over the small arched bridges of Venice. She held Jordan's hand, his palm hot in her own. She tried to push back her fears about him. No matter how feverish he felt, he looked healthy, ready to take on an army.

Once they were alone, she would pry out more details about what had happened in that cavern, and why he seemed to be pulling away from her lately. She suspected the source of these changes came from the angelic essence that Tommy had imbued into him when he had saved Jordan's life. Still, while her mind pondered this possibility, her heart went immediately to more mundane places.

What if he simply doesn't love me anymore?

As if he guessed her thoughts, Jordan squeezed her hand. "Ever been to Venice?" he asked softly.

"I've only read about it. But it's like I always pictured it."

Glad for the distraction, she glanced around. The alleys of this island city were so narrow that only two could walk abreast in some places. Small storefronts displayed antique books, pens fashioned from glass, leather masks, silk and velvet scarves. Venice had always been a trading center. Hundreds of years ago, these same shop windows had dazzled other pedestrians with their wares. Hopefully, they would do the same a hundred years from now.

She inhaled deeply, smelling the sea off the canals, the scent of garlic and tomatoes from some nearby restaurant. Closer at hand, the houses were façades painted in shades of ocher and yellow and faded blues, their window glass rippled by the passing centuries.

It was easy to imagine that she'd stepped into a time machine and arrived a hundred years earlier or even a thousand. She'd been raised on a rural compound by parents whose everyday life was more primitive than the people who lived in this city centuries ago. Her father's faith had caused him to repudiate the modern world, and she sometimes worried that her profession, her curiosity about history, kept her out of sync with time as well.

Am I my father's child after all?

The group finally crossed along a dark tunnel that passed through an ancient wall. At its end, St. Mark's Square opened before them, and she faced the city's famous basilica.

Golden light illuminated the front of the Byzantine building, a fanciful façade of arched portals, marble columns, and elaborate mosaics. Erin craned her neck to take in its breadth. In the center, at the top, stood a statue of St. Mark himself, above a golden winged lion, his symbol. Flanking the Warrior Saint were six angels.

The entire structure was the epitome of opulence and grandeur.

Jordan had his opinion. "Looks a bit gaudy."

A laugh escaped Erin. She couldn't stop it. It sounded like the Jordan she had first met in Israel.

"Wait until you see the inside," she said. "It's called the *Church of Gold* for a very good reason."

Jordan shrugged. "If it's worth doing, I guess it's worth overdoing."

She smiled at him as they headed across St. Mark's Square. During the day, the place would be full of pigeons and tourists, but at this late hour, the square was practically deserted.

Ahead, the countess walked regally next to Cardinal Bernard, her head held high and her eyes fixed on some distant point in front of her. Even in a fairly modern dress, she looked like a storybook princess, stepped from the pages of an ancient book. In the countess's case, it would be a grim book of fairy tales.

As they neared the basilica, Erin pointed to the mosaics at the entrance. "These were installed in the thirteenth century. They depict scenes from Genesis."

She recalled the story on the tablet in the Sanguinist library—and how that story had been altered. She searched the mosaics above for the serpent in the garden, recalling how that ancient account detailed a pact Eve made with that serpent: to share the fruit of the Tree of Knowledge.

Before she could get a good look, an elderly priest stepped out from under a shadowy archway. His white hair was disheveled, and his cassock was buttoned crooked. A ring of keys hung on his belt.

The priest met Bernard at the basilica's threshold. "This is very irregular. Never in all my years—"

Bernard cut him off, lifting a hand. "Yes, it is an unusual request. I am grateful that you are able to accommodate it with so little notice. If it were not urgent, we would never think to bother you."

"I am always happy to be of service." The old priest sounded slightly mollified.

"As are we all," said the cardinal.

The Italian priest turned, led them to the main door, and unlocked it.

As he stood aside, he warned Bernard. "I've deactivated the alarms. So you must notify me when you are finished."

The cardinal thanked him and hurried inside, drawing their group in his wake.

Erin followed, gaping at the golden mosaics that appeared, covering every surface: walls, archways, and domed ceilings.

Jordan let out a small whistle of appreciation at the sight. "Are my eyes playing tricks, or does it look like everything is glowing?"

"The tiles were designed that way," Erin explained, grinning at his reaction. "Created by fusing gold leaf between glass tiles. It makes them more reflective than solid gold."

Elizabeth turned her silver eyes on Jordan, drawn perhaps by his enthusiasm. "They are lovely, are they not, Sergeant Stone? Some of those mosaics were commissioned by my Bohemian ancestors."

"Really?" Jordan said. "They did an impressive job."

Erin didn't like how Elizabeth's smile widened at his attention.

Perhaps sensing Erin's irritation, the countess swung to face Cardinal Bernard. "I suspect you did not bring me here to admire my ancestors' handiwork. What is so urgent that it requires such a nightly sojourn?"

"Knowledge," he answered her.

By now, they had reached the center of the church. Bernard clearly didn't want anyone eavesdropping. Christian and Sophia kept to their flanks, slowly circling the group, likely both to guard them and to keep any stray priest who might be nearby from getting too close.

"What do you wish to know?" Elizabeth asked.

"It concerns a symbol, one found in your journals."

He reached inside his coat and pulled out the worn leather book.

Elizabeth held up her free hand. "May I see it?"

Erin stepped forward and took it herself. She flipped to the last page and pointed to the symbol that looked like a cup. "What can you tell us about this?"

The countess's lips curved into a genuine smile. "If you're inquiring about it now, then I trust you have found the same symbol elsewhere."

"Maybe," Erin said. "Why?"

The countess reached for the book, but Erin moved it out of her reach. A flash of irritation crossed the woman's smooth features.

"Let me guess then," Elizabeth said. "You found the symbol on a stone."

"What are you talking about?" the cardinal asked.

"*You* are a gifted liar, Your Eminence. But the answer to my question is written across this young woman's face."

Erin blushed. She hated being so transparent, especially when she had no idea what the countess was thinking.

Elizabeth explained. "I'm referring to a green diamond, about the size of my fist, with this same marking upon it."

"What do you know about it?" Jordan asked.

The countess threw back her head and laughed. The sound echoed across the cavernous space. "I shall not give you the information you seek."

The cardinal loomed over her. "You can be made to tell us."

"Calm yourself, Bernard." Her use of his common name only seemed to irritate the cardinal even more. She was clearly enjoying pushing his buttons. "I said that I would not *give* you this knowledge, but that does not mean that I shall not part with it."

Erin frowned. "What do you mean?"

"Simple," she said. "I shall *sell* my knowledge to you."

"You are in no position to bargain," the cardinal blustered.

"I believe I am in a very good position," she countered, facing the storm growing in the cardinal's stance with a steady calm. "You are frightened of this symbol, of this stone, of the events even now transpiring against you and your precious order. You will pay me what I want."

"You are a prisoner," the cardinal began. "You—"

"Bernard, my price is a slight one. I'm sure you'll be able pay it."

Erin gripped the journal more tightly, her eyes drawn to the countess's triumphant face, dreading what was coming next.

The cardinal kept his tone guarded. "What do you want?"

"Something of very little worth," she said. "Only your eternal soul."

Jordan had stiffened next to her, as if expecting an attack. "What exactly does that mean?"

The countess leaned closer to the cardinal, her black hair brushing his scarlet cassock. He took a step back, but she matched it.

"Restore me to my former glory," she whispered, her voice more seductive than demanding.

Bernard shook his head. "If you're referring to your former castle and lands, that is not within my power."

"Not my lands." She laughed brightly. "I can get those back myself, should I have need of them. What I require from you is much simpler."

The cardinal stared down at her, revulsion written on his face. He knew what she was going to ask for.

Even Erin did.

Elizabeth reached toward the cardinal's lips, toward his hidden fangs.

"Make me a *strigoi* again."

10

Elizabeth shivered in delight as shock washed away Cardinal Bernard's usual calm composure. For a fraction of a moment, he bared his teeth at her, dropping his mask, showing his true nature. After centuries of sparring, she had finally managed to crack his façade of diplomacy and order, exposing the animal beneath.

I need that animal.

She would risk even death to unshackle it.

To the side, the archaeologist and the soldier looked equally surprised, but the best reactions came from the Sanguinists. The young Christian went stiff; the slim Sanguinist woman with burnished Eastern features curled her lip in revulsion. In their holy minds, such a request was unimaginable.

Then again, a failure of imagination had always been the Sanguinists' chief sin.

"Never." The cardinal's first word was a low rumble—then his voice rose, bursting from his chest, booming through the church. "You . . . you are an abomination!"

She faced his fury, stoking it even more with her calmness. "Your priestly prudery holds no interest for me. And do not fool yourself, I am no more an abomination than *you*."

Bernard fought to bottle back his rage, to tamp it down inside him, but the cracks continued to show. His fists were iron at his side. "We will not discuss such mortal sins in this holy place of worship."

He yanked on her cuffed wrist, hard enough for the edge of the shackles to cut her skin. He stalked toward the back of the church, pulling the rest with him as if they were equally bound to the cardinal.

And maybe they were, in their own ways.

Elizabeth had to run to keep up with him, but she could not keep that pace. Her feet tangled in her long skirt, and she sprawled across the cold marble. Her handcuff bit deeper into the flesh of her wrist.

She kept silent, savoring the pain.

If he was hurting her, he had lost control.

And I've gained it.

She struggled to get her feet beneath her, losing a shoe in the battle. In her efforts to rise, she tore the shoulder of her dress. Aghast, she clutched it with her free hand to keep it from falling.

Christian blocked Bernard, touching the cardinal's arm. "She cannot keep up with you, Your Eminence. Remember, she is mortal now, as much as she might not wish to be."

Jordan helped her to her feet, his strong hands warm against her body.

"Thank you," she whispered to the sergeant.

Even Erin came to her aid, reaching over and adjusting Elizabeth's dress so that it did not hang down so. Despite the woman's low background, she did indeed have a well of kindness, one deep enough to help an enemy in distress. Perhaps that was part of Rhun's attraction to her—her simple kindness.

Elizabeth stepped away from the woman without offering her thanks. She kicked off her other shoe, so as not to walk with a limp. Cold stone pressed against the soles of her bare feet.

Bernard apologized through gritted teeth. "I beg your pardon, Countess Bathory."

He turned and continued onward, but now at a more moderate pace. Still, anger was evident in each exaggerated step. He plainly could not appreciate what she wanted, what she demanded of him. He had been immortal so long that he had forgotten mortal desires, mortal weaknesses. But in doing so, he had also created a powerful weakness inside him.

And I will exploit it to the fullest.

The cardinal reached the far side of the basilica and led them down a set of stairs, likely heading to the buried Sanguinist chapel.

A dark space for dark secrets.

At the bottom of the stairs lay a candlelit crypt. The floor was smooth and clean, an easy walk, even in bare feet. On the far side, Bernard stopped in front of a stone wall decorated with a carved figure of Lazarus.

She guessed it was one of the order's hidden gates.

How they loved their secrets.

Standing before the statue, the cardinal peeled off his left glove and took a knife from his belt. He pierced his bare palm with a small knife and dripped blood into a cup that Lazarus was holding. He spoke softly in Latin, too quickly for her to follow.

A moment later, the small door swung open to the side with a grating sound.

The cardinal faced the others. "I will speak to the countess alone."

Murmurs spread among the others, uncertainty on their faces.

Christian was the boldest, maybe because he was newer to the order, willing to confront his superior directly. "Your Eminence, that goes against our rules."

"We're well beyond rules," Bernard countered. "I can come to a more satisfactory arrangement without the presence of others."

Erin stepped up. "What are you planning on doing to her? Torture the information out of her?"

Jordan supported the archaeologist. "I was against enhanced interrogation techniques in Afghanistan, and I'm not going to tolerate it now."

Ignoring them, the cardinal backed through the door, pulling Elizabeth with him. From the threshold, he called out a command that echoed through the crypt.

"*Pro me*. For me alone."

Before anyone could react, the door slammed closed between them.

Darkness enfolded Elizabeth.

Bernard whispered in her ear. "Now you are mine."

9:20 P.M.

Erin pounded the flat of her hand against the sealed door.

She should have suspected such an underhanded maneuver from Bernard. If there were secrets to be learned, he had shown in the past that he would go to extreme measures to control the flow of information. Erin would not put it past the cardinal to withhold whatever knowledge he gained from Elizabeth, maybe even killing the countess to silence her.

She turned to Christian and pointed to the cup in the statue's hands. "Get this door open."

Before he could obey, Sophia touched the young Sanguinist on the shoulder, but her words were for them all. "The cardinal will question the countess himself. He has experience in such matters."

"I am the Woman of Learning," Erin argued. "Whatever Elizabeth knows concerns our quest."

Jordan nodded. "And this Warrior of Man agrees, too."

Sophia refused to back down. "You don't know with certainty that her information has any direct bearing on your quest."

Erin fumed, hating being cut out of the loop so abruptly. But she also had a bigger concern. She didn't trust the countess, not even with the cardinal. Erin feared Bernard might be outmatched by Elizabeth. It was evident the woman knew how to push Bernard's buttons, but was it just a sadistic game or was Elizabeth manipulating Bernard to her own ends?

Erin took a different tack. "If things go sour in there, how fast can you get us inside?"

"Define *sour*," Christian said.

"Bernard is locked alone in there with the Blood Countess. She's a brilliant woman who knows more about *strigoi* and their nature than anyone."

Sophia raised an eyebrow. She looked a little surprised.

Erin pressed on. "The countess has conducted experiments on *strigoi*, trying to determine their nature. It's all in her journal."

Jordan stared toward the sealed gate. "Which means the countess likely knows Bernard's weaknesses, probably better than he does himself."

Erin looked into Christian's eyes. He wanted to help her, but he clearly still felt a duty to follow Bernard's orders.

"Either way, it doesn't matter," Sophia said. "The cardinal closed the door with the command *pro me*, which means that it will open only to him."

What?

Erin turned worriedly to the door.

"So he's trapped in there with her," Jordan muttered.

Christian clarified. "We can get inside, but not with the blood of only *two* of us." He motioned to Sophia.

"To override the cardinal's command, it would take a full *trio* of Sanguinists. The power of three can open the door at any time."

Sophia's eyebrows drew down in worry. "Perhaps it is best if I fetch a third. Just in case."

"Do that," Erin said.

And hurry.

Sophia rushed across the crypt and melted into the darkness of the stairwell.

Erin met Jordan's eyes and saw her own worries reflected there.

This is going to end badly.

9:27 P.M.

Elizabeth fought against panic. With the door sealed, the darkness was so thick that it felt as if it had substance, as if it could crawl down her throat and smother her. But she forced herself to stay calm, knowing Bernard must hear the pounding of her heartbeat. She stiffened her back, refusing to give him the satisfaction.

She focused on the fiery pain of the shackle on her wrist. Warm blood dribbled from her torn skin and trickled into her palm. The cardinal must sense that, too.

Good.

She rubbed her hands together, smearing them both.

"Come," Bernard said hoarsely.

He tugged on her cuffs and pulled her deeper into this cold lair of the Sanguinists. She shivered against that chill. He half-dragged her through the darkness for what seemed like forever, but was likely only minutes.

Then they stopped again, and a match flared, bringing with it the smell of sulfur. Light illuminated Bernard's pale, set face. He touched the match to a golden beeswax candle set in a wall sconce. He moved along to another, lighting that taper, too.

Soon, a warm, flickering light illuminated the room.

She looked up to a domed ceiling shining with a silver mosaic. Just as the glass tiles in the basilica above had been fashioned of gold leaf, these were made with silver. They covered every surface.

The room glowed with their splendor.

The mosaic depicted a familiar Sanguinist motif: the raising of Lazarus. He sat upright in a brown coffin, white as death, a streak of crimson dripping from one corner of his mouth. Facing him stood a gilded Christ, the only golden figure in the mosaic. Finely detailed tiles showed Christ's luminous brown eyes, curly black hair, and a sad smile. Majesty radiated from his simple form, awing those who had gathered to witness this miracle. And it wasn't just humans. Light angels watched the scene from above, while dark angels waited below, and Lazarus sat forever caught between them.

The Sanguinists' Risen One.

How much simpler her life would be if Lazarus had never accepted Christ's challenge.

She turned her face from the ceiling, her eyes falling on the room's only other adornment. In the middle of the chamber rose a white-clad altar. Atop it rested a silver chalice. The touch of silver burned *strigoi* and Sanguinists alike. To drink from a silver chalice was to intensify a Sanguinist's pain, to increase their penance when they consumed their holy wine.

A sneer rose to her lips.

How could these fools follow a God who demanded such endless suffering?

Bernard confronted her. "You will tell me what I need to know. Here. In this room."

She kept her tone cold, her words simple. "First pay my price."

"You know that I cannot do so. It would be a grievous sin."

"But it's been done before." She touched her throat, remembering teeth ripping into that tender flesh. "By your Chosen One, by Rhun Korza."

Bernard glanced away, his voice dropping. "He was young, new to the fold. He fell in a moment of lust and pride. I am not so foolish. The rules are clear. We must never—"

She stopped him. "Never? Since when has that word ever been a part of your vocabulary, Cardinal? You have broken *many* of your order's rules. Going back centuries. Do you think I do not know this?"

"It is not for you to judge," he said, heat entering his words. "Only God can do that."

"Then surely He shall judge me as well." By now, her bare feet ached from the cold, but she stood her ground. "Surely it must be His will that I am here at this time, the only one who holds this knowledge. A truth that you can receive if you only pay this price."

A flicker of uncertainty crossed Bernard's face.

She took advantage of it and pressed him harder. "If your God is all-knowing and all-powerful, why has He placed me in front of you as the sole repository of the knowledge you seek? Perhaps what I ask of you is His will?"

She instantly knew she had taken a step too far—she read it in the hardening of his features.

"You, a fallen woman, dare to interpret His will?" He scowled at her, his words consigning her to the level of a woman who sold her body for money.

How dare you!

She slapped his supercilious face, leaving a smear of her own blood on his skin. "I am not a fallen woman. I am Countess Bathory de Ecsed, of royal blood that dates back centuries. And I will not be insulted by such slander. Especially by you."

His response was lightning fast. His fist struck her a hard blow in turn. She fell back a step, her face throbbing. She quickly collected herself, drawing her back stiffly. She tasted blood in her mouth.

Excellent.

"I can do anything to you in here," he said in a dark tone.

She licked her lips, wetting them with her own blood. She knew he must already smell the fresh blood drying on his cheek. She noted how his nose lifted slightly, revealing the animal within him, the monster lurking behind that mask.

She had to break that beast free of its shackles.

"What can you do to me?" she challenged him. "You are too weak to ever persuade me to help you."

"Do not mistake my composure for weakness," he warned. "I remember the Inquisition, when pain in service to the church was raised to an art form. I can inflict agony on you such as you have never experienced."

She smiled at his anger. "You can teach me nothing of *pain*, priest. For one hundred years it was forbidden to speak my name in my own country because of the acts I committed. I have given and received more pain than you could ever imagine . . . and received more *pleasure*. These things are entwined in ways that you will never understand."

She stepped closer, forcing him to withdraw, but the handcuffs kept him from moving too far.

"Pain does not frighten me," she continued, exhaling the hot scent of her blood toward him.

"It . . . it should frighten you."

She wanted him to continue talking, knowing to speak required breath. And with each breath, he drew her scent more deeply into him.

"Hurt me," she warned, "and see which of us enjoys it more."

He retreated from her until his back was pressed hard against the silver mosaics that covered the walls. But the handcuffs drew her along with him, ever at his side.

She bit deeper into her bruised cheek, while tilting her head low. She parted her mouth, letting fresh blood run past her lips. She then drew her head back, exposing her neck in a languorous stretch, allowing the candlelight to glisten against that red ribbon as it ran down and pooled into the hollow of her throat.

She felt his eyes follow that warm trail, to the promise it held. Its rich warmth called to the beast buried in every drop of his own damned blood.

She knew how the scent bloomed within the room in ways that she could no longer sense. How the smell could fill one's nostrils, even one's mouth. Long ago, she had felt what he felt now. She knew its immense power. She had learned to embrace it, and in doing so it made her strong.

He denied it—and that kept him weak.

"How would you torture me now, Bernard?" She slurred the words through a mouthful of blood, using the intimacy of his name.

He fumbled his free hand to his pectoral cross, but she blocked him, covering the silver with her own palm, keeping him from touching it, denying him the comfort of holy pain. His fingers closed on her hand, squeezing, as if he thought that her hand was his cross, his salvation.

"I will tell you what you need to know," she whispered, speaking aloud his innermost desire. "I will help you *save* your church."

His fingers tightened, coming close to breaking the small bones of her hand.

"It will be simple for you," she urged. "You have committed blood sins before, and I know that your sins are much darker than anyone suspects. You have committed many sins in His name, have you not?"

His face told her that he had.

"Then do this now," she said. "And your act will give you the power to protect your church, your order. Would you have your world fall, to lose all because you were too frightened to act? Because you placed your own fear of the rules above your holy mission?"

She drew the tip of her tongue along her lips again, freshly coating them, knowing how bright her blood must look against her pale skin, how the sight and smell of it must sing to him.

Without knowing that he did so, he licked his own lips.

"How can saving His world with the tools that He has given you be a sin?" she questioned him. "You are stronger than the rules, Bernard. I know this . . . and down deep, you know this, too."

She drew in a slow breath, never taking her eyes from his. Her words had sunk in, playing on his doubt, stoking his hubris.

He trembled before her—wanting her answers, wanting her blood, wanting *her*.

He might be a Sanguinist now, but he had been a *strigoi* before, and a man before that. He had devoured flesh, tasted pleasure. Those urges were ingrained in every fiber of his being, always.

Her heart raced, and her cheek throbbed with heat from his blow. She had always loved pain, needed it like she would later need blood. She closed her eyes and let the pain beat through her—from her cheek, from her torn wrist.

It was bliss.

When she opened her eyes, he still held her hand pressed against the cross by his heart. His eyes traveled from her blood-bright lips to the pulse in her throat, to the tops of her shoulders, so white against the silken slip. She shifted to the side to let her torn dress fall from her shoulders. Now the candlelight fell on her breasts, so easily visible through her silk underdress.

He stared at her for several long heartbeats.

She leaned forward with infinite slowness—then rose up on her tiptoes and lightly, barely skimming the surface, she brushed her lips against his. For one long breath she stood so, letting him feel her warmth, draw in the scent of her ripe blood.

"If it is not His will, then why am I here?" she whispered. "Only you can be strong enough to get the answer from me. Only you have the power to save your world."

Then she parted his cold lips with hers and slipped her tongue between, bringing with it the taste of blood.

He moaned, opening his mouth to her.

She felt fangs there now, growing as she deepened their kiss.

With their lips still sealed together, he turned and slammed her against the wall, crushing his body against hers. Old tiles broke loose beneath her, the glass edges cutting through her thin silk slip and slicing into her skin. Blood ran warm down her back and pattered to the stone floor.

She pulled her mouth away from his, offering her neck instead.

Without hesitation, he bit her.

She gasped at the pain.

He immediately drew in a great draught of her blood, taking with it her warmth. She shivered as her limbs grew colder. Icy pain shot through her heart. This was not the rapturous joining that she had experienced with Rhun.

This was animal need.

A painful hunger that left no room for love or tenderness.

He might kill her and leave her with nothing, but she had to take that chance, trusting that knowledge was as important as blood to the man that clutched to her.

He will not let me die with the secrets I hold.

But having freed the beast inside of the man, would that hold true?

Her body slumped toward the floor. As her heart weakened, doubt filled those empty spaces—and fear.

Then an eternal darkness took away the world.

11

Rhun strode briskly across the polished floor of St. Mark's Basilica. He had landed in Venice a quarter of an hour ago. From a message left for him, he had learned that Bernard and the others had taken Elisabeta here. Only when he arrived, he found the door to the church unlocked, and no one seemed to be here.

Had they already proceeded to the Sanguinist chapel below?

He stared across the nave toward the north transept of the basilica. As he recalled, a stairwell on that side led down to a subterranean crypt and the secret gateway to the Sanguinists' spaces. He headed toward it, but then movement drew his attention to the south transept. Out of the darkness, the flow of shadows rushed toward him, moving with preternatural speed.

Rhun tensed, crouching, unsure who this party was, wary after the recent attacks.

Surely no strigoi *would dare attack on such holy ground.*

A voice called to him as the shadows moved farther into the light, revealing themselves to be a clutch of Sanguinists: two men and a woman.

"Rhun!" He recognized Sophia's burnished features.

The small woman hurried to his side, drawing the others with her. "You've come just in time."

He read the anxiety in her eyes. "What's wrong?"

"Come with us," she said and headed toward the north transept. "There's trouble at the Sanguinist gate."

"Tell me," he said, checking the *karambit* sheathed at his wrist as he accompanied her, matching her swift speed.

She told him about what had transpired below, how Bernard had taken Elisabeta through the gate and locked it behind him.

"Christian is already down there, but it will take three of us to open the door again." She motioned to the two priests behind her. "I came up to fetch more help, but it has taken me too long to find them. And Erin fears the worst."

Upon reaching the stairwell, Rhun took the lead. He trusted Erin's judgment. If she was worried, there must be good reason. Halfway down the stairs, he heard two heartbeats echoing up from the lower crypt.

Erin and Jordan.

He could easily discern between them, as readily as their voices. Erin's quick heartbeat told him of her fear. He reached the crypt and saw Christian pounding on the far wall, calling Bernard's name.

He knew what had so excited the young Sanguinist.

Past the gate, he detected another heartbeat, one muffled by the stone, but still audible to his sharp senses, the sound amplified by the acoustics of the long crypt.

Elisabeta.

Her heart faltered, growing weaker with each beat.

She was dying.

Christian turned, hearing them approach. "Hurry!"

Rhun needed no such urging. He flew across the crypt. Erin stepped forth to meet him, but he slid past her without a word. There was no time.

He pulled his blade from its sleeve and pricked his palm, dripping blood onto the stone chalice held by the statue of Lazarus. Sophia and Christian flanked him, quickly adding their blood to his.

Together they chanted, "For this is the Chalice of our blood. Of the new and everlasting Testament."

The outline of the door appeared in the stone.

"*Mysterium fidei*," they intoned in chorus.

Slowly—too slowly—the door cracked open. The ripe smell of blood billowed out immediately, thick and heady, redolent with danger.

As soon as the way was open enough, Rhun slipped in sideways and ran, following that scent of blood toward its source.

He reached the threshold to the main chapel—in time to hear Elisabeta's heart stop. He took in the impossible sight. In the sacred room, under the glow of the silver mosaics, Elisabeta lay on her back, her limbs limp and lifeless.

But she was not alone.

Bernard knelt beside her, chained by the wrist to her, his mouth bloody. He turned toward Rhun with anguish etched in his face. Tears ran down the cardinal's cheeks, parting through the crimson stain of his sin.

Rhun ignored that pain and ran to Elisabeta's side, skidding to his knees, lifting her in his arms, cradling her. He pulled her body as far from Bernard as he could with the two of them shackled together.

He wanted to rage against this sin, to let fury burn away the grief that overwhelmed him. Someday he would make Bernard pay, but not this day.

This day was only for her.

Christian was the first to reach his side. He touched Rhun on the shoulder in sympathy then dropped to a knee and fiddled with the shackles. The metal bands dropped from her slim wrist and clattered to the floor.

Now that she was freed from her murderer, Rhun gathered up her cold body and stood, needing to put distance between her and Bernard.

Sophia marched her two Sanguinist companions to the cardinal's distraught form. They drew him roughly to his feet. From their low murmurs, they could not believe that the cardinal could have done such a thing.

But he had—he had killed her.

"Rhun . . ." Erin stood with Jordan, leaning on his arm, holding on to him, to that life inside him that burned so brightly.

He could not face that and turned away, taking Elisabeta toward the altar, wanting her to be surrounded by holiness. He made a promise that she would always remain in such grace from here. He swore to find where her children were buried and rest her near them.

She had earned it.

Long ago, he had stolen her from her rightful place, but now he would do his best to restore what he could. It was all that he could do for her.

Rich silvery light bathed her pale skin, her long lashes, and her black curls. Even in death she was the most beautiful woman he had ever seen. He kept his gaze away from the savage wound on her throat, the blood that ran down her shoulders and soaked into her fine silk nightdress.

Upon reaching the altar, he could not put her down on that cold bed. When he released her, she would truly be gone from him. Instead, he crumpled to the floor next to the altar, pulling down the white altar cloth to wrap her naked limbs.

With the edge of the blessed cloth, he wiped blood from her chin, her full lips, her cheeks. A bruise covered the side of her face. Bernard must have struck her.

You will pay for that, too.

He leaned closer to her. "I'm sorry," he whispered. He had spoken those words many times to her—too many times.

How often I have wronged you . . .

His tears fell on her cold, white face.

He stroked her cheek, gently over the bruise as if she could still feel it. He touched her soft eyelids, wishing that she could simply step back from death, that she could open them again.

And then she did.

She stirred in his arms, awakening like a flower, petals softly opening to a new day. Initially, she began to pull away, then she recognized him and went quiet.

"Rhun . . ." she said faintly.

He stared at her, speechless, hearing no heartbeat from her, knowing the truth.

God, no . . .

He glanced over a shoulder, rage building, replacing his grief. Bernard had not only fed on her—he had forced his own blood into her. He had damned her as readily as Rhun had centuries ago, defiling her. She was a soulless abomination again.

Only months ago, Rhun had sacrificed the return of his own soul to save hers—and Bernard had cast such a gift to ruin and ash.

The cardinal stood, surrounded by Christian and the other three Sanguinists. Bernard had committed the greatest sin, and he would be punished, perhaps even with death.

Rhun felt no pity for him.

Elisabeta dropped her head against his chest, too weak even to lift it. She murmured to him, more breath than words. "I am weary, Rhun . . . weary unto death."

He held her, matching her soft whisper. "You must feed. We will find someone who will give us blood to restore your strength."

Sophia spoke behind him, looming over them. "That is impossible. She cannot be allowed to exist. She is a *strigoi* now and must be destroyed."

Rhun looked to the others, finding no dissent. They intended to slaughter her like an animal. But he found succor from the most unlikely source.

Bernard spoke as if he still had a voice in such matters. "She must drink the wine, become one of us. I took this sin of her creation upon myself . . . because the countess swore to face this challenge. To drink the holy wine and join our order."

Or die in the effort.

Rhun looked down at Elisabeta in shock. She would never have agreed to such a thing. But Elisabeta lay in his arms with her eyes closed again, having faded away in her weakened state.

Sophia touched the silver cross that hung round her neck. "Even if she passes such a test, it will not ameliorate your sin, Cardinal."

"I will accept my punishment," he said. "But she must take the holy wine—and accept God's judgment."

Rhun protested. "This is not her sin."

Christian crossed to join Sophia. "Rhun, I'm sorry. It doesn't matter how she was changed, only that she's now a *strigoi*. Such creatures cannot be allowed to live. They must either face this trial, drink the wine—or be killed."

Rhun considered escaping with her. Even if he could overwhelm those gathered here, what then? A damned existence wandering the earth, fighting to keep her from expressing her true nature, both of them severed from God's grace?

"It must be done, and it must be done now," Sophia said.

"Wait." Jordan held up a hand. "Maybe we all need to step back, talk this through."

"I agree," said Erin. "This is an extraordinary set of circumstances. Remember, she has information we need. Should we not at least obtain that before we risk losing her again?"

"Erin's right," Jordan said. "It seems the countess was paid in full. She got what she asked for, and now she needs to tell us what she knows."

Christian frowned, but he looked like he was being slowly swayed to their side. Unfortunately, Sophia looked little moved, and she was backed by the two Sanguinists at her side.

Then support came from a new direction.

"I will tell you what I know," Elisabeta rasped out, turning her head with what clearly took great effort. "But not if it means my death."

Sophia slipped free two curved blades, their lengths shining in the candlelight. "We cannot let a *strigoi* live. The rules are clear. A *strigoi* is allowed only two choices: to join our order or to be put immediately to death."

Rhun tightened his arms around her. He could not lose her twice in one night. If necessary, he would fight.

Perhaps sensing the tension was coming to a head, Erin stepped between Rhun and the others. "Can we not make an exception for her? Let her keep her current form. The Church was willing to work with her as a *strigoi* before, when we sought out the First Angel. She was allowed to live as a *strigoi* in exchange for her help back then. Are these current circumstances any different?"

Silence hung within the room.

Bernard finally broke it with the truth. "We lied to her before. If she had survived as a *strigoi* after the First Angel was recovered, she was to be killed."

Erin gasped. "Is that true?"

"I was to end her cursed life by my own hand," Bernard said.

Rhun stared at his mentor, the man who had raised him in this new life. He had trusted Bernard for hundreds of years. Now he felt the world shifting beneath him. Nothing was as it seemed. No one was who they said they were.

Except for Elisabeta.

She had never pretended to be anything other than what she was, even when she was a monster.

"So your promises are meaningless, Cardinal," said Elisabeta. "Then I see no reason to adhere to my oaths. I will tell you nothing."

"Then you will die now," Bernard said.

She stared at the cardinal, the two ever at war. "Put the question to me then," she said. "Offer me what you Sanguinists must offer any *strigoi* in their custody."

No one spoke.

She rested her head again, looking up at Rhun, her eyes aglow with sadness but purpose. "Put the question to me, Rhun."

"I will not. You have nothing to answer for."

"Oh, but I do, my love. In the end, we all do." She reached up and touched his cheek with a trembling hand. A ghost of a smile showed on her tired lips. "I am ready."

Bernard interrupted. "You will be burnt to ash if you touch the wine. Tell us what you know first and perhaps God will forgive you."

She ignored him, keeping her gaze upon Rhun.

He read her determination. With cold lips, he asked her, "Do you, Bathory de Ecsed, forsake your damned existence and accept Christ's offer to serve the Church, to drink only His blood, His holy wine . . . for now and forever?"

Her gaze never faltered, even as his tears fell upon her face.

"I do."

12

Erin stared up at the vast cupola in the center of St. Mark's Basilica, raising her face to that golden shine as if it were the risen sun. It was nearing midnight, but here the darkness of the night held no sway.

Earlier, down in the smaller silver chapel, she had watched the others lead the countess away into the darker recesses of the Sanguinist level. Erin worried what they might do to her, but Sophia had been adamant that this was a sacred rite of their order, one Erin couldn't observe. All she knew was that Elizabeth would be washed and dressed in a nun's habit before she underwent the ritual of transformation, which apparently involved prayers, repentance, and drinking transubstantiated wine.

Erin would have liked to witness that event, but she wasn't the only one shut out.

One Sanguinist had not been permitted to go with the others.

At least not yet.

She turned to find Rhun pacing the length and breadth of the vast basilica, stirring the candles in his wake as he passed from one shadow to another. He clasped his rosary with one hand, never letting go. His lips moved in constant prayer. She had never seen him so agitated.

Jordan, in contrast, sat sprawled on a nearby pew. His machine pistol lay within easy reach. She crossed and scooted in next to him, settling her backpack beside her.

"I think Rhun's going to wear ruts in the marble," Jordan said.

"The woman he loves might die tonight," she said. "He's earned the right to pace."

Jordan sighed. "She's not really that great of a catch. I've lost count of the times she's hammered him."

"That doesn't mean he wants to watch her die." She took Jordan's hand, dropping her voice, knowing that Rhun could likely hear them, even from across the nave. "I wish there was something we could do."

"For who? Rhun or Elizabeth? Remember, she *asked* to be turned into a *strigoi*. Something tells me she calculated the angles before she agreed to convert. I say we let the chips fall where they may."

Erin leaned against Jordan's side, noticing again his burning heat. He shifted away from her. It was a slight movement, but unmistakable.

"Jordan?" she started, ready to confront her own fears. "What happened to you in Cumae?"

"I already told you."

"Not about the attack. You're still burning up . . . and . . . and you seem *different*."

That word barely described what she felt.

Jordan sounded faraway. "I don't know what's happening. All I know—and this is going to sound strange—but I feel like what has changed in me is leading me down a good path, a path I must follow."

"What path?" Erin swallowed.

And can I come with you?

Before he could answer, Rhun appeared at the end of their pew. "Could I trouble you for the time, Jordan?"

Jordan took his hand from hers to check his wristwatch. "Half past eleven."

Rhun held his pectoral cross, staring toward the stairwell in the north transept that led below, plainly distraught. The ceremony was to begin at midnight.

Erin stood up, drawn by his anguish. She wasn't going to get anything more concrete out of Jordan. Maybe he didn't know more than he had already told her, or maybe he just didn't want to tell her. Either way, she wasn't doing any good sitting here.

She joined Rhun. "Jordan's right, you know."

Rhun turned his face toward her. "About what?"

"Elizabeth is an intelligent woman. She wouldn't agree to convert unless she thought that she stood a good chance of surviving the transformation."

Rhun sighed. "She thinks that the process is complex, that it leaves room for doubt and error, but it does not. I've attended many of these ceremonies in the past. I've seen many . . . succumb when they drink the wine. She cannot trick her way through it."

He set off again to pace, but Erin kept to his side.

"Maybe she's changed," she offered, not truly believing it but knowing Rhun wanted to.

"It is her only hope."

"She's stronger than you give her credit for."

"I pray you are right, because I—" Rhun's voice broke, and he swallowed before speaking. "I cannot bear to watch her die again."

Erin reached over and took his cold hand. His fingertips were red, blistered from the silver of his rosary beads. He stopped and looked into her eyes. The suffering in those dark eyes was hard to face, but she didn't look away.

He leaned toward her, and she instinctively took him in her arms. For the space of a breath, he relaxed against her and let her hold his cold, hard form. Over his shoulder, she saw Jordan watching them. Knowing how he felt about Rhun, she expected him to be jealous, but he stared past her, clearly lost in his own world, a world where she seemed to be losing her place.

Rhun broke free of their embrace, touching her shoulder gently. The simple gesture conveyed his gratitude to her. Even in his anguish, he was more aware of her than Jordan.

They returned down the nave silently until they reached Jordan.

He glanced over at them, looking infuriatingly calm. "It's almost time," he said before Rhun could ask. "Will you be with Elizabeth when she takes the wine?"

"I cannot," Rhun said, his voice dropping even lower. "I cannot."

"Are you not allowed to be there?" Jordan asked.

His guilty silence was answer enough.

Erin touched Rhun's arm. "You must be there."

"She will live or die regardless of my presence, and I cannot watch if . . . if . . ."

He sagged beside her.

"She's frightened, Rhun," Erin said. "No matter how she tries to hide it. There's a chance that these could be her last moments on earth, and you're the only one left in the world who truly loves her. You can't leave her alone."

"Maybe you are right. If I had let her live out her life as God intended, she would not be suffering this fate now. Perhaps it is my duty—"

Erin squeezed his arm. It felt like clutching a marble statue, but there was a wounded heart somewhere deep inside. "Don't go out of a sense of duty," she urged. "Go because you love her."

Rhun bowed his head, but he still looked undecided. He turned and started on another circuit of the nave. She let him go alone this time, knowing he needed to ponder her words, to make up his mind.

She blew out a breath and sat next to Jordan again. "If we were in this position, would you let me drink the wine alone?"

He lifted her chin with a finger to face him. "I'd break your ass out of here before it got to that."

She grinned back at him, enjoying this moment, but it didn't last.

Christian appeared from the entrance of the basilica and crossed down the aisle toward them. He carried a flat box that smelled like meat, cheese, and tomatoes. His other hand held two brown bottles.

"Pizza and beer," Jordan said. "You're a dream come true."

"Remember that when calculating my tip." Christian handed him the box.

Rhun returned to them, suspecting Christian came with more than just a late dinner.

The young Sanguinist nodded to Rhun. "It's time. But you don't have to be present. I understand how painful that might be."

"I shall go." He gave Erin a long look. "Thank you for reminding me why, Erin."

She bowed her head, acknowledging his words, wishing she could go with him, to be there for him if the countess didn't survive.

Rhun turned away and headed off to face what was to come, to share it with Elizabeth.

Their two fates forever entwined.

11:57 P.M.

Elizabeth stood again in the silver chapel where she had died and been born again. Someone had cleaned her blood from the floor and walls. The room smelled of incense and stone and lemons. Fresh beeswax candles had been lit on the altar.

It was as if nothing had ever happened.

She stared up at the bright mosaic of Lazarus overhead. He had done what she would soon attempt, and he had survived. But he had loved Christ.

She did not.

She ran her palm over her black garments, the uniform of a lowly nun. A silver rosary had been tied around her waist, and a pectoral cross hung from her neck. Both objects burned even through the thick cloth. She felt like she had donned a costume, one she might wear to a ball.

But that wasn't her only masquerade.

Keeping still so that no one would know how she truly felt, Elizabeth reveled at the strength inside. The cardinal had fed deeply on her and had offered little of his own blood in return, not enough to sustain her. Even worse, her sensible shoes stood on holy ground, a place that should have weakened her even further.

But she felt strong—stronger, perhaps, than she ever had.

Something has changed in the world.

Eight Sanguinists shared the chapel with her, watching her, judging her. But she only noted one. Rhun had come to participate in this rite, standing next to her. She was surprised how deeply this gesture struck her.

He stepped closer, his words a faint whisper. "Do you have faith, Elisabeta? Faith enough to survive this."

Elizabeth looked up into Rhun's concerned eyes. For centuries, he wanted nothing more than for her to battle the evil inside her, to devote herself to a joyless existence serving a church she had never trusted. She wanted to comfort him, to reassure him, but she would not lie to him, not when this might be their last moment together.

The Sanguinists behind him chanted a prayer. If she tried to escape, they would kill her—and if she died, then Tommy would die along with her. Down this burning path lay the only chance to save the boy's life and her own.

"I do have faith," she told Rhun, which was the truth. It just wasn't the faith he wanted her to possess. She had faith in herself, in her ability to survive this and save Tommy.

"If you don't believe," Rhun warned, "if you don't believe Christ can save your damned soul, you will die with the first sip of His blood. It has ever been so."

Has it?

Rasputin had been excommunicated from the Church, yet she had seen with her own eyes that he still lived outside of the realm of the Church. Likewise, the German monk, Brother Leopold, had betrayed the Church for fifty years, yet he had drunk the wine countless times and never been burned.

Was it the monk's belief in his purpose, in the one he served, that had sustained him?

She hoped it was so. For her sake, and for Tommy's. She had to trust that there were other pathways to the salvation offered by that holy blood. While her heart was not pure, surely helping Tommy was a noble enough goal.

But if I am wrong . . .

She reached to Rhun's bare wrist, touching it with a finger. "I want you to give me the wine. No one else."

If I'm to die, let it be by the hands of someone who loves me.

Rhun swallowed, fear darkening his face, but he didn't refuse her. "Your heart must be pure," he warned. "You must come to Him with openness and love. Can you do that?"

"We will see," she said, shying from his question.

Satisfied but reluctant, Rhun gestured to the silver chalice resting on the altar. The sharp smell of wine rose from it, cutting through the incense. It was difficult to fathom that such a simple substance, a fermentation of grapes, could hold the secret of life. Or that it might destroy her newfound immortal power and her along with it.

Rhun stood before the altar, facing her. "First, you must publicly repent your sins, *all* of your sins. Then you may partake of His holy Blood."

With no other choice, she listed sin after sin, seeing how each one fell onto Rhun's shoulders, how he took the blame for her acts onto himself. He bore it in front of her, and she recognized pain and regret in his eyes. In spite of everything, she would have spared him that if she could.

By the time she had finished, her throat was hoarse. Many hours had passed. Her *strigoi* body sensed that daylight was not far away.

"That is all?" Rhun asked.

"Is it not enough?"

He turned, picked up the silver chalice from the altar, and held it above his head. He chanted prayers necessary to transform the wine into the blood of Christ.

All the while, Elizabeth searched her conscience. Did she feel fear that these were her last moments? That she might soon be burned to ash and scattered across the clean floor? She came to only one conclusion.

Whatever must come would come.

She knelt before Rhun.

He bent down and brought the chalice to her lips.

13

March 18, 5:41 A.M. CET
Venice, Italy

Jordan stretched a knot out of his back. He had fallen asleep, sprawled across one of the wooden pews of the basilica. He stood now and twisted his spine to and fro, forcing circulation back through his body. He bent down and massaged a spasm in his calf.

I can miraculously heal a mortal wound, but I got nothing for a charley horse.

He hobbled toward Erin, who studied a piece of artwork a few yards away. She stood with Christian, who had kept them company during this long vigil, all of them waiting for word about Elizabeth. From the slight hunch in Erin's shoulders and the puffiness of her red eyes, he doubted she had gotten any sleep.

Christian could have joined his fellow Sanguinists and participated in the rite, but he remained here, either to guard them from some kind of threat or to keep them from interfering with what was happening down below. Or maybe he simply didn't want to watch the countess burn to death any more than Rhun did.

All night long, Christian had been straightforward with them, answering Erin's questions about what was likely going on below. And more important, he also fetched Jordan more beer.

"What are we looking at anyway?" Jordan asked as he joined them.

Erin pointed to the mosaic straight above their head.

He craned his neck. "Is that Jesus sitting on a rainbow?"

She smiled. "Actually, it is. He's ascending to heaven. Giving this section of the basilica its name: the Ascension Cupola."

The three of them continued along the nave. Erin questioned Christian about various pieces of art, but clearly there was a greater question hanging above all three of their heads.

Jordan finally asked it. "Do you think she'll survive the wine?"

Christian stopped, sighing loudly. "She will survive if she truly repents of her sins and accepts Him into her heart."

"That's not likely to happen," Erin said.

Jordan agreed.

Christian had a more compassionate response. "We can never know the heart of another. No matter how much we think that we might." He turned to Jordan. "Leopold had us all fooled, serving as agent of the Belial within our own folds for decades."

Erin nodded. "And he was able to drink holy wine without burning to ash."

Jordan frowned, realizing there was one subject he'd never had the time to address. He had told everyone about Leopold's body missing from that subterranean temple, but he never elaborated on the stranger aspect of that story.

"Erin," he said, "there is something I never mentioned about that attack in Cumae. That *strigoi* who . . . who wounded me . . . just before he died, he said he was sorry. He knew my name."

"What?"

Christian turned sharply to him. Apparently Baako and Sophia had also failed to share this detail with the Sanguinists. Perhaps all of them had been ready to simply dismiss it as a coincidence. Maybe the dead *strigoi* was German, which would explain the accent. Maybe he knew Jordan's name because whoever sent that monster down there knew the Warrior of Man was in that buried temple.

Still, he wasn't buying it.

Jordan, mein Freund . . .

"I swear the voice that came out of the *strigoi* was Leopold's," he said.

"That's impossible," Erin muttered, but she had witnessed enough of the impossible to be unsure now.

"I know how it sounds," he said. "But I think Leopold was using that body like a mouthpiece."

Erin remained silent, her gaze distant as she digested this information. "What sort of connection could there be between them to allow that to happen?"

Christian offered one theory. "Maybe when Leopold died, his spirit leaped into this other *strigoi.*"

Erin turned to him. "Has that ever happened before?"

Christian shrugged. "Not that I know, but since meeting the two of you, I've witnessed many things I thought would have been impossible."

Erin nodded at the truth of his words. She eyed Jordan. "Was there anything else unusual about that *strigoi,* anything that might explain such a psychic link?"

"Besides being supersized in strength and speed?" he asked.

"Besides that."

Jordan remembered one last detail. "Actually there was one other odd thing. He had a black mark on his chest." He mimicked with his own palm. "It was shaped like a hand."

Erin's hunched shoulders grew straighter. "Like Bathory Darabont had?"

"That's exactly like I thought. Some mark of ownership."

"Or possession," Erin added.

Christian looked concerned. "They must have finished with the autopsy on that body back in Vatican City. Perhaps by the time we're back there, they'll have some better explanation. Cardinal Bernard will likely know what to—"

Christian's voice died away. Plainly he had momentarily forgotten that the cardinal was no longer in charge of the Sanguinists. He was now a prisoner.

Jordan shook his head. This was the worst time for the order to have a shake-up in leadership. "What will happen to Bernard?" he asked.

Christian sighed. "He will be taken back to Castel Gandolfo and placed on house arrest until he is ready to stand trial. Because he is a cardinal, a conclave of twelve other cardinals must be gathered to pass sentence. It might take a couple of weeks, especially with the increased *strigoi* attacks."

"What are they likely to decide?" Erin asked.

"Cardinal Bernard is powerful," Christian said. "Few will want to speak against him. Because of that—and the fact that there are mitigating circumstances—penance will likely be assigned."

"What kind of penance?" Jordan asked.

"He committed a grievous sin. Normally a death sentence would be warranted. But the order can also choose to forgive him. Sophia told me that the cardinal has broken our laws in the past, feeding on human enemies during the Crusades."

"The Crusades?" Erin's voice rose in pitch. "That was over a *thousand* years ago."

"You guys have pretty long memories," Jordan said.

"It is a difficult calling." Christian fingered his rosary beads. "And if Countess Bathory has information that can aid you in the quest to reshackle Lucifer, the court may go easy on the cardinal."

Erin looked down the length of the nave. "So Bernard's life might depend on the countess surviving her transformation?"

"Seems fitting," said Jordan.

"Fitting or not," Christian said, "I'm sure we'll know her fate soon enough."

Jordan imagined Bernard was resting no easier this night.

Serves him right.

5:58 A.M.

With both arms shackled in front of him, Bernard braced his legs as best he could against the roll of the boat. The silver manacles seared his wrists each time he moved, filling the dark hold with the smell of his own charred flesh.

I have been imprisoned like a common thief.

And he knew whom to blame for his current state: Cardinal Mario. The cardinal of Venice had always loathed Bernard, mostly because Bernard thwarted his centuries-long campaign to move the center of the Sanguinist order to this decadent city of canals. This harsh trip in the dark hold was the payment for that sin.

Still, this was but an annoyance. Bernard had no illusions of what was to come. While he didn't know what his exact punishment would be for this greater sin, he would be toppled from his lofty post, falling so far that he could not even guess where the bottom might land. He would certainly be stripped of his title.

Death would be a simpler option.

He bowed his head. He had served the Order of the Sanguines for nearly a thousand years. Few Sanguinists of his age remained. In all that time, he had never been tempted to retreat to the Sanctuary, to become one of the Cloistered Ones. That was not a path for him or his ambitions.

I belong among the ranks of the Church, serving the order to my fullest capacity.

He lifted his cuffed hands high enough to touch his pectoral cross with his thumbs. The pain was familiar, comforting. It reminded him that he was not done serving.

He must focus on that—rather than how he had been laid low by the likes of Elizabeth Bathory. Fury flashed through him, but he schooled himself, accepting his faults. The countess had recognized the depth of his pride, used the fires of his ambition against him. Her words rang in his head.

Only you have the power to save your world.

She had tempted him—not just with blood, but with her precious knowledge. Stored in her brain were secrets that he had desired as much as he had wanted her blood. He had been too eager to pay her price. She had known what music to play.

And I was but her instrument.

But no longer.

The others did not understand the depth of evil that the countess carried in her black heart, but Bernard did. He had no doubt the wine would consume her, but if it did not, he must be ready.

He knew one way to control her if she survived. She cared for the boy, Tommy.

Control the child, and you control the mother.

He shifted enough to retrieve his cell phone from his pocket. His captors had stripped him of his weapons, but they had left him with this. He dialed a number in the dark. Even in times such as this, there were those who were loyal to him.

"*Ciao?*" said a voice on the other end.

Bernard quickly explained his needs.

"It will be done," his conspirator said, closing the connection.

Bernard took cold comfort that his plan for the countess would not fail.

This time, I will turn her into an instrument of my purpose.

No matter the cost.

6:10 A.M.

Elizabeth knelt with the chalice poised at her lips, teetering on the brink between salvation and extinction. Above her head, the mosaic of Lazarus stared back down at her, along with Christ, but she found herself looking at those gathered to witness that event. They were Lazarus's family, his sisters, Martha and Mary of Bethany. The small glass tiles captured their looks of terror, not joy.

Did they fear their brother would not survive the act of drinking Christ's blood?

Her gaze drifted to another who matched their fear, who held the chalice to her lips. Reflected candlelight shone on Rhun's tense face, turning his pale skin to silver. She had never seen him look so terrified, save the moment when she had first kissed him in front of the fireplace at her castle, the moment that had set the events in motion that led them both here.

Rhun's dark eyes stared into hers. This was the moment for a poetic farewell, but she could think of nothing to say to him, especially in front of the gathered Sanguinists.

She focused on Rhun, letting everything else go.

"*Ege'sze'ge're*," she whispered over the brim of the cup. It was a common Hungarian toast: *To your health.*

Rhun's eyes softened with the hint of a smile.

"*Ege'sze'ge're*," he repeated with a small nod.

She tilted her head, and he tipped the cup.

A spill of wine poured over her tongue.

It is done . . .

As she swallowed, the liquid burnt a fiery trail down her throat. It felt as if she had sipped molten rock. Tears sprang to her eyes. Her back arched in agony, thrusting her breasts against the rough-spun cloth of her nun's habit. Her arms jerked wide. Fire flowed through her body into her limbs, out to her fingertips. Every vein in her body ran with flame. It was an agony that she had never known.

With that pain, the wine's holiness spread inside her, draining her *strigoi* strength. It fought against the darkness in her blood. But the holiness did not win. The evil was not completely burned away. It still pulsed within her, like a banked fire.

She finally gasped out a breath, casting out some of the fire.

She suspected what might come next, bracing herself against it. From Rhun's account, every time she drank the wine she would be forced to relive her worst sins. He called this experience *penance*. Its purpose was to remind each Sanguinist that they were fallible and that only His incredible grace could carry them through their sins.

And I have so much to atone for.

As the fire receded inside her, she bowed forward across her knees, covering her tear-stained face with her hands. But it was not to blot out any terrible memories.

It was to hide her relief.

She had survived their test—and she saw no scenes of past depredations. Her mind felt as clear as it ever had been. It seemed she needed no penance.

Perhaps because I have no regrets.

She smiled into her palms.

Were the Sanguinists the architects of their own penance and their own pain?

Rhun's hand dropped onto her shoulder as if to comfort her. She let it stay, unsure how long penance normally lasted. She kept her hands in front of her face and waited.

Finally, Rhun's fingers tightened on her shoulder.

Taking this as a sign, she raised her head, careful to keep her expression tragic.

Rhun beamed down at her as he helped her to her feet. "The good in you was triumphant, Elisabeta. Thank the Lord for His eternal mercy."

She leaned on him, notably weaker from the holiness, stripped of the strangely expanded *strigoi* strength. She clutched Rhun's hand, while gazing across the faces gathered here, most remained stoic, but a few could not hide their surprise.

She continued to play the role expected of her. She looked into Rhun's eyes. "Now that I'm reborn, I cannot break my promise to you, to everyone. I will tell you what I know, something that could help you on your quest. Let this be my first act of contrition."

Rhun hugged more tightly to her, thanking her and perhaps wanting to reassure himself that she was indeed still alive.

"Then let us go," he said.

He led her past the others. They touched her shoulders as she walked among them, welcoming her to their ranks. However, one witness could not keep the shock from her face. She was the last to acknowledge Elizabeth.

Sister Abigail gave a small bow of her head.

"I am humbled to have joined you, Sister," Elizabeth said.

The old nun marshaled her features into something resembling welcome. "It is a difficult path that you walk now, Sister Elizabeth. I pray that you will find the strength within yourself to keep to it."

Elizabeth fixed the somber expression on her face. "As do I, Sister."

She headed out of the chapel, bottling the laughter ringing inside her.

Who knew escape would be this easy?

14

The Blood Countess survived . . .

Still coming to grips with this, Erin stared at Elizabeth's back as the former countess led them across the depths of St. Mark's Basilica. She was dressed in a simple nun's habit, accepted now as one of the Sanguinists. Still not believing this sudden change, Erin studied her. Despite the humble clothes she wore, Elizabeth still strode with the haughtiness of royalty, her shoulders thrown back, her neck stiff.

But she did pass the Sanguinists' test.

Erin gave a small shake of her head, accepting this truth.

At least for now.

And if nothing else, the woman was at least proving cooperative.

"This is what I've come to show you," Elizabeth said, stopping beneath a magnificent mosaic that graced the roof above. "It is titled the Temptation of Christ, one of the finest in the basilica."

Rhun kept to Elizabeth's side, shadowing her at every step, his gaze wide upon her, his face full of relief and awe . . . and joy. After all that the countess had put him through, he still loved her.

Jordan stood a little apart from Erin. She wished Jordan would look upon her with that same expression of unquestionable, unquenchable love. Instead, he studied the spread of the artwork.

"So this is showing the three times Satan challenged Christ," Jordan said, "when Christ was out fasting in the desert for forty days."

"Exactly," Erin said. "The leftmost section shows the devil—that's the black angel in front of him—bringing Christ stones and tempting him to turn them to bread."

Christian nodded. "But Christ refused, telling him *Man shall not live by bread alone, but by every word of God.*"

Erin pointed to the next section. "The second temptation is where the devil tells Jesus to jump off a building and have God catch him, but Jesus refused to tempt the Lord. And the last one—showing Christ standing on a set of mountains—is where the devil offers Christ all the kingdoms of the earth."

"But Jesus turns him down," Jordan said.

"And the devil is banished," Erin added. "Then those three angels to the right take care of Jesus."

A new voice intruded. "And that number is significant."

Erin turned to Elizabeth, who kept her hands demurely folded before her.

"What do you mean?" Erin asked.

"*Three* temptations, *three* angels," Elizabeth explained. "Note also that Christ stands atop *three* mountains during the second temptation. *Three* was always an important number to the Church."

"As in the Son, the Father, and the Holy Ghost," Erin said.

The Holy Trinity.

Elizabeth unfolded her hands and motioned to Rhun, Christian, and herself. "And it is why the Sanguinists always move in groups of three."

Erin also recalled how it took the blood of three Sanguinists to open the door that Bernard had sealed. Even the Blood Gospel's prophecy centered on three figures: the Woman of Learning, the Warrior of Man, and the Knight of Christ.

"But that's not the most significant *trio* that is hidden in this mosaic," Elizabeth said and pointed up. "Look closer at the mountains under Christ's sandals."

Jordan squinted. "It looks like He's standing on some sort of watery bubble?"

"And within that bubble?" Elizabeth asked.

With the mosaic so far overhead, Erin wished that she had binoculars, but she still saw clearly enough to understand. Small luminous tiles of white surrounded a trio of objects hidden there, floating in that watery brilliance.

"*Three* chalices," Erin said, unable to keep the awe from her voice.

One hope rose through the questions in her mind: Could one of them be *Lucifer's Chalice*, the cup they were supposed to find?

She turned to Elizabeth. "But what's the significance of you showing us this?"

"Because it might be linked to your quest. Long ago, this artwork was commissioned by men who would later form a court in Prague under Emperor Rudolf II. The Court of the Alchemists."

Erin frowned. She had read about that group, in children's tales about the Biblical golem. They were a group of famous alchemists assembled in Prague, who studied the occult, along with seeking ways to transform lead to gold. In their many labs, they sought to tease out the secrets of immortality.

So far as she knew, they had failed.

"What's the significance of the chalices?" Erin asked.

"I do not know for sure. But I know they are somehow connected to that green stone you found. That green diamond."

"Connected how?" Jordan asked.

"That stone also has a history that goes back to the Court of the Alchemists. To a man I once knew, back when I was performing my own study concerning the nature of the *strigoi*."

Erin scowled at her choice of words. *Study.* It was a despicably clinical way to describe the torture and murder of hundreds of girls.

"He was one of the court's alchemists," Elizabeth continued. "He showed me that symbol you discovered on that diamond, the mark I copied in my journal."

"Who was he?" Erin pressed.

"His name was John Dee."

Erin stared harder at Elizabeth. John Dee was a famous English scientist who lived during the sixteenth century. Through his skills with navigation, he helped Queen Elizabeth set up the British Empire. But later in his life, he would become world renowned as an astrologer and alchemist. He lived during a time when religion, magic, and science stood at the crossroads.

"What was he working on that involved the green diamond?" Erin asked.

"One of Dee's life goals—one that would discredit him in the end—was his quest to speak with angels."

Angels?

A year ago Erin would have scoffed at the idea, but now—she glanced over to Jordan—she knew how real they were.

Elizabeth continued. "Dee worked with a young man named Edward Kelly, who claimed to be a scryer."

"What's that?" Jordan asked.

"A fortune-teller," Erin explained. "They used crystal balls, tea leaves, and other means of predicting what was to come."

"In Kelly's case, he possessed a black polished mirror, said to be constructed of obsidian from the New World. In that mirror, he claimed the angels appeared to him, or so he convinced John Dee. Dee transcribed the words of those angels using a special language that he invented."

"Enochian," Erin said.

Elizabeth nodded. "In time, Dee lost his faith in Edward Kelly and wished to speak to the angels himself. To that end, he sought to open a portal to the angelic world through which he might speak to those beings and share their wisdom with mankind."

"But what does any of this have to do with the green stone?" Jordan asked.

"Exactly," Erin muttered.

"The stone held the power to open that portal. It was full of a dark energy, one strong enough to pierce the veils between our worlds. On the day that Dee was to open the portal, a calamity occurred, and he and his apprentice were found dead in the laboratory. Emperor Rudolf hid the stone so that none could unleash its power again."

"How did you learn of this?" Erin asked.

The countess smoothed the folds of her skirt. "Because Emperor Rudolf II told me."

Christian frowned skeptically. "You knew the emperor?"

"Of course, I knew him," she snapped, clearly angry. "I come from one of the most royal houses in Europe."

"I meant no offense, Sister," said Christian.

Elizabeth quickly collected herself, refolding her hands at her waist, looking like she was trying her best to be that humble nun again. She did a poor job.

"The emperor wrote me a letter," she explained. "He knew that Master Dee and I were the only ones in the known world engaged in the same kind of research— exploring the nature of good and evil."

"How does any of this help us move forward on our quest?" Jordan asked.

"Dee knew much more about this diamond than he was willing to share in letters," she said. "Like that symbol. I suspect he knew its significance. If we could find his old papers, his private notes, we could learn the truth."

Erin nodded. *At least it's a place to start.*

Rhun stared at Elizabeth. In fact, his gaze rarely left her features. "What has you looking so worried?"

Erin tried to read that same anxiety in the woman's stoic face, but failed. Then again, Rhun knew her better than anyone.

"From small details in the emperor's description of the state he found Dee and the boy's bodies, I fear that Dee's portal did not open unto the holy angels, but unto the darkest angel of all—Lucifer himself."

Elizabeth stared up at the black figures above their heads, tempting Christ. Silence filled the vast church as the implications of her statement slowly settled in on them all. The countess finally turned to them again.

"No matter what," Elizabeth warned, "we must keep the stone in one piece."

Jordan exchanged a look with Erin.

"Show her," Erin said.

Jordan slowly pulled the two broken pieces of diamond from his pocket. Elizabeth shrank back from the glittering green shards. Even Erin could read the raw fear on her face. It was unmistakable now.

"It is free," she whispered.

"What is free?" Erin asked.

"There is nothing left for us to do," Elizabeth said, ignoring the question, her voice low and frightened. "Except to plan for Lucifer's return."

10:38 A.M.

Rhun stared at Elisabeta in disbelief, searching for deceit but finding only authentic fear. "Lucifer?" he asked. "You truly think his return is close?"

"The *strigoi* have changed, have they not?" Elisabeta's eyes bored into his. "Possessing more speed, more strength?"

Jordan nodded, rubbing his belly.

"But what does it mean?" Erin asked.

"It means that the danger facing you is greater than you realize." Elizabeth touched the broken stones with one finger. "It has escaped its prison."

"What has escaped?" Rhun asked, drawing her hands away. If any evil remained in that stone, he didn't want Elisabeta near it.

"The gem was filled with dread forces, an energy amassed and distilled across many years as John Dee harvested them."

"Harvested whom?" Erin asked. "What energy are you talking about?"

"The essence of over six hundred *strigoi*. Dee collected their dying energies at the moment of their death and funneled them into the heart of the diamond." She turned to Rhun, clutching his arm. "You've slain enough *strigoi* to have seen the dark smoke that drifts free upon their deaths."

Rhun slowly nodded, glancing to Erin and the others, seeing recognition in their expressions. They had all witnessed it at one time or another.

Erin spoke, "In your journals, it showed you killing a *strigoi* in a glass coffin. You illustrated that smoke rising from their bodies."

"That was as far as I could carry my experiments. But Dee learned to trap those essences using a glass apparatus of his own invention—and to collect them. Somehow, he discovered this green stone could contain such concentrated evil."

Jordan looked down at the two heavy shards in his hands. "And now those forces have been let loose."

"The act of shattering this stone," Erin said, "could it be what the Blood Gospel's prophecy was referencing, that the shackles of Lucifer have been loosened?"

"Perhaps," Elizabeth said, "but it is surely the reason that the *strigoi* have grown more powerful of late."

"Why is that?" Rhun asked.

She turned to him. "Do you truly not know?"

Rhun simply frowned.

"Haven't you ever wondered what it is that gives you your long life, your strength?" Elizabeth asked.

"A curse," he said.

"That is a simple answer," she said. "Surely the Church has scholars who have delved more deeply into this mystery than that."

"If so," said Christian, "we don't know about it. So tell us."

Elisabeta shook her head as if she could not believe their folly. "From my experiments and from Dee's research into angels, we came to believe that all *strigoi* are fueled from a single angelic force—a dark angel."

Rhun stared up at the figures of Lucifer above.

Elisabeta followed his gaze. "Have you not seen how the smoke of a dying *strigoi* does not drift *up*, but worms *down*?"

He slowly nodded. "Returning to Hell."

"Returning to its source. To Lucifer himself."

Rhun lifted his hands, staring at his flesh, thinking of that Satanic energy inside, restrained only by the grace of Christ's holy blood. To the side, Christian looked equally aghast, both of them for the first time perhaps understanding their truest natures.

Thankfully, Erin directed the line of inquiry in a more practical direction. "Elizabeth, you said before that *it was free*, that *it had escaped its prison*. What do you think was released from that diamond?"

"I cannot say for sure, but Dee had collected a specific number of *strigoi* spirits. Six hundred and sixty-six, to be precise."

"The Biblical number of the beast," Erin said.

"Dee believed, when he reached that number, that those essences would coalesce, come together to give birth or perhaps bind a demon."

"The Biblical beast," Rhun said, beginning to fathom Elisabeta's earlier terror.

"Dee believed he could coerce that demon to open that angelic portal, but he failed."

"And now it's loosed upon this world," Rhun said.

Elisabeta squeezed her hands together at her waist. "For any hope of stopping it, we must find Dee's old papers. Only he might have understood what he created."

"Where do we begin to look?" Erin asked.

"His old labs in Prague. That is, if they still exist. Dee knew how to keep secrets. He had hidden compartments throughout his rooms. In the fireplace, false walls, even the caverns underneath his laboratory. We must go to his workshop in Prague and seek out those answers."

Rhun looked to Erin and Jordan. It was a tenuous lead, but it was more solid than anything else. "What do you two think?"

Jordan glanced over to Erin.

She nodded. "I think it's worth a shot. And with everything that's happening, we should head out immediately."

"I can get the helicopter warmed up," Christian said. "But who all's going?"

Erin waved to Rhun and Jordan. "The trio, of course."

Elisabeta stirred, straightening her shoulders. "I should accompany you, too. I have visited Dee's workshop and know many of its secrets."

Christian raised an eyebrow. "You have just joined our order, Sister Elizabeth. It is common for those new to the cloth to spend months in seclusion, to learn to govern the animal forces within. It is a dangerous time."

Elisabeta bowed her head, but Rhun saw a familiar flash of anger in her silver eyes. "If that is the will of the Church, I must obey it. Yet, I do not see how you can succeed on this mission without my aid."

A voice rose behind them, revealing someone who had been eavesdropping on their conversation from the shadows.

"Sister Elizabeth should assist the trio on their quest," Sophia said, as she stepped out the darkness. "No one else in the Church has her knowledge. Risks must be taken if we hope to succeed."

Elisabeta bowed her head. "Thank you, Sister Sophia."

"You have taken the wine. If God trusts you, we can do no less." Sophia nodded to Christian. "But the concerns raised a moment ago are real ones, so I will travel with you. To help you to be alert to temptation."

"I would welcome your expertise in such matters," Elisabeta said.

Rhun suspected Sophia was joining them, not as a tutor, but as a bodyguard—to keep an eye on Elisabeta. And maybe that was wise. Either way, the matter was settled.

Christian turned away. "I'll prepare a flight schedule. Barring any problems, we should be in Prague by noon."

As they prepared to follow, Rhun watched Jordan pocket the two halves of the green stone, reminding him what had been released into this world. If Elisabeta's fears were true, a demon had been set free.

But what manner of beast was it?

15

How much longer must I wait . . . ?

Legion remained hidden under the shadow of an archway. From the darkness, he studied the columned façade of the great church on the far side of the sunlit square. Bright midday sun reflected off its golden surfaces and burned his eyes, but he stayed in place.

I have waited long, and I can wait longer still.

As he kept vigil, rooted inside Leopold, he searched out other eyes, those whom he had enslaved with the touch of his hand. Through those distant branches, those other eyes, he saw a hundred other views, from places that were yet in darkness:

. . . a torn throat of a young girl, pouring crimson over black tar streets . . .

. . . the wet terrified eyes of a man in a metal box anticipating his death at the sharp teeth of a beast of the night . . .

. . . another stalks a dark wood, circling a couple entangled together and oblivious to all but their own lusts . . .

At any moment, he could do more than just see. He could pull his awareness fully into one of those slaves, taking possession of its limbs and body. But he remained where he was, planted firmly in this vessel, his foothold in his world. He searched yet again through the memories cast out by that small flame flickering in the enormity of his darkness.

Leopold had recognized the sanctified stronghold across the square.

And now I know it, too.

St. Mark's Basilica.

Legion had come here from Rome, brought by a trembling Sanguinist priest who listened behind the door of one called Cardinal Bernard. From those ears, he had learned that the trio of prophecy would gather here. Though he wanted to know what transpired within those holy walls, he dared not trespass himself.

Not only was that ground sacred, but the day's fierce sun threatened to burn him to ash. He had brought nothing with which to cloak himself. Even in the shadows, the sunlight tingled against his skin. The sun would soon chase him into a nearby house or perhaps deep below the sea that fed the canals.

I can rest under the cool green water during the heat of the day.

The temptation called to him, to experience that beauty: the sparkle of flitting fish, the dance of emerald veils of seaweed. He wanted to revel within it, to be part of it.

But not yet.

Instead, he must linger in this city of foul canals, a patchwork of human depravity and holiness. The trio he hunted had sought sanctuary here. And despite Leopold's attempts to hide knowledge of them, Legion had slowly gleaned more.

Two of the trio were, of course, mortal.

The *Warrior* and the *Woman*.

But the third—the *Knight* named Rhun Korza—had arrived later than the others. He was a Sanguinist, like Leopold, which meant he was corruptible. Legion was capable of touching that darkness inside the Knight with his own shadows.

Marking him, binding him to my will.

Sadly, it was something he could not do with the Warrior or the Woman, who held no such darkness inside, but Legion only needed the Knight.

Korza would be his way into the trio, his way to destroy the prophecy from within.

A heavy door slammed across the square, drawing his attention.

A troop of silent-hearted Sanguinists poured out of that holiness and into the open square. Legion searched their faces, breathing deeply of the smoke cast out by Leopold's flame. Leopold knew many of them by name and habit.

But his gaze fixed to one in the center, standing with the Warrior and the Woman.

Rhun Korza.

Once he bows to me, we will purge his world, returning it to a paradise.

But his prey stayed ever in the light, frustratingly so. With no other recourse, Legion followed them along the narrow streets of Venice, keeping to the shadows. Through passing doors, he heard the heartbeats of those going about their dreary human lives—but one heart drew his attention more fully.

The Warrior should already be dead. Legion remembered possessing the *strigoi* who had attacked the man: the thrust of the blade into this one's soft belly, the heavy pour of hot blood against his cold hands.

But the Warrior's heart still beat.

Closer now, Legion recognized a foreign note to its rhythm, as if the trumpeting of a great horn echoed behind those stolid beats.

It was a mystery, but one that would have to wait.

The others had reached their destination, hurrying during this last stretch under the merciless sun.

I have no more time.

The others rushed into a building, one smelling of oil, as much of this world does now. A bladed machine rested on the roof. Leopold knew this device.

. . . a helicopter, for flying like a bumble bee . . .

A trickle of awe filled Legion at the mastery of these mortals over their limited world. Man had conquered much in the centuries that Legion had been imprisoned.

Even the skies.

Knowing this, Legion struggled with how he could continue his hunt. The helicopter would soon fly into the sun of a new day, bearing away the trio. He must know where they were headed.

Already those blades had begun to turn.

From the building below, a smaller group of Sanguinists exited. It was the escort who had guarded the trio's passage through the city, preparing to return to their holy roosts. Most headed back from whence they had come, back toward the basilica, but one figure split away, heading another direction.

Her path took her along a canal, whose closest bank still lay in deep shadows.

He quickly circled through other patches of darkness to trail her.

As he ran, he listened to the city, to its shouts and laughter, the growl of its engines, the hammering of its construction. He heard little of the natural world here. No birdsong, no brush of wind through leaves. Mankind had taken over this island—as they had much of this modern world—and tamed it for their uses, destroying the wild gardens, killing the creatures that lived in harmony there.

While God might tolerate such ruin to his creation, I will not.

To that end, he closed in on the swish of cloth as his target continued along the canal, oblivious to the hunter behind her.

He pulled her name from Leopold and spoke it aloud.

"Sister Abigail . . ."

The Sanguinist turned toward him. Her hair was as gray as stone, pulled away from a fretful face. She was plainly irritated, and her anger made her react too slowly. As horror widened her eyes, reflecting back his dark countenance, he was upon her.

He lunged out and touched her cheek, branding his mark into her flesh.

She immediately sagged against him. He caught her, embraced her. As he held her, he flipped through her memories like a book.

. . . *walking the wet streets of London holding a hand above her head. Mother* . . .

. . . *standing before a simple white gravestone. Father* . . .

. . . *joyful people dancing in the streets. The Great War has ended, but so many lost. So many wild fields bombed into stripes of death* . . .

. . . *giant stones falling from the sky. Bombs. Another war, greater even than the last. Weapons that can annihilate everything that man was given* . . .

. . . *a man with eyes the color of thunderclouds and cold skin. He takes her blood and offers his in return* . . .

. . . *a battlefield of mud. Brown eyes, slanted at the corners. Bombs falling, destroying good and evil alike. Another war, Korea, and she hunts with the man with the storm-cloud eyes* . . .

. . . *a choice given by a woman wearing a cross. Repent or die. Wine burning against her lips* . . .

Legion took in the nun's life, breathing it all in, but her past held little interest. He pushed aside those memories and searched for fresher ones.

. . . *The face of a woman appears. She has curls of black, eyes of silver gray. She is beautiful, and the cold form of Abigail hates her* . . .

Legion extracted her name.

Countess Elizabeth Bathory.

She was of no use to Legion. Losing patience, he concentrated instead on a single purpose, focusing it into the woman he embraced.

Where are they going?

Abigail's lips moved, already close to his ear. "They head to Prague."

Legion shivered at that name, a place tied to his own history, where he had been first imprisoned. It seemed as much as he hunted the trio, they were closing in on his past.

He drew his intention into a single word.

Why?

Quiet words reached his ear. "They search for the journals of John Dee."

This time, his own memories overwhelmed him.

. . . *The man with a beard as white as milk and clever dark eyes* . . .

. . . *those eyes smile at me on the other side of the green flame. He is my jailer* . . .

. . . I burn with pain and hatred . . .

He shoved Abigail away from him, holding her at arm's length, his mark emblazoned on her cheek. He now knew where he must go.

To Prague.

He already had slaves nearby and would gather them toward that old city, but he intended to go there himself. Abigail could travel in the daylight, and she could help him do the same.

In that city, he would avenge his past, protect his future *. . . and destroy the hopes of all mankind.*

Third

*For wickedness burneth as the fire: it shall devour
the briers and thorns, and shall kindle in the
thickets of the forest, and they shall mount up
like the lifting up of smoke.*

—Isaiah 9:18

16

Seated at the back of the helicopter, Elizabeth held on to her safety harness with both hands. Rivers, trees, and towns had passed under their tiny aircraft with dizzying speed. Her window showed a toy world, and she was the child who looked down upon it, ready to play.

Within her blood, burning wine pushed against the dark strength. Still, she felt whole again, *right* for the first time in months.

This is who I am, who I am supposed to be.

Perhaps she could even forgive Rhun for all that he had cost her, because he had showed her the way here, led her to this moment.

Throughout the flight from Venice, Rhun cast long looks at her, as if he expected her to disappear. Across the cabin, Erin and Jordan had drifted off to sleep quickly, while Sophia and Christian sat together in the cockpit, piloting their craft along never-ending rivers of air.

This was an amazing time to be alive.

And I will drink it all in.

She searched the lands rolling ahead, knowing they would soon be in Prague. She wondered if she would recognize it or if it would be foreign to her, as so much of Rome had been. In truth, she did not care. She would learn and adapt, flow through the changes to come for all eternity.

But not alone.

She pictured Tommy's small face. In the past, he had taught her much about these modern times. In turn, she would teach him the wonders of the night, of the pleasures of blood, of the march of years that would never touch them again.

She smiled.

Who needs the sun with a future so bright?

The radio crackled in the headphones she wore. Christian's voice woke the others, stirring Rhun straighter. "We're coming into Prague."

Rhun noted the smile still on her face and matched it with one of his own. "You look well."

"I am well . . . so very well."

Rhun's dark eyes were happy and kind. It would pain him when she abandoned the order. She was surprised to discover how much that thought bothered her.

She turned her eyes back to the window. Their helicopter skated over modern structures of glass and ugly buildings, but farther ahead, she recognized an older section of the city with red tile roofs and twisted narrow streets.

As the helicopter followed the flow of the wide Vltava River, she recognized the brick bridge that forded it, spanning the water in a row of majestic arches. She was happy to see not all had changed. It seemed Prague still retained many of its towers and landmarks.

"That's the Charles Bridge," Erin said, noting her attention.

Elizabeth stifled a wry smile. It had once been simply called the Stone Bridge. She watched people strolling along its span. In her days, horses or carriages once thronged the bridge.

So some things have changed.

As the helicopter headed toward the heart of the city, she drank in the sights, searching for streets and buildings that she had known in the past. She recognized the twin spires of Týn Church near the town square. The tower of city hall still bore the majesty of the Orloj, the city's famous astronomical clock.

Erin had followed her gaze. "It's a marvel, that medieval clock. It's said that the clockmaker was blinded by order of the Councilors of Prague, so that he would never build another."

Elizabeth nodded. "With a hot iron poker."

"Harsh," Jordan said. "Not much of a bonus for completing the job."

"They were harsh times," Elizabeth said. "But it is also said that the clockmaker took his revenge, that he crawled into the tower and destroyed the delicate mechanism by touch alone—then died in that tower. The clock could not be repaired for another hundred years."

Elizabeth stared at the clock's fanciful face. It was good that some of the past was still preserved and revered. Though the clockmaker had died, his masterwork had survived the march of years.

As will I.

Christian radioed back to them. "We'll be on the ground in a few minutes."

Elizabeth's phone vibrated deep in her pocket. She covered it with her palm, hoping Rhun hadn't heard it past the roar of the engine and the muffle of the headphones. It had to be Tommy. But why was he calling? Fearing the worst, she shifted impatiently in her seat, wishing she could talk to the boy. But to do so, she needed a moment alone.

As the phone's vibrations ended, she clasped her hands together, squeezing hard, wishing this aircraft would land. Thankfully, it didn't take long. As Christian had promised, they were soon on the ground. After some moments of wrangling, she found herself outside, following the others across hard pavement toward a long, low building.

The air was colder than in Venice, but she still burned. She held her palm open toward the midafternoon sun. As a *strigoi*, her skin would be blistering, burning to ash, but it seemed the holy blood protected her. But not completely. There remained enough darkness inside her that the sunlight still stung. She withdrew her hand and tilted her face down, shading her features in the shadows of her wimple.

Rhun noted her reaction. "You'll grow accustomed with time."

She frowned. Even the daytime was not wholly open to a Sanguinist. Such a life was one of constant accommodation and pain. She longed to shake loose such restraints and limitations . . . to be truly free again.

But not yet.

She followed the others into the airport terminal. She scowled at its unsightly utility, impersonal, gray, and white. Men in this modern age seemed frightened of color.

"May I have a moment to wash the dust from my hands and face?" Elizabeth asked Rhun, seeking to find a private moment to return Tommy's call. "I found the journey most disorienting."

"I will take her," Sophia offered. The small woman spoke a touch too quickly, displaying her distrust.

"Thank you, Sister," Elizabeth said.

Sophia led her down a side hall to a many-stalled bathroom and followed her inside. Elizabeth crossed to the sink and washed her hands in the warm water. Sophia joined her, splashing water on her face.

Elizabeth used the moment to study the dark-skinned woman, wondering what she had been like before becoming a Sanguinist. Did she have a family that she left behind in the passing of years? What atrocities had she committed as a *strigoi* before taking the holy wine?

But the woman's face remained a stoic mask, hiding whatever pain haunted her past. And Elizabeth knew there must be something.

We are all haunted in our own ways.

She pictured her son, Paul, remembering his bright laughter.

It seemed the passage through life was but a gathering of ghosts. The longer you lived, the more shadows haunted you. She stared at herself in the mirror, surprised by the single tear coursing down her cheek.

Rather than wipe it away, she used it.

"May I have a moment by myself?" Elizabeth asked, turning to Sophia.

Sophia looked ready to object, but then her face softened, seeing the tear. Still, she glanced around, plainly looking for windows or another exit. Finding none, she touched Elizabeth on the arm, then retreated. "I will wait outside."

As soon as Sophia was gone, Elizabeth retrieved her phone. She left the water running to mask her voice and quickly dialed Tommy's number.

It was answered immediately. "Elizabeth, thanks for calling back. You caught me just in time."

She was relieved that he sounded calm. "Is everything well?"

"Well enough, I guess," he said. "But I'm so excited that I get to see you soon."

She frowned, not understanding. The boy could not know that she intended to join him as soon as she could escape these others. "What do you mean?"

"A priest came by. He's taking me to Rome."

She went stiff, her voice going hard. "What *priest*?" Her mind was on fire, struggling to comprehend this news. It was unexpected and felt wrong, like a trap. "Tommy, do not—"

"Hold on," Tommy said, cutting her off. She heard him talking to someone in the background, then he was back. "My aunt says I have to get off the phone. My ride is here. But I'll see you tomorrow."

He sounded so eager, but dread filled her.

"Do not go with that priest!" she warned, her voice sharp.

But the line went dead. She dialed his number again, pacing the bathroom. The phone rang and rang, but he did not answer. She clenched a fist around the telephone, imagining reasons why they might have taken him.

Maybe they were whisking Tommy to safety because of all of the strigoi *attacks.*

She cast this hope aside, knowing the Church had no interest in the boy any longer.

So then why were they taking him? Why was Tommy suddenly important to them again?

Then she knew.

Because of me.

The Church knew Tommy was important to her. Someone was taking control of the boy, intending to use him like a pawn, a way to attach a leash around her neck. Only one priest would use such an innocent boy as leverage. Even imprisoned, that villain must still be exercising his power.

Cardinal Bernard.

She slammed her fist against the mirror. It shattered outward in rings from the point of impact.

Elizabeth glanced at the door, knowing Sophia waited out there. It was a rash act, one born of rage. But if she was to save Tommy, she must be smarter. Before Sophia came in to investigate, she turned off the water and hurried toward the entrance.

As she exited, Sophia eyed her suspiciously.

Elizabeth straightened her wimple and brushed her hand down her rosary. A tingle of pain crossed her fingertips from the silver. She used that sting to steady herself.

"I . . . I believe I'm ready to continue," she said.

They returned to the others.

Erin had a map opened on her phone, another wonder of this modern age. "We're not too far from the old palace. Most of the alchemy labs are in its shadow."

"The laboratory that we seek is not there. We must go to the town center, by the Orloj," Elizabeth said, intending to bide her time.

I will wait and watch.

Her time would come.

As would Bernard's.

3:10 P.M.

Erin hiked her backpack higher as they headed toward the terminal exit, very conscious that she carried the Blood Gospel over her shoulder. She worried that she should have left the book in Rome, where it could be locked up safely, but with the book bound to her, she refused to let it out of her sight.

It felt like a part of her now.

Ahead, Rhun walked alongside the countess, as graceful as a panther in his dark jeans and long black coat. Elizabeth, in turn, glided with a measure of command in her step. The two made a handsome couple, and a pang of jealousy struck Erin with unexpected force. It surprised her. Did she want to be the woman at Rhun's side, even if such a thing were possible?

She looked up at Jordan. His blue eyes scanned the room, always looking for danger, but his shoulders were down and relaxed. Golden stubble covered his square jaw. She remembered the scratchy feel of those whiskers against her stomach, her breasts.

Jordan caught her looking, and she blushed and looked down at the floor.

As they stepped out into the cool afternoon, Elizabeth shifted her wimple to better cover her face. Rhun's jacket was hooded, but he didn't bother to pull it up.

Erin leaned toward Christian. "Why does the sunlight seem to bother Elizabeth more?"

"She is new to the cloth," Christian explained. "I don't know if it's simply the passing of time or the many years of penance, but I do know that Sanguinists become more inured to the light as they get older."

"How could you not know exactly how it works?" Erin asked, surprised by the Sanguinists' lack of curiosity about their own nature. "You can't check your brain at the door. What's wrong with finding out what's been done to you?"

Sophia answered from Christian's other side. " *'Trust in the Lord with all thine heart; and lean not unto thine own understanding,'* " she quoted, a touch sharply. "That is not to be questioned."

"Being a Sanguinist is not a scientific process of discovery," Christian added. "Our journey is about faith. *Faith is the substance of things hoped for, the evidence of things not seen.* Not the *proving* of such things."

Jordan rolled his eyes. "Maybe if you had all asked more questions earlier, we wouldn't be in such a mess now."

No one disagreed, and Christian pointed ahead to a small coffeehouse with an outdoor patio. "How about a little refueling? We've got a big day ahead of us."

Only Erin and Jordan needed that *refueling,* but Christian was right. A little caffeine would be good . . . and a *lot* would be even better.

Christian went inside to place an order, while Jordan pushed two small round tables together under a patio umbrella. Christian returned shortly with a tray holding two coffees in wide-lipped ceramic mugs and a pile of pastries. Before placing the tray down, he leaned forward and inhaled the steamy aroma from the cups.

He sighed with appreciation.

Erin smiled, but out of the corner of her eye, she saw Sophia's lips pinch with disdain. The Sanguinists considered any trace of humanity a weakness. But Erin found the lingering traces of Christian's humanity endearing, making her trust him more, not less.

Erin held the mug in her palms, letting it warm her, to steady her. She stared around at the others. "What's the plan from here? It feels like we're tapping through the dark, like a blind man. It's time to change that. It's time we started asking the hard questions. Like understanding the nature of Sanguinists and *strigoi*. That seems to be critical to our quest."

Jordan nodded, looking pointedly at Christian and Sophia. "The less we understand, the more likely we are to fail."

"I agree," Elizabeth said. "Ignorance has not served us in the past, and it will not serve us now. There are things that the Church should know. They have had two thousand years to study such matters, yet they cannot answer the simplest questions. Like what animates a *strigoi*?"

"Or another question: How do you change when you take the vow of a Sanguinist?" Erin added. "How does the wine sustain you?"

Her questions erupted into a brief, but heated discussion. Rhun and Sophia took the side of faith and God. Erin, Jordan, and Elizabeth argued for the scientific method and reason. Christian played reluctant referee, trying to find common ground.

In the end, they all ended up even farther apart.

Erin shoved her empty mug away. All that was left on her plate were pastry crumbs. Jordan had taken only a single bite of his apple Danish, but it looked like he'd had enough—if not of the pastry and coffee, then at least of the conversation.

"We should be going," he said, standing up.

Sophia checked her watch. "Jordan is right. We've wasted enough time."

Erin bit back a sharp retort, knowing it would get them nowhere.

Surprisingly, Elizabeth offered a more conciliatory response. "Perhaps we'll discover the answers to these questions in John Dee's laboratory."

Erin stood up.

We'd better find them . . . or the world is doomed.

17

Rhun stood beside Elizabeth in the center of Prague's old town square. Clouds had rolled in, and a light rain had begun to fall, pebbling against the cobblestones. She had stopped, staring up at the golden face of the astronomical clock, the famous Orloj. Then she turned her attention to the surrounding buildings.

"So exactly where is this guy's lab?" Jordan asked.

"I just need to get my bearings," Elizabeth said. "Much has changed, but fortunately for us, much has not."

Rhun studied the clock's many overlapping dials and symbols. It was already almost four in the afternoon, which left them another two and a half hours of daylight.

Erin huddled in a light blue jacket. "I would've thought John Dee's lab would be somewhere in the Alchemist's Alley, off by Prague Castle."

"And you would have been wrong," Elizabeth said, in a troublesomely haughty tone. "Many alchemists had workshops in that alley, but the most secret work was done not far from here."

"So then where was Dee's laboratory?" asked Sophia.

Elizabeth paced slowly away from the clock tower and into the square. She turned in a slow circle, like a compass trying to find true north. Eventually, she pointed down a narrow street that led off the square. Tall apartment buildings flanked both sides.

"Unless it has been destroyed, his laboratory lies that way."

Erin's brow creased with worry. Rhun understood her concern. If it was gone, they would not only have made this trip for naught, but they would be lost, with no way forward.

Elizabeth headed off, forcing them to follow her. Sophia hurried to keep abreast of her, while Rhun hung back with the others.

Erin stared around, clearly taking in the history, but her mind was on a more recent event.

"Back in 2002," she said, with a wave of her arm, "Prague was hard hit by a flood. The Vltava River broke its banks and flooded the capital. When those waters receded, sections of the city streets— including this one, if I'm not mistaken—collapsed into medieval-era tunnels, revealing long-lost rooms, workshops . . . even alchemy labs." Erin looked at them, then at the wet stones under her feet. "Over the years, probably a million people walked over those tunnels without knowing what was there. It caused quite a stir in the archaeological community at the time."

Ahead of them, Elizabeth uttered a single harsh syllable that Rhun recognized as a Hungarian curse. They all hurried to join her. She had stopped next to a wooden sign hanging over the street. Next to it, two dark blue doors stood open. Her eyebrows were drawn down into a scowl. She looked ready to rip the sign off its metal hinges.

On one of the doors, a bright silver circle enclosed a symbol of two flasks connected by tubes. The words *Speculum Alchemiae Muzeum Prague* were written around it.

"It's a museum!" Elizabeth spat. "This is how your age guards its secrets?"

"Apparently so," Jordan said.

Rhun moved closer. Pear-shaped flasks hung from a wrought-iron rack attached to the doors. A golden shield on the front labeled each one's contents: *Elixir of Memory, Elixir of Health,* and *Elixir of Eternal Youth.*

Rhun remembered similar fanciful potions from his childhood.

Christian planted his fists on his hips, looking dubiously at the museum. "John Dee's papers are here?"

"They *were* here," Elizabeth corrected. "This used to be an ordinary-seeming house. It had a great room in front, and a sitting room in back, where alchemists would receive guests and talk about their works. Including scholars such as Tycho Brahe and Rabbi Loew. Old men with white beards hunched over crucibles and alembics. And of course, charlatans, too, like that damnable Edward Kelly."

Rain ran into Rhun's eyes, and he wiped it away with the back of his hand. "What were they working on?"

Elizabeth shook drops from her wimple. "Everything. They searched for many things that would prove foolish and elusive, like a philosopher's stone capable of turning base metals to gold, but they also discovered much of real consequence." She stamped her small foot on the cobbles. "Discoveries that were later lost.

Things the likes of which your modern mind cannot ever comprehend. And now you have turned it into a child's amusement show."

"Well, we came all of this way," Christian said, slipping past her. "We might as well have a look."

Everyone followed, drawing her with them despite her protests.

Two women welcomed them from behind a counter. The older one, a salt-and-pepper brunette, toyed with a necklace she was beading, while the younger one, likely her daughter, swiped at a glass display with a long feather duster.

Rhun surveyed the room. He ducked from the dried herbs hanging from an arched ceiling. All around, wooden shelves lined the walls, crowded with all manner of old books and more glass and pottery. He noted a large wooden door to the right of the counter. It was currently closed.

Elizabeth swept past him and went straight for the front desk, confronting the older of the two women. "Is it possible to see the receiving room?" she demanded. "And perhaps the rooms beneath?"

"Naturally, Sister." The woman peered at Elizabeth over the top of a pair of half-moon glasses, studying the mix of nuns and white-collared priests with a bit of amusement. "We give tours."

Elizabeth looked aghast, but Christian pushed forward. "I'd like to buy six tickets," he said quickly. "When is the next available tour?"

"Right away," the woman said.

The older woman took the euros Christian handed her and gave them each a large rectangular ticket.

The younger woman smiled at Jordan. She had kind brown eyes and looked about twenty-five. Her long dark hair was pulled back in a bun and tied with a purple ribbon. The color matched her shirt and a tight skirt that ended high above her knees.

Elizabeth stepped between her and Rhun, eyeing the woman's tight garments with distaste.

"My name is Tereza," the young woman said, trying her best to ignore Elizabeth's scathing glare. "I'll be your guide through the alchemist's laboratory. If you'll please follow me."

Using a heavy key, the woman unlocked the door. As she swung it open, a waft of dank and moldy air rolled out. Rhun felt a prickling along his neck as he caught a whiff of something else. He remembered his days spent in the Egyptian desert, recognizing here the same sense of malevolence that he had hunted in the sands.

He searched around but found no evidence of danger. The other Sanguinists showed no such misgivings.

Still, Rhun moved closer to Erin.

4:24 P.M.

With the tour guide leading them, Erin followed Rhun through the door and into a dark hallway. Jordan trailed behind, giving off a resounding sneeze at the dust. Or maybe he had mold allergies. Still, Rhun jumped at the abrupt noise, pushing Erin against the wall with an arm that felt like a bar of steel.

Jordan noted the protective gesture. "Be ready if I burp," he told Rhun. "That's much more dangerous."

They continued onward. Erin studied the oil paintings lining both walls, likely reproductions.

Up ahead, Tereza waved an arm, while walking backward. "These paintings are of—"

Elizabeth interrupted her, thrusting out her arm toward various oils. "Emperor Rudolf II, Tycho Brahe, Rabbi Loew, and Rudolf's physician . . . whose name escapes me at the moment. Not their best likenesses."

She then walked right past their guide and into one of the rooms off the hall, as if she knew where she was going.

"Sister! Wait!" Tereza hurried after Elizabeth, and everyone followed them.

Elizabeth stopped in the center of a medium-size room, her hands clasped in front of her as if she were praying, but Erin couldn't imagine that was true. Her haughty gaze swept the room.

Overhead, a round chandelier held two horned masks and cast an orange-tinted light on a bearskin rug that lay before a marble fireplace. Erin's attention was drawn to an antique case full of old books, skulls, and specimens in glass jars.

Intrigued, she moved closer.

This is what it must have looked like four hundred years ago.

Elizabeth stepped over to the granite-topped desk along one wall, then to a curtained window behind it. She stopped and surveyed the room. "Where is the bell?"

"The bell?" Tereza looked nervous.

"There used to be a giant glass bell in front of this window. Large enough for a man to stand inside." Elizabeth dropped to one knee and examined the tiles underfoot. "It left grooves on the floor. John Dee kept his device here instead of in his main laboratory below because he needed the sunlight for his experiments."

Erin joined her, running her fingers across the floor. "Are these tiles new?"

Tereza nodded. "I think so."

Elizabeth stood with a huff and wiped her hands on her damp habit. "Where was the bell taken?"

"I don't know what you're talking about," Tereza said. "So far as I know, there was never a bell."

Tereza turned slightly away, muttering something under her breath. It sounded like a Czech expletive. Elizabeth answered her sharply in the same language, making the guide gulp.

Jordan stepped to Tereza's side, touching her arm reassuringly. "How about we let this nice young woman tell us what she does know? After all, we paid for the full tour."

Elizabeth looked like she was going to say something, but instead, she clasped her hands behind her back. She glanced over to the spot where she'd expected to find the bell, a calculating expression on her face.

Tereza took a deep breath, then tried to find her groove again. "Th-this room is where the alchemists would have received guests, but it wasn't a simple sitting room. If you'll note that each corner of the room bears alchemical symbols for Earth, Air, Fire, and Water."

Erin turned slowly to examine each symbol. Off to the side, Elizabeth drifted over to the fireplace, keeping her back to the guide. She leaned against the mantel, as if she were about to be sick.

Tereza continued more boldly, apparently glad not to have the irritable nun at her throat any longer. "The energy from these forces was channeled through the chandelier in the center of the room. Those energies were used for all manner of occult and alchemical purposes. If you'll come over to this case, I can show you . . ."

Erin stepped away, slipping toward Elizabeth who had turned away from the fireplace.

"What were you doing?" Erin asked softly.

Elizabeth kept her voice low. "Dee had a secret compartment in that marble mantel. The green diamond was once hidden there, when the stone was intact. I just checked it."

"Did you find anything?"

Elizabeth opened her hand to reveal a scrap of paper in her palm. "Just this."

Erin noted a row of unusual symbols on it.

"It's a name written in Enochian," Elizabeth explained.

Erin stared at the strange letters. She knew that John Dee had created his own language, but she'd never learned it. "What name?"

"Belmagel."

Erin frowned at Elizabeth, not recognizing the name.

"Belmagel was an angel to whom Edward Kelly supposedly spoke with during his scrying sessions with John Dee. Dee eventually had his doubts, and the two men had a falling-out, but Emperor Rudolf was a fierce and unfaltering admirer of Kelly."

"So who do you think left that scrap of paper?"

"Only Rudolf, Dee, and I knew of the existence of that compartment. Rudolf was very secretive about it. He even had the original designer killed to ensure that he never revealed its presence. If Dee had left something there, Rudolf would have taken it after the man died, so I assume that this note must have been left by Rudolf himself."

"What else do you know about this Belmagel?" Erin asked, nodding to the paper.

"Kelly supposedly communed with two angels. Sudsamma was a good angel, a being of light. Belmagel was a dark angel, born of evil."

Maybe this was a clue. Her group *was* searching for the most evil angel of all—Lucifer.

"If Rudolf left this, it may have been a message to me," Elizabeth explained. "Something only I would understand."

"What was he trying to tell you?" Erin asked.

Elizabeth gave a small, frustrated shake of her head. "It must have something to do with that charlatan,

Kelly. Perhaps this was hidden to direct *me* toward the man, to his house."

"Where did he live?"

"He had many houses. Who knows if any of them are still standing today?"

Erin stared toward one person who might know. She lifted her arm. "Tereza, a question, if I might?"

The guide turned toward her. "What would you like to know?"

"Edward Kelly was an associate of John Dee. Do you know where Kelly lived and if that place still exists?"

Her eyes widened, clearly delighted to have an answer. "Certainly. It's quite an infamous place. It's named the *Faustus Dum*, or the Faust House, and it can be found in Charles Square, though it's not open to the public for tours."

Erin glanced to Elizabeth. The countess gave a small nod of acknowledgment, plainly knowing the place. From the darkening of her expression, she wasn't pleased about this location.

As Tereza returned to her lecture with the others, Erin spoke quietly with Elizabeth. "What do you know about the Faust House?"

"It was a place of much infamy. Before Kelly moved in, Emperor Rudolf's astrologer, Jakub Krucinek, resided there with his two sons. Later, the younger one killed the older one because of a supposed treasure hidden in that house. Kelly himself rigged the place with all sorts of trickery. Doors that would open by themselves, staircases that would fly around, handles that would shock you if you touched them."

She made a sharp scoffing sound, then continued. "The man was a fraud and a swindler. But the house . . . it's authentically malevolent. It's why the house was associated with the Faust legend."

"The scholar who made a pact with the devil?"

"Some say Faust himself lived there, that it was in that very house that he was sucked away to Hell, drawn straight through the ceiling."

Erin eyed the countess doubtfully.

She shrugged. "Legend or not, strange occurrences have been associated with that place. Mysterious disappearances, loud blasts during the night, strange lights."

Erin pointed to the paper with the Enochian writing. "Could Rudolf have left that secret message to you, directing you to the Faust House? The green diamond had a connection to a dark angel and so does that place."

"Perhaps . . ."

Tereza spoke louder, stepping to a bookcase. "And now for the next stop on our tour."

The guide shoved the bookcase to one side, revealing a set of steps leading down.

Jordan exclaimed loudly, sounding boyishly excited, "Cool! A secret passageway."

Tereza stood at the threshold of the secret stairs. "This passage leads down to an alchemist's private laboratory. If you'll look down near the floor, you'll see a large metal ring just inside. It is said that the Rabbi Loew chained his infamous golem there when it misbehaved."

Erin smiled at the idea, but the Sanguinists looked down at the ring skeptically. Apparently, they believed in *strigoi* and angels but not in giant clay men brought to life by alchemists. She guessed they had to draw the line somewhere.

Tereza led them down the stairs.

Erin trailed with Elizabeth, who nudged the ring with her toe as she passed it. "Such nonsense," the countess whispered. "Dee chained a wolf to that ring, a beast that answered to no one but Dee himself. On the day Dee died, Rudolf had to kill the animal to get into this room."

Erin followed last down the stone steps. The stairs were narrow so that everyone had to go single file. At the base of the stairs, a tunnel ran ahead, and Tereza directed them onward. But Erin paused to examine a metal door on the left. It had a square opening at eye level, like the door to a prison cell. Through the opening, she could see another tunnel.

"Behind that door," the guide called back, noting Erin's attention, "is a tunnel that leads to the old town square. We discovered that tunnel and others a few years back following a great flood. It took some time to clean out the mud."

Jordan glanced back at Erin, clearly remembering her recounting of that flood.

Tereza continued. "In the furnace room up ahead, we discovered a tunnel that leads under the river and runs all the way to Prague Castle."

Elizabeth nodded. "Rudolf used that tunnel—and others—to come and go under the city, so that no one knew where he was."

Erin could not help but be fascinated by these stories, trying to imagine that time when science, religion, and politics blurred together, wrapped in mysteries and legends.

They continued down the tunnel. Jordan had to keep his head ducked from the low ceiling. The passageway finally ended at a small room with a round metal stove in the center. The stove held metal flasks with long spouts, while a limp set of bellows rested in front of the stove's opening. Soot covered everything:

roof, walls, and even the stone tiles on the floor were black.

This must be the furnace room that Tereza had mentioned. At the back, another doorway led off to a neighboring dark room. Their guide pointed toward it. "In the next room is where the alchemists worked on transmutation—changing base metals to gold."

Elizabeth muttered. "Such foolishness. Who could believe you could change simple metals to gold?"

Jordan heard her, glancing back with a grin. "Actually, it *is* possible. If you bombard a certain kind of mercury with neutrons. Unfortunately, the process costs more than the gold it produces. Plus, the gold ends up being radioactive and decays in a couple of days."

Elizabeth gave an exaggerated sigh. "So it seems modern man has not given up his old obsessions."

"The furnace and the larger flasks are original," Tereza said, continuing her dialogue about the old alchemists' attempts to brew an Elixir of Eternal Youth. "We found a vial of that elixir bricked up in a secret safe in the wall of this room. Along with a recipe to make it."

Now it was Erin's turn to scoff. "You can make it today?"

Tereza smiled. "It is a complicated process, with seventy-seven herbs, gathered by moonlight, infused into wine. The brewing takes a full year, but yes, it can be done. In fact, it is being made by monks in a monastery in Brno."

Even Elizabeth looked surprised by this bit of trivia.

Erin studied this five-hundred-year-old time capsule of the alchemists' world. She moved through the room, examining the furnace and glassware. She spied a small door behind the furnace.

Must be that tunnel to the castle.

Rhun suddenly appeared at her side, clutching her arm. She turned, only now noting how the Sanguinists had gone stone-still, looking up. Even Elizabeth cocked her head, her nose high.

"What is it?" Jordan asked. His hand instinctively went to his waist, where he normally holstered his machine pistol, but due to the Czech gun laws, he hadn't been allowed to pass through customs with any firearms.

"Blood." Rhun whispered, gazing toward the tunnel that led up to the rooms above. "Much blood."

18

The blood is hot upon my tongue . . .

Legion knew it was not actually his own tongue. His body—rooted deep inside the black vessel of Leopold—lay sprawled in the back of a rumbling vehicle. The windows were darkened, shadowing the burn of the late-afternoon sun. He sensed sunset was near, but until then, he must hunt from afar, peering out other eyes, directing his will into those who bore his mark.

Closer at hand, the Sanguinist woman—Abigail—controlled the vehicle, this great rumbling black horse that spewed clouds of poison in its wake. She seemed oblivious of the sun. The wine of the Sanguinist protected her from the light, its holiness acting like a shield.

Legion was determined to brand more like her, to create forces that could move in light and darkness, swelling his ranks for the war to come.

Blood called to him again, drawing his awareness back to the slave who feasted on the old woman in the small room, a space full of dried herbs, dust, and books. He extended his senses farther, seeing out of three more pairs of eyes. Three more slaves, who were bound to his will, skulked through dark tunnels, closing in on the prey hidden below.

Legion had gathered these and others to this city, to destroy that ancient prophecy imbued into the body of the trio: the Warrior, the Woman, and the Knight.

He would allow them no rest, no safe refuge.

The mortals he intended to kill, but the one called Korza . . .

You will be my finest slave, a weapon to wield against Heaven.

But first, Legion needed to flush that Knight out into the open.

He lifted his hand, watching the whorls of blackness swim across his palm. He sent out a command to those who bore his mark.

Kill them . . . but save the Knight for me.

4:50 P.M.

Standing in the furnace room, Jordan pulled Erin behind him. Rhun, Sophia, and Christian drew blades and kept watch on the far stairwell that led up to the museum.

"What are you doing?" Tereza asked, noting the weapons, covering her throat with her hand.

Erin took the woman's other hand. "Stay close."

Jordan stepped over and grabbed the only weapon in view: an old iron fireplace poker that lay propped up against the furnace stove.

Not the machine pistol he missed, but it would have to do.

Elizabeth noted him arming himself and did the same. She picked up a flask by its spout and shattered the bulbous base, creating a glass dagger.

Tereza gasped at the damage, but she kept to Erin's side.

"Smoke," Rhun said by the door.

Jordan shifted enough to peer over his shoulder. From the stairwell on the far side of the tunnel, a roll of sooty blackness flowed from the steps into the tunnel. The upstairs must be on fire.

"My . . . my mother," Tereza said. She began to step forward, but Erin restrained her.

And with good reason.

From out of that pall of smoke, a dark figure appeared. It dropped into a crouch, revealing a large shaven-haired man with a muscular physique. He clutched a long knife in one fist. His white T-shirt was stained with the crimson of fresh blood. He bared fangs, sniffing at the air, hunting for them.

As he did so, Jordan spotted a five-fingered black brand on his throat, marking him as an enslaved *strigoi*, like the one who had attacked them in the cavern in Cumae.

Sophia hissed with recognition.

The *strigoi* lowered his gaze at the noise—then lunged forward, moving with incredible speed.

Rhun leaped forward into the tunnel, meeting the charge of the creature. The priest held a silver *karambit* in each hand, the curved metal blades looking like long claws. He slashed out as the beast reached him— but found only empty air.

The *strigoi* feinted low, then spun, striking out with his knife. But at the last moment, he turned its blade and smashed the steel hilt into the side of Rhun's head. The blow knocked Rhun against the tunnel wall, clearly dazing him.

The *strigoi* barreled past him, going straight for Sophia and Christian.

Elizabeth shifted forward, concern ringing in her voice. "Rhun . . ."

Jordan pushed Erin and Tereza farther back. A moment too late, he realized the error of his defense. The creak of old hinges sounded behind him. He swung around in time to see a dark shape burst forth from the small door that led to Rudolf's secret tunnel.

The *strigoi* ripped Tereza from Erin's grip and tore into the young woman's throat, drowning her surprised scream with blood. Another *strigoi* followed on that one's heels, going straight for Erin with a long blade in hand.

Jordan was already moving by then. He reached Erin, spun her by the arm behind him, and blocked the *strigoi's* blade with the length of his poker. As steel rang off iron, one thought rose in Jordan's mind.

I shouldn't have been able to move that fast.

He had no time to comprehend this mystery, only be thankful for it.

The *strigoi* snarled, drawing back his blade and crouching in surprise. Behind him, the other beast finished with Tereza and joined his partner, hissing blood at Jordan. For the moment, they seemed cautious of Jordan, wary of his speed and strength.

Then Christian and Sophia joined him, flanking him to either side. Christian lifted a long sword, while Sophia carried two daggers, one in each hand.

Three against two . . . I like these odds better.

Then a third *strigoi* appeared from the furnace-room tunnel, a massive giant, an ogre of a beast.

So much for those odds.

To the side, Erin grabbed a pair of metal tongs, readying herself to help. "We must get out into the sunlight!"

Easier said than done.

And the sun was close to setting.

Crashes behind him told him that Rhun and Elizabeth were still struggling with their first adversary in the tunnel. So that way was blocked. Plus the stairs leading up were on fire anyway.

Jordan concentrated on the three enemies before him. Beyond them, smoke billowed into the room through the small door, bringing with it the scent of burning wood and gasoline. It seemed their ambushers had set fire to that tunnel, too, ensuring no one escaped that way.

The huge *strigoi*, clearly the leader of this bunch, pushed past the other two. His face was a map of scar tissue, his fangs yellow. He lifted a broadsword and whirled it in a circle, so fast it became a silver blur.

Christian stepped forward to face the attacker—then one of the smaller *strigoi* leaped low, moving with that preternatural speed, and tackled Christian to the ground. The other hurtled into Sophia, knocking her against the furnace.

Jordan lifted his poker, realizing the giant had used his dramatic swordplay as a distraction, allowing the smaller two to ambush the Sanguinists, eliminating the larger threats.

Leaving only Jordan and Erin.

So then let's see what you've got, big fella.

Jordan lunged at the armed *strigoi*. He struck the whirling blade a resounding blow. He felt the impact from his shoulders to his heels.

Then again, so did the *strigoi*.

The giant dropped the ringing blade and fell back a step. A sneer curled its lip—then it hurled itself at Jordan. It felt like being hit by a truck. Jordan crashed backward into a table, shattering glassware.

Teeth sank into Jordan's forearm, fangs grinding down to bone.

But rather than crippling pain, Jordan felt a blaze of fire erupt along his arm.

The *strigoi* screamed, releasing Jordan's arm. It stumbled back, clawing at its face. Jordan watched as flesh blistered and burned, black blood boiling out. It fell, convulsing to the floor as that conflagration spread, swiftly burning through its body.

Jordan stared down at his wounded arm, then over to the giant.

My blood is poison.

Rather than fear, calm suffused him, growing even stronger, reducing the movement in the room to slow-motion. Sounds became muffled. The light took on a golden hue, turning everything hazy.

The *strigoi* battling Sophia panicked at what had happened to the giant and fled toward the burning tunnel. Christian took advantage of the surprise to cleave the other's head clean from its shoulder.

Jordan picked up a piece of broken glass from the table, and without a thought, he was upon the fleeing *strigoi*. He grabbed it by the back of the neck and sliced its throat open from ear to ear, then let the body drop.

Jordan turned to find Erin yanking on his arm, coughing from the smoke, trying to get him to move.

"It's all coming down!" she yelled at him, her voice sounding like they were both submerged under water. "The rooms above are starting to collapse into the basement level."

He followed her, collecting Christian and Sophia along the way.

Out in the tunnel, Elizabeth held the first *strigoi* in a bear hug from behind, while Rhun lashed out with his knife. To Jordan's eyes, the priest's arm moved slowly, the blade in his hand catching each mote of light. The splash of black blood seemed to hang in the air.

As that last body fell, Erin drew Jordan along. She pointed past Rhun, toward the door near the base of the stairs. "We have to make for the tunnel to the old town square!"

As he watched, an oak rafter broke away from the roof and crashed to the stone floor, scattering fiery embers. More smoke washed into the tunnel.

"We're too late!" Erin yelled.

5:02 P.M.

Erin choked on the smoke, her lungs burning, her eyes weeping. Then Rhun was there, sweeping his jacket over her. Luckily, the Sanguinists did not need to breathe.

"Stay low," Rhun warned her.

She obeyed and lifted the edge of her rain-soaked collar, breathing through the damp fabric. Ahead, Christian and Sophia led the way, using their strength to forge a path through fiery timbers and tumbles of stone. More debris rained down as the rooms above collapsed into the tunnel.

Farther down the passageway, Elizabeth crouched by the door to their only exit, clearly struggling to get the way open. Beyond the woman's shoulders, flames filled the stairwell, turning it into the mouth of a massive fireplace.

Erin glanced behind her, coughing hoarsely. Jordan walked leadenly in her wake, seemingly oblivious to the smoke and heat. She remembered what had happened to the huge *strigoi*, picturing that flesh boiling forth with blood. She had observed such damage before, when angelic blood touched a *strigoi*.

Was that further proof of Jordan's angelic nature? And what did it mean for the man she loved?

A loud tearing of metal drew her gaze forward.

Elizabeth had ripped the door off its hinges. "Hurry!" she called out, brushing fiery embers from the shoulders of her habit. The countess immediately set off into the waiting darkness, vanishing away.

Erin feared the woman might very well use this opportunity to escape.

And I wouldn't blame her.

They all rushed into the tunnel and fled along it, chased by the smoke.

Shoulder to shoulder, Christian and Sophia kept the lead, following Elizabeth's path, clearly watching for any new dangers, any new attack.

Rhun continued to shadow her, followed by Jordan.

As the light faded behind them, Erin dug into her pocket and removed a metal flashlight. She clicked it on, and a small beam of light pierced the darkness.

She coughed hard, her lungs still aflame, bobbling the light. A crashing rumble echoed from behind. She pictured that alchemists' tunnel collapsing completely.

Finally, a door banged up ahead, and light flowed into the tunnel.

Sunlight . . . glorious sunlight.

She sped toward it. With each step, the air was fresher, cleaner, colder.

Once close enough, Erin spotted Elizabeth holding the door open for them.

So she hadn't fled.

They tumbled gratefully out into a sunlit alley— bloody, half-burnt, but alive.

She immediately swung around to face Jordan, concerned that he had not spoken a single word during their entire escape from the tunnels.

She touched his cheek, but his blue eyes were unfocused, staring off into some middle distance. Panic rose up inside her, but she fought it back down.

She kept her palm on his burning cheek. "Jordan, can you hear me?"

He blinked once.

"Jordan . . . come back."

Jordan blinked again, a shudder passing through him. Slowly focus returned to his eyes. He stared down at her. "Erin . . . ?"

He sounded unsure, as if he didn't truly know her.

"That's right," she said softly, wounded and scared. "Are you okay?"

He finally shook himself once like a dog, then swept his gaze across the others. "I'm fine . . . I think."

"Perhaps he was disoriented from the smoke," Elizabeth offered.

Erin wasn't buying it. Whatever was wrong with him, it had nothing to do with the smoke. She took his arm, parting his torn sleeve to examine the ragged bite mark. Already the wound had begun to heal, the flesh knitting together as if he had been attacked days before, not mere minutes.

More disconcerting, she discovered a red line that curled from his biceps down to the wound, forming curlicues around the edges of the healing flesh. She tugged the remains of his sleeve higher, revealing the source.

It extended from the old scarring from when Jordan was struck by lightning. When he was a teenager, he had that fractal pattern tattooed over as a reminder of his close call, creating an almost flowery decoration.

But this crimson tendril was new.

She ran her finger along it, feeling the heat along that trail. "Your tattoo is growing . . ."

Jordan pulled his arm back and shook his sleeve down.

"Tell me what's happening," she demanded.

"I don't know," he mumbled, turning slightly away. "It started back when Tommy touched me, healed me. At first, it was just a burning sensation."

"But since then?"

"It's been stronger since that *strigoi* stabbed me in Cumae. And stronger again when I was bitten just now." Jordan wouldn't meet her eyes.

She took his hand. At least, he let her hold it.

As if he sensed her distress, Rhun touched her gently on the back.

"We must leave," Elizabeth warned as sirens wailed in the distance. "The sun will soon be down."

But where could they go?

5:37 P.M.

Legion studied the burning building as the fires set by his forces spread. He watched red flames dance against a gray sky, remembering this place. It was in a room in this structure that he had been trapped inside that green diamond. Through the tracery of smoke from the six hundred and sixty-six inside him, he drew out snatches of memory of that time.

. . . an old man with a white beard walks on the other side of green glass . . .

. . . sunlight burning skin and bone, leaving nothing but smoke . . .

. . . that smoke being chased by brightness into the dark heart of a cold stone . . .

Beyond the confines of the vehicle where Legion hid, the fire continued to roar, consuming all, turning the painful history into so much ash and smoke.

How fitting.

He sent a command to Abigail. The vehicle growled and glided away from the curb, turning from that fire. Through the eyes of his slaves, he had watched his enemy vanquish his forces below. He did not know the fate of the trio of prophecy, but he had left them with only one path to follow. A single open tunnel. If they survived, the enemy would be flushed into his trap.

Already he had summoned additional forces to Prague, a gathering storm waiting to be unleashed. Legion awaited only one last element. He stared through the darkened window, toward the glaring orb of the sun, sitting low on the horizon.

The day may be theirs, but the night will be mine.

19

March 18, 6:08 P.M. CET
Prague, Czech Republic

Rhun hurried across yet another street, following Erin, who had pulled up a map of Prague on her phone. A chill wind swept down the narrow thoroughfare, as a storm closed in over the city. He smelled distant rain, the crackle of electricity.

Ahead the street ended at a large grassy square dotted with fountains. A verdigris-stained copper sign announced their destination in broad Gothic letters.

Karlovo náměstí

"Charles Square," Erin translated as they stepped into the open.

A sprawling town hall with a tall tower rose to one side, but it was the large Jesuit church, rising in baroque spires, that drew Rhun's attention. It was the Church of St. Ignatius. Rhun would not have minded spending time there, giving them all a chance to recuperate. Christian had a bandaged arm; Sophia nursed several prominent scrapes and bruises. Even Elizabeth had lost her wimple and bore a ragged scratch across her cheek, which she hid with a fall of dark curls.

But they didn't have the time to tarry.

As the group crossed the square, the orange sky faded toward red, then indigo, as the sun was near to setting. If more *strigoi* ranged this city, they would come out before long. Someone had surely sent those *strigoi* into the tunnels to ambush them, and that threat remained.

En route here, he had watched for anyone hunting their trail, but the city was bustling with springtime tourists. Even now, he heard the heartbeat of people wandering the city, eating at its restaurants, shopping in its stores. He attempted to listen for more furtive sounds, rising from those without heartbeats: quiet footsteps, cold breath. Though he did not hear evidence of such creatures, that did not mean they were not there, skulking in the shadows, biding their time for the sun to fully set.

Rhun glanced to St. Ignatius. As soon as their team was done investigating this last spot in the city, they could take refuge in the nearby church.

"That should be the Faust House," Erin announced. "There on the southwest corner of the square."

The structure climbed four stories: gray stone on the first floor, a salmon pink above, with faux Corinthian columns decorating its façade. Once close enough, gold lettering above the arched entrance read FAUSTUS DUM, confirming this was indeed the infamous Faust House.

Elizabeth believed Rudolf had left that message as a code meant for her, directing her to this home. If so, something important might be hidden here, too.

But what?

As they drew near, Rhun continued to maintain a wary vigil as rain again began to fall. They stopped on the opposite side of the street from the house. Cars sidled past, drivers hurrying home before the full storm hit.

As thunder rumbled in the distance, Jordan stared up at the building, looking more himself again, though Rhun noted his heartbeat had subtly changed after the attack, sounding more like a heavy drum tattoo, underscored by a faint ringing. Maybe that aberration had always been there, and whatever transpired during that attack had brought forth that change more prominently.

"That Kelly guy must have been doing pretty well to afford this place," Jordan said.

Erin nodded. "He *did* have the backing and patronage of Emperor Rudolf. Plus, the ground was supposedly cursed."

"What?" Jordan looked sharply at her.

"I Googled this place on my phone during the hike here," she explained. "In pagan times, this ground was used as a gathering place for sacrifices to Morena, the goddess of death. Such a history is probably why the legend of Dr. Faust became incorporated with this house. And likely added further support for Edward Kelly claiming he could commune with Belmagel, an evil angel."

Jordan craned his neck further. "Whatever. All I see is a pricey house with a lot of lightning rods."

Elizabeth stood at his shoulder, shading the rain from her eyes with a slim hand. "What is a lightning rod?"

Jordan pointed to the red-tiled roof. "Do you see the weather vane? And that rod next to it? Both are designed to attract lightning and then channel it down to the ground, where it will be discharged safely into the earth."

Elizabeth's eyes shone. "What a clever idea."

As if on cue, a blast of thunder crackled across the rooftops, booming loudly, reminding them that time was short.

"How are we going to get inside?" Erin asked. "Looks like all the windows on the first floor are barred."

Rhun pointed higher. "I'll climb up, force one of those upper windows open, then come back down and let you in through the front door."

"What about alarms?" Sophia asked.

Christian shook his head. "Place is centuries-old, likely not modernized. At best, they probably only have the second-story windows wired, trusting the lower-level's bars to do most of the security work for them." He pointed higher. "You'll probably have no problem if you can reach those smaller windows on the third level. I doubt those are armed."

Rhun nodded at his analysis. He took quick account of his surroundings. At least, the rain had chased most people out of the open square. He waited until no cars were moving along the street, then hurried across to a drainpipe that ran along a shadowy corner of the façade.

He threaded his fingertips around the pipe and swiftly scaled its length to the third story. Gripping the capital of one of the ornamental Corinthian columns, he edged his foot to the right, sliding across the wet façade of the house like a lizard to reach the closest window.

Once there, he waited until another rumble of thunder burst forth—then used his elbow to crack through the lowermost pane. Glass tinkled to the floor inside. He waited to see if any shout was raised. The house stayed silent.

Still, Rhun proceeded with caution. He reached through the broken glass, undid the latch, and slowly pushed the window open. The inside smelled like mildew and concrete—but something else set his skin to crawling. He remained where he was, listening, but when no alarm sounded, he rolled inside.

Even before his feet hit the floor, he felt the strength drain from his body. He landed in a crouch, remembering Erin's story of this place being built on accursed ground.

It seemed some legends were true.

Rhun grabbed his cross, to center himself. The air in the house was ice cold, and it crackled with malevolence. He searched for any overt threat but found nothing. Light from streetlamps outside revealed an empty room with high white ceilings and smooth plaster walls.

He whispered a prayer of protection—then headed down to let the others in, ignoring a stronger urge to flee this place.

6:19 P.M.

As Rhun held the tall wrought-iron door open, Elizabeth stepped through, pushing ahead of the others who were huddled under the entrance archway. She sensed the ungodliness of this place as soon as the way opened. It drew her like a moth to a flame—but rather than being burnt as she stepped inside, she felt a surge of power flow into her, the unhallowed ground calling to the darkness in her blood.

She noted Rhun sagged on his legs, hanging on the door handle to keep upright.

This unholy place has plainly sapped him deeply.

She saw the same effect as Christian and Sophia entered. It was as if a heavy weight had been dropped upon their shoulders.

So why am I unafflicted?

She stared around, wondering if it was because she was new to the holy wine, but she suspected it was something else, a testament to her true heart.

To hide that, she placed a palm against the wall and leaned upon it, as if beset by the same unholy malaise.

Rhun came to her side, offering his arm. "It is the accursed ground," he explained. "It fights against our strength because it is born of Christ's blood."

She nodded. "It's . . . it's just dreadful."

Jordan gave Elizabeth a suspicious look as he passed them, as if he knew of her deceit.

Sophia spoke with a strained voice. "Let us hurry about our task then."

"Where should we start looking?" Erin asked, looking to Elizabeth for direction, suspecting that she had been here before. "Do you have any idea?"

Jordan clicked on a flashlight, revealing a wrought-iron chandelier and white plaster walls. They stood in a large entryway looking into a grand hall, with a curving set of stairs beyond.

Elizabeth let go of Rhun and headed across the hall. "Kelly's damnable angel, Belmagel, appeared to no one else." She glanced back to the others. "Because, of course, it was all farcical nonsense. Kelly was a charlatan looking for financial gain from the foolhardy. But what I do know is that Belmagel only appeared to Kelly in a room upstairs. If Rudolf left that message for me, perhaps that is where we should look first."

Erin kept to Rhun's side, protectively, concern for him plain upon her face. "This unholiness that you're feeling?" she asked. "Does it emanate from any certain point, or is it everywhere?"

"I felt it stronger upstairs," Rhun admitted.

"Worse than this?" Christian muttered under his breath, looking supremely unhappy.

Rhun nodded.

Elizabeth felt it, too, as she reached the curved set of grand stairs. It was like a breeze flowing down those wooden steps. While it seemed to buffet the Sanguinists back, she had to fight to stop from running giddily upward into its embrace.

"We should follow that unholy trace," Erin recommended. "Whatever has accursed this place might be significant to our cause."

"Or it could take us straight into trouble," Jordan added.

Elizabeth continued to guide them, mounting the stairs first. She climbed slowly, feigning weakness by clutching the carved rail, pretending to have to pull herself up. She did her best to match the pace of the Sanguinists behind her. But with every step, she felt dark strength flowing up from the oak planks underfoot.

Impatient, she distracted herself by examining the passing walls. They were rich ochre and decorated with paintings from the Renaissance. At first glance they seemed to be ordinary court paintings, but a closer look revealed demons dressed in the garb of lords and ladies leering out at her. One demon held an innocent child in his lap; another feasted on the head of a unicorn.

At last, they reached the topmost story. Here the air hummed and crackled with malice. She longed to throw back her head and drink it in. But instead, she kept her hand on the burning silver cross, and her face blank.

"This way," Elizabeth said. "Kelly kept his own alchemy lab just ahead. It's where he purportedly summoned Belmagel."

She led them through a double set of doors to a large circular room with bare plank floors. A stained wooden table had been pushed against one rounded wall.

"Smells like brimstone in there," Rhun said, hesitating at the threshold, leaning on the doorframe.

"Sulfur was a common alchemical compound," Elizabeth explained, as she moved deeper into the room with Erin and Jordan. "Apparently whatever Kelly worked on in here has seeped into the very bones of the house."

It was a reasonable explanation, but even Elizabeth doubted it was true.

It is the evil of this place that infects the house.

She began to wonder if she had been wrong about Kelly. Maybe he had successfully summoned something dark into this space.

While Jordan examined the desk, opening various drawers, Erin circled the walls, noting a series of three frescoes painted on the smooth plaster, examining the Latin inscriptions below each one.

Once done, the woman returned to the room's center and motioned to them with her arm. "These alchemy symbols are similar to those we saw in Dee's receiving room." She crossed back over to one—a circle holding wavy blue lines—and read aloud the Latin found below it. "*Aqua.* Water."

Intrigued, Elizabeth moved to the second, a ring dappled with green, like leaves in summer. "This one says *Arbor.* Latin for tree or garden."

Jordan stepped over to the third, not far from the desk. His circle dripped with crimson lines. "*Sanguis.*" He gave them an ominous look. "Blood."

Erin pulled a camera out of her backpack and began to take pictures of all three. She spoke as she worked. "Over at John Dee's place, there were *four* symbols, representing Earth, Wind, Air, and Fire. Not only are these marks different, but there's no fourth symbol."

Elizabeth searched around. The only other decoration on the walls was an elaborate mural. She shifted over to it, bending down to examine it closely, to see if that missing fourth symbol was hidden somewhere in this lush painting.

The mural depicted a verdant valley surrounded by three snowcapped mountains. A river ran through the valley and emptied into a dark lake. Curiously, a red sun hung at the top of the picture. Underneath the fresco were the Czech words *jarní rovnodennost.*

She ran a finger over the words, translating aloud. "*Vernal equinox.*"

Erin joined her. "What's that coming out of the lake in the center?"

Elizabeth looked closer. From the water's dark surface, limbs and demonic visages seemed to be boiling forth under that red sun.

"Looks like all hell's about to break loose," Jordan said, staring pointedly at Erin.

Erin straightened, looking sickened. "Could this be where Lucifer breaks free? This valley?" She touched that red sun. "It looks to be hanging at high noon. On the vernal equinox." She stared over to the others. "Could that be a warning? A timeline we must meet?"

"When's the equinox?" Jordan asked.

Christian answered from across the room. Even the effort to speak seemed a strain. "March twentieth. The day after tomorrow."

"Talk about cutting it close." Jordan frowned at the mural. "Especially since we don't know *where* that lake is—that is, if it even exists."

Erin glanced again at the three colored circles, as if she expected to find an answer there. And perhaps she would. Elizabeth could not deny the woman's fierce intelligence.

"Why only *three* symbols?" Erin muttered.

"The badge for alchemy is a triangle," Elizabeth offered. "Maybe that's why there are only three symbols."

Erin turned in a slow circle, plainly drawing an invisible triangle between the trio of frescoes. "Back at Dee's place, the four symbols were painted to funnel their supposed energies into the chandelier, the one with horned masks that hung in the room's center. Surely some focal point like that must have once been here."

Elizabeth nodded. "If the three symbols form an alchemical triangle, we should be hunting for something that lies in the center of all three."

With the assistance of the others, they walked off those invisible lines between the frescoes. Erin stood in the center. "The floor," she said. "It's wood. Maybe there's a secret compartment below. Like at John Dee's place."

Christian came forward, drawing his sword. "The planks are old. I should be able to pry them up."

Erin moved aside, crossing her arms nervously. "Be careful not to damage any—"

A thunderous crash of iron and broken glass echoed up from two stories below.

Everyone froze.

Elizabeth heard the traipsing of many feet, amid softer snarls and hisses. She glanced beyond the room's threshold to one of the front windows. Darkness claimed the world beyond the glow of the streetlamps. Thunder rumbled, and a flash of lightning traced the underbelly of black clouds.

The sun had set, and the storm was upon them.

Then a new noise burst forth—one readily heard even by Erin's and Jordan's weaker ears.

The moaning howl ululated up from below, full of bloodlust and fury. It was echoed by another, then a third.

It seemed the *strigoi* forces had not come alone this time.

Jordan recognized the tainted character of that howling, marking a dread beast, one all Sanguinists feared. "Great. They've brought a pack of grimwolves."

6:23 P.M.

Legion stood on the rain-swept street, his palms raised toward the stone building before him, as if basking before a fire. But it was not *heat* he warmed himself against this cold night.

A malignancy flowed from that edifice, pulsing forth from its poisoned heart. He wanted to consume it—and with it, every soul inside.

He watched his forces—a dozen strong—flow into the building. Through his connection to them, he felt their limbs fueled by that evil, growing stronger the deeper they forged.

Earlier, before the sun had set, he had set watchers upon the end of that dark tunnel near the old town square. Through those enslaved eyes, he had spied upon his prey scampering back out into the sunlight, escaping the fires set by his *strigoi* forces, taking the only path left open to them.

Taking them to me.

He had used those many eyes, hidden in shadows and dark rooms, to track the group's path from the old square to this new one, to this grand malevolent structure—where they were now trapped.

He knew from that flicker of spirit—Leopold—still burning inside him that the Sanguinists would be weakened, including the Knight, whom he intended to mark and bind to his will this night. To ensure the prophecy's doom, he would also slay the Warrior and the Woman and let their blood be a sacrifice on this unholy ground.

He raised his face to the storm.

There is no sun to protect you now.

From the entrance, fiery light bloomed, drawing his attention back down. He watched through multiple eyes, flitting from one to another, alighting nowhere for long. He was one and many at the same time, seeing all.

. . . furniture broken into kindling . . .

. . . combustible oil cast everywhere . . .

. . . one flame becomes many, sweeping through the lower floors . . .

He intended to drive his quarry to the roof, to claim the Knight there amid flames and smoke. There would be no escape this time.

To ensure that, he reached out to another of his marked, one closer to his black heart than any other slave, the leader of the wolves. He pulled his awareness more fully into that great beast, savoring its dark lusts, the power in its muscular limbs. He howled through its massive jaws, shrieking his threat into the night.

He sent one command deep into the wolf's blood.

Hunt.

20

"Hurry," Erin urged, smelling smoke rising from the lower stories. She knelt on the floor with Jordan and Elizabeth, roughly in the center of the three alchemical symbols: *aqua*, *arbor*, and *sanguis*.

Moments ago, Rhun and Christian had whisked away, vanishing down the stairs before the howling of the grimwolves had even faded. Sophia kept a post by the door, wielding two swords.

Erin had her own responsibility.

Find out what was hidden here.

Elizabeth edged a dagger between the planks and deftly popped a floorboard free, flipping it far with a twist of her wrist. She then used her fingers to rip boards to either side. She moved swiftly, her strength incredible, even when weakened by the unholy ground.

Erin shone her flashlight into the hole created, revealing floor joists, dust, and rat droppings. Motes floated up into her bright beam as she cast her light around. "Nothing's here."

Elizabeth looked as frustrated as Erin felt.

What are we missing?

Elizabeth rose to her feet, studying the symbols, trying to solve this mystery.

Erin stared up at her—then jolted bodily as inspiration rocked through her.

Up . . .

"The chandelier . . . over at John Dee's place! That's where the energies of those symbols were directed. Toward the ceiling. It's not the *floor* we need to be searching."

Jordan joined her, squinting toward the ceiling. "I don't see anything up there."

She didn't either, but she felt a thrill of certainty.

"Remember the story of Dr. Faustus," Erin said. "A legend tied to this place. According to the story, he was whisked *up* through the ceiling, taken by the devil. What if that story had its roots right here?"

Elizabeth stared up. "I can make out a faint outline of a square. Though I never witnessed it myself, I heard that Kelly had secret doors and stairs throughout his homes."

So why not one in the ceiling?

Jordan looked less convinced. "Even if there's some attic up there, who knows if it's important?"

"It is," Elizabeth said. She dropped to a knee and drew in the dust. "This entire room screams its importance. The circular room, the triangle, and now the square above."

She inscribed the layout of all three in the dust, forming a symbol.

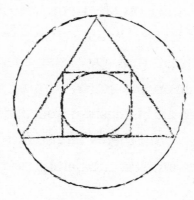

"This is the mark for the philosopher's stone!" Elizabeth breathed.

Erin's heart beat faster, staring up, trying to make out that square. "The philosopher's stone was supposed to turn lead into gold, and also to create the elixir of life.

It's the most important element in alchemy. Something must be up there."

Jordan hurried to the abandoned desk. "Help me with this!"

Before Erin could move, Elizabeth was there, beside Jordan, shoving the desk to the center of the room with little other help.

Once in place, Erin clambered up, reaching toward the roof, but she was still too short. Even Jordan tried, but he was two feet shy from brushing his fingertips against the ceiling. But at least, she could make out that outline of a square herself now.

Erin turned to Jordan. "I'm going to need you to—"

The clash of steel on steel cut her off, echoing up from the lower levels. After setting the fires below, ensuring no retreat that way, the enemy must have started its assault on the stairs, forging upward—only to discover Rhun and Christian guarded those steps.

But how long could their defense last?

The answer came immediately: a pained scream rose from below.

Elizabeth spun toward the noise, recognizing its source. "Rhun . . ."

"Go," Erin ordered, but Elizabeth was already across the room and through the door, shoving past Sophia, rushing to Rhun's aid.

Sophia pointed to them as she grabbed the room's door handle. "Find what's up there!" she ordered, then stepped to the hallway and slammed the doors closed behind her, leaving Erin and Jordan alone.

"Boost me," Erin said breathlessly, staying on task to stave off paralyzing panic.

Jordan lifted her, and she climbed onto his shoulders. Wobbling a little, she pushed against the center of the square above, but it didn't give.

Screams and snarls echoed through the guarded door.

"Hurry," Sophia called from the far side.

"I got you," Jordan reassured her. "And you got this."

I'd better.

She took a steadying breath, pushed off the top of Jordan's head, and braced her shoulder against the ceiling. She shoved hard. Dust and crumbling plaster rained down as one corner of the square budged, raising one inch.

So it is a door!

She repositioned herself closer to the edge that gave way and pushed again. The door lifted higher, enough for her to wedge her foot-long flashlight lengthwise into the crack, propping the way open.

"Got it . . ."

She grabbed the edge of the opening and pulled herself through the narrow crack, worming on her belly past her flashlight, careful not to dislodge it. Once through, she swung around and used her legs to raise the door even higher.

"Don't know how much longer I can hold it!" she called down.

"I can jump for it."

He proved a man of his word. His fingers snatched the edge of the opening and he pulled himself through, clambering up next to her. He then used his own muscular legs to hold it, while she found a stout iron bar nearby to prop it open.

Panting from the effort, Erin retrieved her flashlight and played the beam across the secret attic space. Dust coated everything. From the higher rafters, all manner of ropes and pulleys hung.

She moved away from the open hatch, brushing aside a drape of rope, stirring up a snowstorm of dust motes. "All this must be some of Kelly's secret mechanisms, used to move doors and stairs."

"Too bad none of it is functional," Jordan said. "Maybe we could've used it to make our escape."

Reminded of the threat, Erin accidentally bumped a toothed metal gear from its hook. It clattered to the floor. The noise was explosive in the confined space.

She continued deeper. The attic space appeared to be half the diameter of the room below. It didn't take long for her flashlight's beam to reveal a tall object, upright in a corner, filmed by grime and age.

There was no mistaking its shape.

"The bell," Erin said.

She stared at the large artifact, at the protruding length of glass pipe, remembering Elizabeth's story of hundreds of *strigoi* dying inside, their smoke collected and funneled down that pipe. She was momentarily fearful of approaching it, knowing its awful history. But she set such superstitions aside and moved over to it.

"Rudolf must've had it hidden here after John Dee died," she said.

"So was that the emperor's message for Elizabeth, to show her how to find this blasted thing. Why? So she might continue the work that Dee had started?"

"I hope so," Erin said.

Jordan glanced sharply at her. "Why would you wish that?"

With the cuff of her sleeve, Erin rubbed away the centuries of filth and dust from the glass. Once she had cleaned a large enough window, she peered through the thick greenish glass.

"That's why . . ."

Jordan leaned next to her. "There's a whole pile of papers inside there."

"If Rudolf brought John Dee's bell here," she said, nodding to the stack, "he would've certainly also included the old alchemist's notes."

"Like its operation's manual. Makes sense." Jordan ran his palms over the bell's surface, searching for a way inside. "Look! There's a door over here. I think I can get it open."

He yanked at the catches and bands and the door came off in his hand.

She reached inside the bell and grabbed sheaves of paper, dragging them out.

"Most of this looks like it's written in Enochian," she said, stuffing the papers into her backpack, next to the case that held the Blood Gospel. "Hopefully, Elizabeth can translate it."

"Then let's get out of here."

Together, they moved back to the hatch—only to hear a blast of shattered wood.

As they stared below, a broken door skittered across the floor. Sophia flew into view, deftly sliding on her feet, turning to face the entrance, her blades raised.

"Stay there!" she shouted to them without looking up.

The reason stalked into view.

Through a roll of black smoke, a hulking beast lumbered into view, its head low, teeth bared, a mane of dark hackles shivering along its neck and spine.

A grimwolf.

Jordan swore and kicked the iron bar that supported the hatch door.

It crashed down.

Trapping them in the attic.

6:37 P.M.

Pinned down on a wide landing of the stairs, Rhun held his position, his right arm hanging uselessly at his side. He had failed to even *see* the blade that had wounded him. His blocks and counterstrikes felt slow and clumsy. In his weakened state, he felt like a child playing at war against these curse-strengthened soldiers.

And in turn, they seemed to be toying with him.

They could have killed him by now, but they held off.

Why? Was it purely out of malice or some other reason?

Three *strigoi* closed a triangle around him. They were all bigger, muscle-bound, covered with scars and tattoos. Each carried a heavy curved falchion. None was particularly skilled with his weapon, but they were faster and stronger than Rhun. First one, then another would dart forward and slice Rhun's arms, his chest, his face. They could have killed him at any time, but they chose instead to play with him, like a cat with a frightened mouse.

But I am no mouse.

He took their cuts, watched their actions, and searched for any weaknesses.

Smoke billowed up from the stairs below. Christian fought somewhere down there, but Rhun had lost sight of him after attempting to pursue a grimwolf that had bounded past him a moment ago. He had heard it crash through the door a floor above, heard Sophia's shout. Still, he could not break free of these three to go to the others' aid.

At least not by myself.

A sharper cry and the ringing of steel told him Christian still lived. But what about Elizabeth? She had come to his rescue a few breathless moments ago, flying down the stairs like a black falcon, taking down two opponents, including the *strigoi* who had incapacitated Rhun's right arm. She and her two combatants had vanished into the smoke.

Did she still live?

Distracted by this thought, he moved too slowly as the largest of his opponents lunged yet again. His sword cut a swath across Rhun's ribs. Another came at him from his injured side. Rhun had no way to—

Suddenly, that second attacker vanished, yanked back into the pall of smoke. A gurgling scream echoed out. The other two *strigoi* closed ranks, as a small, dark figure stalked into view, climbing from the lower stairs to the second-floor landing.

Elizabeth.

She carried a broadsword that dripped black blood. The blade looked absurdly huge in her dainty hands, but she held it easily, as if the weight did not concern her.

The largest of the *strigoi* charged toward her, his falchion cleaving through the air faster than Rhun's eye could follow. But she melted away at the last second, pirouetting on one toe, swinging her sword around, and cutting her attacker cleanly through his throat. The creature's headless body went tumbling down the steps behind her.

Rhun used the distraction of her dance to lash out at the remaining *strigoi*, planting his *karambit* through the back of its neck, severing the spine with a deft twist of his wrist. As the body went limp, he kicked it over the landing's rail.

Elizabeth joined him, both arms soaked in blood, her face spattered. "Too many," she gasped. "Scarcely made it back."

He thanked her with a touch on her free hand. She squeezed his fingers.

"Working together," she said, "we could still make the front door."

Rhun sagged against the wall. Blood trickled from a hundred cuts. If he had been human, he would have been dead a dozen times over. As it was, he felt terribly weak. He pointed an arm up.

"Erin and Jordan," he said. "We cannot abandon them."

The howl of the grimwolf reminded him of the danger.

Elizabeth put an arm around his shoulders, holding him up. "You can barely stand."

He could not argue about that. Rescuing the others would have to hold a moment longer. He pulled his wine flask from his thigh and drained it in one long swallow. Elizabeth stood sentinel next to him, patient and silent in the smoke. He remembered a long ago day when they had walked across fields enveloped in a late-spring fog much like this. She was yet human, and he was yet the Sanguinist who had never fallen.

He closed his eyes and waited for his penance.

It tore him back in time to his worst sin. Memories washed over him, but he had no time for penance now, and he fought it, knowing that it would claim him all the stronger with his next drink of wine.

Still, snatches of the past flashed through his body.

. . . *the scent of chamomile in Elizabeth's long-ruined castle . . .*

. . . *firelight reflected in those silver eyes . . .*

. . . *the feeling of her warm flushed skin against his as he claimed her . . .*

. . . *her body dying in his arms . . .*

. . . *his foolish, dreadful choice . . .*

He returned to himself, with the taste of her blood still on his tongue: rich, salty, and alive. He gripped the cross around his neck, praying through the pain, until the taste of her was gone.

He then stepped free of Elizabeth's arm, standing straighter, feeling renewed strength in his veins. Her silver eyes met his and it was as if she saw straight through him to that night and the passion and pain they had shared. He leaned toward her, his lips touching hers.

A chunk of the ceiling crashed down across the upper stairs, chasing them both back. Fiery embers billowed up, surrounded him, lighting in his cassock and on his hair.

Elizabeth beat them out with both hands. Anger flashed across those silver eyes, then resignation. "We cannot return upstairs . . . at least not from *inside* the house. We will best serve your friends if we leave this place now, then climb to the roof from the outside."

Rhun acknowledged the logic of her suggestion. He must get to Erin, Jordan, and Sophia before this cursed building came down, turning this place into their fiery grave.

He pointed below, into a maelstrom of fire and blood, praying he wasn't already too late. "Go."

21

Legion strode across the flat roof of the malevolent structure, while overhead the vault of the sky crackled with lightning. Below, fires burned through the house, flames blew out its lower windows, and smoke choked up into the rainy night. Under his feet, the evil of this place flowed through his bones of his vessel, filling him with power and purpose.

Over the rooftop, he tracked his prey, closing in on them: two heartbeats, marking the only two humans within the fiery structure.

The Warrior and the Woman.

As he had planned, the enemy had fled the flames he had set, chased ever higher.

Toward me.

If the two humans were nearby, the Knight would not be far from their sides. But as this immortal did not have a heartbeat to track, Legion could not be certain of his exact whereabouts. So he intended to hunt down these two and await the Knight.

And he did not hunt alone.

Heavy paws padded alongside him, splashing in the pools of rainwater. The wolf growled with each boom of thunder, as if challenging the heavens.

Legion shared the beast's senses, staring equally through its eyes, straining with its sharper ears, smelling the lightning in the air. He reveled in its wild heart. Even corrupted by black blood, the wolf reminded him of the beauty and majesty of this earthly garden.

Together, they homed in on those two heartbeats underfoot. He intended to slay the Warrior first, listening even now to the strange beat to that one's heart, how it pealed like a golden bell—bright, clear, and holy. He also remembered how the Warrior's blood had burned through one of Legion's enslaved. He must not be allowed to live.

And the stone the Warrior possesses will be mine.

But the Woman . . . she could yet prove useful.

Leopold had supplied Legion her name: *Erin.* And with that name came more details of the prophecy concerning her, this Woman of Learning. Leopold's respect and admiration for the woman's keen mind was easy to read. Merged as one, Leopold equally knew Legion's purpose, flickering with the knowledge that Legion needed all *three* stones. Leopold believed that she of all people possessed the skill to find those last two stones. And though he could not possess the Woman and bend her to his will, he would find other ways to persuade her, to make her submit.

At last, they reached the spot on the roof directly above those two beating hearts. Legion sent his desire to the wolf. Powerful paws began to dig through the clay roof tiles, then sharp caws tore away the green metal nailed beneath.

Once there was only a thin sheaf of wood remaining, Legion touched the wolf's flank, sending it appreciation and respect.

"This prey is mine," he whispered aloud.

The grimwolf submitted, lowering its muzzle, ever faithful. Legion felt his love for the great wild beast echo back to him. Knowing it would guard him with its very life, Legion stepped to the ravaged section of tiles and stamped his powerful heel through the last of the wood, breaking the way open—and dropped heavily through the hole.

He crashed to the floor below, landing on his feet, not even buckling a knee.

He found himself facing the Warrior, who carried an iron bar in his hands. The Woman huddled past his shoulder, holding a beam of light in her grip. Both were unsurprised, ready, having heard the wolf digging, but still Legion enjoyed the looks of horror on their faces as they gazed upon his dark glory for the first time.

He smiled, showing teeth, revealing Leopold's fangs.

Legion felt the flutter of recognition in the Warrior's heart—and the confusion.

But one emotion was strongest of all, shining in both of their faces.

Determination.

Neither would yield this night.

So be it.

All that truly mattered was the Knight, and the one called Korza was not yet here.

The Warrior pushed the Woman—Erin—farther behind his golden heart, as if his body alone could shield her from Legion. Her light skittered to the side when she moved. The beam struck a tall object to Legion's left, reflecting off its mired surface, shining brightly from one section that was recently polished.

The emerald hue caught Legion's eye, igniting fury deep inside him.

It was the hated bell.

The smoke of the six hundred and sixty-six roiled inside him, recognizing the infernal device. They writhed up like a black storm, stirring memories into a whirlwind. Legion's awareness splintered, between past and present, between his own recollection and that of the many.

. . . he crawls across the smooth sides of a green diamond, searching for an opening . . .

. . . he fails six hundred and sixty-six times . . .

Before Legion could fully recover from the shock, the Warrior fell upon him. Impossibly strong hands grabbed his wrists. As that sun-blessed flesh touched his shadowy skin, a golden fire burst forth between them, flaming up his arm to his shoulder.

For the first time in eternity, Legion screamed.

7:10 P.M.

Erin clapped both hands over her ears, dropping her flashlight, falling to her knees at the assault. Tears rose in her eyes, as she fought not to pass out.

Must help Jordan . . .

Steps away, Jordan grappled that ebony-faced monster. He slammed his opponent's body hard against the wall, knocking the air from those lungs to stop the ear-shattering wail.

The impact jarred loose roof tiles from the hole above, sending them crashing to the attic floor. She looked up—to find a pair of eyes glaring down, shining crimson, marking the corruption inside the massive beast.

A grimwolf.

For the moment, the hole was too small for its huge body, but the wolf dug at the edges, widening the hole, plainly intending to come to its master's defense. On the far side of the attic, Jordan continued to wrestle with their shadowy assailant.

Erin retreated until her back was pressed against the grime-slick surface of the glass bell. Her hands searched the floor for a weapon, but only found the metal gear she had knocked off its hook earlier. Her fingers closed on it, useless though it may be.

Still . . .

With her back against the bell, she scooted up until her fingers could reach a long glass pipe that protruded from the bell's side. She swung around and smashed the gear through the base of the pipe, where it connected to the larger bell. Its length broke free and clattered to the ground, shattering into shorter pieces.

She snatched up the longest and thickest.

With the glass spear in hand, she faced the wolf. The beast was almost through. Reacting to her challenging stance, it shoved its head as far as it could, snapping toward her, saliva flying from its snarling lips. But its massive shoulders still restrained it.

At least for the moment.

Intending to take full advantage of that moment, she pushed off the bell and headed toward where Jordan grappled with their adversary. It looked as if he were wrestling his own shadow. They were on the floor, rolling and thrashing, moving with a speed that defied her eyes.

She gripped her spear, fearful of striking out, lest she impale Jordan by mistake.

And what exactly was he fighting?

She had caught a look at the enemy's face when he first crashed down. His skin had been black, darker than coal, and it had seemed to suck in the feeble glow of her flashlight. She remembered seeing a similar shadowy figure on Cardinal Bernard's computer, from the video of the attack at that disco in Rome, but the feed had been too fuzzy for true details.

Not any longer.

She had recognized those features now, blackened though they may be.

Brother Leopold.

Jordan got a fleeting advantage in his fight and pinned that mystery to the floor under him. On top,

Jordan let go of Leopold's black wrist and grabbed his throat.

Erin noted how the freed wrist had turned pale, matching Jordan's palm and fingers, as if those shadows had fled from Jordan's touch. As she watched, the darkness filled back in, flowing like oil over the pale wrist.

Then Erin heard Jordan gasp, pulling her attention to Leopold's face.

As Jordan gripped the man's neck, those shadows bled away from the hand that gripped that black throat. Darkness receded across Leopold's chin, over his mouth and nose, revealing the monk's pale features.

His face contorted in agony, his lips struggling to speak.

"Kill me," Leopold wheezed.

Jordan glanced over his shoulder to her, unsure what to do, but refusing to let go.

Erin rushed forward, hoping for some explanation. "What happened to you?"

Desperate blue-gray eyes stared toward her. "Legion . . . a demon . . . you must kill me . . . can't hold—"

His voice died away as a smoky oil began to swim across his eyes. The freed hand lashed out and grabbed Jordan by the throat—and twisted hard.

Bones snapped in Jordan's neck.

No . . .

A savage growl erupted behind her. A glance revealed the grimwolf plunging its bulk through the hole, coming to finish them off.

7:14 P.M.

Elizabeth raced across the rain-slick rooftop, trailing Rhun. Though unholy power fueled her limbs, she could not keep up with him now. He was a black raven sweeping ahead of her, his speed stoked not by damnation but by fear and love.

The pair of them had managed to fight their way out of the house, collecting the severely wounded Christian along the way. Once outside, they had barricaded the door, trapping as many of the *strigoi* inside as they could. Christian still kept a post down there, protecting their rear.

But once the pair of them had reached the roof—following the sounds of fighting and the heartbeats of Erin and Jordan—they had spotted a grimwolf burrowing through the tiles, trying to reach the attic.

Rhun reached the beast ahead of her, slamming into its flanks, knocking it away from the hole. She did not slow and leaped over them, swinging her sword low as she flew, lopping off one of the beast's ears as it raised its head.

She landed, skidding on the wet tiles, turning to face the grimwolf as it howled its rage.

To her right, Rhun rolled to his feet, baring his silver *karambit*. As if sensing the weaker of the two, the beast lowered its head and shifted its weight to face Rhun.

Elizabeth took a step forward, intending to dissuade the wolf of this action—when a shift of shadows drew her attention to the left. A dark figure appeared through the veils of rain, as if brought down from the clouds. The newcomer wore a black habit that matched what was left of Elizabeth's.

"Sophia . . . ?" Rhun called out, but he was mistaken.

Lightning flashed, and in its quick light, Elizabeth found an older face beneath a damp nest of gray hair. The nun carried a curved scimitar in one hand.

"Abigail?" Elizabeth struggled through her surprise.

What was that sour-tempered Sanguinist doing here?

Lightning burst even brighter, revealing a new feature on the old nun's face: a black handprint emblazoned on her wet cheek.

Abigail rushed Elizabeth, moving with that unnatural speed of the possessed.

Elizabeth's blade barely parried Abigail's first blow. The cantankerous old nun spun to the side with a speed and grace that Elizabeth admired as much as she feared. Abigail raised her blade again, her eyes as dead as a corpse's.

Rhun tried to come to her aid, but the grimwolf slammed into him. The two rolled across the tiles. Yellow teeth gnashed at Rhun's face, while the silver *karambit* flashed.

Abigail lunged, moving swiftly, no longer slowed by the holiness of the Sanguinists. Instead, she was strengthened by an evil much darker than Elizabeth's own heart.

Elizabeth feinted right and managed to slice Abigail's left shoulder.

The nun gave no sign she was hurt. Her sword lashed out again and again. Elizabeth did her best to parry the flurry of blows, but Abigail's strikes were quick and sure.

The last thrust cut deep across Elizabeth's thigh, striking bone.

Her leg buckled under her.

The nun moved toward her, as implacable as the sea.

7:18 P.M.

Erin heard the fighting and howling from the rooftop. A moment ago, a dark shadow had knocked the grimwolf away from the hole above, protecting her. Only one person was that foolhardy and brave.

Rhun . . .

Taking courage from his efforts, she closed upon Jordan and the possessed form of Leopold. Jordan remained atop that monster, but the demon's black hand throttled him, turning his face purple, setting his eyes to bulging.

Jordan saw her approach, and with all of his remaining effort, he rolled to the side, dragging Leopold's body up and around, presenting the former monk's back to her.

She wanted to hesitate. Leopold had been her friend; he had saved her life more than once in the past. But she hurried forward instead, raising her only weapon: the spear of broken glass.

She stabbed downward with the strength of both arms, impaling Leopold through the back, aiming for that dead heart.

A pained gasp burst from Leopold's throat. The choking hand loosened from Jordan's throat. Leopold's body toppled to his side, as if a string had been cut. His fingers twitched once and went still.

Though freed now, Jordan remained on his back, his face turned away. Erin dropped to her knees next to him. His neck was bruised to the bone. A hard knot protruded from his cervical area. His spine had been broken.

"Jordan?" she called softly, her hands out, too afraid to move him.

He did not answer, but another faint voice did. "Erin . . ."

She turned to see Leopold staring at her. The darkness had bled from his face, draining along with the black blood that flowed from his impaled chest. She knew Sanguinists could control their own bleeding, willing it to stop.

Leopold did not, plainly wanting to die.

Grief welled up inside her, knowing there was goodness inside the former monk, misguided though it might have been.

"You saved me before," she whispered, remembering those dark tunnels under St. Peter's.

A cold hand touched her wrist. ". . . saved me." He gave her a small nod of reassurance.

A sob escaped her.

Even in death, he sought to comfort her.

His voice became as faint as a breath. "*Legion . . .*"

She leaned closer, hearing the urgency even now.

"*Three stones . . . Legion seeks them . . .*"

"What are you talking about? What stones?"

Leopold seemed deaf to her, already far gone, speaking across a vast gulf. *"The garden . . . defiled . . . sewn in blood, bathed in water . . . that is where Lucifer will . . ."*

Then those blue eyes went glassy, those lips forever silent.

Erin wanted to shake more answers from him, but instead she touched Leopold's cheek.

"Good-bye, my friend."

7:20 P.M.

Collapsed on the rooftop, Elizabeth cursed her wounded leg.

Abigail loomed over her, smelling of wet cotton. Lightning flashed off her raised blade. Her dead eyes stared down at Elizabeth, not coldly, but with the gaze of an uncaring predator.

Across the roof, Rhun battled the grimwolf, both bloodied, but still fighting.

Unarmed, Elizabeth braced herself for the attack. Regret flashed through her. Her death would seal Tommy's fate. She had been unable to save her own children, and she would not save this child either.

Then the wolf howled, a sound unlike any heard before.

A noise full of rage and pain and shock.

She saw the grimwolf barrel into Rhun, knocking him far, then turned and fled—straight toward Elizabeth and Abigail.

"Run!" The word was spoken with a familiar authority, coming from above her.

Elizabeth looked up at Abigail. The nun's eyes were sharp now, shining with fury. Her cheek was free of any blemish, the mark vanished from her flesh.

Abigail grabbed Elizabeth, dragged her up, and shoved her to the side. "Go!"

Elizabeth stumbled away as Abigail raised her scimitar and faced the beast as it reached them. The grimwolf slid on its paws, claws gouging and shattering clay tiles. It stared at Abigail, looking momentarily dumbfounded at this threat from a former ally. But confusion quickly stoked to rage—and it leaped at the old nun.

Abigail swung her blade. Much slower now, she missed, and teeth snatched her arm. Still, she forced her legs to push, dragging the massive beast by sheer strength. She reached the roof's edge and flung herself and the beast over its lip.

Elizabeth hobbled forward in time to see their bodies strike the pavement four stories below. Abigail looked like a broken doll, limbs akimbo, neck twisted. Black blood washed into the gutter. The grimwolf somehow survived the fall. It rose up drunkenly, then loped off into the shadows.

Below, Christian stumbled into view on the street below. A pair of *strigoi* was on his heels, but like the wolf, these beasts took flight, dropping their weapons and fleeing into the night.

Across the way, Rhun rushed to the ragged hole dug by the grimwolf and dropped into the attic below, checking on the others.

Alone on the roof, she remained standing, wondering what had so suddenly turned the tides of this war. She pictured the mark vanishing from Abigail's cheek. The woman had clearly broken free of her possession.

Is that why the others had fled, too?

But something struck her as odd. Elizabeth had briefly locked gazes with the grimwolf before it attacked and fled. She had read the intelligence shining there— far more than any ordinary beast should possess, even one so corrupted.

But what did that mean?

She shuddered, fearful of the answer.

7:25 P.M.

"I can't get Jordan to respond at all," Erin told Rhun, glad to have him at her side. "And look at his neck."

Jordan lay stretched out on the floor next to Leopold's body. The bruising had faded, but there remained a disturbing crook to his cervical vertebrae. She gently checked his pulse. It throbbed steadily under her fingers, as slowly and evenly as if he were merely asleep.

"Jordan!" she called, afraid to shake him. "Come back!"

Jordan showed no response, his open eyes just stared straight ahead.

Rhun looked equally concerned. He had already examined Leopold, pressing his silver cross against the monk's forehead. The silver didn't burn into the skin, suggesting the evil had truly fled him.

But where it went was a concern for later.

A muffled shout rose from below, coming from under the attic floorboards. "Erin! Jordan!"

Erin straightened, twisting to stare toward the attic's trapdoor, suddenly remembering. "Sophia is still down there."

With a grimwolf.

But that wasn't the only threat.

Erin noted the smoke rising through the planks from below. Rhun stepped over and hauled the trapdoor open and flung it wide. A wash of heat rolled up, bringing with it a fresh clot of smoke.

She coughed, holding the crook of her arm over her nose.

Rhun reached down and helped haul Sophia into the attic. The small Sanguinist was soaked in blood— some her own, some the grimwolf's. She did her best to straighten the shreds of her clothing.

"The wolf fled," Sophia said, her eyes still panicked-looking. "Don't know why."

Erin stared over at Leopold, guessing what had changed.

A trampling of feet overhead drew their attention up to the hole. Everyone tensed, expecting more trouble, but then Christian poked his head through.

"Time to go," he warned. "Whole place looks like it's about to go."

Working quickly, Sophia and Rhun hauled Jordan up. They passed him up to Christian, who caught his shoulders and dragged him to the roof with the help of Elizabeth.

Rhun turned to Sophia. "Help them get Jordan to the street. Erin and I will follow. We can make for St. Ignatius. We should be able to find refuge there."

With a nod, Sophia leaped up, caught the edge, and vanished.

Rhun turned to Erin.

"What about Leopold's body?" she asked.

"The fires will take care of it."

Regret panged through her, but she knew they had no other choice. Rhun helped get her through the hole to the roof. The cold air and clean rain helped push back her sense of hopelessness.

Jordan will heal.

She refused to believe otherwise. She searched the roof, but the others had already vanished, climbing down with Jordan's comatose form. Not wanting to leave him out of her sight for long, she hurried toward the edge with Rhun.

"I'll carry you down," he said, already reaching an arm toward her.

She turned to him with a grateful smile—when the roof collapsed under her.

She plummeted into hot, smoky darkness.

22

Rhun fell with Erin.

He grabbed her arm and pulled her hard against his chest. He wrapped his limbs protectively around her as they crashed through fiery timbers, smoke, and raining plaster. Then they struck a floor that was still intact. He did his best to roll, to bleed away the force of that impact.

He ended up on his knees, cradling Erin's limp form. She was dazed. Blood ran from a deep scalp wound across her face. Flames and smoke roiled around him, but he recognized the round room where they had landed: Edward Kelly's old alchemy room.

He lifted Erin, feeling her lungs laboring in the smoke, hearing the fluttering of a weakening heart as she suffocated. He stumbled, half blind, toward the wall, intending to follow it to the door, then to a window.

Overhead, a crack sounded as another roof beam gave way. Something huge crashed through from above. Flames lit its greenish hue, glowing through the glass.

The bell.

Instinctively, Rhun raised his arm against its evil, protecting Erin, shielding her with his body. The bell struck his arm, his back, and drove him to the floor. Thick glass shattered over him, cutting into his arm, his shoulder, slashing muscle and breaking bone.

Pain blinded him as he cried out.

Erin heard, stirring with a jolt under him. "Rhun . . ."

He rolled off her, slicing up more of his flesh. "Go," he moaned.

She crawled free, but instead of following his order, she grabbed his good arm and tried to drag him away from the ruins of the bell. Before she could, the fire-weakened floor gave way under the weight of the broken bell. As burning boards fell away under him, he twisted and saw the limp form of Leopold tumble from the attic above and follow the wreck of the shattered bell, chasing it down into the fiery pit of the house.

Rhun's body slid to follow, but Erin dragged him away from the gaping hole, keeping him in this round room. Pain consumed him, but he forced himself to fight through it, to stay in this room with Erin. He could not leave her. He might yet be of service to her.

Smoke boiled into the room from the hole left by the bell. Wind drew it up through this makeshift chimney to the roof. Most of the floor had already been burned through. Flames roared beneath them.

Erin held him, cradling *him* this time. She had dragged him to the wall. Rhun wished that she had left him and escaped.

"Leave me," Rhun forced out, turning his face toward the door, toward the faint glow of a streetlamp through the smoke. "Make for the window . . ."

Cold blood gushed down his side. He had been in enough battles to recognize a fatal wound. But perhaps Erin could climb out that window, scramble down the front, and escape to safety. She did not have to die with him.

Still, she did not let go of him. Instead, she yanked off her leather belt, fastened it around his shoulder, and pulled it tight.

Rhun gasped as new pain flared.

"I'm sorry," she said, coughing. "I had to stop the bleeding."

Rhun looked past the belt's tight constriction.

Below the leather strap—his arm was gone, severed by the broken bell.

7:33 P.M.

Erin pressed her wrist against Rhun's lips. "Drink," she ordered.

The tourniquet had slowed the hemorrhage to a trickle, but he would not survive long without a fresh source of blood.

Rhun turned his head weakly to the side, refusing.

"Damn you, Rhun. You need the strength found in my blood. Sin now, repent later. I won't leave you, and I can't move you on my own."

She shook him, but he had sagged against her, unconscious.

She tried to slide him toward the door, but his bulk was too much for her. She could barely breathe; her eyes wept with stinging tears, born equally of smoke and frustration.

A few feet away, a floor joist cracked and gave. Another section of floor fell into the fire below. Heat blazed against the side of her face, as hot as the mouth of an open furnace. Flames roared at her.

Then the smoke shifted by the door, swirling open to allow a dark shape to fly into the room.

Christian fell upon her like a dark angel. He must have followed her heartbeat. He went to grab her, but she pushed Rhun into his arms.

"Take him," she coughed out.

He obeyed, tossing Rhun over one shoulder, and hauled her up with his other arm. He dragged her stumbling form along with him toward a wash of fresher air. Her heels crackled across broken glass to a third-story window. Christian must have crashed through it to reach them.

"How are we going to—?" she started.

Whipping around, Christian scooped her up and threw her headlong out the window.

She plummeted with a scream trapped in her throat. The ground rushed toward her—then Elizabeth and Sophia appeared below. Hands caught her before she struck the cobblestones, softening her landing, but she hit the pavement hard enough to jar her teeth.

She twisted to see Christian strike the ground yards away, rolling across the cobblestones, then smoothly to his feet, Rhun in his arms.

Relieved, Erin remained on the wet cobblestones, coughing. Between coughs she drew in as much of the fresh outside air as she could. Her lungs ached.

A shape loomed over her, then dropped to a knee. "Erin, are you okay?"

"Jordan . . ."

His eyes shone brightly at her. He had come back to himself again. Fresh tears rose to her eyes, but concern still rang through her.

"Your neck?"

He rubbed the back of his collar, looking sheepish. "Still hurts like a motherfu—I mean, it hurts bad."

He smiled at her.

He had healed.

Again.

"C'mon," he said, changing the subject. "We need to go."

He lifted her to her feet, his arms wrapped tightly around her. Her knees trembled, barely holding her upright. She stared up at him, drinking in the sight of him.

"Don't do that again," she whispered. "Don't leave me."

But he didn't seem to hear her.

Instead, he drew her toward Christian, where Elizabeth helped the Sanguinist with Rhun's body. Rhun already looked dead, his head hanging loose, his limbs lifeless. Blood still dripped from Erin's makeshift tourniquet.

Sophia swept up to Jordan's side. "We must get him to St. Ignatius. To our chapel there. Hurry."

The small woman led them quickly across the dark, rain-swept square. Erin stumbled after them, Jordan holding her up. The Faust House raged behind them as the fire ate its secrets.

Ahead, firelight flickered off the golden halo surrounding the figure on top of St. Ignatius Church. Sophia skirted to the side of the baroque façade and headed for a section of wall sheltered under a large tree. A small marble basin protruded from the wall, like a font that might hold holy water at the threshold of a church. The nun bared a seeping laceration on her arm and let her blood drip into it.

Stone scraped against stone, and a small door opened for them.

Elizabeth took Rhun in her arms and carried him in first. They all followed, but Sophia lingered behind at the gate, where she whispered, "*Pro me.*"

Erin glanced back, remembering Cardinal Bernard had spoken those same words to lock himself in the chapel at St. Mark's, so that only a trio of Sanguinists could open the door. Sophia must have done the same, fearful of Legion's enslaved forces that might still be nearby, especially any that might be Sanguinists.

Even here, their group might not be safe.

The door closed behind Sophia, and darkness swallowed them all.

A rasp of a match sounded, then a candle bloomed ahead of Erin. Christian used that flame to ignite more, slowly illuminating a simple stone chapel. She moved into it. A whitewashed-brick roof arched above their heads, while plain plaster walls surrounded them. The scent of incense and wine enveloped her, offering comfort and promising protection.

Between rows of rough-hewn pews, an aisle led to a white-clad altar crowned by a portrait of Lazarus receiving his first wine from the hands of Christ. His brown eyes blazed with certainty, and Christ smiled upon him.

Christian strode to a cupboard beside the altar and removed a white metal box with a red cross on the front. A first-aid kit. He tossed it to Jordan, while Sophia went behind the altar to a silver tabernacle. She opened it and pulled out flasks of blessed wine, the equivalent of first-aid kits for the Sanguinists.

Elizabeth draped Rhun's limp form on the floor before the altar. She tore away the remains of his jacket and shirt, exposing his arm and chest. Hundreds of deep wounds shone dark against his pale skin, but none were as serious as his severed arm.

Elizabeth examined the tourniquet, then her silver eyes met Erin's.

"You did well," the countess said, "thank you."

Erin heard true appreciation in the woman's voice. No matter how much she strove to deny it, Elizabeth cared about Rhun.

Erin nodded, covering a deep cough with a fist. Jordan moved to her side and drew her to a pew. As she set down her backpack, he opened the first-aid kit, searched through it, then removed a pair of small water bottles. He passed her one. While she took a long drink, he used the other to dampen a cloth.

He gently wiped Erin's face clean. His hands slid gently across her body, checking for serious wounds, his touch awakening feelings that were completely inappropriate in a chapel full of priests. She found herself staring into his eyes.

Jordan matched her gaze, then bent down, and gave her a long, slow kiss.

As much as she wanted to believe this gesture of affection was one of passion, she could not help but feel he was also kissing her good-bye. When he finally leaned back, his brows crinkled ever so slightly. He wiped away the fresh tears from her cheeks, plainly not understanding their source.

"Are you all right?" he whispered.

She swallowed, nodded, and wiped at her eyes. "Just too much . . ."

She tried to take a deep breath, but a sharp pain in her chest stopped her. She might have a cracked rib. But her injuries were minor compared to Rhun's.

The Sanguinists knelt around his body.

But were they trying to heal him . . . or were they also saying good-bye?

8:04 P.M.

Elizabeth dripped wine into Rhun's mouth, as frustration rankled through her, trembling her fingers. Wine splashed down his cheek.

Christian reached and steadied her hands. "Let me," he whispered, slipping the silver flask from her burning fingertips.

She let him, rubbing her palms on her knees, trying to wipe away the holiness of the wine and sting of the silver. She stared aghast at the ruins of Rhun's body. They had stripped him nearly naked, leaving little more than the loincloth that Christ wore on the cross above the altar. But even Christ had not suffered so severely. She read the map of Rhun's agony in the hundreds of cuts and torn skin. Her gaze ended at the stump of his arm. It had been severed between shoulder and elbow.

Tears rose to her eyes, blurring her sight, as if trying to erase the horrible image.

She wiped them angrily away.

I will bear witness . . . for you, Rhun.

While Christian continued to trickle wine between Rhun's bloodless lips, Sophia bathed a wine-infused cloth over his wounds, cleaning them, burning them with holiness. Each touch caused Rhun's skin to twitch in pain.

Elizabeth found his hand, holding him, wanting to take this agony from him, but at least it was evidence that Rhun still lived, buried somewhere deep in his ravaged body.

Come back to me . . .

Sophia picked up a flagon of wine and poured it over the ragged stump of Rhun's arm. His body clenched upward, lifting his buttocks off the stone, his mouth open in a scream. His hand tightened on Elizabeth's fingers. Her bones ground together, but she accepted that pain if it would help him even a little.

Finally, his body sagged back to the floor.

Sophia sat on her heels, her face a mask of concern.

"Will he recover with the wine?" Elizabeth asked.

"He needs rest," Sophia said, but it sounded like the nun was trying to convince herself.

"He needs to drink blood," Elizabeth said, letting a note of fury enter her voice. "You all know this, yet you're doing nothing but torturing him."

"He must not drink," Sophia said. "Sinning in this chapel would strip him of the strength of the holiness of these grounds. Such an act could kill him faster."

Elizabeth did not know whether to believe her or not. She considered taking his body and running from this place. But the holy ground weakened her, and these other two Sanguinists had drunk deeply of their wine, taking additional strength from Christ's blood.

And what would I do with Rhun alone on those empty streets?

If he must die, let it be in a place he loved.

And beside those who loved him.

She squeezed his hand.

A voice spoke behind her. "Elizabeth is right," Erin said. "Rhun needs blood if he's going to live."

Christian looked up sadly at her. "Sophia spoke the truth. He must not drink, the sin would—"

"Who says he has to *drink*?" Erin said, dropping to her knees among them. She carried a dagger in her hand. "What if I bathe his wounds with my blood? I would take that sin—if it is a sin—onto myself."

Christian exchanged a hopeful look with Sophia.

"No," Sophia said, her voice firm. "Blood sin is blood sin."

Christian looked less sure.

Erin shrugged. "I'm doing it."

Elizabeth felt a surge of affection for the woman's pluck.

"I won't allow it," Sophia said, moving to stop her.

Christian blocked Sophia with an arm. "We have nothing to lose for trying."

"Except his eternal soul." Sophia tried to shove him aside, but Elizabeth joined him, bodily keeping the nun from Erin.

Elizabeth met Erin's eyes. "Do it."

With a nod, Erin drew the blade across her palm. The archaeologist winced at the pain, but remained steady. The smell of fresh blood—pushed forth by a strongly beating heart full of life—filled the small chapel.

Elizabeth felt the two Sanguinists stir, gasping at the scent. Their still-wounded bodies called for them to drink the life offered in that crimson pool in Erin's palm. Elizabeth smelled it, too, drawing its sweetness inside, but she had not denied herself for as long as these others had. She could withstand it.

And this blood is not meant for me.

Erin leaned over Rhun's naked form. She dipped her fingers into the darkness pooled in her palm and reached down to gently paint her hot blood over Rhun's cold skin. Again Rhun's flesh twitched with each touch, but it was not pain that shivered through him.

It was pleasure.

His lips parted, letting out the softest moan.

Elizabeth remembered hearing that same note in her ear, long ago, remembering him atop her, clasping to her.

Erin continued her labors, working meticulously, missing no wound. Finally, she stared down at the ragged stump of bone, muscle, and slowly weeping black blood. Erin turned toward Elizabeth, as if asking permission.

She gave the archaeologist the smallest nod.

Do it.

Erin massaged her forearm with her good hand, milking more blood into her palm. Only after trickles of crimson spilled from her overfilled fingers did she grasp the end of Rhun's arm, pouring her life over that savage wound.

Rhun convulsed, his back arching high, while Erin kept her grip on his arm.

A cry escaped him, a gasp of ecstasy so raw that Sophia turned away from it.

Or maybe the nun shied away from the harder evidence of Rhun's pleasure. The loincloth did little to hide his rising ardor, revealing the man inside the beast, the lust that the white collar of his station could never fully restrain.

Elizabeth remembered that, too, falling instantly into the past, feeling him deep inside her, swelling there, the two of them becoming one.

As Rhun crashed back down to the stone floor, Erin finally let go. Rhun lay there, his entire body quaking softly, spent but clearly stronger for it.

The many small cuts had closed.

Even the ruins of his arm had stopped bleeding, the flesh already hiding bone.

Christian let out a long sigh. "I think he'll make it . . . with more rest."

Even Sophia acknowledged this. "The wine should help him the rest of the way to healing."

Erin stayed kneeling. Jordan came to her and tended to her life-giving wound, bandaging it up. Erin leaned into his tender ministrations.

"His arm," Erin asked, her gaze still on Rhun. "Will it . . . will it . . . ?"

Jordan finished for her, his voice firm. "Will it grow back?"

"In time . . . many months, if not years," Christian said. "For that miracle, he will still need much more rest."

"What does that mean for our quest?" Jordan said.

No one had an answer, only more questions.

"We don't even know where to go," Sophia said, defeat in her voice. "We learned nothing from all this bloodshed."

Erin shook her head. "That's not true."

Eyes turned to her.

She spoke with certainty. "I know what we're look-ing for."

8:33 P.M.

"What do you mean?" Christian asked.

"Give me a moment." Erin stood up, helped by Jordan, but she pushed free of his arms. She needed some distance from him, from everyone. She shud-dered, remembering what she had felt when she had held Rhun's arm. For a few breaths, she had felt his aching passion, the strain of his lust, the wracking plea-sure of her blood suffusing through him, dissolving her into him, the two becoming one.

She closed a fist over her bandaged palm, cutting off that memory.

Jordan touched her shoulder. "Erin?"

His blue eyes looked at her with concern. She paced away, needing to keep moving.

I did what I had to . . . nothing more.

Still, a pang of guilt shot through her. She and Rhun had shared another intimacy in this church in front of everyone.

She crossed to her pack and opened it with trembling fingers. She reached inside and let her palm rest on the case holding the Blood Gospel. She took strength from its presence, then pulled out the sheaves of papers she had recovered from inside the bell. She stacked them on the pew.

"I believe these are Dee's old notes," she said. "But I can't say for sure as they look to be written in Enochian."

Elizabeth rose and joined her. "Let me see." She gave them a cursory look, flipping through. "These are indeed Dee's. I recognize the handwriting."

"Can you translate the Enochian?" Erin asked.

"Of course." Elizabeth settled into the pew. "But it will take time."

"For now, can you skim through for any reference to the green diamond?"

"Yes, but why?"

Christian echoed her question. "Erin, what do you know?"

She faced him, letting the grief center her. "Very little. But before Leopold died, he broke free of the demon that possessed him."

"What demon?" Sophia asked.

Erin took a deeper breath, remembering that only she had heard Leopold's final words. "He called it *Legion*."

Christian glanced to Sophia. "There was such a demon mentioned in the Bible."

Sophia nodded. "Christ cast it out, but not before confronting it, demanding its name. *'And he answered, saying, My name is Legion: for we are many.'*"

"*For we are many,*" Erin repeated, considering those words. "Could that be this demon's nature? To possess many."

"It certainly seemed capable of enslaving others to its will," Elizabeth said, as she began to peruse the stack of old papers. "Even Sister Abigail."

"But not us," Jordan said, waving to Erin. "I grappled with him, but he couldn't possess me."

"It could be that he can only control those who are already tainted," Sophia said with a worried expression. "A weed needs soil to grow in. Perhaps he needs that darkness to be already there before he can root into someone."

"If this demon is like a weed," Christian asked, "could he have survived the death of Leopold?"

"I don't know," Erin admitted. "But Leopold said that Legion was seeking *three* stones." She looked pointedly at Jordan. "He sent one of his enslaved down into that temple in Cumae. Maybe he wanted the remains of that green diamond."

"Maybe," Jordan agreed. "Or maybe he just wanted to kill me. Heck, he came pretty damned close."

"No, I think he wanted the stone."

"Why do you sound so sure?" Christian asked, then added with a soft smile. "Not that I'm doubting the Woman of Learning."

"Leopold's last words, just before he died. He mentioned something about a *garden defiled* . . . one *sewn in blood, and bathed in water.* It sounded like that was where Lucifer would rise."

"But what garden?" Christian asked. "What does that mean?"

"Perhaps the Garden of Eden?" Sophia offered.

Erin looked off into space, mumbling, "It can't be just a coincidence."

Jordan touched her shoulder. "What?"

She faced the others. "Those three frescoes in Kelly's alchemy room. *Arbor, Sanguis,* and *Aqua.* Representing *garden, blood,* and *water.*"

Christian rubbed his chin. "Symbols that mirrored Leopold's last words."

"And Legion is seeking *three* stones," Erin added. "Perhaps they mirror the same. *Arbor, Sanguis,* and *Aqua.*"

Jordan pulled out the two halves of the emerald-hued diamond. "You think this might be *arbor.* It is *green* like a garden."

She nodded. "And we know it's not a simple diamond. There's that strange symbol infused into it. Plus it was capable of holding the smoky spirits of over six hundred *strigoi*."

"And eventually Legion himself," Christian added.

Erin touched the diamond with a fingertip. "Maybe that's why Leopold described the *garden*—this stone—as *defiled*. It was polluted with evil."

"If you are correct," Elizabeth said from the pew, "then there must be two more gems. *Sanguis* and *Aqua*."

Erin heard a tick in the countess's voice and turned toward her. "Do you know anything about them?"

"I do not," Elizabeth said, but her expression remained thoughtful. "But perhaps we should ask the man who sent John Dee the green one."

Erin turned to her. "Who was that?"

Elizabeth held up a yellowed sheet of old paper with a smile. "This is a letter to Dee from the man who sent him that stone."

Erin crossed to see it, but she found the page was written in Enochian.

Elizabeth used a finger to underline a set of symbols.

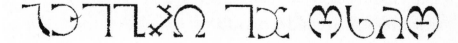

"This is his name," Elizabeth said. "Hugh de Payens."

The name struck Erin as familiar, but she could not place it. Exhaustion made it harder to think.

Christian stepped closer, his face pinched. "That cannot be."

"Why not?" Jordan asked.

"Hugh de Payens was a Sanguinist," Christian explained. "From the time of the Crusades."

Erin suddenly remembered the man's name and his prominent place in history. "Hugh de Payens . . . wasn't he the one who, along with Bernard of Clairvaux, formed the Knights Templar?"

"One and the same," Christian said. "But he actually formed the *Sanguinist Order* of those Knights. Nine knights bound together by blood."

Erin frowned, reminded yet again that the history she had been taught was nothing but a play of shadows and lights, and that the truth lay somewhere in between.

"But Hugh de Payens *died* during the Second Crusades," Christian added.

"Who told you this?" Elizabeth asked. "Because the date of this letter from Dee is dated 1601, four centuries *after* the Second Crusade."

"I heard this story from Hugh's fellow founder of the Knights Templar, Bernard of Clairvaux, a man who witnessed that noble death." Christian lifted an eyebrow toward Erin. "Or, as you better know him, *Cardinal Bernard.*"

Erin's eyes widened. "Bernard is *the* Bernard of Clairvaux?"

It made a certain sense. She had known the cardinal had fought during the Crusades and had been in a high-ranking position in the Church ever since.

"It sounds like Bernard has not been entirely truthful," Elizabeth said with a wry smile, tapping a finger on the letter. "Again."

"That can wait for now." Erin nodded to the paper. "What does the note say?"

Elizabeth's eyes scanned down the page, translating the archaic letters. A smile grew on her face. "It seems Hugh wished *me* to have the stone if anything happened to John Dee. The alchemist must have shared the nature of my work with his secret benefactor."

"So if Dee failed," Jordan said, "that guy wanted you to finish his work?"

"It would seem so. The plan was for Edward Kelly to take possession of the stone upon Dee's death, to protect it and bring it to me. This must be why Emperor Rudolf gave the stone and the bell to Kelly." Elizabeth scowled. "But that greedy charlatan kept them both for himself. He probably secretly sold the diamond. It is worth a king's ransom."

"Still, after that," Erin said, "the cursed gem somehow found its way through history back to you."

"Fate is not to be thwarted," Elizabeth said.

Erin had to force herself not to roll her eyes. "Does that letter say anything about the other two stones?"

"Not a word."

"So, a dead end," Jordan said.

"Unless Hugh de Payens still lives," Erin said. "We know he didn't *die* when Bernard said he did. So maybe he's still knocking around."

Jordan sighed loudly. "If so, how do we find him?"

Erin put her fists on her hips. "We ask his oldest friend. Bernard of Clairvaux." She turned to Christian and Sophia. "Where is the cardinal?"

"He was sent to Castel Gandolfo," Christian said. "Awaiting his sentence."

"Let us pray," Sophia added, "that they haven't already put him to death for his sins."

Erin agreed.

They couldn't afford for anything else to go wrong.

23

March 18, 9:45 P.M. CET
Prague, Czech Republic

The wolf digs through smoke and fiery embers.

Its massive paws churn up mud and push aside broken beams. Rough rocks rip its pads to bloody shreds. Sparks fall and burn through its thick pelt.

A knot of blackness grips the thunder of its heart, drawing it ever deeper.

There are no words, no commands, only yearning.

The source of that black desire waits below, curled tightly around the tiniest flicker of flame, nestled within the cold carcass that holds it safe.

The wolf burrows toward it.

One craving draws it ever deeper into the fiery ruins.

Free me.

Fourth

They have deeply corrupted themselves, as in the days of Gibeah: therefore he will remember their iniquity, he will visit their sins.

—Hosea 9:9

24

March 19, 6:19 A.M. CET
Castel Gandolfo, Italy

Erin thrashed wildly out of a nightmare of fire and demons.

She woke into a room shining with the light of a new day. It took her a few panicked breaths to recognize the simple room, to recall their midnight flight from Prague to this idyllic countryside south of Rome. She was in the papal residence at Castel Gandolfo. She drank in the familiarity: the plain white walls, the wood floor that shone in the morning sunlight like warm honey, the solid mahogany bed with a crucifix hanging above the headboard. She and Jordan had stayed in this very room the last time they had come here.

I'm safe . . .

Maybe that wasn't exactly true, but it was the safest she had felt in a long time.

The windows were secured with thick wooden shutters, but a pair of them had their slats opened enough to let in the sunrise. She welcomed the golden light after the long night of terror. They had taken a private jet—a Citation X—that whisked them under papal orders from that medieval city to here. They had landed, exhausted and worn, bloodied and bruised.

Her first thought was of Rhun.

Upon landing, he had been rushed by stretcher to a Sanguines infirmary. Erin had wanted to follow, but she could barely stand. Jordan had half-carried her here in the middle of the night. They had both collapsed in bed, limbs wrapped around each other. For once, she had not worried about the heat from his naked skin, curling against it like a warm fire.

Still, a twinge of guilt at abandoning Rhun remained with her. She did her best to shake it off, shying away from the memory of touching Rhun, sharing that momentary blood bond with him.

Rhun is in the best hands, she reminded herself. He certainly had a nurse who would brook no ill treatment, who would watch over him. Elizabeth had refused to leave Rhun's side. Though he had never woken, the woman had kept hold of his hand the entire flight and had shadowed Rhun's stretcher down to the infirmary, despite the clear fatigue in her face and body.

Erin might not trust Elizabeth, but when it came to Rhun, there was no better guard dog while he recuperated.

The *clunk* of a shower shutting off drew her gaze to the bathroom door. It was the noise of that running water that had woken her. She reached to the rumple of bed sheets next to her, feeling the fading warmth of Jordan's body. She rested a palm on the imprint of his head on the pillow.

Concern for him ached through her, but she had to admit she felt much better after a night's sleep next to him. She stretched out and sighed.

Pretty good . . . considering.

But was it just from the rest? Though bruises peppered her back and a scalp wound had been closed with butterfly bandages, she felt immensely better—better than she should.

She shifted to the patch of residual warmth from Jordan's body, luxuriating in the memory of his skin against hers, wondering if the night spent bathed in that heat had anything to do with how she felt now.

Or was it simply having this time alone with Jordan?

He had certainly seemed more like himself.

The bathroom door opened with a creak, and she turned.

As if summoned by her thoughts, Jordan stood in the doorway, outlined in steam, wearing only a white towel. She smiled at him, still nestled in the sheets, which suddenly seemed much warmer.

He cocked one eyebrow and let the towel drop, wiping a rivulet of water from one temple with his hand. Her gaze took him in, appreciating every ripple, every damp trail.

Everyone in their party was covered in bruises and cuts. But not Jordan. His smooth skin was unmarked, and he practically glowed with health. Soft light reflected off the blond hairs on his arms and muscular legs. He looked like a Greek statue—too perfect to be real.

He crossed the room to stand in front of her. His bare skin was only inches away from hers. She wanted to touch him.

"How are you feeling?" he asked.

"Ready for anything," she said, her grin widening. "Starting with you."

She stared up into his bright blue eyes. They had stood like this many times before, but it always felt new, always gave her a flutter in her chest. She touched the twining tattoo that covered his shoulder and upper chest. His heart beat against the soft skin of her palm. She traced those curling blue lines, her fingertips sliding down the smooth skin of his stomach.

She knew the tattoo's shape and size. It was now unmistakably larger than it had been a few days before, extending in dark crimson coils and vines—a visible sign of how he was changing. She was especially concerned about the lines that now encircled his neck, as if those new vines were choking him as surely as those demon's black fingers had. But she knew those same crimson lines had likely healed him, fading his bruises, and repairing a crush of cervical vertebrae.

She should appreciate those lines, but instead they terrified her.

"Don't look so worried." Jordan took her hand from his chest and kissed her palm. His soft lips burned against her skin. "We're here, together, and alive. It doesn't get any better than that."

Erin couldn't argue with that.

His tongue traced up her hand to the inside of her wrist. Her breath caught in her throat. He dropped to a knee, kissing along her arm, his mouth light as a butterfly against her bruised skin. Tingling traveled up her arm to her breasts and body.

She wrapped her arm around him and pulled him closer. She wanted to feel his skin against hers again, to forget everything that had happened, and believe, even for a moment, that everything was all right.

Jordan slid into bed next to her, his warm hands caressing her, exploring her, moving ever lower. She wanted to lose herself in him completely, but his feverish heat reminded her how he had retreated from her, how those eyes had looked at her without seeing her.

She shuddered.

"Shh," he whispered, mistaking her reaction. "You're safe now."

He rolled on top of her. His smoldering blue eyes told her that he wanted nothing else but her, and that he still loved her. As his eyes drifted closed, she reached toward him for a kiss.

His lips whispered gently against hers, soft as the wind. "I missed you."

"Me, too," she answered.

Her mouth opened to his, hungry for the taste of him. His arms tightened around her, holding her so close that she could barely breathe. It wasn't close enough.

When he pulled his head back, she moaned. She didn't want the kiss to end. *Ever.* She couldn't bear to lose him, to lose this closeness. She traced the curve of his jaw, his cheekbones. Her fingertip lingered on the tiny indent in his upper lip that was shaped like a bow. Those lips smiled at her and kissed her again.

For a long time, nothing existed but the two of them, lost in the heat of each other's bodies. Time became meaningless. It was just the taste of him, the stubble of his cheek on her thigh, the press of their bodies, of him inside her, making her feel whole, not that she needed him to be complete, just that it felt so very right.

Then for a moment, lost in the passion, her body responding to his every touch and movement, she closed her eyes—and flashed to that time with Rhun in the chapel, recalling the fiery ardor of her blood flowing through him, until his body became hers.

She gasped, arching under Jordan, pulling him tighter to her with her legs. She rode that moment like a wave, lost in a blur of ecstasy, unsure where her body began and ended.

Finally, she collapsed, gasping, trembling.

Jordan kissed her, calming her, smiling down at her.

She stared up at him, loving him more than ever. Still, guilt flickered inside her, knowing not all of her response rose from Jordan's touch.

"Is something wrong?" he asked, running a finger along her cheek.

"No . . . it was perfect."

Too perfect—and it scared her.

They cuddled together as sunlight crept across the room. At some point, Erin dozed off into a dreamless slumber. When she woke, she listened for the shower, for some sign that Jordan was still here, but she knew he was gone.

A flicker of panic rose inside her.

He's probably off getting breakfast.

She pushed back her fears and climbed from the bed, needing to move. She took a quick shower. The steaming hot water massaged the remaining aches from her body, waking her more fully. Afterward, she buffed her skin dry and climbed into a fresh set of clothes supplied to them last night, pulling on a pair of jeans and a white cotton shirt.

Lastly, she donned a leather jacket. The coat had been fashioned from the hide of a grimwolf. From past experience, she knew it was as strong as armor. She let some of that strength sink into her, centering her for the day ahead.

A knock sounded from the door. She turned as it opened. Her body tensing, until she saw Jordan.

"I come with breakfast," he said, holding up a tray of coffee, fruit, and croissants. "Along with marching orders."

"Marching orders?"

"Ran into Christian. He says we've been granted permission to speak to the prisoner."

Cardinal Bernard.

"It's about time," she said.

Jordan gave her a mock scowl. "It wasn't like any of us were up to an interrogation last night."

True.

"When can we talk to him?"

"At eight o'clock . . . in about an hour." He crossed to the bed with the tray, sat down, and patted the mattress. "So how about I serve you breakfast in bed?"

She dropped next to him. "I think it only counts if we're naked."

He placed the tray on the nightstand. "I like that rule . . . and you know how I'm a stickler for rules."

He began to undo the buttons of his shirt.

7:20 A.M.

Elizabeth carefully changed the wine-soaked bandage on the stump of Rhun's left arm. She removed the old wrap and examined the wound. Already the skin knit over most of the raw muscle, but much still needed healing. She covered the damage with a compress soaked in holy wine, earning a small gasp of pain from Rhun, but still his eyes did not open.

Come back to me, Rhun.

She secured the compress with a fresh wrap, then leaned back. She sensed that the sun had risen an hour or so ago. She had spent the entire night with him in this windowless cell. It reeked of incense and wine, with a hint of hay and brick dust and reminded her of the time she had spent imprisoned here. Still, she stayed, wanting to be here when Rhun awoke.

She scowled at the room, finding it unfit.

The cell contained a simple wooden bed covered with a pallet of straw, a stand holding a lit beeswax candle, a flask of wine, clean white gauze, and jars of ointment that smelled of wine and resin. The room was a match to her own that neighbored this one, not that she had used it this long night.

The scuff of leather on stone drew her gaze to the small door. A short chubby monk with a gray friar's tonsure entered, carrying fresh wine and more bandages.

"Thank you, Friar Patrick."

"Anything for Rhun."

The friar had assisted her in her ministration of Rhun, coming and going throughout the night. Genuine sorrow crossed his face at the sight of Rhun's still form on the bed. He cared for Rhun, more than simply as a fellow Sanguinist. Perhaps the two were friends.

"You should take some rest, Sister Elizabeth," he offered for the eleventh time. "I can watch over him. If there's any change, I will inform you immediately."

She opened her mouth to refuse—when she felt a soft buzz from the pocket of her skirt, rising from the phone hidden there.

Tommy.

She had used many moments during the night—when she was alone—to try to call the boy, but she only heard the same mechanical voice over and over again, asking her to leave a message. She never had, fearing who might retrieve her words.

"Thank you, Friar Patrick." Elizabeth stood from her bedside stool. "I believe I shall go rest."

His expression was a mix of surprise and relief.

She gave him a bow, then turned on her heel and left the room. She crossed to the neighboring cell and closed the stout door. Only then did she pull out the phone. Words glowed on the small screen.

> *It's me.*
> *I saw that you called many times.*
> *Phone or text me*
> *when you're awake*
> *Trouble here.*
> 😫

She didn't understand how to respond to Tommy's message, nor did she understand the small symbol at the end. But she understood the word *trouble*.

Fearfully, she gripped the phone and dialed his number.

7:32 P.M.
Rome, Italy

C'mon, already . . .

Tommy sat on the closed seat of the bathroom toilet, the shower running noisily nearby. He wore only a towel. He stared at his phone, praying for Elizabeth to respond to his text. He watched the locked door, fearful of the guards out in the hallway of this apartment in the outskirts of Rome. The windows of the place were barred. The only way in or out was past a pair of Sanguinist priests, both wearing civilian clothes, who stood post before his door.

Finally, the phone vibrated in his hand.

He answered it immediately, keeping his voice down to a whisper. "Elizabeth?"

"Tommy, where are you? What's wrong?" As usual, the woman never bothered with the usual pleasantries that everyone else used on the phone.

"I'm somewhere in Rome."

"Are you in danger?"

"I don't think so, but something's wrong with this whole setup. The priest who came with me from Santa Barbara didn't take me to Vatican City. He dumped me in some apartment instead. It's locked up tight . . . with guards."

"Can you tell me anything about where they've taken you?"

"It's an old building. Yellow. Smells like garlic and fish. I'm on the third floor. I can see a river from the bedroom window and a fountain with a fish spewing water. Also I think there's a zoo nearby. At least, I heard lions roaring."

"Good. I should be able to find such a yellow building. It might take time, but I will get to you."

Tommy lowered his voice even more. "They say I'm in danger . . . from *you*, but I know that's wrong."

"I would never hurt you, but I will make them pay if you come to harm while under their care."

Tommy grinned. He had no doubt that she would come and kick their asses, but he didn't want to see her get hurt.

As the room grew steamy from the running shower, he listened for a moment to see if anyone noted their conversation before continuing. "I overheard them saying that Bernard wanted me kept under lock and key until you do what they want. I don't know if that's true or not. But if it is, don't give in to them."

"I will do what I need to do to get back to you. I will free you, and we will find a way to make you well again."

He sighed, baring his arm. The single melanoma lesion had multiplied, spreading like wildfire up his arm. He had new lesions on his legs and left buttock. With his angelic blood gone, it was like the cancer was making up for lost time.

"It's not so bad," he lied. "Just get tired easily, but they let me sleep."

"Save your strength."

Yeah, easier said than done.

Knuckles rapped against the bathroom door, making Tommy jump. He hadn't heard anyone approach, but those Sanguinists could move like ghosts.

"I gotta go," Tommy hissed. "I miss you."

"I . . . miss you as well."

He pressed the disconnect button, pushed the phone behind the toilet's water tank, and dashed into the shower. He splashed around loudly before shouting.

"Can't a guy take a shower in peace?"

"You've been in there a long time," a gruff voice said. "And I heard talking."

"I'm a teenager! Sheesh. I'm always talking to myself."

There was a long moment of silence, then his guard spoke in a more fatherly tone. He must have known Tommy was lying, covering something up, but the guy went for the wrong explanation.

"If you are touching yourself in there, young man, it is nothing to be embarrassed about. But you must confess such sins to your parish priest."

"First of all, I'm Jewish. Second of all, screw you!"

Tommy stood under the spray, his face hotter than the steam.

Okay, now I really do want to die.

7:35 P.M.
Castel Gandolfo, Italy

Elizabeth headed back to Rhun's room, resting a palm over her concealed phone. Anger flared inside her, but she banked it. When the time came to rescue Tommy, she must act with icy clarity. Emotion had no place until then.

She intended to confront the cardinal, but first she wanted to check on Rhun.

As she entered, she smoothed her skirt and adjusted her sleeves. She found Friar Patrick kneeling next to Rhun's bed, holding his hand.

The friar raised his head and beckoned her forward. "He still rests."

Stepping to the bed, she studied Rhun's face, relaxed in sleep. He looked much as he always had, untouched by the many years and tragedies that had made up his long life. Would that he had lived the life of an ordinary priest, dying with only a single lifetime of cares at the end. He did not deserve the fate that had been thrust upon him.

"I'm sure he'll rouse soon," Patrick continued. "The prompt care in the field saved his life."

She pictured Erin painting her blood over his wounds. As frail and mortal as she was, the archaeologist had saved him.

"You may sit and pray with me if you like," the friar offered.

She wanted to stay, but she glanced back at the wooden door. "I must speak with Cardinal Bernard first."

"I heard the others are meeting with him soon."

This she had not heard.

Anger built inside her, knowing what that villain had done with the ailing boy, turning him into a pawn.

She backed out of the room, then hurried down to the end of the corridor. A trio of unfamiliar Sanguinists—two men and a woman—guarded this section of the residence. But was it to protect Rhun or keep her in place?

She spoke to the woman, an African, with skin darker than Elizabeth had ever seen. "I must speak to Cardinal Bernard. I have information vital to the security of the order."

The woman's round eyes studied Elizabeth. "Access to the prisoner is restricted. Only his personal aide, Father Gregory, is permitted to speak to him, to attend to the cardinal's requests. I could give such a message to Father Gregory to pass on."

"I must speak with the cardinal myself."

The other's lips pinched. "Given his crimes against you, I'm afraid that is forbidden."

Elizabeth kept her voice soft, as meek as she could manage. "But I understand that my companions are scheduled to meet with him this morning. Surely, I may address him in the company of others?"

"The edict was firm." The nun's expression turned sterner. "As the victim in the charges against him, you are not to be allowed to see him under any circumstances."

"Then it appears I must permit my companions to pass on that information themselves." Elizabeth gave a small bow of her head, hiding her fury, and walked slowly back to her cell.

Once alone in her room, she slammed a palm against the brick wall.

I will make you pay for taking Tommy, Bernard . . . even if I have to destroy everything you hold dear.

A knock on the door drew her attention back around. Friar Patrick called through the stout planks, his voice stoked with happiness.

"Rhun . . . he wakes!"

25

Rhun struggled through a fog of pain and blood. He smelled wine, incense. He heard excited voices, naggingly familiar. His vision swam, then slowly settled to reveal a small room, lit by candlelight.

Where am I . . . ?

He tried to raise his head, but that only set the world to spinning even faster. Cold hands touched his forehead, encouraging him to lie back down.

"It's okay, Rhun, my son. Not too fast."

He focused on the gently smiling face, recognizing the friar.

"Patrick . . ."

"That's right." The friar turned enough to reveal someone bent behind him.

"You're finally awake, I see," Elizabeth said sternly, but her eyes shone with clear relief.

"I am."

He barely recognized his voice. It was deep and hoarse, the voice of another man, a weaker one. He tried to sit up, but he fell back as pain flared up along his left side. He gritted his teeth against it, reaching to massage the source—only to find nothing there. He turned to see.

My arm is gone.

The shock returned a kaleidoscope of memories: the bell shattering atop him, Erin pulling him to safety, fire and smoke closing in on them both.

That was as much as he recalled.

"What happened?" Rhun gasped out. "How are we in Castel Gandolfo? Why are we—?"

Elizabeth sank to a stool and took his right hand. He gripped her fingers, and she, in turn, squeezed reassurance.

He took several breaths, steadying himself. "How long have I been out?"

"Just the night." Elizabeth slowly explained all that had transpired, telling him what they had learned from John Dee's papers, and how they connected him to

Cardinal Bernard. "That's why we're here. To find out what he knows. But you, the famous Knight of Christ, need to rest."

She smiled at him.

He turned his head and studied the bandaged stump of his limb. "I remember . . ."

He let his voice die away, recalling a vague vision of writhing in pleasure, of hot fingers, steeped in blood, gripping him, bringing him to the height of rapture.

He stared up at Elizabeth. "Erin."

A wounded look shadowed her eyes. "Yes, it was the archaeologist who saved you. Used her blood to draw you back from the brink of death."

Patrick touched Elizabeth on the shoulder. "But it was you, my dear sister, who never left his side all night, tending to his wounds, ministering Christ's blood through his lips."

Rhun touched Elizabeth's knee. "Thank you."

She dismissed his gratitude with a toss of her head. "Erin and Jordan are scheduled to meet with Bernard this morning."

"When?"

Elizabeth glanced to Patrick, who checked his watch.

"In another twenty minutes or so," he said.

"I should be there." Rhun used his remaining arm

to push himself up. Agony flared, but he withstood it this time. "Where are my clothes?"

"I do not believe that is wise," Patrick said.

"Wise or not, I must go."

Recognizing his determination, Patrick slid an arm around his shoulders. The friar glanced to Elizabeth as Rhun's blanket slid down, exposing his naked state. "Perhaps, Sister, you should leave him to me for the moment."

Elizabeth turned to the pile of clothes, picked up a folded pair of trousers, and shook them out. "Not to be immodest, but who has been cleaning his wounds all night? I am not so faint a woman as to go weak at the sight of a naked man."

Patrick lowered his face, hiding a grin. "As you wish." The friar helped Rhun stand. "Go slowly."

It was sage advice. The room swayed as he attempted a few steps, but after several tries, he could soon stand on his own and move with little assistance. Still, he needed help dressing, especially with only one arm.

Once finished, Elizabeth knotted his loose sleeve and tucked it into his belt. She eyed him up and down. "You've looked better, Rhun."

"I've felt better."

Patrick took him by the elbow, helping steady him

toward the door. "I'll go with you, take you to where they are holding Cardinal Bernard."

Rhun glanced to Elizabeth. "Are you coming?"

She looked hopeful, but Friar Patrick quickly quashed it. "That is not allowed, I'm afraid. The cardinal has insisted that he will only speak with the trio of prophecy."

Elizabeth scoffed. "As a prisoner, can he set such conditions?"

"He can," Patrick answered. "He is not without his allies in the Holy See. Even now. I am truly sorry, Sister."

"So be it." Elizabeth crossed her arms, looking more defiant than the acquiescence of her words.

Rhun understood her frustration. Bernard had wronged her, stolen her very soul, and yet he was free to set the terms of their contact, while she was restricted and confined. Who truly was the prisoner here?

"Go," she said, dismissing them both, her words bitter. "Perhaps I shall take up needlepoint while I wait."

With no other choice but to leave her behind, Rhun headed out the door and down the corridor. Even with Patrick's support, he trailed fingers along the whitewashed bricks to keep his balance. His right arm was gone. Even though he could see the stump and feel the pain, he did not seem able to come to terms with his new state.

A new limb will grow.

He had seen such miracles in the past, but he also knew it might take years.

How can I properly protect Erin and Jordan in this maimed state? What will become of our quest?

Patrick led him through the papal residence, letting Rhun set the pace. Thankfully he grew stronger with every candlelit hall they crossed, every winding stair they climbed. Eventually, he walked free of Patrick's support, but the friar stuck to his side.

Rhun sensed his friend wished to speak. "What is it, Patrick? If you keep looking over your shoulder like that, you'll get a permanent crick in your neck."

Friar Patrick tucked his hands into his wide sleeves. "It concerns your *other* friend."

It took Rhun a moment to decipher his words. "The lion cub . . ."

He remembered the creature's plaintive cry, how the small cat had nudged the body of its dead mother.

"He has changed much. Growing far faster than any natural creature should." Patrick looked at him. "What haven't you told me about him?"

Rhun knew he could no longer keep the secret of the cub's birth. "His mother was a *blasphemare*."

Patrick drew to a sudden stop in the hallway, forcing Rhun to do the same. "Why didn't you tell me?"

Shame flared through him. "I thought if you believed the cub to be tainted you wouldn't take him in."

"Nonsense. He is clearly not *tainted*. If anything, I'd say he is *blessed*."

"What do you mean?"

"I have never seen his like before. He is a gentle soul. Full of mischief, yes, but there is no corruption. I see only a sweetness about him."

Rhun felt a deep measure of relief. He had sensed the cub's essential goodness back in the desert, and he was glad to hear it borne out. "I've wondered about him since I found him."

"And do you know anything more about him?"

"Very little. His mother was badly wounded by the angelic blast following the battle in Egypt. I suspect the cub was spared in her womb, a testament to its innocence. And perhaps some of that angelic essence was instilled into him."

Patrick touched his arm. "I don't doubt it. Thank you for sharing this miracle with me. I never thought to see its like, a creature the mirror opposite of the *blasphemare*, a beast blessed by purity. It is a wonder."

"Can you still keep it a secret . . . at least for now?"

"Do not trouble yourself on that account." Patrick

waved ahead and set them in motion again. "I am happy to have this miracle all to my own for now."

They continued through to a far corner of the residence.

"The cardinal is being kept in a private apartment around the next corner," Patrick said.

As they turned into another hall, Rhun spotted a pair of Sanguinists, both hooded and cloaked, with blades drawn, at the end of the passage. They guarded a stout wooden door, marking Bernard's current prison cell.

Rhun started toward it, noting the windows lining the way looked out upon the blue majesty of neighboring Lake Albano. Rare Renaissance paintings dotted the walls, their oils aglow in the sunlight. He imagined Bernard's *cell* had the same view and was likely equally well appointed.

The cardinal certainly did have allies who were looking after him.

A call rose from behind, coming from another hallway that ended here.

"Rhun!"

He turned to see Erin rushing forward, her jacket winging open. Jordan stalked after her, looking less thrilled to see him.

"Shouldn't you still be in bed?" the big man said as they gathered together in the hall.

Friar Patrick bowed his head toward Erin and shook Jordan's hand. "He has mended well enough for now, but I'll trust the two of you to take charge of him from here." The friar turned to Rhun. "I will leave you with your companions. But I will be on the estate should you need the council of an old fool such as myself."

"You have never been a fool," Rhun answered.

Friar Patrick shrugged, tucked his hands into his sleeves, and walked briskly away.

Erin's eyes studied Rhun anxiously as they headed toward the guarded doors. "How do you feel?"

"Stronger," he answered truthfully. "It seems I have you to thank for my life."

She gave him a small smile. "It was my turn."

"Gotta admit," Jordan said, "for a guy who counts his birthdays by the centuries, you're a tough old nut."

Rhun felt himself relaxing in their camaraderie. Admittedly, they were a team that had survived much together, but they were more than that.

They were friends.

As they reached the doors, the guards parted. From under his hood, one spoke, sounding none too happy at their intrusion, nor to whom they had come to see.

"The cardinal has been expecting you," the guard said, his contempt for the prisoner plain.

The other guard removed a large key from under

his cloak and unlocked the door. He did not bother to open it.

Rhun shifted forward, but his balance betrayed him. Erin caught his arm.

Jordan moved to the door and shoved it open, speaking to the guards. "You both need to work on your hospitality skills. Trust me, my Yelp review about this place will sting."

Jordan held the door for Erin and Rhun.

They passed into a sumptuous entry hall, decorated with plump furniture and heavy silk drapery. Beyond that space, a short passage led to bedrooms, a small parlor, and a powder room. The place was kept dark, except for candlelight glowing through a door at the end. Rhun heard a faint voice rising from there. The words were too inaudible to understand, but the accent was unmistakable.

Bernard.

Was someone with him? Patrick had told him on the way up that Bernard's assistant, Father Gregory, had been coming and going at all hours of the day and night, likely running errands for the cardinal as the man fought to keep his position, to control the gears that his sin had set in motion.

Jordan heard the cardinal, too, and strode briskly down the hall. He took in the surroundings as he went. "Talk about a pretty bird cage," he mumbled sourly.

Rhun followed.

Erin hovered at his side, clearly worried about his stability, but he waved her forward.

Jordan reached the half-closed door first and rapped a knuckle on it. When his knock went unchallenged, Jordan pushed inside. Erin kept close at his heels, plainly full of questions for Bernard.

Rhun hurried after them. He had much to ask Bernard himself about his lies and half-truths, especially concerning the cardinal's old friend, the crusader Hugh de Payens.

As Rhun slipped into the room, he saw the disheveled state of Bernard's temporary desk, the pools of melted candle wax on top, the heavy silk drapes that had been tied closed over the windows.

Something's not—

The door slammed shut behind him.

He turned too slowly to block the shoulder that rammed into him, knocking him to the floor. Agony lanced through him as he landed on his left side, jarring his stump and closing his vision to a knot.

A dark shape sped past him and struck Jordan a blow to the skull with the bust of a statue. As Jordan collapsed, Erin was grabbed and tossed over the desk, where she hit a draped window and crashed to the floor.

Before Rhun could even sit up, a hand grasped his neck with iron-strong fingers and yanked him high, until only his toes brushed the carpet.

A ghastly chuckle cut through his pain.

Cardinal Bernard leered at him. His scarlet robes hung in tatters on his nearly naked form. Madness crazed his brown eyes.

"Welcome, Knight of Christ . . . welcome to your ruin."

26

Dazed by the sudden attack, Erin grabbed the edge of the desk and pulled herself up, ignoring the ache in her side. Her flung body had knocked over the lone candle. The room was now dark, lit only by filtered light coming from the shuttered windows.

Her first thought was: *strigoi.*

She stumbled to the window behind her and yanked on the drapes. A sash had been knotted over them, keeping them from opening completely, but she managed to part the heavy silk enough to bring sunlight into the room.

Twisting back around, she saw an impossible sight. Cardinal Bernard had Rhun clutched by the throat, pinned against a bookcase. Rags of scarlet draped the man's nearly naked body, revealing scores of scratches on the white skin beneath, as if he had torn his own robes from his shoulders in a rage.

On the rug behind them, a figure lay unmoving on the floor, blood seeping from his scalp.

Jordan . . .

Rhun seemed to recover from his surprise. A silver blade appeared in his right hand and bit deep into the cardinal's arm. Fingers released his throat. As Rhun slumped down the bookcase, he lashed at the cardinal—but only swiped through empty air.

Bernard was already across the room, ripping a sword from the wall. The unearthly speed with which he moved told her that the cardinal no longer obeyed the vows of a Sanguinist. Like the *strigoi*, his power sprang from a darker source.

What had happened?

Jordan stirred, his eyes fluttering open. In the darkness, they shone with a faint golden gleam.

Before Jordan could gather his wits, Bernard rushed Rhun.

Rhun leaped to the side, crashing clumsily into a giant Chinese vase. His natural grace was plainly thrown off balance by his missing arm.

She drew a dagger from an inner sheath in her jacket, ready to defend the others. But she wasn't a fighter. Her best weapon was her mind. Bernard went after Rhun again, but Jordan broadsided the cardinal, knocking him over a large standing globe.

As the cardinal sprang back up with a snarl—his body framed in a sliver of sunlight—Erin searched his exposed nakedness, looking for a telltale black handprint.

Nothing.

She wasn't surprised.

How could Legion have possessed the cardinal? Especially while the man was imprisoned here? But if Legion wasn't the source of this corruption, what was?

Must think . . .

Jordan joined Rhun, both facing down the raving beast that was the cardinal.

Erin studied the room, searching for whatever held the cardinal in thrall. Her gaze swept across the chaos atop his desk. She saw nothing unusual: papers, books, a leather-bound journal. She looked around the base of the desk. As she did so, her toe nudged a black pouch on the floor. Something rolled out the open end.

A piece of black glass.

It seemed to exude darkness. She had seen such a poisonous artifact before: in the Egyptian desert. Rhun had recently led a team to rid the sands of such evil. She dropped to a knee, knowing what rested on the carpet.

A drop of Lucifer's blood.

She used a piece of paper to scoop the stone up, while grabbing the ties of the bag. Straightening, she rolled that black tear into the pool of sunlight atop the desk and emptied the pouch's contents beside it. The pile of dark drops seemed to suck in the light, creating little voids in the fabric of the universe. She didn't need to touch them to sense their malignancy, their *wrongness.*

But how could she vanquish it?

Sunlight clearly had no effect.

And why should it?

Millennia ago, these drops of Lucifer's blood had fused with the Egyptian sand, creating a black glass that sealed in their malevolence, protected the darkness within from the light of the sun. If two thousand years of desert heat hadn't harmed them, then simple Italian sunlight wouldn't have any effect.

But what if—

Her eyes fell on a toppled stone paperweight on the corner of Bernard's desk. It was in the shape of an angel—but more important, it was *heavy.*

She grabbed it, lifted it high, and smashed it down on a dull black drop, shattering it to dust.

Across the room, Bernard howled and hissed.

So you feel that, do you?

She lifted the paperweight again and again, crushing drop after drop. With each strike, a tendril of black smoke rose up from the crystalline powder. It swirled in a circle, snaking away from the exposure of the sun, then over the edge of the desk, where it plunged through the floor.

She remembered Elizabeth's recounting how the essence of a *strigoi* would do the same upon the beast's death, returning to its source.

Lucifer.

As she shattered the last obsidian piece, Cardinal Bernard gave out a final gasp, toppling over, his body thudding to the floor.

8:12 A.M.

Rhun knelt over Bernard's body, his knife at the cardinal's throat, ready to kill his old friend. Jordan had collected the abandoned sword and stood guard by his shoulder. By now, the two cloaked guards had rushed into the room, sweeping in with weapons bared, drawn by the clatter of the brief fight.

Fearing what other evil might be about, Rhun shouted. "Guard the doors! Let no one in without my word!"

They gave him curt nods and returned to their posts.

As Rhun watched, madness faded from the cardinal's eyes. It was replaced with something that Rhun had never seen there before.

Doubt.

Rhun leaned back, lifting his blade away, but keeping it ready.

Bernard sat up, gathering the shreds of his robes around himself, as if trying to do the same with his dignity. He ended with his hands trembling in his lap.

Erin came over, still holding a small angelic sculpture. The bottom was cracked, coated with black dust. "It was those drops of Lucifer's blood."

Rhun nodded, understanding. "I left them after I returned from Egypt. Locked up in the cardinal's safe. It's my fault."

"No . . ." Bernard shook his head. "It was my hubris, believing I could dabble with such darkness and remain untouched."

"But why mess with them in the first place?" Jordan asked.

"I hoped to learn something from them, something about Lucifer." Bernard stared at Rhun. "Last night, when Father Gregory brought word that you were headed back from Prague, that you were coming with questions about stones associated with Lucifer, I remembered what you had brought back from Egypt."

"The glass stones," Rhun said.

"I was going to wait until you were all here before examining them, but after Father Gregory fetched them for me from my safe in my old offices, they called to me. I could not resist."

Rhun nodded, turning to the others. "I saw the same affliction strike members of the team who had traveled with me to Egypt."

Bernard stared around, a hand rising to touch his forehead in confusion. "I don't know how long I was under its power. It took me, but it gave nothing in return."

"But you're free now," Erin said. "And we have questions."

"About Hugh de Payens," Bernard said with a sad nod. "Father Gregory informed me of this, too. You want the truth about my friend."

Erin brought a gentler tone to her voice, possibly responding to the pain and sorrow in the cardinal's voice when he mentioned this figure from his past. "So Hugh didn't die, as you claimed, during the Second Crusades?"

Bernard's voice was barely above a whisper. "He did not."

Erin held an arm toward the cardinal, helping him up. "Jordan, fetch him a blanket."

Rhun guided Bernard to a set of chairs by the fireplace, careful of the broken pieces of vase on the floor. Jordan returned from a neighboring bedroom with a woolen throw and handed it to Bernard, who wrapped his nakedness, sighing his gratitude, slowly regaining some of his dignity. He looked, again, like the man Rhun had known so long.

Erin sat in a chair across from Bernard, leaning forward. "Tell us what really happened."

Bernard looked at the cold fireplace, his gaze still lost, slipping into the past. "Hugh took me in when I was a savage beast. He prayed for me when I was lost."

Rhun had not heard this story. "Are you saying he was the one who converted you, brought you into the Sanguinist fold?"

A small nod confirmed this.

Rhun knew such a monumental act's significance, how it could deeply bond a pair. It was, in fact, Bernard who had brought Rhun to this holy path, becoming his mentor and friend, and despite the cardinal's recent actions, he would always owe Bernard a debt of gratitude. The bonds between Bernard and Hugh de Payens must have been equally strong.

"I was a lost savage until he saved me," Bernard continued. "Together we brought many into the order. Many. We founded the Knights Templar. We did much good."

"Nine men, bound by blood," Erin said quietly. "A Sanguinist order of warrior monks."

"What were these Sanguinist Templars exactly?" Jordan asked.

Bernard glanced to the big man, a touch of pride stiffening his bowed back. "We were a knighthood within a knighthood, capable of fighting a double battle against both the adversaries born of flesh and those spirits risen out of evil. Our armor was our faith, as much as it was our chain mail. We feared neither men nor demons."

"So you truly are Bernard of Clairvaux?" Erin asked.

"I am. And together, Hugh and I performed great acts, uniting the scattered Templars under a single banner, giving them unity and strength of purpose." Bernard stared around at them. "You must understand, Hugh was a great leader. Charismatic, sympathetic, empathetic. Men and Sanguinist fell in line behind him, willing to give their lives upon his word. But over time, it became too much."

"I knew men like that," Jordan said. "The characteristics that make a man a good leader—like empathy—sometimes make them more susceptible to battle fatigue, to PTSD."

"What happened to Hugh?" Erin asked.

Bernard sighed heavily. "He abandoned the Templars. After the Second Crusades." He stared at Rhun. "In truth, he left our order entirely."

"He left the Sanguinists?" Rhun could not hide his shock.

Sanguinists didn't *leave*. They were either killed in service to the Church, or they forsook from their vows, returning to their unholy natures so that they had to be hunted down and slain. The only Sanguinist who had escaped such a fate was Rasputin, who had built his own twisted version of the order within the Russian Orthodox Church, safely entrenched in the city of St. Petersburg, beyond the reach of the Sanguinists.

But apparently there had been one other.

"Where did he go?" Rhun asked.

Bernard looked to his hands. "He sojourned far and wide at first, alone, both hermit and nomad. Eventually he settled in the remote mountains of France, to a hermitage of his own making. There, he found some measure of peace, discovering grace in the wild places of the world."

"So what are you saying?" Rhun asked. "That he reverted to a *strigoi*?"

Bernard shook his head.

Rhun struggled to understand. "Then how did he come to live beyond the protection of the Church?"

"He simply did," Bernard answered evasively, not meeting Rhun's eye.

It was Erin who clarified some of this story. "That's why you spread the lie of his death, wasn't it? Hugh de Payens abandoned the order, but he didn't return to his savage ways. He found his own path to grace, independent of the Church."

Rhun stared at her, unable to accept her words. There could be no other path to grace than humble service to the Church. He and all the Sanguinists had been taught this simple truth since the days of Lazarus.

"I could let no one know," Bernard explained. "What if more Sanguinists were to leave the order? So I made up a story of a noble death, of a life given in service to the Church. But that was only half the reason for the lie"

"What's the other half?" Erin asked.

"When Hugh spoke of leaving the order, I knew that they would kill him for it. To save him, I made up that story." Bernard looked to Rhun, as if searching for absolution. "I lied to the order. I lied to the Church. But they would have hunted him down like an animal, and he was no animal. He was my friend."

Rhun settled heavily to another chair, weakened both by his injuries and by the revelations.

This Sanguinist had found grace outside the Church.

Rhun's mind whirled. He had joined the Sanguinists because he had thought that it was the only way to live with his curse. The choice offered to him had been a simple one: die as a *strigoi* or live as a man of the cloth, helping to protect others. At the time, centuries ago, Rhun had already been on the road to the priesthood, studying in a seminary, so his decision had been an easy one: he would serve. He had thought it the only way.

When Rasputin had left the Church nearly a century ago and built up an army of followers strong enough to protect him from the Church's justice, Rhun's faith had not faltered. Rasputin's life was one of wickedness and deceit, and Rhun would not follow his example. But to hear that there might be another path frightened him and made him angry.

He stared toward the sunlight flowing through the windows.

Has my entire existence been a lie?

8:25 A.M.

Erin noted how Rhun sagged in his chair, reading the forlorn look etched on his face. She knew he had been through too much. He had nearly died and lost his arm, but she suspected this news was a deeper wound, one that would take some time to heal, if it ever did. She could almost see Rhun's foundation and faith in the Church crumbling beneath him.

But for now, they had more pressing matters to discuss.

She confronted Bernard. "Does Hugh still live?"

"He does."

Rhun looked sharply at Bernard, but the cardinal would not meet his eye.

"He still maintains his remote hermitage in those mountains," Bernard admitted.

"Do you know anything about the stones?" Erin nodded to Jordan, who pulled out the pieces of green diamond. "Hugh gave this one to John Dee, and maybe two more like it."

"I know nothing. It was why I thought to dabble with those cursed drops."

Jordan pocketed the diamond. "So it sounds like we're going to have to go to the horse's mouth. Pay this old guy a visit, if we want any answers."

Exactly.

"Tell us how we can find him," Erin urged.

Bernard lifted a hand, but he let it drop to his knee in a gesture of defeat. "One does not simply *request* an audience with Hugh de Payens. He has no interest in worldly concerns, and his hermitage is well guarded."

"Guarded?" Jordan frowned. "How?"

"What you must understand, what made Payens such a great leader, was his ability to read another's heart, to know them often better than they know themselves. And it wasn't just the hearts of men. He had a keen affinity for all God's creatures and became a great admirer of St. Francis of Assisi."

"The patron saint of nature and animals," Erin said.

She knew of the legends associated with the Italian saint, how even the birds would flock to listen to his preaching, landing on his shoulders. It was said Francis even tamed a wild wolf that was terrorizing a village. It made sense that Hugh would admire such a figure.

Bernard looked down, a wistful smile on his face, revealing how much he truly loved this man. "It was said in jest that Hugh could talk to animals. During the Crusades, the warhorses would follow him around like dogs. They would do anything for Hugh—charge into the thickest fighting or even into fire if he commanded it. I think . . . I think their blood stained his hands more heavily than the blood of the men who died alongside him. To Hugh's mind, they were innocents, slaughtered for their loyalty to him. Eventually, it became too much."

Erin could understand that all too well, flashing back to the deaths of her former students in Egypt.

"Eventually Hugh could not bring himself to kill even the *blasphemare*."

"I thought you had to kill all cursed creatures," Jordan said. "That you had shoot-on-sight orders."

"We do," Rhun said. "They are beasts corrupted by evil. And, unlike *strigoi*, they cannot be turned to good. To end their suffering, they must be destroyed."

"But do you know that for sure?" Erin asked, recognizing now more than ever how many of these set-in-stone edicts were wrong. "Why can't there be different paths to salvation for those poor animals? Maybe even for the *strigoi* themselves?"

"Hugh would have agreed with you," Bernard said. "I suspect it is that sentiment that perhaps explains why *blasphemare* are drawn to his hermitage. They come from far and wide, lone creatures severed from their blood-bonded creators, who seek the comfort and protection he offers."

"What?" Rhun sat straighter, looking horrified.

"And not just such tainted creatures," Bernard said, "but *strigoi*, too."

Rhun stood up. "And you kept this secret from us all?"

"Let me guess," Jordan exclaimed, "when you said his place was *guarded*, that's what you meant. He has an army of *strigoi* and *blasphemare* loyal to him, guarding him."

Bernard bowed his head, acknowledging this truth.

"Great," Jordan mumbled.

Bernard stared at them. "But I tell you this because it also offers you a way to reach him." He turned to Rhun. "You yourself have brought the *key* that will unlock Hugh's heart."

27

Jordan watched the cardinal lower the phone atop his desk.

"It is done," Bernard said, then crossed back to his chair on legs that were still shaky. "The key will be brought here."

Jordan glanced at Rhun, waiting for some explanation. Erin knelt next to Rhun's seat, checking the bandages on his stump. The gauze was stained with fresh blood from the recent fight. Rhun had once told Jordan that all sensations were heightened in a Sanguinist, including pain. If that was true, Jordan could only imagine the agony Rhun must be suffering now.

"Okay, Cardinal," Jordan said, "how about you tell us more about how Hugh's place is guarded, what we might be facing?"

Bernard rubbed his chin. "To understand that, you have to understand Hugh's philosophy. I had many long talks with Hugh on this very subject before he abandoned the order. When it came to *blasphemare*—or *strigoi*, for that matter—he came to believe that they were all God's creatures, whose only sin was that their innocence had been stolen from them."

"He might have a point," Erin said. "It's not like either really had a say regarding their corruption. It was usually forced upon them against their will."

"It does not matter," Bernard argued. "We are all born with Original Sin, a sin that stains our innocent souls because of the defiance committed by Adam and Eve in the Garden of Eden. It is only through the holy rite of baptism that this sin is cleansed from us."

Erin didn't look swayed by this argument.

"At the time," Bernard continued, "I thought Hugh's arguments were only theoretical in nature. Then when he left, wandering the world, I heard not a single word from him. I assumed that he had perished, as so many do without the protection of the Church."

"But he survived," Jordan said.

"One day, I received a letter from him. He told me that he had settled in the mountains of France, that he had found his peace in caring for the lost and broken creatures of the world."

"That includes both *blasphemare* and *strigoi*?" Erin asked.

Bernard nodded. "I told no one. Hugh only wished to be left alone—to live on his mountain like St. Francis of Assisi. I only tolerated it because he forbade killing on its slopes. Not even those under his protection are allowed to kill unless provoked to defend their hermitage."

Jordan didn't like the sound of that. "Even with this supposed key in hand, how do you propose we get through that gauntlet?"

"You must go to his mountain, not to lay siege, but as supplicants." Bernard stared hard at Jordan, then Rhun. "Which means you must take care not to *harm* anything that confronts you on that mountain, no matter how sorely you are pressed. If you fail doing that, not only will Hugh refuse to see you, but you'll likely be struck down before ever leaving those forested slopes."

"So we're supposed to climb a mountain full of monsters," Jordan said, "and turn the other cheek when they try to attack us."

Bernard held up a finger. "And you must come bearing a gift, one that Hugh will never be able to refuse."

What could that be?

"Once you have his attention," the cardinal stressed, "it will be up to you to convince him to help you, to prove your mission is a worthy one, one that serves the interests of all—not just the Sanguinists, but *all* God's creatures."

"So a walk in the park," Jordan said. "And we only have a day or so to convince him to help us save the world."

Bernard frowned, looking confused.

Erin explained. "From a painting we saw in Edward Kelly's lab, we think we have until noon or so on the vernal equinox to stop Lucifer from breaking free of his chains."

Jordan checked his watch as she explained more details about this deadline. "That leaves us roughly twenty-seven hours."

"But it might not be *this* year's vernal equinox," Erin offered. "That mural was painted centuries ago. Who knows for sure what inspired it?"

Bernard wasn't buying it—neither was Jordan, for that matter.

"Matters grow worse around the world with every passing hour," the cardinal said. "The balance between good and evil is tilting toward ruin. Even the stars are aligning against us, suggesting tomorrow's equinox is important."

"What omen?" Erin asked.

"Have you not heard?" he asked.

"We've been busy," Jordan said.

"There is to be a solar eclipse . . . only a partial one."

Erin frowned. "The sun painted in that mural was bloodred. Maybe the artist was trying to signify an eclipse."

Before it could be discussed further, a knock sounded from the front of the apartment. They all turned as the entry door swung open down the hall.

One of the guards stepped halfway through and called to them, his voice oddly nervous. "Father Korza, this visitor says he was summoned by you. That you wanted to see *both* of them."

The guard stepped aside, revealing the first visitor: the pudgy shape of Friar Patrick entered. Rhun stood up, raising his arm in welcome.

So who else had the friar—

A snowy shape bounded past the friar's legs, almost bowling the man over.

Jordan blinked in surprise at the sight. The creature was a half-grown lion, the size of a German shepherd, with snowy fur, silvery claws, and golden-brown eyes.

As the lion charged toward them down the short hall, Jordan shifted to protect Erin. But the cat immediately pounced on Rhun, knocking him to the floor, licking the priest's face.

Jordan heard a most peculiar sound.

Rhun was laughing.

Then the cub looked up at Jordan and bounded in one leap, sniffing around his ankles, up his legs. Jordan had to push the inquisitive lion's nose from his crotch.

"Yeah, hello to you, too." Jordan swung to Bernard, remembering his story about Hugh de Payens's love of animals. "Let me guess. Here is your *key* to your friend's heart."

Bernard gazed upon the animal with clear longing. "This beast is so much more than that."

Jordan dropped down to one knee and rubbed his fingers into the scruff of its immature mane. He would be a stunning adult. The cat responded, bumping his head against Jordan's forehead.

When their heads touched, a jolt shot through Jordan's body. The scarring across his shoulder and chest flared with fire.

What the hell?

The golden eyes locked on to his, and Jordan couldn't look away, sensing a kindred spirit, one similarly touched by the angels.

Bernard was right.

You certainly are much more than you seem, little guy.

Then the lion growled at him, baring fangs.

9:04 A.M.

Rhun reached for the young lion, surprised by his sudden aggression toward Jordan. But before his fingers could grab the animal, the cat twisted and bounded away. Trailing a growl, the animal stalked back out into the hall. The hackles along his snowy back stood on end.

Friar Patrick watched his behavior and held up a hand. "Leave him be! He's caught some scent!"

The lion turned off the hall into one of the dark bedrooms.

"I was just in there to get a blanket," Jordan said. "Room's empty."

In case his friend was wrong, Rhun retrieved his *karambit* from the floor and followed the hunting cat. The others hovered behind him.

"Patrick," Rhun called to the friar, "fetch the guards."

The lion padded low to the ground, tail swishing angrily. He led the way to a standing antique wardrobe on one side of the bed. The growl died as its gaze remained fixed on the doors.

Something's in there.

Rhun waited until he heard the guards join them, then edged past the cat.

Jordan came up on the cub's other side, his sword in one hand. He reached his free hand to the wardrobe's handle. He glanced to Rhun, his eyes questioning.

Rhun nodded.

Jordan tugged the door open—and a small, dark figure burst out at them. It shouldered hard into Jordan, knocking him back against the bed's frame. Rhun lashed out with his curved blade, slicing flesh, but only dealt it a glancing blow.

The attacker moved with the preternatural speed of a *strigoi*. But Rhun caught a flash of a white collar. A Sanguinist.

Bernard shoved Erin to the side, then spun—grabbing one of the guard's swords and swinging full around, catching the lurker in the neck. The head went flying into the hall, while the body toppled to the floor. Rhun glanced around the room to make sure there were no other threats.

"Lights!" Bernard shouted and pointed his sword. "Open those hall drapes!"

The two guards stripped the heavy silk from the windows. Fresh sunlight flowed into the hall.

Bernard crossed and turned over the head to view the face of their attacker. The cardinal fell back a step in shock. "It's Father . . . Father Gregory."

Rhun drew Bernard away, pulling him toward the office, away from the head of his former assistant. Rhun called to the guards. "Search the rest of the apartment. And the body. Look for any black marks upon his skin."

The others followed Rhun back into the office, even the cat.

Erin stood, hugging her arms around her chest, her eyes shining with the knowledge that nowhere was safe any longer. Rhun wished that he could comfort her, but she was right.

Bernard spoke, his voice slightly trembling. "Could . . . could it be the drops of Lucifer's blood? Maybe he was afflicted like I was. Gregory did bring them to me."

"No," Erin said with certainty. "Your assistant would've been freed when I destroyed the stones. Like you were. I think it more likely that he brought you those stones on purpose last night knowing the evil would claim you. Some other darkness held him in thrall."

Confirmation came when one of the guards returned to the door. "The other rooms are clear. But we found a black handprint on the base of Father Gregory's spine."

"Legion," Erin said.

"So his evil still lives." Rhun had feared as much.

"Apparently so." Erin stared down the hall. "And if he was spying on our conversation, we have to assume he now knows as much as we do."

Jordan crossed to her side. "Then we need to get to Hugh before Legion reaches him."

Bernard nodded. "You have one advantage."

"What's that?" Jordan asked.

The cardinal stared down at the lion. "He is a blessed creature."

Surprised, Rhun glanced to Patrick.

"I did not divulge our secret," the friar said.

"That is the truth, Rhun," Bernard said, as if Rhun would trust the cardinal. "But nothing is far from the eyes and ears of those loyal to me, both here and at the Vatican. Besides, a lion on the papal premises is not something to pass unnoticed. Especially this one."

Bernard placed a hand on the cub's head, but the animal shook it off.

A clear sign of good judgment.

"He is a creature utterly new," Bernard said, "and that is why he will fascinate Hugh de Payens."

The lion rubbed against Rhun's thighs, a loud purr rising from his chest. Rhun touched his silky head. Smiling, Erin held out a hand. The cub sniffed, then bumped his nose playfully into her palm.

"Where did you find him?" she asked.

Rhun told a quick version of the story, ending with, "I believe it was that angelic fire that spared the cub in the womb and blessed his current form."

"If you're right," Jordan said, his gaze thoughtful upon the beast, "then that would mean it was that same fire that healed me, a gift from Tommy." He looked down at the cub. "Sort of makes us blood brothers, little fella."

Rhun stared between Jordan and the lion. Both were indeed blessed from the same font. Perhaps there was a reason they were brought together in the same room. He took hope from that small bit of providence.

But at the same time, he felt a trickle of fear, knowing their adversary was still out there, the dark mirror to the brightness found here. The enemy had managed to infiltrate the very heart of their order, to poison it.

So whom could they trust?

Rhun stared at Erin and Jordan, knowing one certainty.

I can place my trust in them, in their hearts.

28

Legion felt the severing of that black tendril, cut
by silver. As it withered and retracted, it returned his
awareness to the darkness of an icy cellar beneath an
old building in Prague. Those that lived in the floors
above were already dead, their heartbeats forever
silenced.

He opened his lips and let more blood run over his
parched tongue, down his burnt throat. His servants
were few now, only those whom Legion could still hold
firm to when his vessel was so damaged. The gaping
wound through his chest had already closed. His
broken bones callused and healed. His fire-blackened

skin peeled in great sheets, shedding their past like a snake.

But he held on to that past, letting it burn through him as surely as the fire had seared this frail body.

He remembered claws and teeth dragging him from the smoking rubble of that malevolent house. He was pulled down steps into darkness. He knew his benefactor. It slumbered next to him, heaving great breaths, but still alert, still protecting him.

The grimwolf.

Once here, Legion had uncoiled his shadows from around the faded flame of Leopold, where he had been forced to protect that ember of life, stoking it back to a small flame. If Leopold had died, Legion's foothold in this world would have evaporated, casting him back into formless darkness. So he nurtured that flame, preserving this vessel. It had taken all of his efforts and concentration, costing him many of his branches, freeing those he had previously enslaved.

But not all of them.

While the tree had starved, withering away its branches, the root had survived.

And I will grow anew, all the stronger for it.

After the wolf had dragged him here, Legion had reached to those who still bore his yoke and drew them to this place, slaughtering everything above, bringing fresh blood to revive and strengthen his vessel. He searched out other eyes, finding how many remained across other lands, reaching those who had not broken free when he fell. He set them in motion, toward a single direction.

All except one.

Legion had pulled his awareness into a priest within the Sanguinist order. He had marked the man before he left Rome. He had learned of him from the Sanguinist whom he had branded in the shadow of the Vatican's walls. It had been so simple to lure that other out into the open, exploiting the simple trust of the victim in the fellow Sanguinist who led him to Legion.

How that priest had screamed when he first saw Legion—but it had ended when the man was held down, stripped of his robes, and Legion placed his palm on the priest's lower back, hiding his mark there.

Through those same eyes and ears he had spied upon his enemy, learning what they knew.

What I know now . . .

His attempt to corrupt them with the black blood of the dark angel might have failed in Prague, but he knew where they were headed next.

Where I will go . . .

To find the stones.

He needed all three, to multiply their power in order to forge the key to Lucifer's chains. Then he would bring the reign of mankind to a fiery end.

His hand found the wolf next to him, reading the wildness behind the corruption, making a promise to it.

I will return paradise to you—and to myself.

Your new dark king.

Fifth

The wolf also shall dwell with the lamb, and
the leopard shall lie down with the kid; and
the calf and the young lion and the fatling
together; and a little child shall lead them.
And the cow and the bear shall feed; their young
ones shall lie down together: and the lion shall
eat straw like the ox.
And the sucking child shall play on the hole of the
asp, and the weaned child shall put his hand in
the cockatrice's den.
They shall not hurt nor destroy in all my holy
mountain: for the earth shall be full of the
knowledge of the Lord, as the waters cover
the sea.

—Isaiah 11:6—9

29

March 19, 2:14 P.M. CET
Pyrenees Mountains, France

Jordan stood in the open meadow, as the helicopter's engines whined down behind him. He took in a deep draw of the pine-scented breeze flowing down the tall mountain before him. Winter snow still frosted its granite pinnacle, while below verdant spring forest fringed its slopes, glowing in every shade of emerald under the afternoon sun.

"Got to say," Jordan concluded, "crazy or not, this guy picked a beautiful patch of God's green earth to make his home."

Erin joined him, moving stiffly through the clover and grass. The fall through the roof in Prague had

clearly taken its toll. She needed more time to heal—
time they didn't have. He looked at the sun, knowing
they hoped to be out of these mountains before the
sun set.

He glanced behind to his fellow teammates. The
Sanguinists looked little better than Erin: Rhun
moved awkwardly with his missing arm, Sophia had
a slash across her face, and Christian's long sleeves hid
bandages.

The last member of their group appeared to be the
strongest of the Sanguinists. Elizabeth had shed her
religious garb for hiking boots, pants, and a knee-
length black leather coat. She could easily be mistaken
for some day hiker, eager to tackle this mountain.
They had brought the countess along because of her
past history with Hugh de Payens. They needed every
advantage.

Including bringing along the team's mascot.

Rhun had freed the lion from a crate in the back
of the helicopter, and it gamboled across the field,
chasing a blue butterfly. Jordan noted Rhun's soft
smile as he took in the carefree nature of the young
lion, how it erased the lines of tension and pain that
had marked the priest's face during the flight. Jordan
had never seen anything that made Rhun as relaxed as
that big cat.

Christian finished securing the aircraft and headed over to them. "This is as close as we can get. According to Bernard, Hugh de Payens allows no modern vehicles past this point."

It was a sobering reminder that they were in the middle of enemy territory.

The plan was for Christian to remain behind with the aircraft, both to guard against anyone tampering with the helicopter and to be close by if a quick evacuation off the mountain became necessary.

Erin stared up at the mountain, shadowing her eyes from the glare off the snowy peak. "Where do we go from here?"

Rhun pulled out a map, and they clustered around it. He tapped a point on the topographic map, a fair distance up the mountain, where a river coursed down its face, tumbling from the snowline into a series of pools and waterfalls.

"The exact location of Hugh's hermitage is unknown, but Bernard believes it lies somewhere in this area. We'll head there and hope for the best."

"I wager this Monsieur de Payens already knows we're here," Elizabeth said. "Our arrival in the helicopter was not a quiet one."

"That's why we're adhering to the Boy's Scout motto," Jordan said. "Be prepared."

For anything.

Jordan hiked the shoulder strap of his Heckler & Koch MP7 machine pistol higher on his shoulder. He also had a holstered Colt 1911 sidearm, loaded with silver ammunition, and a silver-plated dagger strapped to his ankle.

While Jordan took to heart the warning from Bernard—*no killing*—he didn't want *turning the other cheek* to be his only option in a fight.

The others were equally armed. Erin had her own Colt 1911, and the Sanguinists had all manner of knives and blades sheathed on their bodies.

"Let's move out," Jordan said. "Before we burn any more sunlight."

As a group, they marched across the meadow toward the tree line, led by their enthusiastic mascot. The chirping of birds greeted them when they entered the shadowy woods. Within yards, the beeches grew so thick that at times they had to turn sideways to pass between their gray trunks.

Here was definitely an old-growth forest, untouched for centuries.

Hugh had clearly protected his lands against any molestation.

As the canopy grew higher and the shadows thicker, there was no escaping the primeval feeling of the forest.

It was as if they were traipsing through some natural cathedral.

It would also be easy to get lost.

The lion rubbed his chin against various tree trunks, as if leaving scent markings to help find their way back. Otherwise, the cub acted more like a kitten: kicking up leaf litter and bouncing through bushes. Still, when an owl hooted overhead, the lion jumped a foot in the air and landed in a rustle of leaves and cracking twigs.

The cat was plainly tense, too.

Or maybe he's just picking up on our anxiety.

They marched for a little over a mile, climbing over logs, and weaving through beeches and the occasional silver pines, never moving in a straight line for long. If they kept up this pace, they should reach the site on the map within the hour.

After another ten minutes, Jordan discovered an old deer trail.

Should be able to make even better time on it.

"Over here," he whispered, afraid to raise his voice—less because of any fear of alerting the enemy, and more out of a strange reverence for this forest.

They headed along it, moving more quickly now.

Then a twig snapped ahead and to the left of the trail, sounding as loud as a gunshot.

He pushed Erin behind him and turned toward the sound. The Sanguinists flanked him, while the lion stuck to Rhun's legs, giving off a growling hiss.

Ten yards ahead, a giant shaggy dog bounded onto the trail and faced their group. Its black fur was more shadow than substance, the perfect camouflage for this forest.

Except for the unnatural crimson glow of its eyes.

A *blasphemare*.

The beast's shoulders rose higher than Jordan's hip. As it lowered its head and pulled back its ears, it revealed a long powerful neck and muscular body. It looked more bear than dog.

A well-fed bear.

Even its dark coat looked polished.

This was no stray animal.

Though it was freakishly large with a black coat, Jordan recognized the breed as a Great Pyrenees. Originally bred to herd sheep, they were usually gentle creatures, but they were fiercely protective of their masters and their territories.

Other shadows moved to either side of the trail, clearly letting themselves be seen.

He counted four more out there.

So a pack.

The first order of business was getting Erin some-where safe.

Jordan shifted slowly, interlacing his fingers. He turned to offer Erin a hike up. "Get into that tree," he warned.

Erin didn't bother with any false bravado and gave a quick nod. She planted her boot in his hand and pushed off him as he shoved her higher still. Reaching up, she snagged an overhanging limb of a stout beech tree, pulled herself up, then clambered higher.

Jordan never let his gaze leave the dogs.

The pack stirred, but didn't approach.

Jordan swung his machine pistol to his shoulder, while knives and blades bristled from the Sanguinists, silver shining in the dappled shade.

After a long tense stretch, the pack began to move in unison, as if obeying some silent whistle. The first dog stalked down the trail, aiming for Jordan. The others split off, flanking toward the Sanguinists.

"Remember that we are not to harm them," Rhun warned.

"Okay, I promise not to bite him *first*." Jordan kept his machine pistol up, pointed straight at the snarling dog's face.

Unimpressed by the threat, the pack leader stepped closer, panting out foul breath, its muzzle rippling up into a snarl.

Jordan's finger tightened on the trigger.

He had a choice to make.

Kill it, wound it, or make peace with it.

Jordan remembered his training as a soldier.

He lowered his weapon.

Obey your orders.

His heart pounded as he held out the back of his hand to the animal. "I'm not going to hurt you," he whispered softly. "I promise."

With a shift of muscles, the dog jumped at him, snapping at his hand, catching his fingers.

Jordan managed to yank his arm back. Blood dripped heavily from his fingertips.

But, at least, I still have fingers.

He watched his adversary closely. Maybe his blood was poisonous to the dog, as it had been to the *strigoi* back in the tunnels under Prague. The dog simply curled a corner of its lips and licked its chops.

No such luck.

The dog lunged at him, leaping for his throat.

Jordan dropped onto his back, brought his feet up, and caught the dog in the stomach. He kicked it up and over his head. By the time the dog landed and turned back around, Jordan was standing up and facing it again.

Saliva dripped from the beast's fangs as it padded in a slow circle around him, its steps noiseless on the thick mat of dead leaves.

Jordan touched his palm against the butt of his machine pistol—then let his arm drop again.

Can't shoot it.

"Good boy," Jordan called out, stepping toward the dog again, his hands open, showing no threat.

From the corner of his eyes, he saw the Sanguinists fending off attacks from the other dogs with various nonlethal means of defense, which mostly involved running and leaping.

But how long could that last?

As if knowing its target was distracted, the dog launched himself straight for Jordan's chest and knocked him to the ground. He managed to raise an arm to protect his throat, but teeth sank deep into the meat in Jordan's forearm. Contorting to the side, he grabbed the dagger from his ankle sheath.

He had taken enough punishment in the name of peace.

The dog growled, grinding harder to the bone. Red eyes stared down into Jordan's. He didn't see anger or malice there, only a savage determination.

Bernard's words echoed in his ears: *harm nothing that you find on his mountain.*

Their mission was to get Hugh's help. Whatever happened to Jordan was insignificant compared to that. He let the dagger drop from his fingers.

Beyond the dog's ears, he spotted Erin sprawled flat on a tree branch. Her brown eyes were wide with horror. She aimed her pistol at the dog.

"Don't shoot!" Jordan croaked out past the pain.

To ensure she obeyed, he heaved to the side, rolling the dog under him, shielding it with his body. He had to protect the dog. If the dog died, the mission would fail.

But no one told the dog this plan.

The snarling muzzle unlatched from his arm and snapped at his face. Jordan yanked his head back.

Bad move.

Yellow teeth fastened on to Jordan's exposed throat.

3:18 P.M.

Erin screamed as the dog shook its head, its teeth ripping deeper. Blood gushed from Jordan's throat and poured down the muzzle of the dog under him.

She kept her pistol trained but was still afraid to shoot, of hitting Jordan by mistake.

A frantic search told her that the three Sanguinists had their own troubles. Each one battled a dog of his or her own, and none of them could get free to help Jordan.

Below her branch, the beast growled and rolled, throwing Jordan under him like a rag doll. Jordan no longer moved, his head lolling from the monster's jaws. She steadied her aim, having a clear target now. She remembered Jordan's earlier warning.

Don't shoot!

To hell with Hugh de Payens and his rules.

Her finger tightened on the trigger.

Then a flash of white speared through the shadows under the trees and struck the much larger dog in the flank, slamming the beast off Jordan.

Rhun's lion.

Shadow and light battled in a tangle of limbs, then the dog rolled free, back to its feet, facing the cat with a growl. The cub looked so small. Still, the cat hissed and raised a paw, exposing silver claws.

Apparently unimpressed, the dog advanced one stiff-legged step—then the cub lashed out, striking as fast a cobra, raking claws across the dog's black nose. The pack leader yelped and backed away. Dark blood welled up from four ragged lines across its nose.

The cub shifted to stand before Jordan's body. His snowy fur stood on end, and a deep growl rumbled from his chest. He lifted a threatening paw again, clearly ready to fight some more.

With a whimper, the dog turned and fled away, melting back into the shadows of the forest. The rest of the pack followed its example, breaking off from their various battles and vanishing away.

Erin clambered quickly out of the tree, falling next to Jordan, collapsing to her knees beside him. The cub stalked on the far side, looking equally scared. The cat leaned his small muzzle down and nudged Jordan's face. A small flash flared between them, like a static-electric shock in a dark room, only this was distinctly golden, reminding her of the pair's angelic nature.

C'mon, Jordan, you can heal from this.

She wiped at his neck with the cuff of her sleeve. The cub licked Jordan's cheeks and forehead. Already the blood had stopped flowing. As she watched, the torn flesh began to knit together. The crimson tendrils that had spread outward from his tattoo and had encircled his neck grew thicker yet again, weaving through the damage, healing his flesh.

She touched his cheek with her fingertips. His skin felt impossibly hot. No one could survive long with a fever like that.

"Jordan."

He opened his eyes, their hue as blue as a sky peeking between dark clouds.

She knew everything about those eyes—how the ring around the outside of his iris was a darker blue, like denim, but the rest of his iris was much lighter, with pale lines running through it like tiny rivers. Those eyes had laughed with her, cried with her, and promised her a future together. But now they looked at her as if she were a total stranger.

"Jordan?"

He groaned and pushed to a sitting position, one hand patting the cat absently. His other hand rose to touch his neck. Under the residual blood, the tattoo looked like a vine strangling a tree. Through the ripped sleeve of that same arm, she saw the damage there had healed, too. As she stared, a crimson tendril bloomed into a curlicue on the back of his hand.

Erin reached for that hand, but he pulled away from her and stood.

Rhun rushed up to them. "Is Jordan all right?"

Erin didn't know how to answer that.

Elizabeth and Sophia joined Rhun. The Sanguinists looked roughed up, but not nearly as wounded as Jordan. Perhaps their dogs had been playing with them versus trying to rip out their throats.

Elizabeth frowned at the forest, straightening the shreds of her jacket sleeve. "Why did the dogs abandon their fight?"

Erin kept her gaze fixed to Jordan. "The cat . . . I think he scared them off."

Rhun stroked the lion's head, mumbling his thanks.

Erin shifted in front of Jordan, forcing him to look at her, gripping his strong shoulders. "Are you okay?"

He finally glanced down at her, blinked a few times, then nodded. His eyes focused on her, seeing her. He touched his neck, looking vaguely bewildered.

"I'm fine."

She hugged him, squeezing him hard to her chest.

He was a moment slow in responding, but his arms finally wrapped around her, too. "I'm even better now," he whispered to the top of her head.

She smiled into his chest, while also holding back a sob.

Elizabeth brushed leaves from her skirt, looking impatient.

Erin broke away, but she kept one hand in Jordan's grip, doing her best to ignore the burn of his palm and fingers, fearful that he might not come back the next time.

She took a moment to rub the lion's velvety ears, knowing who had truly saved Jordan's life. "Thanks, little guy."

In the distance, a dog howled out of the deeper forest, reminding them that they weren't out of danger. Not even close.

"Time to go," Jordan said. "If those dogs are retreating back home, we might be able to follow their tracks."

"He's right," Rhun said. "If these beasts are the emissaries of Hugh de Payens, then perhaps they were sent to bring us to him."

"Or they're simply wild *blasphemare* who came to kill us," Erin added bitterly.

But with no better plan, they set off with Rhun in the lead. His eyes watched the ground, likely picking out prints in the damp loam or noting snapped twigs. He would occasionally lift his nose, drawing in the scent of the cursed pack.

"At least we got our own personal bloodhound," Jordan whispered beside her.

But where is Rhun taking us, what new horrors were on this mountain?

30

Rhun tracked through the forest, doing his best to ignore the throbbing ache of his stump. He took measure of those around him after the battle, knowing he would need to lean on them.

Now more than ever.

Elizabeth walked easily behind him, having sustained only a small wound on her hand. He had seen how swiftly she had fought against the *blasphemare*, a reminder of how fierce a warrior she was. Still, he sensed a reluctance from her to be here, an edgy impatience that was new. Like Jordan, she had grown withdrawn, her mind elsewhere. He had tried to question her about it on the flight, but she dismissed him.

Still, he sensed something had happened back at Castel Gandolfo, something that both angered her and worried her at the same time.

She was hiding something.

But aren't we all?

Behind him, the leaves rustled as Erin and Jordan trod more heavily through the forest, unable to move as lightly as the Sanguinists. Rhun listened to the beat of Jordan's heart, hearing again the undertone of a war drum. Whatever held him in its grip, it did not seem to frighten Jordan. Instead, it seemed to lend him strength and peace. The same could not be said of Erin, who could scarcely take her eyes from Jordan, evaluating him with every step, her heartbeat threaded with fear.

Trailing them, Sophia guarded their rear, her small form shadowing them like some elfin spirit. But Rhun knew the slight woman was as sharp as she was lithe, both deadly with her blades and quick to read an opponent's weaknesses. Back in Prague, she had tangled with a grimwolf all by herself and lived to walk away. Few could make that claim.

Flanking Rhun to the left, the cub darted through the silvery-gray trunks of the beeches, as much on the scent of the *blasphemare* pack as Rhun was. The forest air was thick with their tainted smell, but oddly the rank odor did not set him on edge as it usually did.

Something is different about these creatures.

Clearly, the shade of the deep forest provided ample cover for the dogs, reminding Rhun how numerous such beasts were in the past, when the deep places of the forest remained dark even under the bright sun. Since his own mortal days, so many wild places had fallen before the axe and plow of civilization. And so many creatures, *blasphemare* and natural alike, had vanished with the trees.

The beech forest gradually gave way to silver pine as they climbed higher up the mountain. Somewhere to his left, a stream tumbled over rocks, smelling of snowmelt and ice. The sound of running water grew louder as they went, roaring up into what could only be a vast waterfall up ahead.

Finally, a glimmer of sunlight sparkled through the shadowy bower, drawing them forward. Rhun sensed the pack splitting off, melting back into the thicker trees, their duty apparently done.

They brought us here for a reason.

Rhun continued toward the light. Ahead, the lion pranced more brightly on his paws, showing no fear at what might lay ahead.

The trees quickly grew thinner, spaced more widely apart. A meadow opened ahead. Grasses waved along the rolling slopes, like an emerald sea. Small white flowers glowed out there, pristine and clean in the sunlight.

After so long in darkness, that brightness stung. Rhun squinted against it, while Elizabeth drew in a sharp breath. She was still more sensitive to the light. As they stepped out of the forest, she pulled the hood of her jacket over her head, shadowing her features.

Rhun looked around. The open space formed a rough oval of green, dotted with white blooms of gentian flowers. A handful of gray boulders poked through the grass like wary sentinels. Meandering through them was a silvery stream, flowing from a tall waterfall on the far side where sheets of water plummeted from a sheer cliff into a wide blue pool.

The team gathered at the forest edge, all eyes searching for threats.

Rhun nodded ahead. "This is the place Bernard marked on the map, where he believed Hugh de Payens built his hermitage."

"Nothing's here," Jordan said. "Place is empty."

"No," Elizabeth said. "That's not true. Bernard was not mistaken about this location . . . a rarity for him."

Rhun heard the spike of bitterness in her voice when she mentioned the cardinal.

She pointed to the towering cascade. "Beyond the veil of the waterfall, I can make out the outline of a structure."

Erin squinted. "Are you sure?"

Even Rhun could not discern anything and cast a doubtful glance at Elizabeth.

"Over there!" she said with an exasperated sigh.

She leaned closer to Rhun, aiming her arm, allowing him to follow her graceful finger. She outlined the watery shadow of an arched doorway in the rock behind the falls, halfway up the cliff face.

Once pointed out, he saw it as well.

Two windows flanked that door, with a larger round window centered above them.

It looked like the façade of a church, sculpted out of the rock behind the waterfall. Its bottom edge hovered two stories above the blue pool. It would be a precarious climb to get up there, especially through the pounding of that water.

Rhun became all too aware of the ache in his stump, reminded of how impossible such an ascent would be for him with only one arm.

Erin took a step farther out into the meadow. "I see it now, too!"

"We should proceed as a group," Jordan warned, drawing Erin back, wisely reining in the woman's eagerness. "While this Hugh guy has let us get this far, let's not take any unnecessary risks."

Rhun bowed to the wisdom of the man's words and waved them all onward toward the waterfall. No one spoke as they marched across the field, marking the team's tension. Rhun was sure eyes were watching their approach across the meadow. As they neared the waterfall, its roar grew deafening, which only heightened Rhun's apprehension.

Reaching the small lake, they assembled along its edge. The water was a pristine blue, clear enough that Rhun spotted dappled trout deep below the rippling surface, flitting for cover as his shadow fell over the pool.

He searched the base of the rock behind the falls for any carved steps, for some way to reach the façade of the church far above their heads. He spotted no way to gain access without a slippery climb through a heavy cascade of water.

Jordan voiced all their concerns, shouting to be heard above the roar. "How do we get up to that friggin' place?"

It was Elizabeth's keen eyes again that discovered the answer, pointing down instead of up, into the pool's depths. "The mouth of a tunnel is hiding in the rocks below the falls. Perhaps there is an underwater passageway there that leads up to the church above."

Erin eyed the water with clear trepidation, crossing her arms. Rhun knew from past experience that the archaeologist was not a strong swimmer and had a fear of water.

Erin swallowed. "There's got to be some other way into this place. I doubt those dogs swim in and out through that tunnel. Especially here, exposed to the sunlight."

Rhun agreed with her. Hugh de Payens had been here for centuries. The mountain was probably riddled with tunnels and hidden entrances and exits. But his team did not have time to hunt them down.

Jordan sighed. "Hugh guided us to this meadow with his dogs. Something tells me this is another test. We find our way inside through that underwater tunnel, or we don't go in at all."

"Then we swim for it," Erin said, uncrossing her arm and steeling her face.

"As a group," Jordan said. "All or nothing."

The big man stripped off down to his pants, even kicking off his boots. Rhun was taken aback at the transformation of his blue tattoo, following the new crimson lines that extended from it, wrapping his neck, entwining down his arm. It was a darkly beautiful design, as if the angels themselves had inscribed his flesh.

And maybe they had.

Rhun and the others followed his example, shucking off jackets, and shedding heavier clothes.

Once done, Elizabeth stood next to him, wearing only her pants and bra, showing no shyness, her back straight. She ran one hand through her dark curls, pushing them back from her face and tying them with a bit of string. Her breasts were firm and white under the thin silk, and her pale skin shone even in the shadow cast by the overhanging rock.

Rhun remembered how it had felt to have that smooth skin pressed against his, his lips against hers. He had wanted to devour her then, possess her wholly.

He still did.

Still, he averted his eyes, turning his attention to their pile of discarded clothes and abandoned weapons. They would go unarmed to this meeting. Perhaps this was why Hugh had led them to this entrance—to force them to strip down.

Rhun recovered only one weapon.

He took his silver pectoral cross from the pile and hung it back around his neck. It burned hot against his bare skin. Elizabeth stared at him. He felt suddenly self-conscious with his bandaged stump exposed. But she looked at the cross, instead, then went and recovered her own, donning it as he had done. The silver left a pink line against the pearly whiteness between her breasts. It burned her skin as much as it did his, but she did not remove it.

"Let's go," Jordan said and plunged straight in, coming up like an otter.

"Wait," Erin said and grabbed her backpack from their discarded clothes. She turned to Rhun. "Can you take this? I don't want to leave it abandoned here, but I'm not really a strong enough swimmer to take it myself."

Rhun knew her bag held the Blood Gospel, sealed in an airtight and waterproof case. She was right not to leave it unattended, especially here. He pulled the pack over his good shoulder. "I'll keep it safe."

"Thank you."

Erin swallowed, faced the pool, then waded in, gasping at the cold.

Rhun and his fellow Sanguinists joined her. The water was snowmelt, barely above freezing—but at least the icy chill numbed the ache from his stump.

The party set off across the pool toward the thunder of the falls. Even the lion cub jumped in and swam steadily beside him. Its giant feet pushed through the water like paddles. Its heartbeat was quick and steady. The animal showed no fear of the water.

Erin, on the other hand, fought to keep up, splashing more than moving, her heart racing. Rhun dropped back next to her, as did Sophia.

"I didn't learn to swim until I was one hundred and five!" Sophia shouted to Erin. "So I'm still not very good at it myself."

Erin gave the nun a quick smile and kept swimming.

Rhun appreciated the gesture, but unlike Erin, Sophia did not need to breathe. Whereas Rhun had seen Erin nearly drown once before. He knew she would not stop going, even past the point of no return.

Ahead, Jordan and Elizabeth had reached the falls. Elizabeth glanced up at the cascade, as if taking her bearings, then dove. Jordan followed immediately.

Rhun did a one-armed sidestroke next to Erin until they reached the falls, too. He treaded water with Sophia to let Erin catch her breath. Her lips were set in a hard line, going blue from the cold.

Rhun glanced to Sophia. The thunder of the cascade made talk impossible, but he got a small nod back from the woman, acknowledging his request.

Keep Erin safe.

Erin gave them a weak smile of bravado and upended herself, her pale feet shining in the sun for a moment before she vanished underwater.

Rhun and Sophia followed her down, lashed by the turbulent water.

Rhun quickly found it vexing to swim with only one arm, eventually settling for only kicking his legs. Still, he easily kept up with Erin.

He felt something bump his leg, felt a snag of claws in his pants. A glance revealed the cub digging down after them. It seemed the cat was not going to let them go alone.

They reached the mouth of the tunnel that Elizabeth had spotted. He saw no sign of the other two. Erin hesitated, but the cub shot past her and entered first, his paws snagging the rocky walls and propelling him deeper.

Perhaps taking courage from the cub, Erin followed.

But how much farther could she truly go?

4:24 P.M.

Erin's lungs burned as she swam after the cat.

Though, in truth, it felt more like *crawling*, as her hands clawed the walls and her toes pushed off along the bottom of the tunnel.

How far did this passage run?

It was a question that terrified her.

Her chest already ached for breath. She doubted she had enough air left to return to the pool, to sunshine and fresh breezes. It left her with only one way to go from here.

Forward.

She kicked, following the paddling rear end of the cub. The filtering sunlight behind her quickly faded to a gloomy murk, but the cat's snowy fur glowed ahead of her, like a will-o'-the-wisp in the dark. She placed all her trust in the cub. It needed to breathe, like she did. If it turned around, she would, too.

So she continued, commanding her cold arms to pull and her numb legs to kick.

Then suddenly the lion's hind legs disappeared upward into darkness.

She felt the tunnel dissolve around her into a larger space, as dark as pitch.

Blindly, she headed up.

Seconds later, her head broke the surface. She gasped in a new breath, then another, taking in the small cavern around her, illuminated by slivers of daylight seeping through cracks in the roof.

Jordan and Elizabeth climbed out on a ledge on the far side, next to a plain wooden door set into the granite wall. The cub paddled over and scrabbled at the edge, until Jordan helped pull his sodden form out of the water.

Jordan spotted Erin and waved one arm, while holding out the other. "I got you."

Yeah, well, you could've got me sooner . . . or at least, hung around.

Like some others.

Rhun and Sophia surfaced behind her.

Still, as much as it stung that he had abandoned her, she knew it wasn't his fault. Whatever was happening would eventually pass, and he would be his old self again.

Now if only I could truly believe that.

She hurried to the ledge, and Jordan pulled her up as if she weighed nothing. He quickly hugged her, the feverish heat of him welcome for the first time. She shivered and shook in his embrace, remaining there until the cold tremors in her limbs warmed away.

To the side, Sophia helped Rhun onto the ledge, compromised as he was with only one arm.

"We must find a way to open this door," Elizabeth said, running her palms over it.

With her teeth still chattering, Erin moved over. If there were warm towels and a roaring fire behind it, she would kick it down herself.

She examined the door alongside Elizabeth. It

was made of a single thick wooden plank, sanded smooth as glass, with no visible hinges or lock on this side.

"Looks like it can only be opened from the other side," Erin said.

"Or we batter it down from this side," Jordan offered.

She suspected such an action would win no favors from the owner, Hugh de Payens. "I think we must wait," she said. "Show patience."

"So then we wait," Rhun said. He dropped to a knee to fondle the cub's ear, who looked none too happy with his wet status.

Jordan stepped to the door. "Or we do this."

He raised his fist and knocked on the thick plank, then stepped back, cupping his lips. "Hello!" he hollered, his voice booming in the small cavern.

Erin held her breath, but after there was no response, she let it sigh out.

"Maybe no one's home," Jordan said with a shrug.

Another member of their party tried.

The cub leaned back his head and let out a massive roar.

Erin jumped slightly, wincing at the noise, shocked that such a huge outburst came from such a small creature.

It sounded like a challenge.

When the echoes died away, a deep voice intoned, seeming to rise from everywhere. It made Erin's skin crawl.

"Only the lion may enter."

A scraping sound came from beyond the thick plank, as if a bar had been drawn back. The door swung slowly inward.

Erin tried to see past the threshold, but it was too shadowy, the space lit by flickering torchlight.

Still on one knee beside his cub, Rhun pointed to the door. "You can do it."

The lion rose timidly, then turned and gently gripped Rhun's wrist with his teeth. The cub tugged Rhun toward the open door.

"Doesn't look like the little guy wants to go into that creepy place by himself," Jordan said. "Can't say I blame him."

Rhun tried to resist, but the cub refused to unlatch from him.

The voice returned, slightly softened by amusement. "It seems your companion will not enter without you, priest. So you may all enter, but you may not proceed beyond the first room."

Jordan patted the cub. "Good going, bud. And here I thought I might get to sit this one out."

Led by Rhun and his cat, the group edged one by one over the threshold.

Erin studied the antechamber beyond the door. Two torches hung from iron brackets, revealing a space the size of a two-car garage, carved out of the granite of the mountain. An archway opened on the far side, but plainly they weren't allowed to pass through there.

At least, not yet.

From that archway, a figure stepped out to join them. "Be at ease," he greeted them, but he kept a wary distance. "I am Hugh de Payens."

His appearance and demeanor surprised Erin. She had expected to confront a medieval hermit, someone dressed in simple rough robes, someone like Francis of Assisi. Instead, the man wore khaki-colored pants and a thick woolen sweater. He looked like a farmer or a fisherman, certainly not a former priest.

She studied his round face, his wide brown eyes, his mop of curly black hair. In spite of his cautious expression, he looked kind. He held his thin hands clasped loosely in front of him, plainly carrying no weapons.

"It has been long since the Order of the Sanguines has troubled itself with me," he said, his voice rough and deep, as if he didn't use it often. He stared at Elizabeth, then gave a slight bow of his head. "And I see you've brought someone from my distant past. Be welcome, Countess Bathory."

"It is Sister Elizabeth now," she corrected him, touching the cross on her chest.

He lifted an eyebrow in surprise. "Truly?"

She gave him a demure shrug.

"Then these are strange times indeed," the man said. "And it seems Countess . . . rather *Sister* Elizabeth is not your group's only intriguing companion."

Hugh de Payens approached, staring down at the cub. Once close to the cat, he eyed Rhun. "May I?"

Rhun backed a step. "He is his own master."

"Well spoken," Hugh said, holding out a hand for the cub to sniff.

The lion looked back at Rhun, who gave him a small nod. Only then did the cat lean forward and huff at the man's outstretched fingers. Seemingly satisfied, the cub licked the hermit's hand.

Hugh beamed at the lion. "Remarkable," he murmured. "Something wholly new. A creature tainted not by *darkness*, but rather illuminated by *light*. May I ask how you came by him, Father Korza?"

Rhun looked surprised that Hugh knew his name, but Erin suspected the man knew much more than his pleasant demeanor implied. One didn't survive for centuries, hiding from the Sanguinist order, without honing some talent at subterfuge

"I killed his mother in the desert in Egypt," Rhun explained. "She was an injured *blasphemare*."

Hugh straightened. "I imagine she was one of those unfortunate beasts caught by that holy blast in the desert."

"That's right," Rhun said slowly.

Even this surprised Erin. Only a handful of people knew about that event. Most of them were right in this room. So this hermit was more attuned to current events than anyone would have guessed.

"After I slew his mother, the cub came to me," Rhun explained. "I brought him away to keep him safe."

"By the rules of your order, you should have killed the child. Yet, you did not." Hugh shook his head in mock disapproval. "Did you know that the Buddhists consider lions to be *bodhisattvas*—sons of the Buddha? They are thought to be beings who have attained a high level of spiritual enlightenment. They stay in this world to free others from their suffering. You are fortunate indeed, Father Korza, that this beast chose you. Perhaps it's because you wear the crown of the Knight of Christ."

Hugh eyed Erin and Jordan. "And travel with the Warrior of Man and the Woman of Learning."

Jordan spoke up. "How come you know so much about us?"

His question was ignored as Hugh ran his fingers

along the cub's side, eliciting a steady purr. Only then did he rise again and face Jordan, but instead of answering his question, he held out a hand.

"May I see the gemstone you carry in your pocket?"

Jordan took a step back, but Erin grabbed his elbow. There was no reason to keep any secrets, especially as this man seemed to know theirs anyway. And they needed any answers that Hugh de Payens might provide.

"Show him," Erin urged.

Jordan dug around in his pants pocket and pulled out the two pieces of the broken green stone.

Hugh took them and nudged the two halves together in his palm. He held the stone up to the torchlight, as if to verify the design infused into its surface. "It's been centuries since I last saw this stone, when it was intact, uncorrupted."

He lowered his hand and passed the pieces back to Jordan. He paused only long enough to cock his head, staring at the design twined across Jordan's skin. "It seems you are indeed a fitting bearer of this particular gem," he said cryptically.

Erin used this statement as a way to broach the reason they had traveled here. "We are looking for *two* more stones. Very much like this one."

Hugh smiled at her. "You are mistaken. The other two are *nothing* like this one."

"So you know of them?" Rhun moved closer. "We believe that they are key to—"

"To fulfilling your latest prophecy."

"Will you help us?" Erin asked.

Before Hugh could answer, the cub let out a mewling cry of simple hunger.

"It seems there are more immediate concerns to address first." Hugh gestured toward the archway that led farther into the mountain. "Join me in my home. I have dry towels, along with food and wine for those in need of nourishment."

He rubbed the lion's head with one knuckle. "And of course, meat and milk for you, my friend."

Erin followed Hugh de Payens, as he led them deeper into the mysteries locked within this mountain.

But can we trust him?

31

Rhun dropped his hand on the lion's head as they followed Hugh through the second doorway, which revealed a winding staircase heading up, cut through the same stone. As the group ascended, they passed landings leading to other levels, each sealed with stout doors. He pictured the labyrinth of tunnels that likely coursed through this mountain.

But their host led them ever upward, holding aloft a smoky torch.

The stairway ended at another door, this one wood strapped in iron.

"Open!" called Hugh through it.

The thick portal swung wide. Rhun followed Hugh over the threshold into what appeared to be a church. To the far left was the tall door they had spotted through the waterfall. It was presently closed, but he still heard the muffled roar beyond, picturing what it must look like when those massive double doors were thrown open upon that cascading veil, the waters lit by the eastern sun when a new day dawned.

Through the windows on either side and above the door, he could catch some glimpse of that spectacle, but the glass was stained, the work of a true master. The circle over the door displayed a perfect rose, its petals blooming in every shade of red. The smaller flanking windows showed flowering trees, their bowers full of doves and ravens, their shadows hiding deer and wolves, lambs and lions, all living in harmony.

Rhun stepped farther in the room, but he cautioned the others to hang back.

They were not alone.

In the deeper shadows at the other end of the church stalked the four shaggy dogs that had attacked them in the forest. Other beasts stirred back there, crimson eyes glowing, revealing their accursed natures. He spotted a pair of grimwolves, a black leopard, and hulking on one knuckle was a mountain gorilla.

"Do not be afraid," Hugh said, standing to the side with the torch. "You are my guests . . . until I say otherwise."

Rhun moved out with the others, but he kept everyone back from that dark menagerie, whose eyes watched their group with equal suspicion. He frowned at the state of this small cathedral. The nave held no pews, and the stone floor was spread with straw. A dozen cots lined the walls, while smaller side chapels were penned off, revealing troughs and thick beds of loose hay.

Sophia nudged Rhun, nodding toward tall, thin figures hovering near marble statues.

Strigoi.

At least a dozen.

The *strigoi* had no weapons that he could see, save perhaps those garden tools leaning against the walls—rakes, hoes, and spades.

"You need fear no one here, Father Korza," Hugh tried to reassure him.

Rhun hoped that he was telling the truth. He glanced around at the building itself. Rather than raw rock, the walls were covered in white bricks, soaring up into great gothic vaults. Huge wrought-iron chandeliers hung down, dripping with candlewax.

Even up there, creatures stirred.

Hugh noted his attention, lifted an arm and whistled.

A shred of black shadow broke away and swept down, landing on his wrist.

It was an ebony-feathered raven with glowing eyes. Its beak was a spear, its claws true talons. Hugh used a finger to gently ruffle the feathers along its neck. The bird bowed, rubbing back in turn.

"This is Muninn." Hugh glanced upward, searching the roof. "Huginn is up there, too. Or perhaps he's off hunting."

Erin must have recognized the names. "Odin's ravens," she said. "They were said to be able to fly around the world, bringing information to the Norse god, keeping him informed of everything. You're not suggesting these are—"

"The same ones? No, my dear," Hugh said with a smile. "It just amuses me to call them by those names. And the pair is but two of a great flock that haunts these forests, a mix of *blasphemare* and natural birds."

"Amazing," Erin said, her gaze searching the ceilings.

Rhun suspected she wasn't looking for more birds, but her attention was captured by the decoration across the vaulted roof. The ceiling was white, but red stars and blue wheels had been painted across its surface, forming an elaborate, fanciful design.

"The frescoes above," Erin muttered, confirming Rhun's guess. "They're extraordinary. They look Middle Eastern—with the wheels and stars—but not quite, somehow."

She wandered off a few steps to better take them in.

Jordan kept to her side. Elizabeth trailed after them after Rhun quietly signaled her to do so.

Sophia waved to the beasts and *strigoi*. "How did they come to be here?"

Hugh looked lovingly upon his flock, as Muninn hopped to his shoulder. "It is my experience that creatures seek out their true masters. To reach my sanctuary, many *blasphemare* and *strigoi* traveled hundreds of miles. I did not call them. They are drawn to me, just as this sweet lion was drawn to Rhun."

Rhun rubbed the cub's head. "But how do you keep them from killing in these mountains?"

Hugh lifted his arms. "Because, like you, they have made *peace* with their nature. Instead of being ruled by their savage blood, they control it. They are no longer killers."

Sophia looked little convinced by the man's words.

Rhun could not blame her. "How does one find peace outside the bounds of the Church?"

"Acceptance and mindfulness," Hugh answered. "I was taught certain techniques during my travels long ago, ways to open your mind and develop patience and love. I can teach them to you, if you like. All are welcome here."

Hugh motioned gently behind him. "Francesca, would you join us? I've found truths are best heard from the lips of those who have experienced them firsthand."

A slim woman parted from the shadows only yards away. Rhun had not even known she had been there. She was likely once beautiful, with long pale blond hair and supple limbs, but there was a gentle frailty about her thin frame. She smiled at Hugh, love shining from her eyes.

Rhun noted the hint of fangs, the lack of a heartbeat.

"Tell them," Hugh said.

"We were first taught *awareness,*" she whispered reverently. "Awareness of our nature, of who we are. To know we are one of God's creatures."

Sophia made a scoffing noise. "You are predators, preying upon the weak."

Francesca smiled sadly at her. "No one judges a lion for bringing down a gazelle. It is the lion's nature, and the lion need feel no guilt or shame."

Hugh moved to a stool and sat down. A three-legged gray fox scurried over and jumped onto Hugh's lap. A clean white bandage had been fastened around its stump, and Rhun felt a twinge of sympathy for it. When Hugh stroked its back, the fox leaned against him, showing no fear, not even of the lion, whose ears had perked up at the sight of the injured animal.

"But how do you sustain yourselves?" Rhun asked.

"Somewhat with wine," Hugh answered. "Like you."

"Monsieur de Payens, can you still consecrate wine, even after turning your back upon the Church?" Elizabeth asked.

"A priest bears an indelible mark upon his soul," Rhun explained, "which means that one remains a priest and can consecrate wine even after one leaves the Church."

Sophia picked out a guileful detail to the man's explanation. "You said wine *somewhat* sustains you. What else does it take?"

"Blood, of course." Hugh showed no sign of shame or guilt at this admission. "As Francesca has told you, we are all predators and must accept our natures."

Rhun felt sickened, remembering how Rasputin's followers mixed wine with human blood to survive. They remained killers. It seemed Hugh had fallen into the same sinful trap. He remembered too well the taste of Rasputin's blood-damned wine.

Hugh held up a hand. "Understand, we take as little

as we need to survive—but we also have a right to survive. As I mentioned *awareness* is but one half of a whole. *Mindfulness* is just as important."

Francesca nodded in agreement, explaining, "While we accept and are aware of our nature, we must be *mindful* not to lose control. We meditate, learn to separate need from desire, taking only what is necessary and right."

"How can any killing be *right*?" Rhun asked.

Francesca folded her thin hands. "We only take the blood from those who are suffering or those who inflict suffering upon others."

"Our purpose is to *end* suffering," Hugh expounded. "We find those who are in terrible pain and wish to die. Those who are so wracked with disease and will never recover. We end their lives with mercy, grace, and joy."

As a priest, Rhun had spent time with the dying. While he balked at such a concept as killing as an act of mercy, he knew how man had created technology to stave off death, but so often it seemed these methods were used to extend suffering, to prolong an inevitable end to an unnatural length.

Hugh sighed. "And when we can find no others, we sometimes take the lives of those who inflict suffering on the innocent. Rapists, murderers. But in truth, we rarely need to resort to such means. Like

I said, we sustain ourselves on as little blood as possible."

Jordan spoke up, reminding them that this was not why they had come. "All well and good, but what about those other two stones?"

"I am in possession of one of the stones," Hugh admitted. "But it must be earned. To prove you are worthy to bear it from here."

"Earned how?" Jordan asked.

"Your Woman of Learning must show her worth." Hugh's eyes settled on Erin. "She must prove her grasp of *awareness* to find where the stone has been hidden— and demonstrate her *mindfulness* to discover where it must be taken."

5:07 P.M.

Great, Erin thought sardonically. *Should be a walk in the park.*

On the helicopter flight, she had read up on Hugh de Payens and his history with the Knights Templars, but she likely hadn't learned even a tenth of what she might need to know to face his challenge.

Hugh stood up from his stool, sending the injured fox back to his den in the shadows. "So, Woman of Learning, what can you tell me of this place?"

She glanced around the surrounding chapels, vaults, and walls, noting the crosslike shape typical of all great churches, but her gaze settled on the most unique detail: the roof.

"Medieval churches aren't my specialty," she admitted. "But some of these decorations are similar to those at St. Christophe's Chapel in Montsaunes, France, a building built by the Templars, the order you founded."

"I remember that chapel's construction."

She took this as a positive sign and studied the frescoes above more attentively. Was this the test of her *awareness*? Was she supposed to decipher the riddle up there?

Tilting her head, she searched for clues. Amid the kaleidoscope of red stars and blue wheels overhead, other fanciful designs had been painted there: moons, suns, and a variety of geometric shapes. She saw influences from both Islamic and Egyptian culture. That multispoked wheel definitely looked Buddhist. Her eyes began to blur at the sheer volume, the disharmony of its design.

Staring up, she suspected this was done purposefully, to make the viewer miss the forest for the trees. It would indeed require *awareness* to ignore the chaos and see through to the inner truth.

She stared up and slowly stripped each culture's iconography from that vast fresco, turning it in her mind's eye, judging it on its own. Unfortunately, she found nothing significant in this exercise. She wondered if these were examples of the cultures that Hugh had visited after leaving the Church. Cardinal Bernard said Hugh had traveled much of the globe before settling in France.

But how does that help me? She closed her eyes. *What am I not seeing?*

Then she knew.

She opened her eyes, clearing those symbols off the roof, looking for the truth hidden behind the noise, behind the cacophony of mankind.

The forest behind the trees.

Once the fanciful decorations were stripped away in her mind's eye, only one display was still left painted up there, in the background of the clutter.

The stars.

They were eternal.

"Paper," she said, holding out an arm. "And a pen."

Rhun rummaged through her pack and passed her a notebook and a ballpoint. She set about mapping those stars, noting the constellations. Several were larger, more prominently displayed. The stars painted in those constellations were six-pointed, not five like the others.

As she worked, she heard Jordan confront Hugh. "Why can't you just tell us?"

"It is a test," Hugh repeated adamantly. "The trio must show themselves to be worthy."

"Then what's my test?" Jordan pressed.

"You already passed it. In the forest, you sacrificed yourself without a fight, proving you were a Warrior who could achieve his goals through peace and nonviolence."

"Then what about my test?" Rhun asked.

"It came with you." Hugh bowed his head toward the cub. "You, a Knight of Christ, took pity and mercy on a creature you believed to be born of darkness, defying the edicts of your order to kill it on sight. For such mercy, you came away with a miracle of light and grace."

And now it's my turn.

Erin suddenly wished she had gotten a simpler test. But she was the Woman of Learning. She must figure this out on her own.

She did a final comparison between the star map painted on the ceiling and what she had copied down. Satisfied, she headed back to Hugh with notebook in hand. She felt like a student coming to the front of the class to solve a problem on the blackboard.

"It's the stars," she said. "That's what you wanted me to be *aware* of through all that noise above."

Hugh smiled, but remained silent.

I'm on the right track.

She remembered a Hermetic principle often associated with the Knights Templar: *As above, so below.*

Stars had been a tool for navigation since the beginning of civilization, to use the positions of the stars above, to find meaning down here on earth.

She worked it out aloud, pacing. "I'm supposed to figure out *where* on earth this sky would be visible, but to do that I would need to know which *date* this particular sky would appear."

She studied her page in the notebook. The more prominent constellations depicted above were those associated with spring: *Cancer, Leo, Virgo . . .*

So this must be a *spring* sky.

Then she remembered what had been painted beneath the mural at Edward Kelly's house, the one showing a mountain lake and all hell breaking loose. Elizabeth had translated the Czech writing below: *vernal equinox.*

Perhaps that was the answer, but she wanted confirmation. She frowned, remembering seeing Latin words painted on the ceiling. She half-ran, searching anew, stirring up the straw on the floor. She felt eyes on her, both from her party and those that glowed a deep crimson. Finally, she found the inscription, one painted in red on the eastern side of the church, the other in blue on the western side.

Two words.

Aequus and *Nox.*

She closed her eyes with relief.

Equinox.

She joined the others, her legs shaking. "It's the spring equinox. That's the date." She waved her notebook to encompass the star map. "So I have to figure out where in the world this particular night sky is visible during tomorrow's equinox."

From his back pocket, Jordan pulled out his cell phone, slipping it from a waterproof plastic bag. "I've got an app for that. Any good soldier keeps a means of navigation handy."

Erin glanced to Hugh to make sure it was kosher to use this technology.

He shrugged.

She held her page open for Jordan. "Can you map this?"

"I'll try." He took a snapshot with his phone, then spent some time fiddling with the application program, apparently trying to find a match. "Already I can tell that the constellation of Leo is in the *wrong* place up there. At least for the skies over France."

"Then find out where it's *right*," she urged.

She noted Hugh looking quizzically at her, as if she were missing something.

So the teacher wants me to earn extra points.

She pursed her lips and returned her attention to the

ceiling, picking through the constellations, especially focusing on the spring ones. Three of the lesser spring constellations were connected together, woven by flowing lines.

Hydra, Crater, and *Noctua.*

"The snake, the cup, and the owl," she mumbled, naming the shapes they represented. She had no trouble understanding the significance. *The snake likely represents Lucifer, the cup could easily be the Chalice mentioned in the prophecy, and the owl had been the symbol of knowledge across many cultures, going back eons.*

She glanced to her pack. The Blood Gospel was prophesied to have all the knowledge of the universe locked between its covers. She returned her attention above, noting the smaller lines that formed fanciful curlicues and whorls around the three constellations, weaving them together.

"They're connected together into one whole," Erin said.

A glance revealed a broad, congratulatory smile on Hugh's face. She wanted to smack that smug look off him and get some real answers.

Luckily Jordan interrupted, holding up his phone. "Got it!"

She moved closer.

"Here's the night sky over France."

She looked at the screen, seeing that he had labeled the constellation Leo.

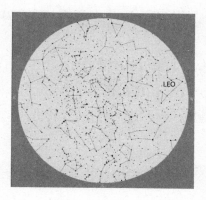

"We're at about latitude forty-three," he explained. "This time of year, Leo should be at the westernmost edge of the sky, but clearly it's not in the star map on the ceiling."

She looked to the roof, recognizing how different that star map was up there. "Then *where* on the planet does it match this sky?"

"Far to the east, about twenty-eight degrees north latitude."

"Could it be Tibet?" Erin asked. "Or maybe Nepal?"

Jordan whistled his appreciation and held up his phone for her to see, revealing the name that his phone app had pulled up.

KATMANDU, NEPAL
27°30'N 85°30'E

"Keep in mind," Jordan cautioned, "this is a rough approximation. But that's the region of the world referenced above. Basically it could be anywhere in the Himalayas."

Erin pictured the mural painted on Kelly's wall, showing a trio of mountains surrounding a dark lake. It must be somewhere in the Himalayan range of Nepal.

But where?

"How did you already guess Nepal?" Rhun asked her.

"Because of the wheels and the stars on the ceiling. They're Buddhist symbols. Of all the cultures depicted above, they're the most numerously represented." Erin talked quickly now, certain of what she was saying. "That wagon wheel over there is Buddha's wheel of transformation. The rim is limitation, the hub represents the world, and the eight spokes are the Noble Eightfold Path, which is what you need to tread to end suffering."

Erin turned to Hugh, challenging him. "That's where you learned your meditation techniques, wasn't it? You went east, during your travels before you settled in France. You learned these techniques from Buddhists monks."

Hugh bowed his head in acknowledgment.

Rhun frowned. "But how could Buddhists help you deal with your cursed nature?"

"Because the monks were *strigoi* themselves."

Shock rang through the Sanguinists' faces, even Elizabeth's, but hers settled into a look more curious than horrified.

Hugh looked up at the lit windows. "After I left the Church, I wandered for many years, trying to make sense of what I was. I followed legends of eternal monks rumored to reside in the Far East, immortals like ourselves. I endured great hardship to find them, but always I was directed onward, until eventually I reached a valley between three peaks where I would learn much about my nature and the nature of the world."

Into the stunned silence that followed, Elizabeth spoke. "And you left a record of that, didn't you?"

Hugh lifted his brows in surprise, likely a rare expression for the man. "I did."

Elizabeth turned to Erin, as if she should know this, too.

Then she did.

Three peaks.

Everything fell into place in her head.

32

"What is Elizabeth talking about?" Jordan asked Erin, noting a familiar expression dawning over her features, one of understanding. She had figured something out.

She took the phone from his fingers. "You have copies of my photos on here, don't you? From back in Venice."

"Yeah . . ."

She flipped through the files, pausing at one recent picture that showed her half-naked, stepping from the bathroom. He had secretly snapped it when they were at Castel Gandolfo. He couldn't resist taking it.

I mean, look at that body.

She glanced over to him, giving him a quick smile, but that wasn't the picture she was looking for. Finally, she found it and lifted the phone. "There were three peaks painted on Edward Kelly's wall. At the time, it reminded me of something Elizabeth had shown us in Venice, but then things got a little crazy in Prague."

Erin faced Hugh. "There's a famous mosaic at the cathedral in Venice, which I understand from your history was your favorite city in Italy. You spent a lot of time there."

"How could I not?" he admitted. "It is a rare city, one blended into the sea itself. It speaks to the dichotomy of man's relationship with the natural world. Venice is an example of man's struggle to both circumvent nature and be a part of it."

"And the basilica there," Erin continued. "St. Mark's. Elizabeth said that this particular mosaic was commissioned by alchemists in Prague, the very men to whom you gave your green diamond."

Erin showed everyone a picture of one of the basilica's mosaics. It showed a triptych of a black devil confronting Christ in three different ways.

Jordan remembered it himself now. "The Temptations of Christ."

"You were behind this commission, weren't you?" Erin said. "The three peaks of that valley of the monks, that's what Kelly had painted on his wall, something you must have shared with those alchemists when you gave them that diamond, something you also had represented in a mosaic of a timeless city, in a basilica that would stand for centuries. You made a record of that valley in the gold glass tiles."

Jordan still didn't understand what she meant.

Erin zoomed in on the third temptation—*it's always the number three*—and expanded the view under Christ's sandals. He was standing on a set of mountains, with a snow-globe-shaped bubble under his feet, like he was walking on water.

"You are correct," Hugh said. "Such knowledge could not be lost to time. It is too important."

"What's so important about it?" Jordan asked Hugh.

Erin answered instead. "That dome of watery light under Christ's legs, it holds *three* chalices." She stared hard at Hugh. "Those *three* chalices represent the *three* stones, don't they?"

"They do," said Hugh.

"That's where you first saw them," Erin said, "where you found them. *Arbor, Aqua,* and *Sanguis.* The gems of Garden, Water, and Blood."

"It is indeed. In that most holy valley, one of divine enlightenment."

"Enough riddles," said Rhun. "Where are these mountains?"

Hugh ignored him. "You have proven yourself adept enough, Woman of Learning. Those mountains surround a place known as the Holy Hidden Valley of Happiness."

Erin closed her eyes and gave an amused shake of her head.

"Do you know this place?" Sophia asked.

"Only by reputation. I wish I could say that such knowledge came to me from study and research, but it actually came from reading an article in a travel magazine. A pure coincidence."

"No," Hugh said. "There are no such *coincidences.*"

"So what then?" Erin asked disdainfully. "My coming upon this article was fate?"

"No. There is no such thing as *fate*. We are masters of our own destinies." Hugh waved to encompass the shadowy audience, stirring the raven still perched on his shoulder to an irritated ruffle. "It was your *awareness* and inquisitive nature that made you see and read that article, when others might have skipped it. It was your *mindfulness* that made you remember it. You have always been that way, Erin Granger. I suspect that was what drove you to abandon your family, to take a path away from one of blind obedience to the father's faith, to discover your own road to knowledge and wisdom. *Fate, luck, coincidence* . . . none of these matter. You are simply a Woman of Learning. That is your true nature. That is what brought you to me."

Erin had shifted closer to Jordan during this revelation, plainly shaken not only by this man's knowledge of her past, but also by how quickly he exposed the essential core of her being.

Jordan pulled her closer, feeling her tremble, beginning to understand how even monsters and beasts could bow down to this guy.

"Where is this valley?" Rhun pressed.

Erin answered, "Tsum Valley in Nepal. It was only recently opened to tourists due to its sacred history. It is said to be the home of Shambhala, a legendary

Buddhist kingdom. Or as it is more commonly called in Western culture: *Shangri La*."

Jordan knew that story, but only from movies. "That's supposed to be a place lost in time, where no one ages or dies."

This made him wonder: *were these* strigoi *monks the basis for that legend?*

"But there's a more important story about Shambhala that bears more directly on our situation," Erin said. "I read that the second Buddha, Padmasambhava, blessed the valley as a place that would be rediscovered when the earth was nearing it destruction, when the world grew too corrupted to survive."

"That pretty much sounds like right now," Jordan said.

"And this valley truly exists?" Rhun asked.

"It does," Erin said. "The valley has long been a sacred Buddhist place. Monks and nuns still live there, and all killing is forbidden on its slopes."

"Like here," Jordan added, wondering if Hugh had set up this hermitage as his own personal Tsum Valley.

"The monks who taught me," Hugh explained. "They lived in a monastery in that valley, built between two great trees, trees as eternal as the monks themselves. Under one bower the monks sat to meditate.

That tree was called the *Tree of Enlightenment*. Under the other, the monks drank their wine. That tree was called the *Tree of Eternal Life*."

Erin stepped free of his arm. "In other words, *the tree of knowledge* and *the tree of life*. From the biblical story of the Garden of Eden."

Even Elizabeth looked aghast. "Are you claiming this place—Tsum Valley—is the actual location of the Garden of Eden?"

Sophia scowled. "How could the Garden of Eden be in the Himalayas?"

"There is a school of thought that places it there," Erin told her. "Some scholars think that the legends of Shambhala are similar enough to the stories of Eden that they might be the same place. Like Eden, Shambhala was said to be a garden where there was no death and only the pure could remain."

"The Nazis sent an expedition to Tibet in the 1930s," Jordan added, drawing upon his knowledge of World War II. "To look for the origin of the Aryan race, a race of supermen. Those immortal Buddhist *strigoi* would definitely fit that bill, too."

All eyes turned to Hugh for confirmation.

He shrugged one shoulder. "I am merely saying that the valley has two trees. I cannot presume to know where the Garden of Eden was, or if it ever existed."

"Still," Jordan said, drawing them back to the more pressing issue, "from Edward Kelly's mural, that valley is also where all Hell is supposed to break free."

He pictured that lake and the dark shadows boiling out of it.

Hugh gave him a small nod. "The monks told me that this garden was at an intersection between good and evil. That they were guardians of that gateway."

"And what about the three stones?" Erin asked.

"According to my teachers, that trio of gems hold the power to open and close that portal between worlds. But as modern man began to encroach farther and farther into their territory, threatening to expose them, the monks feared that they might not be strong enough to guard those stones. So they gave me two of the gems, to disperse them apart in the wider world."

"In other words," Jordan said, "don't keep all your eggs in one basket."

"Timeless wisdom," Hugh concurred.

"But why did you hand such a powerful artifact to John Dee?" Elizabeth asked.

"A foolish conceit in hindsight," Hugh said with a sigh. "As the world of scientific inquiry rose out of the ashes of the Dark Ages—as alchemy became chemistry and physics—I thought I could discover more about the stones myself."

Jordan knew Cardinal Bernard had fallen into the same trap just recently, dabbling with those drops of Lucifer's blood. It was no wonder these two characters had once been best buds. They shared a similar nature.

"John Dee was a wise man and a good one," Hugh continued. "I thought that he was using the stone to contain evil, imprisoning it drop by drop. I could not fathom where that might lead. After he died, I tried to recover the gem, but the greed of Edward Kelly drove the man to sell it. From there, I lost track of the stone."

"So our goal must be to take your stone and the one in Jordan's pocket and bring them back to that valley," Erin said. "Where the monks are still safeguarding the third one. But why?"

"I only know what I have told you," Hugh said. "Perhaps the monks will know more."

"And don't forget," Jordan reminded everyone, glancing to the windows, happy to see the sunlight still shining through the waterfall, "we're not the only ones looking for those stones."

Legion was still out there.

"But why does that demon care?" asked Sophia. "What is his role?"

Rhun looked dour. "With those stones, he could possibly open the portal in that valley and unleash Hell's forces upon the world, freeing Lucifer in the process."

Erin nodded. "And apparently it'll be up to us to use those same stones to find a way to secure that demonic horde in its place, to bottle Hell back up."

"Sounds easy enough," Jordan said with exaggerated bravado. "Of course, first we'll need that gem you hid here, Hugh."

The man opened his arms wide. "You are free to seek the stone in my church."

"If Erin passed the test," Elizabeth asked, her eyes flashing angrily, "why not simply give her the stone?"

"She must find it on her own."

Jordan stared at Erin. "Sorry, babe, looks like it's time for part two of your test. So take out a Number Two pencil and begin." He looked to the shine of the lowering sun, knowing they had about an hour of daylight left.

And you'd better hurry.

6:04 P.M.

Erin scowled at Hugh de Payens.

No wonder he and Bernard were such close friends.

They both were masters of secrets and manipulation.

She faced her challenger. "Let me guess. *Aqua*, the stone of Water, is still up at that mountain lake. Which means you possess *Sanguis*, the gem of Blood. It only makes sense the monks would send that particular one with you, a *Sanguinist*."

"The gem was never meant for me," Hugh answered. "You must decipher the riddle so that you may retrieve the stone that belongs to *you*."

Belongs to me? What did that mean?

She shoved that thought aside for now and turned to face the church. If Hugh had hidden it somewhere in here, it would be somewhere significant.

"*Sanguis* . . . blood . . ." she muttered to herself.

Rhun watched her, his worried fingers rising to touch his pectoral cross. The crucifix rested over his silent heart, the silver burning his skin, the pain meant to eternally remind him of his oath to Christ and the Church. She stared a moment at his bandaged stump.

Was that not enough pain for any god?

She returned her attention to the church, recognizing it was laid out as a cross.

Like Rhun's crucifix.

A thought rose inside her. She paced it off, striding through the straw. She moved to the center of the church's cross, to where the transept intersected with the nave.

She stared back at Rhun, seeing the burn over his heart.

She stood now in the *heart* of Hugh's church.

And wasn't the purpose of a heart to pump *blood*?

The *Sanguis* stone had to be here.

Erin glanced directly over her head, back to the ceiling. Did Hugh hide it somewhere up there?

No, she decided, *that riddle's been solved.*

A previous principle echoed in her head.

As above, so below.

She stared down to her toes, then dropped to her knees. She leaned down and swept the straw from the floor, searching. She scuffled around until she found a stone with a distinct scalloped indentation.

Like a cup.

"It's under here," she said hesitatingly, then louder and more certain. "You've turned the *Sanguis* into the heart of your church, Monsieur de Payens! You've hidden it here."

The others rushed over, stirring a flight of dark birds across the bricked vault.

Hugh followed.

Rhun reached her first, lowering beside her. He held his palm over the chunk of stone she had found. "She is right. I can even feel a whisper of holiness rising from here."

Sophia joined him, warming her hands with that glow. Of all the Sanguinists, only Elizabeth hung back, her arms crossed, showing little interest.

Even the lion trotted over. The cub had kept close to Hugh, mostly eyeing the bird on the man's shoulder with a natural feline curiosity. The cat licked its chops a few times. Still once near, the cub pawed at the cupped indentation, batting at whatever it felt.

The motion drew Erin's attention back to that small feature. She ran a finger along the scalloped rim, reminded that *blood* was likely the key here, too.

"This is a Sanguinist gate, isn't it?" Erin stated. "The only way it can be opened is with the blood of a Sanguinist."

"You are truly a remarkable woman," Hugh admitted. "With a mindfulness that is impressive."

She stared at him, sensing there was still more. "Something tells me opening this particular gate isn't that simple."

"Indeed, such gates can be locked in many unique ways."

Erin remembered Bernard shutting them out with the *pro me* command.

"Even I can no longer open it," Hugh admitted. "I've secured it with a command few Sanguinists still remember. Not even my dear friend Bernard."

Erin nodded. At least that made sense. It was locked in such a way that no one could force Hugh to open it under duress.

"I am too tainted to open it now," Hugh said. "It will take purity to unlock the holy stone."

"Purity?" Erin asked.

"It will only open for a Sanguinist who has never supped of blood before drinking the wine and accepting Christ's offer." Hugh stared at them. "It will take the blood of the Chosen One."

Erin turned to Rhun.

6:18 P.M.

Rhun backed from the gazes of the others.

I am no Chosen One . . . at least, no longer.

It was true that he had not tasted human blood before becoming a Sanguinist. He remembered being attacked at his sister's gravesite by a *strigoi*, only to be saved by a trio of Sanguinists who brought him before Bernard. There, on his knees, Rhun had taken his vows, drank the wine, and accepted his mantle to join the order.

But I am far from pure now.

"It can only be you," Erin pressed him.

"It cannot be. I have sinned. I have tasted blood."

"But you were forgiven your sins in the desert," she said quietly, touching his bare shoulder. "It is *you*."

Elizabeth frowned at him. "You are the purest of us all, Rhun. What is the harm of trying? Does the fear of failure, of being found wanting, frighten you so? I thought you were of stronger mettle than that."

Rhun felt shame rise in him. Elizabeth was correct. He was scared, but he also recognized that he could not shirk from this task if there was even a chance it might do good.

He reluctantly knelt on the cold stone and bowed his head. He gripped his silver pectoral cross. The searing in his palm reminded him of his unholy nature and how it ruled him. But he must try anyway. He held his palm above the indentation in the stone, and realized that he did not have another hand to hold the knife to slice his own palm.

How far I have fallen . . . a Knight with only one arm.

Sophia came to his aid, accepting a small knife from Hugh. She pricked the center of Rhun's palm. Dark blood welled up from of the wound. Rhun turned his wrist, squeezing a fist, and spattered his cursed blood into the hollow of the stone.

Once done, he crossed himself and went through the ritual, ending with *mysterium fidei.*

Everyone stared.

Still, the stone did not move.

I have failed.

Despair drove him down, crushing him with certain truth.

My sins have doomed us all.

33

Elizabeth stared down at Rhun, his back bowed, his head hanging. He was the very sigil of defeat. She sighed at the fragility of these Sanguinists, leaning upon their faith like a beggar's crutch. Knock it away by casting doubt, and they fall so easily.

Sophia played the Greek chorus in this drama. "Rhun was our only hope. He was the only member of our order—going back millennia—who never drank blood before accepting Christ's gift."

That is not true.

At least, the archaeologist fought. "There must be another way. If we took chisel and hammer to the floor . . ."

"I will not allow the church to be desecrated in such a manner," Hugh said. "And in any such attempt, the gem will be dumped into a river that flows through the heart of this mountain, where it will be lost forever."

"So you booby-trapped your secret vault," Jordan said. "Gotta say, you covered your bases well."

As Elizabeth watched Rhun's lips move in futile prayer, she pitied him. He had given everything for his God, and his sacrifice had been wasted. In the eyes of the Lord, he was judged as impure as any feral *strigoi*. This failure was his reward for centuries of service to Christ.

So Rhun would certainly find it particularly galling at who would save them now, who could open this vault when he could not.

"Step aside," Elizabeth said, slipping the knife from Sophia's fingers.

Elizabeth knelt beside Rhun and used a fistful of straw to scrub his blood from the receptacle in the stone.

Rhun watched her. "What are—?"

"Quiet," she scolded.

Still on her knees, she cut her palm and studied the blood as it pooled. In its glossy surface, the reflection of her own face shone back at her.

Sorry, Rhun, I know how this will pain you.

She chanted the proper Latin words. *" 'For this is the Chalice of My Blood, of the new and everlasting Testament.' "*

She then turned her hand and let her blood drip into the indentation on the floor. It quickly filled the shallow reservoir. Once it was full, she chanted the final words of the incantation. *"Mysterium fidei."*

With a soft scrape, the stone sank into the floor, then moved to the side.

She heard the gasps of disbelief.

Only Erin laughed.

The others turned to her.

"I get it," Erin said. "Elizabeth was made whole when Rhun returned her soul in the desert. Then back at St. Mark's, when Bernard stripped her of that new soul by making her a *strigoi* again, she wasn't allowed to drink any blood. Instead, she was forced to drink the wine that very night."

"And I've not touched a drop of blood since then," Elizabeth added, as she turned to Rhun. "By the dictates of the Church, my being remains pure. I am the Chosen One. And here is your proof."

She shifted aside to allow a beam of sunlight from the church's windows to fall inside the hollow. Fiery light reflected back from the surface of a dark red gemstone hidden inside, setting its facets ablaze. The brilliance seemed to pour forth from the stone's heart.

Though her eyes were dazzled, Elizabeth gazed deep into the crimson stone, stunned by its beauty. She had beheld many gems in her lifetime. In her mortal life, she had been one of the richest women in the world. But none of those gems had held the same fascination as this one.

She was not the only one so captured.

Jordan crashed to his knees, the light dappling his face, looking like fresh blood.

"It sings," he moaned.

6:27 P.M.

Jordan's heart sang to the fiery stone, and it answered in a holy symphony, drawing him ever deeper into its melody, into its light. Around him, the world faded to shadows before such brilliance.

How could it not?

Distantly he heard the others chattering, but their words were mere undertones before the glory of that singing.

"Can't you hear it?" he asked, trying to get them to listen.

A sharper voice cut through the melody, ringing between the individual notes. "Erin Granger, take the stone! Cover it from the light before he's lost to it forever!"

He recognized the voice of the hermit.

Then moments later, the radiance dimmed, muffling that eternal song. The world found its substance, weight, and shadows. He saw a woman wrapping the gem in white linen, dousing its fire. Her eyes looked upon him with fear and worry.

Another carried a bag to her, and she stuffed the treasure into it. The sound of the zipper closing was loud in the quiet church.

Jordan's arms lifted toward the woman, toward the pack. He ached to take the stone from its hiding place, to bare it to the sunlight, to hear its song to the end.

The woman took another step back. "Did any of you hear *singing*?" she asked.

A chorus of denial answered her.

Slowly, more of the world grew solid around him. But if he strained, he could still hear a faint whisper of that song from the pack, even an echo from his own pocket. That echo was a darker emerald, full of verdant life, and the promise of root and leaf, flower and stem.

"Jordan," a sweet voice said at his ear. "Can you hear me?"

Yes.

"Jordan, answer me. Please." Then softer as she turned away. "What's wrong with him?"

"He is unbalanced." *The hermit again.*

"What does that mean?"

"He was touched by angelic blood. While it protects him and heals him, it also consumes more of his humanity each time it saves him. You can see a map of this war written on his skin. If the angelic force prevails, he will be lost to you forever."

A hand touched his forehead, as icy as snowmelt against his hot skin.

"How can we help him?" *Her name is . . . Erin.*

"Do not let him forget his own humanity."

"What exactly does that mean? What do we do?"

He heard a change in that faint song, drawing his attention away. It was a whisper of minor chords, a darker thread woven through the song, inserting deeper notes of warning.

He forced his lips to move. "Someone's coming."

Silence followed, letting him listen more closely.

"Impossible," the hermit started again. "I have guards posted all around. In the shadows of the forest, in the dark tunnels. They would have warned me. You are safe."

The black notes beat louder in his head.

The lion growled, its white fur bristling with warning.

Jordan stood, strode to a wall, and grabbed a long-handled weapon.

"Put down the hoe," the hermit said. "There is no need for violence."

Jordan turned to face the deep shadows at the rear of the church.

Too late.

He is here.

6:48 P.M.

Legion stepped into the dark tunnel from the shadowy bower of the old forest. Others led him, those he found lurking in the woods, those of a corrupted nature who had thought to find peace on this mountaintop. Instead, they ended with Legion's palm resting upon their cheek, where he branded them, claimed them. He took in their memories, their knowledge of the lair of the hermit, learning the secret ways into that mountain.

Earlier in the day, after gaining knowledge of this place through the eyes and ears of Father Gregory, Legion had left Prague, his still-weak body carried by those who bore his mark. A trio of branded Sanguinists had secured a vessel, a helicopter with windows shaded against the sun so he could be whisked over lands bright with the new day.

They had landed on the far side of the mountain from where the enemy's helicopter sat. From there, this old forest protected him from the sun's touch. As he had climbed, he had basked in the scent of the rich loam, the mold of decaying wood, the sweetness of leaf and bark. His eyes drank in the dark emerald of the canopy, the soft petals of flowers. His ears heard every rustle, chirp, and scurry of life, reminding him of the paradise this world could be, if untouched by the molestation of man.

I will return this to a true garden, he had thought. *I will reap and weed and burn until it is paradise once again.*

In that forest, he had discovered the hermit's guardians—both beast and *strigoi*—those loyal to a man who promised a path to serenity. It only took a touch to free them from such conceit, to make them his own, so no alarm would be raised.

Legion entered their tunnels now, amused that the enemy had sought such a refuge, surrounding themselves with the corrupted, those who could so easily be turned against them. He continued into the mountain, spreading with every touch, a storm growing within the dark heart of this mountain.

With every step deeper into the hermit's lair, his eyes multiplied, his voice expanded. His enslaved called others to him. They came to him, like moths to his cold flame, swelling his ranks further.

He followed his forces ever deeper—until he heard familiar heartbeats.

The Woman's frantic flutter, the Warrior's thunderous beat.

Here was the pair who came so close to destroying his vessel.

Fury fired through him as he lifted an arm.

Go, he commanded.

His storm raged through the tunnels, preparing to break upon those below. He knew the others had already obtained the second stone. Its fiery song had echoed up to him as he fell toward it. Knowing that the stone had been found, he no longer needed any of these others, not even the Knight.

Legion cast out his final order, filling his desire into his army's silent hearts.

Kill them all.

6:50 P.M.

With the cub at his side, Rhun snatched a scythe from among the garden tools.

Sophia grabbed a wood axe in one hand, a hammer in the other.

Elizabeth raised a shovel.

Rhun turned, just as figures boiled out of a tunnel at the rear of the church, falling upon those *strigoi* and *blasphemare* gathered there, like a wave crashing on rocks.

If not for Jordan's warning moments ago, they would have been unprepared, ambushed before they could react.

One of the attackers broke through the fighting, flying through the air toward Erin. She was down on one knee, pulling up the backpack holding the stone and gospel, protecting them both.

Rhun swept to her side, swinging high with the scythe, cleaving through the leg of the beast and knocking its body away. The *strigoi* crashed to the floor, black blood pouring from its severed limb. Still, it struggled to come at them, clawing and kicking, a furious scream ripping from its throat, exposing a black handprint branded on its pale cheek.

The mark of Legion.

Then Jordan appeared, moving as swiftly as a striking hawk. He swung down with his hoe and split the creature's skull.

Rhun pulled Erin to her feet, as Jordan spun away, breaking his weapon over the back of a *blasphemare* panther. Then he twisted around to stab the splintered end through the animal's eye. Before Rhun could even react, Jordan turned and ripped the scythe from his hand.

Rhun did not protest, retreating instead with Erin, knowing he had to keep her and what she carried safe.

Sophia and Elizabeth guarded his sides, while Jordan took the fight to the enemy as more beasts and *strigoi* flooded into the back of the church. Their numbers were overwhelming. It was a fight they could not win.

Then light burst brighter behind Rhun's back, accompanied by a great roaring.

"To me!" Hugh shouted.

Rhun glanced back to see Hugh drag the second of the church's double doors open, revealing the thunderous cascade of water beyond the threshold. Rhun also noted how shadowy that light appeared. While a few minutes of the day remained, Hugh's church faced east. With the sun setting to the *west*, the shoulder of the mountain shadowed the threshold. The light was too meager to offer true protection.

Proving this to be true, another *strigoi* broke through and came at them.

But a flash of white shot through the air and tackled the thin form to the floor, raking its face and throat with silver claws, as if trying to erase Legion's mark from that flesh.

Hugh grabbed Rhun's elbow and shoved a rolled sheet of leathery vellum at him. "An ancient map, etched on calfskin. It will show you the way to the valley."

Rhun accepted the scroll and shoved it through the belt of his pants to secure it. He then grabbed Erin around the waist, knowing there was only one way to survive this assault.

"We must jump," he said.

Erin twisted in his grip, facing the dark church and the war inside. "Jordan . . ."

Rhun spotted the man, a rock in the middle of a black maelstrom. Jordan moved with incredible speed and ferocity, bleeding from a thousand cuts, spattering that darkness with his holy blood, burning and cutting a swath around him with his scythe.

But even the Warrior of Man could not stand long before such a storm.

As Rhun watched, Jordan collapsed to one knee, about to be swamped.

"We'll get him," Sophia said, waving to Elizabeth.

Hugh whistled, and from the shadows, the pack of black dogs appeared. "Defend them," Hugh ordered, pointing to the two women. "The Warrior of Man must not fall."

The pack took off with Sophia and Elizabeth.

Rhun tightened his hold on Erin. "They will not fail," he promised her.

She stared up at him, her eyes shining with fear, but she trusted him enough to nod.

Across the way, a new figure emerged into the church, darker than the shadows, a black sculpture of a former friend.

Erin spotted that monster, too.

Legion wearing Leopold's skin.

So the demon still lived.

Rhun did not wait and took the only path left to them.

He pulled Erin close, backed to the thunderous roar, and leaped out of the mountain.

6:55 P.M.

Erin gasped at the icy cold, only to have the air pounded from her chest by the force of the water. She tumbled as she plummeted, but Rhun's one arm was iron around her shoulders, his legs were steel around her lower waist, his cheek against hers.

Then they hit the pool below with an impact that jarred her every bone. They plunged deep, to where the waters grew dark. She sucked in water, choking. Then she felt herself propelled upward. Rhun kicked with his legs, but he kept his arm around her, never letting go.

They breached the surface, greeted by the roar of the falls.

She coughed out water, gasping great gulps of air.

Rhun dragged her toward the shoreline. She finally caught enough breath to kick and paddle on her own. They crawled on hands and knees out of the pool. She turned, sitting on a hip, staring upward. With the sun almost set behind the mountain, the waterfall was dark, hiding the church behind it.

"Jordan," Erin choked out.

Rhun stood and staggered to their pile of clothing and gear. Erin recognized the wisdom of his action and followed, her limbs shaking from cold and fear. She grabbed her Colt 1911. The steel butt in her grip helped settle her.

Rhun recovered his silver *karambit*. "The sun will be down in minutes. We must go."

"What about Jordan and the others?"

As if summoned by her words, a tangle of figures burst from the dark cascade. They fell through the air and crashed into the pool below, plunging deep. Erin rushed to the shore, searching the water, watching a storm of bubbles rise—then from the depths, a figure burst forth.

Elizabeth.

She dragged up the limp form of Jordan, rolling him to his back. He wasn't moving. Blood spread around him, staining the blue waters like an oil slick. Lacerations and scratches crisscrossed his chest. White bone shone through one huge gaping wound.

Then Sophia popped into view behind them, pulling up the waterlogged form of the young lion. The cat paddled and thrashed, momentarily panicked, hacking out water. But the cub regained its wits and followed the others.

Erin waded in with Rhun to help pull Jordan out.

Jordan's eyes stared up, shining blue but clearly seeing nothing.

Was he dead?

Then his chest heaved once, then again.

"He still lives," Elizabeth said. "But his heart weakens with every beat."

"She's right," Rhun said. "Even his miraculous healing might not be able to save him without help."

Erin wished she had their senses, to hear his heart, to be even that much closer to Jordan.

Sophia pointed toward the dark forest and the lower slopes. "We must get off this mountain. Already the path is shadowed enough to allow Legion's forces to hunt us down."

A loud watery splash jerked them all around.

A massive black shape leaped into view through the falls, thick limbs outspread. Everyone backed away.

Jordan remained sprawled on the banks of the pool, his blood still seeping into the water.

The huge figure hit the water not far from the shoreline, crashing only waist-deep, its muscular legs showing no effect from a fall from that height.

Erin lifted her Colt, pointing it at the chest of the *blasphemare*. She had spotted this creature earlier in the church, one of Hugh's menagerie.

The black-coated mountain gorilla waded toward Jordan.

"Don't," Sophia said, pushing Erin's arm down. "He remains uncorrupted. He was at Hugh's side when we leaped out of the church."

The gorilla scooped Jordan up and gently draped his bloody body over its shoulder. The beast made a chuffing noise, nudging the muzzle of his face forward.

"Hugh must have sent him to help us," Sophia said.

"Then grab weapons," Rhun ordered.

Sophia and Elizabeth quickly armed themselves. Erin took the strap of Jordan's machine pistol and hung it around her neck.

For you to use when you're better, she promised Jordan.

They fled across the meadow as a group, led by the gorilla, which loped ahead of them, knuckling his way through the grasses.

"What about Hugh?" Erin asked.

Elizabeth looked back, her face oddly mournful. "He would not abandon his flock."

"He also intended to buy us time," Sophia said, hurrying forward.

As they reached the tree line, screams rose behind them. A tumble of dark shapes burst out of the falls, like ants boiling out of a flooded hill.

Looks like we're out of time.

34

Legion lifted his palm from the woman's cheek, brushing the fall of blond hair from her face. He watched as her eyes became his. He could now see through her eyes to view the glory of his own face. He knew her name now, too, as her memories filled him.

Francesca.

Through scores of other eyes, he spied upon his hunters as they chased down their prey in the forest outside, heard their howls echoing down the mountain slopes.

Legion remained in the church, facing his own target.

By now, he owned all the beasts and *strigoi* in the chapel.

Save one.

The hermit faced him, his back against the wall, bloody but standing firm. No trace of fear marked his smooth face. His brown eyes gazed calmly into Legion's.

"You can stop," the man said. "Even now. Peace and forgiveness is not beyond anyone. Even you, a spirit of darkness."

"You seek to absolve me," Legion said, mirth rising inside him. "But I am beyond sin and damnation, so need no forgiveness. But for you"—he held up a hand—"let me take away your pain, your suffering, even your false sense of peace. You will find true serenity in mindless obedience. And in doing so, you will share with me all you know, all you told them."

"I will tell you nothing."

The hermit turned away, as if to shun his offer. But instead, the man's hands grabbed hold of a giant wooden lever hidden in a crack. With a tremendous heave, he hauled it down. A loud crash echoed from below, setting the floor to quaking—then it gave way beneath them both.

Legion lunged forward as great sections of brick and loose stone broke away under his feet. The hermit leaped high to snatch the thick iron braids of a wall sconce. Legion followed, catching the man's boot with a black hand.

As he hung there, the remainder of the floor crashed into a vast pit hidden below the church, taking with it all his remaining forces. A great cloud of brick dust and exploded bits of broken timbers burst upward, bringing with it the rumbling sound of water. It echoed from far below, marking some subterranean vein of this peak, a great river that washed into the roots of the mountain.

If Legion fell below, he would be trapped forever in the bowels of the earth, imprisoned as surely as he had been in the heart of that green diamond.

Terror bubbled up inside him.

Legion stared upward, finding the face of the hermit shining down at him.

Don't, he willed to the man.

But Legion's fingers only clasped leather, not skin. The hermit's will was still his own. And using that will, the man uncurled his fingers and let go.

Together, they plummeted into the darkness below.

7:10 P.M.

"Keep going!" Rhun shouted to the others.

A moment ago, he had heard a muffled explosion, a great grinding of stone and splintering woods. He did not know what that meant, only that his group was still hunted, pursued by a howling, slathering mix of *strigoi* and *blasphemare*.

Rhun kept beside Erin. Ahead, the gorilla lumbered with Jordan over one shoulder, moving quickly down the side of the mountain, barreling through bushes, shouldering aside saplings like twigs. His bulk broke a path through the dense forest before them, like a boulder rolling downhill.

Sophia had borrowed Jordan's weapon and strafed behind them as they fled. Silver rounds ripped through pine needles and shredded leaves from trees. Elizabeth haunted their path to his left, lashing out with a sword and knife. To the right, the cub protected their flank, moving like a ghost.

Still, they were losing ground quickly.

The enemy threatened to crash over them at any moment.

Sophia appeared next to Rhun, throwing her smoking weapon across her back.

"Out of ammunition." Fear shone in her face. "We'll never make it. We'll have to—"

A booming shout cut her off. "EVERYBODY DOWN!"

Rhun obeyed, recognizing the voice. He threw Erin into a thick pile of leaf litter and piled on top of her.

The others dropped low. Even the cub slid to Rhun's side and mimicked him. A white tail slashed angrily through the leaves.

Only the gorilla continued its course, pounding down the slope.

In the beast's wake, Christian stepped into view several yards down slope. He crouched low, balancing the butt of two machine guns on his thighs—and opened fire.

The silvery barrage tore apart the forest, raining bits of wood and leaves over them. The chattering roar deafened Rhun. Even when it finally ended, his ears still rang with the noise.

"Go!" Christian yelled, tossing the spent weapons aside. "That'll only buy us a little time! Make for the helicopter!"

They gained their feet and paws and ran even faster.

Finally, they burst out of the forest into the open meadow. The helicopter rumbled ahead of them, the engines already warmed and ready, the rotors slowly spinning.

By now, the sun had fully set.

They needed to be off this mountain.

The gorilla waited for them by the aircraft, leaning on one thick arm, huffing loudly, plainly exhausted.

They joined the beast. Sophia and Christian helped lift Jordan into the back cabin. Erin clambered up with him, hovering over him.

Rhun stepped to the gorilla and placed a palm on his massive shoulder. "Thank you."

A part of him had still questioned the work of Hugh, believing the redemption for such cursed creatures to be impossible.

No longer.

The gorilla nudged Rhun in the chest, as if it understood.

Then it turned and headed back toward the forest, its gaze raised toward that distant waterfall, intending to return, to protect the man who had offered the great beast not only a home—but also his heart.

Rhun looked to that mountain as he climbed into the helicopter.

May the Lord keep you safe.

7:22 P.M.

Legion lay broken across a nest of broken timber and shattered chunks of the church floor. The jumble of debris had caught on a craggy ledge along one wall of the cavernous pit, building into this precarious perch. He had crashed here, not by luck, but by sheer strength of will. He had spotted the buildup as he fell and hurled his body toward it, hoping it would hold him.

And not just him.

He had never let go of the hermit's boot as he plummeted. The man's body lay sprawled beside his own, even more broken. His adversary's neck was twisted at a wrong angle; his blood seeped through the stones and trickled into the river far below.

But faint life still remained.

Perhaps enough.

Legion carefully rolled to his side, grinding bones.

I will know what you know.

He reached to the man's pale cheek as brown eyes stared back at him, weak but defiant still. Legion ignored that gaze and placed his palm upon his victim. With a touch, he sensed how feeble the flame remained inside the hermit, barely a flicker.

Was it enough?

Concern grew in Legion as he pulled his hand away. As he feared, his palm had left no mark. The hermit was too close to death to hold his brand. Legion tried again, but his darkness could find nothing substantial enough to claim.

The hermit closed his eyes, a smile playing across the old priest's lips, believing he had bested Legion.

You are wrong.

Legion crawled higher. While he might not be able to claim the man as a demon, there were other paths to knowledge.

My vessel is still a strigoi.

He bared those fangs. As if sensing the predator at his throat, the man's eyes reopened, showing fear as understanding came too late.

Legion sank his teeth deep into that cold flesh. He drank fully of that fading font, building a blood bond between the two of them, between predator and prey, between *strigoi* and victim. With each drop, Legion drew more of the man's life into him, sopping up the last of the man's strength, willing him to share all that he knew as they became one.

Even as that knowledge was gained, Legion continued to feed, draining his victim in great draughts until there was nothing left. Only then did he sprawl back and cast his will to those who still survived, calling for rope to haul him up, for more blood to heal him.

He smiled into the darkness.

He had learned something from the hermit, something not shared with the others. Whether this was done purposefully or from simple disregard, he did not know.

Still, he would use that knowledge against his enemy.

But first I must be free . . . and reach the valley ahead of them.

35

Erin held Jordan's slack hand as their helicopter landed hard in a cow field on the outskirts of the
French village of Lasserre. Moments ago, their aircraft
had hurtled out of the mountains and into the foothills,
sweeping over this darkened hamlet, a quaint settle-
ment of stone homes, stretches of vineyards, and small
farms.

Once on the ground, Christian popped from behind
the helicopter's stick and went around to unfold a
stretcher from a cargo hold. Sophia and Elizabeth
helped get Jordan's body off the backseat and onto the
padded board outside. Erin followed them, trying not

to stare at the amount of blood soaked into the aircraft's seat and pooled on the leather.

Jordan, don't die on me.

On the flight, Erin and Elizabeth had used a first-aid kit to clean and bandage the largest of the wounds. The countess had moved deftly, apparently experienced with treating battle wounds. But they ran out of supplies before they could finish covering his wounds. Afterward, Erin had wrapped his body with a red emergency blanket, but she checked beneath it periodically, quickly realizing even the smaller cuts weren't healing this time. Jordan was dying.

Terrified, she climbed out and joined the others. She searched around, noting a small homestead beyond a fencerow. All its windows blazed with light.

Why did we land here?

"Jordan needs a hospital," Erin demanded, expressing her confusion and frustration. "A team of doctors."

"This'll have to do." Christian hauled up one end of the stretcher. "Nearest hospital is too far."

Sophia took the other end, while Rhun secured the lion in his crate in the helicopter. Christian didn't wait and headed toward the house. Erin had to run to keep alongside Jordan in the stretcher.

"Then where are we taking him?" she asked.

"A retired doctor lives here," Christian called back to her. "A friend to the order. He's expecting us."

As they neared the front door, a grizzled old man opened it for them and gestured them inside. He wore brown corduroy pants and a blue plaid shirt. He had a shock of thick white hair and whisky-brown eyes under shaggy eyebrows. His lined face was grave when he looked at Jordan.

The doctor barked at them in French.

The Sanguinists hurried the stretcher through a rustic hall and into a back kitchen. Erin kept pace behind them.

In the kitchen, a cast-iron stove took up one corner of the room. Heat radiated from its surface, and a pot of water steamed on the stovetop. A stack of folded rough-spun towels sat on a chair, and on top of them rested a cracked leather medical bag. It looked like a movie prop and not something that could help them.

The Sanguinist lifted Jordan from the stretcher and onto the kitchen table.

Seeing Jordan under these brighter lights, Erin felt faint. The crimson lines had spread much farther by now, stretching across his chest, up his neck, and onto his face. Angry-looking curlicues looped over his chin and up to his lips. The lines stood out in stark contrast to his ashen face.

But at least, the smaller cuts *did* appear to be finally healing.

Then the doctor peeled back a patch of bloody gauze, and Erin's stomach clenched. A deep slash extended from Jordan's right shoulder to his left hip. It still gaped open, revealing bone and bloody muscle.

The doctor's gnarled hands moved quickly as he washed Jordan's chest with one of the towels, handing it to Erin when he was finished. She held the warm, bloody cloth in her hands, not sure what to do until Sophia took it away.

"Will he be all right?" Erin asked.

"He's lost a lot of blood," the doctor answered in English. "But I'm more concerned about the big wound there. It's not bleeding much, but it's not clotted either. It's as if the blood vessels have closed down."

"What can you do to help him?" Erin hated the note of hysteria in her voice. She took a deep breath to drive it down, needing to stay calm, for Jordan.

"I'm going to stitch up the arteries and close the wound. But he's burning with fever. I don't understand why. With this much hemorrhaging, his temperature should be plummeting. I'll have to get it down."

"No," Erin and Rhun said at the same time.

"The fever is not caused by any disease," Rhun explained.

"It's something beyond physiology," Erin added, trying to find the words to explain the inexplicable. "Something in his blood, something capable of helping him heal."

At least, I hope so.

The doctor shrugged. "I don't understand—and I'm not sure I want to—but I'll treat him like a normal patient and see if he comes round. I can't do anything else."

As the doctor worked, Erin pulled the remaining chair next to the table and took Jordan's hand. It burned in her palm. She ran her fingers through his short blond hair, his scalp soaked now with fever sweat.

Christian joined the doctor. "Let me help, Hugo. You know my skill."

"I would welcome it," the doctor said. "Fetch the instruments out of that pot of boiling water."

Erin wanted to help, too, but she knew her place, holding tight to Jordan's hand. Physically, the doctor was doing all he could, but she knew Jordan's wounds went deeper than that. She traced her finger along the whorled line on the back of his hand, both hating that mark and praying for the power that ran through it to save the man she loved. She knew that same power could consume him completely, steal him from her as readily as death, but was that a bad thing for Jordan?

He might be transcending his humanity and becoming wholly angelic. His transformation had never seemed to bother him like it bothered her. How could she weigh her selfish desires to keep him against his chance to become an angel?

The warning from Hugh de Payens echoed through her: *Do not let him forget his own humanity.*

But what did that mean?

9:21 P.M.

Jordan drifted within an emerald fog, lost to himself, lost to everything but a faint whisper of melody. It sang softly to him, promising peace, drawing him ever deeper into its sweet embrace.

But the smallest sliver of him remained, a single note against that mighty chorus. It coalesced into a hard knot of resistance, around a single word.

No.

Around that word, memories aggregated, like a pearl forming around a grain of sand.

. . . arguing with his sister about who would get the front seat of the car . . .

. . . fighting hard to drag a wounded friend to safety as bullets flew . . .

. . . refusing to give up on a cold case, to find justice when all others gave up . . .

A new word formed out of those fleeting glimpses, defining his nature, a core from which to build more.

Stubborn.

He accepted that as himself and used it to struggle, to twist and kick, to search beyond the promise of the song, to want more than peace.

His thrashing stirred the fog—clearing it enough to catch a pinprick of reddish light in the distance. He moved toward it, sensing enough of himself now to add a new word.

Longing.

The fiery mote grew larger, occasionally wavering, sometimes disappearing entirely. But he focused on it, anchoring more of himself to it, knowing it mattered, even when the faint notes told him it didn't.

Finally, that ruby particle grew close enough, steady enough, to discern a new noise: a drumbeat. It thrummed against the chorus, a counterpoint to those soft notes. That drum pounded and galloped, full of chaos and turmoil, everything that the music wasn't.

A new word formed, defining its messy perfection.

Life.

He felt himself born again with that thought, a birth accompanied by lancing pain that shot through the fog and gave him limbs, and chest, and bones, and blood.

He took those new hands and covered his ears as they formed, too, shutting out those sweet notes.

Still, that red drumbeat grew louder and louder.

He recognized it now.

A human heartbeat, fragile and small, simple and ordinary.

He opened his eyes to find a face staring down at him.

"Erin . . ."

9:55 P.M.

"The hero awakes," Elizabeth said, trying to sound disdainful, but even to her own ears, her words appeared thankful, even happy.

How could they not?

Joy suffused Erin's face as she kissed Jordan. The woman's relief shone from her skin; tenderness glowed from her eyes. Rhun had once looked upon Elizabeth in such a manner. Unbidden, her fingers rose to touch her lips, remembering. She forced her hand back down.

After almost two hours in the makeshift surgery, Jordan now rested on a small bed in a back room of the farmhouse, his body swaddled in bandages, his face a map of sutures. The doctor had done good work, but Elizabeth knew the true healing went beyond those many stitches.

Rhun stirred on a lumpy chair in the room's corner, disturbing the young lion curled at his feet. He had let the cat join them inside as they set up this bedside vigil. Christian and Sophia had prayed over the man, until eventually they drifted outside, to stretch those pious knees of theirs and to make further plans.

Rhun rose now, touched Erin on the shoulder, then turned toward Elizabeth. "I will share the good news with Sophia and Christian."

As he left, Elizabeth stepped over to Erin, standing behind her with her arms crossed. The archaeologist's love for her man was revealed in her every touch, her every whisper. Erin said something that raised a smile on Jordan's face, crinkling his sutures, causing him to wince, but not stop grinning.

Despite all the good cheer, Elizabeth studied the crimson lines wended across his body, over his face.

It is true that you still breathe, but you are not well.

But she kept such gloomy thoughts to herself.

The doctor returned, having apparently heard word about his patient, and set about examining Jordan: shining a light in his eyes, listening to his heartbeat, placing a palm on his forehead.

"*Incroyable,*" the man muttered as he straightened and shook his head.

A door slammed, and Rhun rushed in with his fellow Sanguinists. Earlier, they had all consumed wine, even Elizabeth. She felt restored now and saw the same vitality shining in the others, but beneath that, she read the anxiety in their faces, the impatience in their postures and movements.

They knew the truth.

The world was falling into darkness this night, with dreadful stories of bloodshed and monsters being told on the television, on the radio. Warnings and panic were growing by the hour.

They dared not tarry very much longer.

Christian spoke hurriedly as he entered with Rhun. "Our Citation jet is fueled and waiting. We can be at the tarmac in fifteen minutes and wheels up immediately after that. If I push the engines to the red line, we can reach Katmandu in under seven hours. We'll be coasting in on fumes by then, but we should be able to make it."

That plan depended on one crucial detail.

Christian asked it now, dropping to sit at the foot of the bed. "How are you doing?"

"Been better," Jordan answered.

Rhun faced the doctor. "How soon will he be fit enough to travel?"

The man looked aghast at Rhun, swore sharply in French, then answered, "Days, if not weeks!"

"I'm ready now," Jordan said, struggling to sit up—and actually succeeding. "I can sleep on the plane."

Erin turned to Rhun, worry shining in her eyes, clearly begging him to discourage Jordan, to agree with the doctor.

Instead, Rhun turned his back on her. "Then we leave now. Be ready."

Only Elizabeth glimpsed Rhun's face as she brushed past her. She saw how speaking those words to Erin had left him demolished.

And upon seeing that look, a part of Elizabeth was crushed, too, recognizing how much Rhun still loved that woman.

So Elizabeth let Rhun go—both from the room and from her heart.

There is another who needs me more.

36

March 19, 10:04 P.M. CET
Rome, Italy

Tommy ran across the dark street toward the glowing dome of St. Peter's Basilica. The square in front of it was normally full of tourists, wandering around and gawking at everything, but tonight it was empty due to the curfew. Scores of patrols traveled the city, a mix of armed men and Sanguinist priests in civilian clothing.

But they were losing this night.

Sirens echoed over the city, punctuated by screams. Fires burned out there, casting up ribbons of smoke from countless spots.

Tommy tripped on a curb and fell to a knee. He was hauled immediately back to his feet by one of his three

Sanguinist guards. They were moving him from his apartment by the river to Vatican City.

For your protection, he had been told.

He had tried to object, fearing that Elizabeth wouldn't know where he was being moved. He had tried calling after sunset, growing scared as the chaos grew, but the lines were busy, overloaded.

Ahead, somebody had set up barricades across the entrance to St. Peter's Square. Metal plates had been bolted in place, standing ten feet tall. Armed snipers stood in special bulletproof cages on top. Giant lights shone out from the base of the barrier, illuminating the surrounding streets.

The city was under siege.

But by whom?

Earlier, he had watched BBC news, glued to the television, seeing reports of nighttime attackers all across Europe and beyond. Troops patrolled the major cities, especially after dark. Rome wasn't the only city falling under martial law.

To Tommy, it sounded as if the *strigoi* had gotten stronger and were out of control.

As his small group reached the barricade and were whisked through, Tommy gawked at the sheer number of Swiss Guardsmen and robed Sanguinists inside, both on the walls and up on the balconies surrounding the plaza. More armed men rushed in after them, before the gates were resealed.

It seemed the Church was pulling back a majority of its soldiers, protecting itself, leaving everyone else pretty much on their own.

Tommy was marched across the square toward the basilica. Even those massive doors had been covered in new metal plates.

"You'll be safe in St. Peter's for the night," one of his guards tried to reassure him.

Maybe . . .

Worry for Elizabeth burned through him. She was out there. Somewhere. Who knew what trouble she faced? Tommy selfishly wanted her at his side. Only then would he truly feel *safe*. But he also knew there were some things even Elizabeth couldn't protect him against.

He coughed into his hand, hacking loudly, doubling over in pain.

He stared at his palm.

Blood.

Sixth

Ye serpents, ye generation of vipers, how can ye escape the damnation of hell?

—**Matthew 23:33**

37

March 20, 10:48 A.M. NPT
Airborne over the Himalayas, Nepal

Erin held her breath as their helicopter climbed toward the knife-edge of the snowy mountain. The icy wall ahead soared to an elevation of twenty thousand feet, the outside limit of their aircraft's ability to fly. When they reached the crest, their rotors kicked up swirls of snow, as wind batted the craft back and forth. The helicopter seemed trapped, balancing on that icy razor—then the nose dipped and they slid down the far side of the mountains.

Erin let out a loud breath, rolling her neck from side to side, trying to let go of the tension.

"Landing in ten," Christian radioed back from the pilot's seat, his voice irritatingly calm.

They had just crossed over the last range of mountains—the Ganesh Himal—and descended now toward a long valley. Giant sharp peaks surrounded them on all sides, which explained why this place had remained untouched by the modern world for so long. According to the ancient map that Hugh de Payens had supplied, a river should be meandering through the valley's center, but below, Erin only saw a glaring blanket of uninterrupted whiteness. The river was likely frozen over and covered in snow this time of year. Maybe in summer this valley was a lush and verdant place, but right now it looked like an inhospitable wasteland.

Definitely no Garden of Eden.

Working circulation back into her legs, Erin stomped her heavy snow boots. The steel ice crampons clanged against the metal floor. Even though she was warmed by the cabin heater and decked out in winter gear, the cold of these mountains found its way down to her bones.

Or maybe it was simply the fear.

She glanced to the others, huddled in white parkas. While the cold-blooded Sanguinists had no need for such insulated gear, the snowy color offered good camouflage for this wintry terrain. Even the lion cub, with his white ruff and fur, seemed built for this expedition.

Everyone stirred, readying themselves for what was to come.

Erin craned her neck by the window and stared up at the sun. It hung in a bright blue sky, marred by a few smudges of cirrus clouds. It was a little more than an hour until noon.

Jordan noted her glance skyward and reached to squeeze her knee. "Who says the deadline is midday anyway? We may have more time than that to close the gates of Hell."

She turned to him. His face bore only faint scars from the recent attack, but now his pale skin whorled and ran with crimson lines, covering half his face. Jordan had his parka unzipped, seemingly oblivious of the cold. Erin imagined if she took off her snow gloves, she could warm her hands off the heat flowing from him.

She took a deep breath and turned away, unable to stare at those lines any longer, knowing they marked how little of Jordan's humanity remained. Still, a part of her felt guilty, even selfish, at her reaction to Jordan's state. He had come back from the edge of death in France because of his angelic power and his human stubbornness. When the time came, he would have to decide which path to walk. And she would have to let him, no matter how much she feared to lose him.

To distract from these worrisome thoughts, she answered his question. "We have only until noon today."

"Why do you sound so certain?" Rhun asked from across the cabin. His lion stretched on the neighboring seat, arching his spine into a bent bow.

Elizabeth answered Rhun before Erin could. "Look at the moon."

Faces turned toward the various windows. A full moon hovered at the sun's blazing edge.

Jordan leaned against Erin to see out. "Bernard mentioned that there would be an eclipse today," he muttered. "But only a partial one, if I'm remembering right."

"A *partial* one in France," Erin corrected him. "This far east, it will be a *total* eclipse. I checked during the flight here. Totality will reach the Himalayas at one minute past noon."

She remembered the mural painted on Edward Kelly's wall. That bloodred sun above that black lake could have been the artist's representation of a full eclipse.

Knowing this, she wished they had made better time getting here. Piloted by Christian, their Citation X jet had raced across Europe and Asia. En route, Bernard had regularly updated them by satellite phone on the conditions on the ground, about the surge of attacks erupting across the dark cities they flew over. The *strigoi* and *blasphemare* had grown bolder and stronger as the tide of evil spread, shifting the balance in their favor. But those monsters were only the spark of this firestorm. Simple panic did the rest, stoking those flames of chaos even higher.

As Christian swung them around a shoulder of a mountain, a small village appeared, tucked against the slope. Atop the peaked slate roofs, chimneys cast ribbons of smoke into the air, showing people inside cooking, laughing, living. It reminded her of what they were fighting to preserve.

A lone yak walked along a narrow snow-covered path. A brightly clad figure walked at its side, a cap pulled tightly over a round head. Both the dark-skinned man and the yak stopped to stare up at their helicopter.

Erin pressed a palm against the glass, wishing them both a long and happy life.

As the village vanished behind them, the last sight of habitation was a Buddhist temple, its gutters strewn with lines of fluttering prayer flags.

But it was not the temple they had come to find.

Christian continued onward, heading for the spot marked on Hugh's map. "I don't see any lake, unless it's under all that snow. I might have to circle around."

As he lifted their aircraft higher, Erin spotted a

bowl-shaped gorge to the right. "Over there!" she called to Christian, leaning forward and pointing.

Christian nodded. "Got it. Let's check it out."

He angled toward that basin, sweeping between two peaks. At the bottom of this smaller valley spread a flat expanse of snow, about half the size of a football field, but its surface was not unbroken. Black ice reflected up at them, like dark cracks in the glaze of a white vase.

"That's got to be it," Erin said.

"Only one way to find out." Christian manipulated the helicopter's stick and lowered their aircraft to a hover over the snow.

Wind from the rotors blew the fine snow away to reveal an expanse of frozen lake. Its surface was black, like obsidian, like the black lake painted on the mural in the Faust House. But here there were no monsters crawling forth.

At least not yet.

Erin checked the sky, noting the moon had already taken a bite out of the sun.

"Think we got the right place?" Christian asked.

Sophia spoke up from the far side of the cabin and pointed. "Look up by the cliffs on this side."

Erin wriggled to see better. It took her a moment to note what had drawn the small nun's attention. But then she spotted it, too. Half hidden by the shadow of the sheer rock face, two giant trees hugged the cliff. Both were leafless with pale gray trunks, their branches crusted with ice and frosted with snow.

Sophia faced them. "Didn't Hugh de Payens mention that the valley home of those *strigoi* monks had two mighty trees growing in it?

Possibly the Tree of Knowledge and the Tree of Eternal Life.

Erin felt a sinking of disappointment at the sight of them. The pair looked like ordinary trees, certainly old, but nothing spectacular. Still, they matched Hugh's description.

"Put us down," Erin said. "This must be the right place."

Christian obeyed, warning them. "Let's hope the ice is thick enough to hold us. It's the only place to land."

He was right. All around, the banks sloped steeply, rising and merging with the cliffs of rock. He lowered their craft cautiously until the skids gently kissed the ice. Only when the surface seemed to support their weight did he allow the aircraft to fully settle.

"Looks good," he said and powered the aircraft down.

Erin took off her headphones and waited while the Sanguinists, even Elizabeth, exited first, wary of any dangers. As soon as the door was open, a frigid breeze blasted inside, sweeping around as if trying to flush her out. She shuddered in her parka, but not from the cold. Instead, every hair on her body seemed to suddenly stand on end.

The Sanguinists reacted even more strongly: Christian crashed to a knee out on the ice, Sophia gasped loudly enough that Erin heard her above the sharp whistling of the wind, Rhun clutched for the cross hidden under his coat, wavering drunkenly as he took a few steps. Elizabeth caught his elbow and steadied him, frowning at the others.

Erin remembered seeing the Sanguinists react the same at the Faust House. The unholiness here was much stronger.

Even I feel it, she thought, shivering with unease.

Next to her, Jordan clenched his shoulders toward his ears and cocked his head, wincing. "That noise . . . like fingernails on a chalkboard. No, make that steel claws digging into a blackboard. Gawd . . ."

He looked sick to his stomach.

Erin didn't hear what he heard, but he alone had heard singing from the stones. His ears were clearly tuned to an entirely different wavelength than hers.

She climbed out of the aircraft to join the others, with Jordan hopping out after her. As her steel crampons touched the ice, her legs went cold, as if the heat of her body were sucked out through her feet.

Behind Jordan, the cat leaped free, jumping high as if trying to avoid the ice, but the shore was too far. The cub landed on his silver claws, then crossed toward Rhun, lifting each foot daintily before placing it down again, as if he were trying not to touch that black surface.

"Something's wrong here," she whispered.

"A powerful evil resides in this lake," Rhun agreed. "Let us be away quickly."

Despite the desire to run for the shoreline, they proceeded cautiously, careful of the ice's slipperiness and fearful of disturbing what lay below. Rhun aimed them for the bank closest to those shadowy trees.

Erin sighed when her legs finally stepped from ice to rock. She immediately felt pounds lighter, as if the backpack over her shoulders had been lifted free.

Rhun joined her, his spine straighter now. The Sanguinists looked revived as they left the lake, like flowers opening to sunlight.

"I can still feel it," Sophia said. "Wafting off the lake, filling this valley."

Rhun nodded.

Christian wiped his brow with a glove and looked longingly toward the helicopter. "Now I wish I'd parked closer. Don't look forward to hiking back out again."

Hopefully we'll get a chance to.

Erin looked to the sky, squinting at the sun's glare as the moon continued to edge farther over its face. She lowered her gaze to the steep rocky slope that led up toward those massive trees. Only now did she note that the boulders looked artfully placed, framing a snowy trail that wended up toward the cliffs.

"There's a trail," she said and began to head toward it.

Jordan stopped her. "Stay by my side."

She glanced at him, glad to see his protective nature showing itself again. She took his hand, wishing they didn't have to wear gloves.

With the lion at his side, Rhun took the lead. They slowly climbed through the boulders, careful of patches of ice. As the trail took its final switchback near the top, Rhun suddenly stopped, the lion let out a low growl.

"We're not alone," Rhun said.

11:12 A.M.

Rhun had almost missed them.

Three men knelt between the huge boles of the trees, so still and unmoving that they could be statues. Snow rested upon their shoulders and atop their bald pates, creating powdery skullcaps. Rhun heard no heartbeats from them, but he knew they still lived.

Eyes stared toward him, shining out of the shadows under the leafless bower.

Knowing they had been seen, they rose in unison, unfolding smoothly, snow sliding from their white-robed bodies. They stepped into the sunlight to greet Rhun and the others, pale hands folded at their waists.

Rhun knew these were *strigoi*, but they walked under the sun as easily as any Sanguinist. As Hugh de Payens had claimed, these monks had found another way to make peace with the day.

Rhun stepped forward and bowed. He held his empty hands out so that they could see he had no weapon. "We have been sent by Hugh de Payens," he said. "We bring his blessings."

The lead monk had a round face with dark, soft eyes. "Have you returned the stones our friend was given to safeguard?"

"We have them," Rhun admitted.

Erin slipped her backpack from a shoulder and unzipped it, clearly ready to produce her stone, but Rhun cautioned restraint. Hugh had said that they could trust these monks, but the palpable evil that rose off the lake made him cautious.

Even the lion stuck close to his knee, plainly unnerved by this entire valley.

All three monks bowed in unison, as if hearing a silent bell. "Then be welcome," the leader said as he straightened, a soft beatific smile on his lips. "My name is Xao. Please come into our temple and let us reunite your stones with their blue brother. Time, as you know, runs short."

The monks turned and led them toward the trees. Closer now, Rhun noted the two trees were nearly identical, with thick gray trunks and smooth bark. The pair stood so closely together that their higher branches grew entwined, forming a natural archway overhead. The gnarled limbs trembled in the cold wind that blew off the mountains, but they appeared strongly rooted.

Around the trunks, the ground had been swept away. The broom's bristles had left circular patterns in the thin layer of remaining snow. The deliberate arrangement of lines looked like patterns raked into sand in a Zen garden, but the patterns themselves—curlicues and arches—reminded Rhun of the tattoo on Jordan's chest and neck.

The monks stopped at the wall of rock centered behind the trees. They chanted together in a language he did not recognize, but Erin whispered behind him, her voice full of awe.

"I think they're speaking Sanskrit . . ."

Xao withdrew a small silver sculpture of a rose from a pocket. He clenched his fist around its stem, piercing his flesh on its thorns. He then dripped his blood atop a rock that jutted from the cliff, and a heavy grinding of stone sounded.

"It's like a Sanguinist gate," Christian murmured.

Or the precursor to one, Rhun thought.

As the rock groaned and cracked, a small round door pushed out and rolled to the side. Snow crunched under its weight.

The monks entered, clearly intending for them to follow. The door was so low that it required bowing to enter. It was likely purposefully constructed that way, to imbue humbleness into those who entered.

Rhun and the lion went first, followed by the others.

Once over the threshold, Rhun straightened and found himself facing a cavernous expanse, illuminated by the glow of a thousand candles and scores of fiery braziers that smoked with incense. He immediately recognized that this was no natural cavern, but a massive space hewn from the surrounding rock, sculpted by hand into a masterpiece. It must have taken centuries.

Erin gasped at the sight as she entered with Jordan and the others.

It was as if a small village had been sculpted out of the rock, their foundations still attached to the stone floor, as if the buildings had grown out of the cavern. Then there were the hundreds of statues, their bases similarly merged seamlessly with the stone. They depicted ordinary villagers going about their daily life, including a full-size yak pulling a cart, and herds of goats and sheep grazing on patches of stony grass.

"It's like they took that village we passed," Jordan said, "and turned it to stone."

The monks ignored their stunned reactions and led them to the village's center, where a massive Buddha sat, rising at least thirty feet tall. Those stone eyes were closed in peaceful meditation. His face was not stylized but appeared to be representative of a real man, with wide-set eyes, a strong straight nose, delicate arched eyebrows, and the hint of a smile on his overly full lips. His features were perfect; it looked as if he could open his eyes at any moment.

Rhun felt peace, order, and calm emanating from that sculpture—a welcome contrast to the evil that hovered outside.

As one, the monks put their hands together and bowed to the statue, then marched them behind the Buddha to a tall temple. Its bell-shaped tower rose gracefully, almost to the ceiling. Lines strung out from it, hanging with flags, all made of stone, sculpted to appear as if they were still flapping to a long-lost wind.

Closer at hand, two statues guarded the door to the temple. On the right side, a stylized dragon coiled on a plinth, its mouth slightly open to display teeth that looked sharp enough to cut. To the left, a shaggy creature stood upright on its hind legs, its powerful arms raised, exposing heavy claws. It looked like a cross between an ape and a bear. Rhun had never seen its like.

The cub sniffed at the dragon, his hackles slightly raised, as if expecting the winged beast to come alive at any moment.

Jordan ran his fingers over the other's monstrous features. "Looks like some sort of bigfoot."

"No," Erin said, drawing closer herself. "I . . . I think it's a yeti. A creature said to haunt the Himalayas."

She looked to Xao for confirmation.

His face remained inscrutable. "It is the likeness of a creature, one of several of its ilk that escaped from the lake. Beasts of various guises periodically crawl into our world from that darker space. Some are naked and quickly succumb to the cold. Others, like this one, roam the mountains for years before we can bring them back, inspiring fireside legends."

"What do you mean by *bring them back*?" Jordan asked.

"We capture those that have escaped and return them to the lake. We try to keep them from being harmed or harming others, although we all too often fail."

"But aren't they demons?" asked Sophia.

"Our philosophy cannot condemn such beasts for their natures," Xao answered piously, sounding much like Hugh de Payens. "We are here to protect all."

Xao turned and waved toward the open temple doors. "But let us continue. We have important tasks before us."

Rhun did not argue. With his Sanguinist senses, he felt the dying of the sun outside, its blaze slowly being consumed by the moon's shadow.

They were almost out of time.

38

Elizabeth trailed the others into the temple, following them like some lowly commoner. She hated to be pushed to the back, but it also allowed her time to study everything, free of the judgment of Rhun and the others. Hugh de Payens had shown her another way to live, another way to balance the light and the dark, the night and the day. These monks clearly embodied that same path.

I could teach the same to Tommy.

So for the moment, she bided her time, hoping to learn as much as she could before she made her escape and returned to Tommy, to save the boy from a death that he did not deserve.

As she entered the heart of the temple, the flowery smell of jasmine drifted across the wide room. Underfoot, the stone floor had been carved to resemble wooden planks, a task that must have taken years of devotion. A serene Buddha waited at the far end of the long room. Unlike the statue outside, this one had been carved with its eyes open.

She wondered why this temple complex was so large, if only these *three* monks lived here. She listened for others, but she heard no telltale scuff of sandal on rock, no brush of robe against skin, no rustle of prayer beads. It seemed only these three sentinels of the valley remained.

The monks took them to a large crimson table, topped by a shallow silver tray. The table sat in front of the Buddha. Within the tray, sands and salts in a multitude of shades and colors had been artfully combined to create a sand painting. It showed a perfect replica of the outer winter valley: white sands for snow, black salt for the lake. Two gray trees stood on one shore, each gnarled limb perfectly replicated.

The young lion sniffed at the tray, until Rhun waved the curious animal back.

The three monks then stepped around the table and took Erin, Jordan, and Rhun by the hand and led them to different corners of the tray. Each stood in one corner, while the trees anchored the fourth.

Xao pointed, rolling his wrist, allowing a finger to hover over a tiny figure painted in the sand on the same side of the lake as Erin. The monk dropped a tiny ruby in front of that figure.

"The sun rises in the east," he intoned.

Another monk stepped past Rhun's shoulder, and with a tiny silver dropper, placed a perfect pearl of water upon the sands in front of a figure on that side.

"The moon sets in the west," Xao added.

The last monk leaned by Jordan and gently blew a green seed from his small palm. It wafted down and landed before a figure painted there.

"The garden collects light from the south," Xao said. The monk then stepped to the remaining corner himself and pointed to the pair of painted trees in the sand. "While eternal roots anchor the north."

"What does this mean?" Jordan said, squinting at the figure before him.

"It's how we open the gate, isn't it?" Erin asked.

Xao gave the smallest bow of his head in acknowledgment. "The stones must be placed on pillars, each at their proper compass points. When the sun rises to its zenith and its light falls upon the stones, the gems will cast back their brilliance, lancing out over the lake.

Once their individual rays strike together, a new light will be born, one of the purest white."

Erin looked vaguely skeptical. "So you're saying, the three colors of reflected light—red, blue, and green—will merge to produce a *white* light."

Jordan straightened. "Makes sense. It's like old TV screens. Built with RBG emitters. Red, blue, green. From those three hues, all other colors can be made."

Xao offered a more elegant answer. "Darkness is the absence of light, while within white light hides a rainbow."

"The full spectrum," Jordan concurred with a nod.

"What happens then?" Elizabeth asked, not truly understanding such matters, but accepting them for now.

Xao explained, "This pure light will pierce the eternal darkness that shrouds the lake. And like lancing a sickly boil with a hot needle, the evil below will rise to the surface. But fear not, the pyramid of light created by the three gems will contain those creatures born of such malevolence, stopping them from entering our world."

Elizabeth began to understand. "Like a cage with bars of light."

"Just so," Xao said. "But we must take great care. If the stones are moved while the gate is still open, the bars of light will break, and the evil will be set loose upon the world."

"Sounds like you've done this before," Jordan said.

"Is that how you returned those creatures who escaped in the past?" Erin asked. "Like the yeti?"

A mournful expression shadowed Xao's features. "It is the only way to return them to their dark lands, to return balance here."

Another of the monks gently touched a finger to Xao's robe, as if prodding him to hurry. For these quiet souls, the simple gesture was likely the equivalent of a violent shake.

Xao nodded. "And now we face an even greater task. The darkness has been growing stronger for the past several months. The dark king who reigns below—the one you call Lucifer—has loosed his bonds, enough to crack the surface of the lake. We must open the gate and repair his broken chains before he shatters fully free."

"And how do we do that?" Erin asked.

"We must summon him into that gate, lured by that which he can't resist." Xao looked across at the three of them. "The scions of this world: Warrior, Woman, and the Knight who has mastered the king's own dark blood."

Erin looked aghast.

Jordan gave a small shake of his head. "So in other words, we're *bait*."

Even Rhun appeared shaken, still staring at the tray, as if searching for answers in those squiggles of sand. "And once Lucifer is summoned, what must we do? How do we shackle him anew?"

"We have prepared for this day. Millennia ago. This blessed temple was carved at the edge of this valley to hold not just the three gems, but to protect and hold sacred a great treasure, one sculpted by a single pair of hands. Only the Enlightened One could create such perfection."

Xao turned and bowed to the statue.

"The Buddha," Erin said, awe filling her voice.

The three monks stepped over to the statue, and Xao opened a door in the belly of the Buddha, the hatch so seamlessly built that even Elizabeth had failed to note it. From the hollow inside, two of the monks withdrew a large chest of polished white wood, with lotus blossoms painted along its sides.

From the strain in the bearers' faces, it was of immense weight. Still they held it aloft, as if fearful of letting it touch the floor. As the pair supported it, Xao opened the lid—and a wash of holiness flooded forth.

The Sanguinists gasped. Rhun leaned closer to the

chest, drawn toward that blessed font. Elizabeth backed away, wanting to escape it, the chest's sanctity exposing the dark places inside her.

Even the lion bowed down before the open chest, sinking to his belly.

Jordan and Erin stepped closer to view the treasure inside.

"Chains," Jordan said. "Silver chains."

His words did pale justice to their beauty. The chains were the purest silver, burning forth with holiness. Each link was perfection, sculpted and etched to show every leaf and creature that lived under the sun. It was the natural world, rendered in silver.

"And we can reshackle Lucifer with these chains?" Erin asked.

Xao looked to her, then Jordan. "Not you two. Only creatures such as ourselves, such as your companions, can ferry this treasure through the planes of that pyramid of light. It would be death to those whose heart still beats to cross that barrier. Only the damned may pass unscathed, those who have balanced light and darkness within them."

Xao bowed to his fellow monks, then to the Sanguinists.

Christian stepped forward. "Let me go. Rhun must

guard his pillar of this pyramid. But I can enter that pyramid and take those chains to Lucifer."

"But not alone," Sophia said. "I will go with you."

From the strain in the shoulders of the two monks who carried the chest, it would take two Sanguinists to haul that load. Possibly three. But Elizabeth held her tongue. She would not go unless ordered, and perhaps not even then.

Xao came forward and abased himself before Christian and Sophia, dropping to one knee to kiss both their hands. "Our blessings will go with you. The journey into the darkness within that pyramid of light is not an easy one."

Erin muttered to herself. "Hmm . . ."

"What is it?" Jordan asked.

The archaeologist turned her back on the monks and held a hand out to Jordan. "Let me see your green stone."

Jordan reached to his pocket and extracted the two halves and passed them to her. While the Sanguinists remained entranced by the chest and what it held, Elizabeth joined Erin. Erin fitted the two halves together and rotated the gem to expose the design imbedded in the stone. Only this time, she reversed the image, turning that chalice-shaped symbol upside down.

"Could this symbol be some representation of that pyramid of light?" Erin asked.

Erin swung around to Xao, plainly seeking confirmation. In her hands, the stone slipped askew, separating into the two halves.

The monk stared down, and for the first time, he showed a strong reaction, his placid features wrenching into a look of horror and dismay. "No, it can't be." His face went hard with fury, stepping menacingly toward Erin. "What have you done?"

Erin backed away as Rhun rushed to stand between the woman and the monk.

"She didn't do anything," Rhun said, his tone full of warning.

Xao shook his head. "The Garden Stone is shattered. In such a state, it cannot open the gate." The monk gaped at them, his face lost. "With this key broken, there is no future. The world ends this day."

11:34 A.M.

Erin stared down at the two halves of the gem in her palms, tamping down the despair rising inside her. *Was their journey doomed from the start?* She refused to accept that, not after all the blood and sacrifice needed to reach this valley.

"There must be some way to fix it," she said.

Jordan took back the pieces. "And here I left my tube of superglue in my other pants."

"You do not understand," Xao said. "The stone is not just broken, it is *defiled*. I can sense the shreds of darkness that still shadow its heart."

Erin pictured John Dee's bell and the hundreds of *strigoi* burned to ash inside, all so their dark essences could be gathered inside the sacred gem.

"Can it be purified?" Erin asked. "Baptized?"

The holy rite of baptism could wash away original sin from a soul. Couldn't the gem be equally cleansed?

"Only good can vanquish evil," Xao said. "Only light can rid the darkness. To purify such defilement, it would take the *greatest* good and the *brightest* light."

The monk turned to confer with his brothers. They whispered back and forth to each other in

Sanskrit. Erin wished she could understand, but she sensed that the answer would not come from these three.

I am the Woman of Learning.

She stared at the emerald reflection off the pieces in Jordan's hands—then back to the sand painting. She studied the three figures, each with a representation of *Arbor, Aqua,* and *Sanguis* before it, and recalled something Hugh had said.

You must decipher the riddle so that you may retrieve the stone that belongs to you.

She returned her attention to Jordan, noting how the light dappled his features. The motes of shimmering green appeared like tiny leaves shooting forth from his crimson lines. It was as if the stone was indeed a *seed,* one that had sprouted inside Jordan.

She spoke aloud. "These stones . . . are they bonded to us individually?"

Xao faced her. "So it is said in the proverbs of the Enlightened One. *The Daughter of Eve will be bound to the red stone by her blood. The Son of Adam will be rooted to the green stone by his connection to the land. And the Immortal One will join with the blue stone because he has tamed his nature to walk under the blue sky.*"

Erin wished she had time to read all of these ancient proverbs herself, but instead, she focused on their current problem.

"If the Son of Adam's stone is broken, then maybe the Son of Adam can fix it," she said. She stared between the snowy lion and Jordan, knowing the common bond the two shared. "Jordan's blood holds the essences of angels, beings of light and righteousness. Maybe such purity can cleanse the darkness from the stone."

"And if that blood can heal Jordan," Rhun added, "perhaps it also holds the power to heal the stone."

Jordan shrugged. "And if that all fails, I can always just hold those two halves together with my bare hands."

Erin could tell he was only half-joking. "What other choice do we have?" she asked.

"She's right," Christian announced loudly, glancing toward the roof, likely sensing the sun. "Whatever we're going to try, it'd better be soon."

"Then let's see what my blood can do." Jordan pulled a dagger from his boot. "It's not like I can defile the stone any worse than it already is."

He lifted the blade to his wrist.

"No, not here!" Xao exclaimed loudly. "It is forbidden to shed blood in our sacred temple."

"Where, then?" Jordan asked, pausing with the knifepoint on his skin.

Erin knew they had no more time for second-guessing. She pointed to the sand painting. "We'll have to attempt it once we're in our proper positions." She turned to Xao. "Where is the third stone? Your blue gem?"

The one meant for Rhun.

Xao nodded to one of his brothers, who returned to the belly of the Buddha and removed another box, also white, but painted with a sky full of fluffy clouds. It was easily held in the palms of the monk, who carried it to Rhun and offered it to him.

Rhun began to open it, but Erin stopped him.

"Don't," she warned, remembering the effect that the *Sanguis* stone had on Jordan back in Hugh's church. She didn't want this holy gem singing Jordan into a swoon like before.

Instead, she pointed in the direction of the open gate.

"Xao, take us where we must go."

39

March 20, 11:44 A.M. NPT
Tsum Valley, Nepal

Rhun hurried with the others out of temple and back through the stone village. His inner clock felt the approach of the noon hour, while the holiness in his blood responded to the moon's passage across the sun. As darkness approached, his strength faded with each passing second, like sand sifting through the pinch of an hourglass.

Ahead, beyond the open gate, the day's brightness had dimmed to a dull twilight as the moon's shadow swept over these mountains. The group rushed forward and bowed their way back into that wintry valley, the evil even more palpable now.

As Rhun straightened, he looked to the sky, noting only a thin crescent of sun remained. The brilliance burned his eyes, searing him with certainty.

We're out of time.

Under the bower of the two massive trees, the group quickly divided. One monk led each of the trio. Rhun split away with the tallest of the brothers, who hurried him at a fast clip along the base of the icy cliffs toward the western bank of that black lake. Xao took Erin by the hand, and another marched with Jordan. Both headed in the other direction, toward their respective positions on the eastern and southern shores.

Between their parties, Sophia and Christian strained under the weight of the chest and its sacred silver chains and climbed straight down, staying in the shadow of the trees at the north end.

The two remaining members of their party followed at Rhun's heels. One did not surprise him. The young lion padded through the snow behind him, growling softly, his head lowered from the evil wafting off the lake. Clearly this valley assaulted the cub's senses as thoroughly as Rhun's.

His last companion surprised him. Elizabeth strode behind him, taking large steps, her back straight, her eyes on the lake. Unlike Rhun and the lion, he read a longing in her face, as if she wished to run to that lake and skate across its dark surface.

Why does she seem so little bothered by the evil here?

She noted his attention, reading the question on his face, but misinterpreting it. "I'm not about to let you do this without someone at your back. Especially with you missing an arm."

He offered her a grateful smile.

She scowled at him. "Watch your step, Rhun, or you and that stone will go rolling away."

He turned around as the monk led them down a thin path to a tall marker that stuck upward from the shoreline. It was a plinth of gray granite, frosted with ice, rising as high as his chest.

The monk brushed the snow off the pillar's crown with reverent fingers, revealing the sculpture of a small cup, identical to the chalices depicted in the mosaic back in Venice. Like the structures in the Buddhist temple, the base of the stone chalice merged with the stone, making cup and pillar one piece.

Rhun imagined if he cleared the snow from around the foot of plinth that it, too, would be a part of this mountain.

The monk stepped to Rhun's side, collected the box from his one hand, then turned it so the latch faced Rhun.

"The Sky Stone is for you," the monk intoned, bowing slightly. "You must place the sacred gem in its place. At the same time as the others."

The monk nodded toward the chalice.

Rhun understood.

I must set the Aqua *stone into this receptacle.*

Rhun reached his hand to the box, undid the latch with his thumb, and tilted the lid open. For a breath, he expected to find nothing, some final act of betrayal by these monks. But instead, resting in a bed of silk, lay a perfect gem. It shone with the brilliance of a bright blue sky, as if the most perfect day had been captured in that stone, preserved for eternity.

A small sigh of reverence slipped his lips.

The lion stepped closer, placing his paw on Rhun's knee to lift his nose higher so that he could peer at the stone. Elizabeth merely crossed her arms.

Rhun pushed the lion off his leg and closed his fingers over the gem, feeling a sinking sense of unworthiness.

How could such beauty be meant for me?

Still, he knew his duty and took the stone in hand, feeling the holiness warm his fingers, his wrist, and up his arm. As it suffused his chest, he almost expected it to start his heart beating again. When it did not, he turned and faced the pillar and that carved chalice.

Across the lake, he saw the others were already at their positions. Xao was bent near Erin's ear, whispering, likely passing on the same instructions to her.

Erin looked up toward him. Though she was fifty yards away, he could see the fear in her face. He knew the source of her anxiety and turned toward it now, too. The trio needed to act in unison, but there remained one final task.

Rhun stared over at Jordan.

Would the man's blood purify and heal the broken gem?

11:52 A.M.

Jordan touched the cold point of the dagger against the skin of his wrist.

This had better work.

A glance up revealed what was left of the sun: a fiery crimson blaze shooting from the edge of the moon's dark shadow. The brilliance stung his eyes, leaving his vision dazzled when he glanced back to the blade poised at his wrist. By now, the valley was smothered in the moon's umbra, turning the snow a soft crimson and the ice of the lake an even darker shade of black, reminding him of those drops of Lucifer's blood.

The lake looks like a hole in this world.

His blood ran cold at the sight of it, sensing its *wrongness*.

Knowing what he must do, he pressed the point of the dagger into his flesh and drew its edge along his wrist. A thick line of blood welled up. He sheathed the knife and withdrew the pieces of the green stone, handing one to the monk at his side. Jordan took the remaining piece and held it under his wrist, catching the first falling drop into the gem's hollow center.

He steeled himself against some dramatic reaction, but when nothing happened, he continued filling that stone's cavity. Once his blood was spilling over the gem's lip, he exchanged that half for the still-empty one and repeated the same.

Still, there was no blinding flash of light, no crescendo of song.

Jordan looked at the monk for help, but the guy appeared equally lost—and scared.

Only one thing left to do . . .

Pushing aside his worries, Jordan took the two halves in hand. With his blood sloshing over the facets, he fitted the two pieces back together.

C'mon . . .

For a moment, there was no better outcome—then the stone began to warm between his palms, growing quickly hotter, not unlike the feverish heat when his body healed. Jordan prayed this was a good sign. Soon the inner fire grew to a burn, as if he had plucked a coal from a campfire. Still, he held tight, grimacing from the pain.

He watched new crimson lines appear across the back of his hands, burning whorls across his skin, twining up his fingers. He almost expected his hands to fuse together over the stone, to become a husk for the burning seed he held.

When he thought he could withstand that heat no longer, the fire subsided, replaced instead by a singing that passed through him, drawing him closer, rooting him in a new way to the gem in his hands. That faint echo he had heard from the stone before grew into a great chorus.

It sang of warm summer days, the smell of hay in the barn, the sound of wind blowing through cornfields. It rang with the buzzing of bees on a late afternoon, the soft honking of geese migrating with the changing tide of seasons, the low bass notes of a whale seeking a mate.

Jordan cocked his head, hearing a new song merge with the gem's melody. A warm red ribbon of hope and life flowed and danced into his song, the new notes sounded of heartbeats and laughter and the soft whicker of a horse greeting a loved one.

Then a third voice joined the chorus, as blue as the bright plumage of a jay in sunlight. This refrain ran deeper through the chorus: flowing with the thunder of falling water, the soft patter of rain on dry earth, and the sighing of a tide as it waxed and waned, a motion as eternal as the earth.

The three songs wove together into a great canticle of life, one that revealed in each note and chorus the beauty and wonder of this world, of its endless harmony and variety, how each piece fit together into a whole

Jordan felt himself a part of that song, yet still an observer.

Then through that majesty, a command rang forth, reaching his ears.

"Now," Erin called. "On three."

Jordan tore his gaze away from the emerald depths of his stone to see Erin standing before her pillar, her arms upraised, bearing aloft a shining red gem that defied the darkness of the eclipse.

Jordan's heart ached at the sight of her, allowing the song to fade enough to listen and obey. She looked like some ancient tribal goddess, her figure lit by that crimson shine, turning her golden hair to fire.

To the west, Rhun also held his stone aloft.

"*One.*" Erin's clear voice ran across the lake.

"*Two,*" Rhun answered her, as if they had rehearsed it.

Jordan added finality to this moment. "*Three.*"

11:59 A.M.

Erin lowered the *Sanguis* stone into the chalice before her.

As soon as its facets touched the granite, the ruby gem burst forth with a blazing light, echoing the crimson fire of the eclipsing sun. Flames ignited from the gem's surface and danced around the stone chalice. Heat and holiness washed across Erin's face. She feared if she got too close it would burn her to ash.

Xao showed no such worry. He stepped to her side and held his palms before those flames. As he basked his cold flesh in front of that warm fire, the monk chanted loudly in Sanskrit. She heard it echoed by his brothers.

As the moon fully eclipsed the sun, sinking the valley into a shadowy twilight, the gem fought back against the darkness. The flames flared higher, wafting wildly, as if stoked by some great bellows into a fiery whirlwind. Erin wanted to run from that inferno, but she knew her place was here.

Then, just as suddenly as they had appeared, the flames were sucked back into the stone, setting it to shining even brighter, as if a piece of the sun rested within that chalice. Then the fires ignited again—not along the gem's facets this time, but all around her.

Erin craned her neck, looking everywhere, realizing those flames defined a ruby bubble that surrounded her, its surface chased by crimson fire. It was as if the gem itself had suddenly expanded, swallowing her whole.

And I am but a flaw in its heart.

A glance across the lake's dark surface revealed Rhun standing in a sphere running with blue fire—Jordan in a globe of emerald.

She took a step toward them, but Xao was still next to her and placed a hand on her shoulder, holding her firmly. She stared at the liquid fire roiling over the sphere's surface, remembering the monk's warning about the danger of humans crossing these barriers of light, how they would be consumed by that fire.

Or maybe Xao was cautioning her to watch what was still to come.

The flames suddenly swirled and gathered near the top of her bubble—then shot skyward, angling out over the lake. Similar spears of fire—blazing azure and emerald—ignited from the other spheres, lancing upward to meet the ruby column.

All three crashed together above the center of the lake, ringing out with a resounding note that staggered Erin, but Xao helped her hold her feet. She gaped at that giant pyramid of fire. At the top, those three infernos whipped into a great maelstrom, swirling their flames together, blending and merging their colors, revealing a slurry of every combination of light. Then that spinning grew even more intense, moving too quickly for the human eye to follow, until all colors became one, creating a pool of pure white fire.

Erin remembered the reversed symbol she had shown Jordan and Elizabeth.

Here it is, brought to life.

Then from that pool above, a column of light shot down to the lake below, striking the black ice. The ice broke with the impact, cracks shooting across the lake. The ground bucked underfoot.

In its wake, the world went quiet.

Erin heard no breath of wind, no creak of tree limbs, no sound of any life.

Except for the pounding of her own heart in her throat.

She watched as the white column of light expanded outward across the ice, forming a cone shining down from above, creating a pyramid inside a pyramid.

Within that conical blaze of brilliance, the black ice rippled like water under a stiff breeze.

Erin remembered the mural at the Faust House, showing all manner of monsters heaving into this world. She steeled herself against what was to come—but even then, she knew she would be unprepared.

12:01 P.M.

With his skin prickling with warning, Jordan's hand went to the Colt 1911 holstered under the edge of his parka. He knew the weapon would likely do squat against what he felt rising from the dark depths of that lake, but he wanted to feel its solidity in his hand, a counterpoint to that hole in the world wavering before him.

To his left, Erin looked scared, locked within her fiery sphere. She must have felt his eyes on her, because she turned her head to look at him. He gave her what he hoped was a reassuring smile, and she mustered up a small smile in return.

To his right, Rhun stood with one of the monks in a sphere running with blue flames. Behind him, Elizabeth had drawn her sword. The lion paced beyond the sphere, apparently caught outside it when the gem ignited, the only one of them wise enough not to get trapped.

And Jordan knew he was trapped, sensing he dared not pass out of this barrier of emerald light, that he would be burned to ash if he tried. So all he could do was grip his weapon harder in his hand.

Out in the center of the lake, that rippling darkness began to steam forth with shadows and smoke, slowly filling the confines of that white cone of brilliance. Eventually he could no longer see through it to the lake's north side, where Christian and Sophia waited with the chest of silver chains.

As he watched, that darkness began to coalesce at the core, shadow and smoke becoming substance. A dark figure formed there, rising two stories tall, seated on a throne of obsidian. It features were blackened, its naked skin running with shadows as dark as pitch. From behind strong shoulders, a set of massive wings unfurled, feathered with black flames. Where those fiery tips brushed the light, black bolts of lightning chased across the inner surface of the cone—but the barrier held.

The winged creature shifted up from his throne, straining against the coils of silver chain, its body weighted from the waist down.

Jordan knew whom he faced.

The king of that bottomless pit.

Lucifer himself.

And Jordan could not help but find this dark angel—

12:03 P.M.

—so beautiful.

Erin marveled at the perfection of the figure on the throne. Every muscle in his arms and chest was flawlessly defined, his wings blazed with black fire. But it was his face that drew her full attention. Cheekbones rose high, sculpted into graceful arches, flanking a straight narrow nose. Higher still, long lashes fringed eyes that shone with a dark majesty, seeing everything and nothing.

She found it impossible to look away.

One of their group was not so afflicted and awed.

"Why do you wait?" Elizabeth yelled from across the lake, breaking the spell.

Erin watched Rhun shake free of the trance and shout to the north side of the lake. "Christian, Sophia! Go!"

The pair set off from the rocky bank, hauling the heavy chest between them. As Xao had promised, the pair of Sanguinists passed through that outer plane of the fiery pyramid with no trouble, though once out on the ice, the malevolence clearly weakened them, setting their legs to stumbling. The new cracks in the ice also made the trek more treacherous, forcing the pair to take a circuitous route through the damage, slowing them even more.

As fear rang through her, Erin turned to Jordan, wishing he was beside her.

Jordan noted her attention and cupped his mouth to shout something to her—but a length of silver flashed into view behind his shoulders.

Erin screamed a warning. "Jordan! Watch—"

Then cold hard fingers clamped around her neck, strangling away her words.

40

Jordan was moving as soon as he heard Erin's shout, responding with years of instinct as a soldier. He ducked low—as a long curved blade swept over his head.

While the sword missed its intended target, the steel still struck the emerald stone a glancing blow, knocking the gem loose, causing it to roll drunkenly along the rim of the granite chalice. Jordan hit the ground at the base of the pillar and twisted to one hip, bringing up the Colt and firing into the chest of the monk who wielded the sword.

Knowing his adversary was a *strigoi*, Jordan unloaded his entire magazine. The monk went flying backward, falling out of the emerald bubble. The monk landed on his back in the snow, his chest smoking from the silver rounds, black blood pouring from beneath his body.

Jordan spun around, his body thrumming with warning, still attuned to the stone.

He lunged with his arm outstretched as the rolling gem rocked free of its perch and plummeted downward. Unfortunately only his fingers brushed its facets before it landed into a bank of snow at the foot of the plinth.

As it struck, a resounding *boom* shook the ground. He crawled toward the gem as it continued to blaze from the snowbank. But the damage had been done. While the emerald bubble around him remained intact, still blazing with fire, one of the columns of the pyramid had been dislodged from its foundation.

Must get it back up there, before it's too—

A series of sharp pops exploded near at hand, ringing out as loud as rifle fire, echoing from the lake's surface.

Jordan looked up and watched the ice shatter, breaking apart like a dropped mirror. But what that mirror was intended to reflect was something much darker, something not meant for this world.

And it burst free.

Creatures boiled to the surface of the lake: lumbering, slithering, and shoving through the ice. The horde clambered toward shore, mostly toward him and the broken foot of the pyramid, sensing a way to escape.

Jordan flinched away, responding with the lizard part of his brain, refusing to accept what he was seeing, but unable to deny it at the same time. His stomach roiled at the sight, at horrors his mind could not fully grasp. But when his fingers reached back and brushed the inside surface of the flaming sphere that surrounded him, agony shot up his arm to his chest. He yanked his hand back. Smoke rising from his blackened fingertips.

He realized he was trapped in this sphere, unable to escape, remembering the monk's warning.

It would be death to those whose heart still beats to pierce that brilliant veil.

But the abominations that crawled out of the lake had no such hearts, no such limitations.

Something sloshed out of the lake to the right, lumbering forth like an ordinary person, but with a flat black face, showing no eyes or mouth—yet still it screamed, howling at the world. To his left, a massive creature bounded to the rocks, clinging there, with cloven hoofs and a malformed head, then it leaped away.

He wanted to cover his eyes, but he feared the unknown even more.

Directly ahead of him, a black crocodilian shape slithered and clawed its way from the broken ice. But it had no head, only a puckered sucker at the front, showing a ring of teeth. It left a glistening trail of bile-colored slime behind it. Seeming to sense him, it clawed faster in his direction, passing unharmed through the emerald veil of his bubble, bringing with it the stench of sulfur and rotted meat.

Jordan's mind struggled with the impossibility of it, tipping toward insanity. Still, one greater fear kept him grounded, momentarily anchored.

Erin.

But trapped here, Jordan could never reach her.

Only one person could.

12:06 P.M.

Rhun lashed out with his *karambit*, parrying aside the monk's sword—but the impact staggered him. This enemy was far more powerful and faster than any *strigoi* that Rhun had ever fought, its strength likely fueled by the malevolence wafting off the lake and the looming presence of its master of darkness, Lucifer.

To keep his feet after that blow, Rhun stumbled out of the blue veil of light. Beyond that sphere, the air reeked of death and pestilence. Revulsion crawled along his skin like a thousand spiders.

The monk pursued him, his long sword flashing down in a streak of reflected blue, but that strike never landed. Instead, something struck the monk in the side, knocking him down. The cub rolled away, but twisted back around, hissing loudly. The monk rose with the speed of a striking cobra, thrusting his blade at the cub's throat—but instead, the monk toppled forward, his head flying off his body, while his sword harmlessly impaled a snowbank next to the cat.

Elizabeth stood there, dark blood dripping from her blade.

Again, she had saved his life, probably the cat's, too, but he had no time to thank her.

During the heated skirmish, he had seen Jordan dispatch the monk alongside him, his pistol blazing. He also saw the gem fall, causing the lake to shatter on that side, allowing hell to break loose into this world. Even now beasts were clambering along the banks, spreading wider. Others bounded across the ice, gibbering around the foot of their master. Several spotted Christian and Sophia with the chest and went in pursuit, either enraged by the holiness of the chains or perhaps commanded by that dark angel himself.

"Defend the stone," Rhun commanded Elizabeth.

He had to reach Erin. A moment ago, he had watched her get attacked as she tried to warn Jordan, and even now she still struggled in the iron grip of Xao. The monk's fingers were wrapped around her throat, lifting her high, until only her toes brushed the snow.

Rhun raced along the shoreline toward her. A reptilian creature lunged off the ice at him, but Rhun smoothly stepped aside, striking out and decapitating its scaly head with a single stroke. Yellow smoke boiled out of the stump, while a splatter of blood dissolved through his parka and burned his skin like acid.

Still, he kept going, trailed by the lion.

A few other creatures threatened, but they seemed more interested in escaping the lake into the larger world, than truly attacking him. The same was not true for Christian and Sophia deeper out on the ice. The pair had set down the chest and battled a growing horde. Their robes were slick with blood.

Across the lake, a fresh spat of gunfire revealed Jordan had reloaded and was shooting at some beast within his emerald glow, still holding his own for now.

Rhun charged the last of the distance toward that ruby sphere.

Erin still lived, her heart hammering in her chest, her breath ragged in that chokehold.

Xao saw Rhun coming and smiled. Rhun knew the monk could have snapped Erin's neck like a twig at any time, but Xao had refrained—perhaps only to better savor this moment.

The monk freed one hand and lifted a dagger to Erin's throat.

No . . .

The blade sliced deep and wide, carving open that tender neck. Blood burst forth like a fountain as the monk let her go.

Erin dropped like a sack, falling to her side, her life steaming into the snow.

Rhun's legs stumbled with the truth, knowing it was too much to stop, too much to heal. Still, he fought to close the last of the distance. He would not lose her. He had sworn to protect her—not only as a Knight of Christ, but as one who loved her, one who could not imagine the world without her in it.

Xao met his fury with a larger smile, his eyes shining dark with malice.

Here was not the work of Lucifer.

Rhun knew who stared out those eyes at him.

12:07 P.M.

From across the lake, Legion savored the look of horror and defeat in the Knight's face. He witnessed it both through the gaze of the possessed monk and through the eyes of this vessel now.

Legion still remained hidden among the rocks on the southern side of the lake, where he had been manipulating events from afar, lying in wait for the right moment to show himself.

Deep inside him, the small flame of Leopold quavered, shaken by the sudden death of the Woman at the hands of the monk. Legion imagined that feeble flame weeping smoky tears.

How easy it had been to make the trio dance to his wishes!

Using the stolen knowledge of Hugh de Payens, Legion had sped here ahead of the others, coming upon the monks unprepared.

With a touch, they were mine.

Legion had thought to take advantage of a secret, one that Hugh had not shared with the others. The hermit had known that the broken stone could no longer open the gate in this valley. Hugh had trusted that the monks would know how to repair it, so Legion came to believe it, too. Unfortunately, once he took in the monks' long memories, he found no such knowledge.

Frustrated, Legion made new plans. Leopold and Hugh de Payens both trusted the Woman of Learning, held her in the highest esteem. If anyone could figure out how to repair the stone, it would be her. So he hid himself away and carefully manipulated the three monks, using them to wheedle the truth out of the trio, to make them do the work for him.

And how perfectly that had worked.

The Woman did indeed provide the answer, and the Warrior gave his blood to make it so. Together, the trio had opened the gate—which left Legion the simple task of shattering the stones, to ensure this portal was never closed again. This world would be claimed for the dark one. Once that black angel was freed, the garden would be purged of mankind, leaving this paradise for Legion alone.

A promise sworn to Legion by Lucifer.

Legion stepped from the small cave in the rocks and lifted his arms to the eclipse-darkened sky. He only had a handful of moments to complete his task. The sun was already being born again in the sky, rising fiery from the ashes of the eclipse. Knowing time would be short, he had chosen this spot to hide earlier, a shelter closest to the green stone, the closest to the Warrior who still guarded it. Though mended, that stone was still the weakest. Legion would shatter it first—then he would destroy the others one by one.

To ensure his success, he had lured the Knight astray by threatening the Woman. Legion had waited until the

Sanguinist priest was drawn close before slaying the first of the trio. Next, Legion would destroy the Warrior, who remained trapped by the emerald light, a bird in a cage. Only then would he dispatch the Knight, after breaking his will by killing all those he held most dear.

But Legion wouldn't do so alone.

As he stepped under that blasted sky, the denizens of the dark land came to him, gathering to him like shadows. They licked his tattered boots, bowed and scraped before him, bit each other in wild joy in his wake. Of course, they loved him.

He had freed them.

And now he would free this world of the plague of man.

Legion eyed the Warrior.

Starting with this one.

12:08 P.M.

Sprawled on her side, Erin clamped both hands to her throat. Hot blood slicked between her fingers, as cold snow cushioned her cheek.

She could only watch as Xao stepped over her body and met Rhun's charge with a bloody dagger in one hand and a curved sword in the other. Beyond the fiery sphere, steel and silver clashed in a flurry of blows, counterstrikes, and parries. The cub helped, flying in to snag the edge of the monk's robe to throw Xao off balance or bowling into the man's legs.

Even now, she understood the source of this betrayal, knowing how artfully they had been played in this sacred valley, used like puppets by Legion, as surely as if they had been possessed by the demon themselves. Legion had needed them to bring the two stones, repair the broken one, and open the gate so that Lucifer could rise from the darkness of the lake.

And we did all of that.

Anger kept her warm as the blood continued to seep through her fingers.

Xao backed toward her, passing through fire to reenter the sphere. The demon inside seemed oblivious of her, perhaps believing she was already dead, or at least, too weak to fight.

But I am more than the Woman of Learning.

She lashed out with a leg and tripped Xao, catching the demon by surprise. As he fell and lost his guard, Rhun struck fast with his *karambit*, jamming it deep into the monk's eye. Rhun used that new handle to swing Xao's skull and crack it hard against a neighboring granite pillar. He smashed it over and over again, until the monk stopped moving.

Only then did Rhun swing around and fall to his knees next to her.

At least I won't die alone.

But ultimately she did not matter.

"Jordan . . ." she croaked out.

Rhun took her hand, refusing to leave her side.

She let her other hand drop from her throat and pushed at his knee, urging him to help Jordan. Instead, he placed his own hand to her wound. His stronger fingers applied firmer pressure, as if knowing where to push to close the largest arteries.

She wanted to fight him, but she did not have the strength.

The cub paced outside that fiery veil, anxious, plainly wanting to help.

Erin gritted her teeth, hating to fail them both. She was the Woman of Learning, and she still had a job to do. She would fight in the only way left to her.

She shifted to better expose the pack on her back.

"The Gospel," she whispered.

Surely there had to be some answer in that book. She had carried the volume this far, not just because she didn't trust Bernard, but also because she knew that the book must still have a role to play. She had been bound to the book. That had to be important.

But if I die, the potential of the Gospel dies with me.

She could not let that happen without trying everything.

Perhaps believing he was granting her dying wish, Rhun released her neck, taking her hand and showing her where best to apply pressure. Only then did he pull the gospel out of her backpack and free it from its case. He laid the book open in front of her in the snow, then quickly reapplied pressure to her neck, whispering a prayer over her.

Erin turned her head until the edge of the cover touched her cheek. Most of the pages were empty, still waiting to be filled with the words that Christ had written long ago. Bernard had once told her that the Blood Gospel might contain the key to unleashing the divinity within each person, knowledge locked in those blank pages. If so, because of her, the world would never know it.

Rhun had opened the book to the page that held the last lines of prophecies, perhaps hoping she would find extra meaning there. But those words glowed golden and bright, as if mocking her for her failure.

With one trembling fingertip, she turned that page of prophecy and laid her bloody hand on the next blank page. She felt that paper grow warmer under her palm, its surface strangely smoother.

Rhun gasped as golden words appeared under her fingers, inscribing across the paper as if being freshly written, line by line, flowing down the page.

Rhun turned that page for her, then another.

More words, more lines.

Rhun flipped through rapidly. "The entire book is full," he said with awe.

Erin studied the page that was still open, realizing she could not read the words. The letters looked Enochian—the language developed by John Dee to talk to the angels.

Erin closed her eyes, struggling to understand why Christ chose to write the rest of the gospel in Enochian, when the previous prophecies had been written in Greek, the language of man. Why write the rest in the language of angels? Only one answer made sense. Perhaps these new words—perhaps the entire gospel— were not meant for mankind, but for the angels.

No, not *angels*, she realized opening her eyes. *Angel . . . one angel.*

No wonder the pages only appeared now, in this valley.

She turned her face toward the only angel present.

Lucifer sat upon his dark throne, staring straight at her.

Erin clutched Rhun's knee with her fingers. He leaned closer.

"I . . . I know," she croaked softly. "I know what I must do."

41

Jordan reseated the emerald stone in its proper place. As the gem touched the granite chalice, the column of fire on this side of the pyramid flared brighter. The ice reformed over the lake, sealing the portal between worlds. Several creatures were caught halfway between this plane and the other, their bodies frozen and contorted in the ice.

But his efforts did nothing for the hundreds that had already escaped.

Christian and Sophia were still under siege by a mass of them, unable to make headway across the lake to reach Lucifer. Elizabeth held her position by the blue stone, bloodied but still defending her post. Across the lake, Rhun knelt beside Erin, who still lived, although the lake of red blood that surrounded her told him that she did not have much longer. Jordan ached to rush to her side, to take her in his arms one last time.

But even if he could have broken free of his emerald prison, another adversary seemed determined to stop him.

As Jordan turned his back to the granite pillar, Legion stalked down from the cliffs toward him. He was surrounded by a shadow of abominations, a cloak of living flesh. Jordan used his last rounds to fire at the demon, but each time he shot, one of those shadows leaped up and threw itself in the way, blocking his slug with its twisted body.

Out of ammunition, Jordan held his KA-BAR dagger in one hand. He dropped his pistol and bent down to collect the monk's abandoned sword, glad it had fallen inside the green sphere of light.

"Come on!" Jordan shouted over the tide of the demon's screaming beasts. "Come and get me."

Black eyes locked on to Jordan's. "Do not be in such a hurry to die, Warrior of Man, I will be there soon enough."

Good . . . I'm ready for you this time.

Jordan burned with a golden rage, one ignited by both his angelic blood and his lust for revenge. As Legion approached, Jordan lifted the stolen sword—a long curved blade with a green piece of jade set in its pommel. Jordan set his legs in a wide stance and prepared to meet the demon.

Legion also carried a sword, something with a poisonous-looking black blade, shining like a long sliver of obsidian. It was not of this world, probably carried here and gifted to the demon by one of his horde.

Jordan motioned with the tip of his own weapon. "Just the two of us," he urged. "Unless you fear one man?"

"While you are more than a mere mortal," Legion answered, "I will not be caught off guard again. So yes, let us end this."

Sword held high, Legion shed his monsters and entered the emerald sphere. Without preamble, Legion thrust his sword at Jordan, forcing a quick parry that numbed Jordan to the elbow. Legion struck again and again, slowly forcing Jordan toward the edge of the sphere.

If that blade doesn't kill me, the green fire will.

A quick flurry of blows followed. Steel rang against black crystal. Legion darted back and forth through the barrier, using the fiery veil as his own personal shield, knowing Jordan could not follow.

A quick thrust finally penetrated Jordan's guard and sliced across his side. Hot red blood drenched his shirt. Another series of attacks ended with Legion's blade cutting deep into his upper arm. Legion retreated through the barrier, smiling back at him.

Jordan realized a hard truth.

Legion is toying with me.

Jordan lurched away, dropping his dagger and hugging an arm around his wounded side, while still keeping his sword up.

Legion stalked forward, clearly ready to finish him.

As soon as the demon pierced the barrier's edge, Jordan lunged forward, hoping that the flames of the veil might have blinded the demon for a fraction of a second. As Legion's leg stepped through, Jordan kicked out and smashed his steel crampons into the demon's knee. The limb gave way with a crack. As Legion pitched to the side, Jordan grabbed the demon's sword arm, rolled Legion under him, and rode the black body to the ground.

Once they struck, Jordan used the momentum to jam his sword into the soft belly, thrusting up toward that quiet heart. Legion screamed and threw him off with the force of a bull's kick. Jordan went flying, rolling across the snow. All that saved him from striking the fiery barrier was the granite pillar. He hit it broadside, hard enough to break ribs.

Legion was already on his feet. The demon dropped his own sword into the snow and unsheathed the monk's blade from his black belly and came at Jordan, the weapon raised high. Jordan lunged away, going for the dagger he had abandoned. Only too late did he realize his mistake.

Legion stepped past him and brought the sword down, slamming the jade-encrusted pommel onto the green diamond. The gem shattered beneath it, as did the granite chalice underneath. The column of green fire extinguished, blown out like a snuffed candle.

Again the lake exploded along this bank. The entire surface buckled upward as if punched from below. Larger beasts rose to the surface, things still barely seen: the roll of an immense black eye, a flurry of black tentacles. Jordan sensed these creatures were older and darker than the minor demons loosed so far.

Beyond that monstrous upwelling, Lucifer looked down from his throne, his face unreadable. The cone of white light still held the dark angel trapped, but for how long? That purity of whiteness now ran with streaks of shadows, reflecting the damage done to his prison.

As if knowing this, Lucifer shifted higher in his throne, breaking more links in the chains that bound him.

The ground quaked and trembled with his efforts.

Legion faced Jordan, the demon's smile triumphant. "The time of man is finally at an end."

12:10 P.M.

Erin huddled under Rhun as the quakes subsided. She had watched the emerald column go dark, saw the ice on the far side shatter open exposing a roil of monstrous beasts. New cracks skittered across the lake.

Christian and Sophia dragged the chest to a patch of solid ice, hounded by more creatures, the beasts plainly growing bolder at the change of circumstance.

Erin searched for Jordan, but a heavy black steam rose from the lake by that shore, obscuring her view.

Rhun still clutched her throat with his one hand as he leaned back. "Erin, what do you mean you know what to do?" he asked.

She understood the subtext to his question: *What do you believe you can do this close to death?*

She answered him silently, *What I can.*

She clutched the Blood Gospel to her chest with one arm, picturing the lines of Enochian script filling its pages. She knew the truth with absolute certainty, but still the words refused to come out. She was too stunned at what she had come to understand: the true purpose behind this lost Gospel of Christ.

The book was not written to help *humans* unleash their divinity. It had been written for a single being, one angel, to redeem himself: *Lucifer*. She remembered the tablet Lazarus had revealed to her in the Sanguinist library, telling an alternate version of the story of the Garden of Eden, how Eve had promised to share the fruit of the Tree of Knowledge with the serpent, but in the end, she had broken that promise.

Lazarus's words returned to her now, as the world grew darker around her.

When Lucifer stands before you, your heart will guide you on your path. You must fulfill the covenant.

She hadn't understood those words back then, but she did now.

The serpent—Lucifer—had been denied secret knowledge, knowledge that might have led the dark angel to make different choices: *the knowledge of good and evil.* He had asked for that understanding, been promised it by Eve herself, but she had not given it to him, and so he had never learned it.

But Christ had sent it here for him.

"I must fulfill the covenant of Eve," she muttered with dry, cold lips.

Beyond the edge of the sphere, the lion stared back at her, stirring as if he had heard her, mewling softly. The cub reminded her of her first cat, a giant barn tom named Nebuchadnezzar. He'd been snowy white, too.

"Hey there, Neb," she whispered, momentarily lost in time.

Rhun bent closer, drawing back her attention. The sorrow in his eyes made her want to reach up and touch him, to comfort him. "What covenant do you speak of?" he pressed her.

She forced her eyes to focus. "The book . . . the gospel . . . must go to Lucifer."

Rhun's eyes widened with disbelief, even outrage. "How can Christ's gospel go to an angel cast out of Heaven by God himself?"

She didn't have the strength to argue, but she exhaled faint words with each fading breath, knowing his sharp Sanguinist ears would hear them. "Christ wrote it to redeem Lucifer. If Eve had given him the fruit of the knowledge of good and evil, he would have known good. He could have chosen good. The covenant of Eve must be fulfilled. Rhun, you must give him this knowledge."

Rhun looked up at the blackened sky. "I cannot leave you to die alone."

"You must . . . this is what we were chosen for."

Rhun lifted the gospel from her as she let it go, glad to be free of this burden. Her empty fingers returned to clutching her throat, as useless as that gesture was by now. She concentrated on Rhun. His face told her how much he wanted to stay with her, and what it cost him to leave her. His eyes flicked to the book hanging open in his one hand, then his face looked scared.

What's wrong?

He answered her silent question. "The writing is gone." He tipped the book, fluttering through the pages, all blank. "Remember, the gospel is bound only to you, Erin. The words are not revealed to any other."

She was so cold now. She didn't know what to do, what to say.

"Perhaps I can carry you and the book to Lucifer," Rhun suggested. "We can give it to him together."

No . . .

He quickly understood, too, sagging over her. "That won't work. While you live, the light will burn you to ash. Only Sanguinists or *strigoi* may pass through such barriers unharmed."

Erin's vision faded. She used her last breath to whisper the ultimate truth.

"You have to turn me . . . it's the only way."

I must become a strigoi.

12:12 P.M.

Jordan had lost sight of Erin as a heavy black mist rolled across the shattered lake, rising with distant screams and howls, its darkness broken by flares of blacker flames. Giant forms stirred that fog, things he knew whose very sight would strip him of his sanity, what little there remained.

Still, even with the emerald sphere collapsed around him, he remained on his knees. The gate was forever damaged with the gem's destruction, never to be closed again.

Jordan saw no reason to keep fighting, especially knowing Erin was likely dead.

If not now, soon.

Without Erin, Jordan wasn't sure if he wanted to live or die.

But he did know one thing with absolute certainty.

He wanted revenge.

Jordan stared up as Legion fell upon him. The demon lifted the monk's sword high, his face shining with triumph. That blade still steamed with the demon's own blood.

It was what had given Jordan this idea.

Retreating from that assault, Jordan sprawled backward to the ground, as if prostrating himself before Legion, accepting death. Instead, Jordan threw himself atop the blade he had propped up a moment ago behind him. The blade pierced his back and thrust out of his belly. That black obsidian sword burned through him like a spike of ice. It was Legion's own sword, abandoned in the snow earlier, the blade now slick with Jordan's fiery blood.

As the demon came at him, hobbled by the broken knee, Jordan kicked out again. His crampon struck Legion's good ankle—not enough to break it, but enough to trip the demon, to send him crashing atop Jordan.

Jordan opened his arms in a giant bear hug. Legion crashed into him, impaling his body on the bloody sword, coated with Jordan's angelic blood. The demon screamed and writhed on that pike, but Jordan wrapped his arms around Legion and rolled to the side, pouring the pool of fiery blood from his belly wound into Legion's cold black body. Jordan willed all of his angelic essence to follow, to burn this demon from Leopold's body.

"Go back to Hell, you bastard."

Legion thrashed and howled, casting out gouts of dark smoke, as if the demon blazed atop the coals of Jordan's body. Slowly, the black drained from Legion's face, from his body. Leopold's watery blue eyes looked at Jordan.

"*Mein Freund . . .*" Leopold said, lowering his forehead to Jordan's cheek. "You have freed me."

Jordan held him, not to keep the man from escaping, but to let Leopold know he wasn't alone, that he was forgiven in the end, even loved. Jordan held him, until the body of his friend fell limp in his arms, finding true peace at last.

12:13 P.M.

Rhun watched as Erin's hands fell slackly from her neck, too weak now to hold them to the ruins of her throat. Rhun lifted his hand to apply that pressure for her, but he knew from each feeble beat of her fading heart that such an effort was useless. Instead, he scooped her into his lap, cradling her body against his, and clutched her blood-slicked fingers. Her head lolled back, her face bathed in the crimson fire of the stone.

How could he turn her, a woman he had grown to love, still loved?

Strigoi were soulless abominations, and it was a sin to create them. He had slipped from that path long ago when he had taken Elizabeth, and only evil had come of that. She had turned from a healer of man into a killer of men, slaughtering hundreds of innocents.

Rhun glanced in Elizabeth's direction—but by now, those dreadful mists had spread, consuming her position. Still, the azure column of fire continued to blaze into the dark sky. He hoped that meant she still lived. He knew that there was still good in her, even if she could not fully see it yet. He prayed she lived long enough to discover it.

His eyes stared out into the deeper darkness, toward where that fiery emerald column had gone dark. Did Jordan yet live? Either way, with the gateway damaged, what hope did any of them have?

The lion yowled at him from outside the fiery bubble, as if scolding him. Those golden eyes stared deeply into his, reminding him that there was hope, that it lay limply in his arms.

"But it is forbidden," he told the young creature. "Look at these soulless demons. Would you have her join their ranks?"

The answer rose like a sigh from Erin's lips, likely her last.

"Please."

42

Erin hovered at the edge of oblivion. Though her eyes were open, she saw only shadows now. Still, she could make out a silhouette of Rhun's face against a fiery backdrop. Past his shoulders, the blaze of the fading eclipse pierced those shadows, but even that fire was slowly being wiped away by a rising tide of black mists from the lake, a darkness that if unchecked would grow to consume this world.

She had no arguments left to convince Rhun, no breath to speak them, but her mind ran with them anyway.

She knew this battle had played out a hundred times before. Even if the others succeeded in rebinding Lucifer's chains, this would not end.

What was forged could be shattered again.

She knew there was only one path to truly end this.

Lucifer must be redeemed.

Erin stared up at Rhun, trying to get him to search her face for that truth, to accept what must be done.

Don't let my death mean nothing. Free me, so I may do what I must.

Instead, Rhun pressed his cold lips gently on her forehead. She wished it was Jordan who kissed her now, who held her now. But Jordan couldn't do what had to be done. Only Rhun could.

Please . . .

As Rhun straightened, stroking the hair back from her brow, she used the last of her strength to let her plea shine in her dimming eyes.

Tears ran down Rhun's cheeks. He shook his head, as if he indeed knew what she was thinking. She could read him just as readily, knowing the scripture that likely held him back from acting, from stripping her soul: *For what shall it profit a man, if he shall gain the whole world, and lose his own soul?*

She tried to get him to understand.

I am not gaining the world . . . I'm saving it.

She let that shine from her.

Rhun drew her closer to him, gazing deep inside her. She saw for the first time that his eyes weren't black. They were dark brown and threaded with cinnamon-colored lines, like the bark of a redwood tree, vibrantly alive in his pale face.

"I'm sorry," he whispered to her.

His lips brushed softly against hers, like a cold breeze from the mountains.

She let her eyes close, defeated.

Then those lips lowered to her neck and sharp teeth bit deep into her flesh.

The little blood left inside her surged out in a single blissful wave.

Thank you, Rhun.

12:15 P.M.

Rhun took great care, knowing death shadowed Erin's heart. As he drew those last embers of life from her cooling body, he ignored the surge of ecstasy and focused instead on the erratic final beats of her heart. He needed enough blood of hers in order to transform her, but not so much to kill her.

A moment ago, he had read the determination in Erin's eyes, saw the knowledge there, the certainty—but most of all, he witnessed the love, that bottomless well of compassion in her heart, not just for Jordan, not just for him.

For everyone.

To save all, she was willing to sacrifice herself.

And had not Christ made that same decision in the Garden of Gethsemane and upon the cross?

How could I not honor her choice now?

He felt her go slack under him and withdrew his teeth from her flesh, his lips from her skin. He stared down, still cradled against him, a woman he loved so very dearly in turn.

Even now he hesitated, knowing what he must do next, yet terrified of it.

Both for his sake and her own.

Then he heard a heavy thump of her heart, the last of her life demanding him to act.

He slashed with his *karambit,* slicing the silver deep into his throat. As his dark blood flooded forth, he dropped his blade, cupped the back of her head, and drew her mouth to that black font. He let his blood pour between her slack lips, down her open throat. She was too gone to swallow on her own, but he held her there, waiting, praying.

He stared up at the dark sky, watching the sun die again, consumed not by the moon, but by the dread smoke rising from the lake, through the very gates of Hell.

Then he felt a surge of hope—as soft lips firmed upon his flesh and began to drink, drawing him into a crimson bliss.

Still, cold tears ran down his face.

What have I done?

12:16 P.M.

Erin woke to cold blood in her mouth, tasting of salt and silver. She swallowed strength with each sip. More blood followed, awakening a dark passion inside her. Fingers rose to grasp Rhun by the hair, to pull him closer. Her tongue probed and stirred a heavier flow. She drank like she once breathed, in great gulps, as if she had been drowning and finally reached air.

It was life as much as it was death.

And it was ecstasy.

Her body screamed for more, her arms clasped harder to Rhun, as if to pull him inside her, to draw everything out of him. She flashed to that intimate moment in the chapel when she had bathed him with her blood. It paled before this crimson rapture, as two fully became one.

She felt him harden against her, rolling atop her, crushing her under him.

Yes . . .

But it was still not enough.

She wanted *all* of him.

Her teeth now tore into his neck, demanding, accepting no refusal.

But then iron fingers snagged her hair and pulled her lips and teeth away from that blissful font. She struggled against it, straining to reach that throat, but Rhun was much stronger.

"No . . ." he gasped out and rolled off her.

Cold air blew between them, and she wanted to weep with loneliness. She craved that intimacy, that connection, almost as much as his blood. Her tongue licked her lips, searching for an ember of that rapture.

Rhun covered his throat with his hand. "Wine," he croaked hoarsely.

Her sensibilities slowly returned, along with the fear that she had drunk too deeply from him. She stripped the silver flask from his thigh, uncapped it, and poured it over his lips. The silver burned her fingertips, but she held it steady, gasping as drops of wine spattered her hand, as fiery as acid.

That fire burned the truth into her.

I am strigoi.

Rhun swallowed convulsively, finishing the last of the flask, then knocking it aside. He stood shakily and pulled her to her feet next to him.

She rose into her new body, accepting it. Her senses expanded in an amazing manner. She heard every noise, felt every breeze, every scent was a symphony. The darkness seemed to shine around her.

The malevolence wafting from the lake drew her, called to her.

But that was not all.

Hunger spiked inside her, drawing her gaze across the lake, to a heavy booming in her ears. A heartbeat. Marking the only human left in the valley.

She wanted, needed it, longing for the heat it promised, for the blood it pumped, craving to slake that gnawing hunger inside her. She felt the source drawing nearer, coming slowly toward her.

She took a step to meet it, but Rhun stopped her.

"It is Jordan," he told her.

She blinked at the name, remembering, taking an impossibly long time to let warmer memories calm that craving to a dull ache. Still, it would not go fully away. She was not safe around him, especially not now, maybe not ever.

Rhun clamped his hand on her wrist. "You must fight it."

She was not sure she could, finally coming to understand Rhun's struggle.

Without a free arm, Rhun nudged the Blood Gospel closer to her with the toe of his boot, pushing it ignobly through the snow. Erin was still archaeologist enough to instinctively reach down and pluck the ancient artifact out of the snow before it was damaged. But as soon as her fingers touched that worn leather cover, golden light burst forth, washing over her, dimming the worst of her craving.

She straightened, noting how even Jordan's heartbeat grew muffled.

She searched along the shoreline, longing filling her anew, not for Jordan's blood—but for the man she loved.

"We must go," Rhun urged.

She allowed him to gently guide her through that fiery veil, letting her old life burn away behind her.

12:17 P.M.

As Jordan lurched along the shoreline, he clutched a fist against the wound in his belly. He was unsure if he was healing. He feared he had cast most of his angelic essence, along with his blood, into that demon. Still, an ember of fire burned in his belly, suggesting some dregs remained, but he felt even that fading fast.

Still, he kept marching onward. His other hand dragged Legion's black sword behind him, still dripping with the demon's blood. He continued through the damnable fog as it smoked out of the broken piece of the gate behind him. After slaying Legion, he had fled the worst of that gibbering, maddening horde, as they gathered in those mists, greeting the larger abominations that slowly slouched into this world.

Let them . . . as long as they leave me alone.

He followed the only path open to him, sticking to the bank of the lake, cautious of the two remaining planes of the pyramid that still blazed across the ice.

Farther out, the cone of Lucifer's white light continued to shine, but even through the black mists, Jordan knew the purity of that white light was dissipating. With the gateway broken, it would only be a matter of time before that dark angel broke free.

When that happened, Jordan was determined to be at Erin's side, if only to hold her cold body one last time. Still, a glimmer of hope remained inside him, driving him forward, one hard step after another.

Maybe she's still alive . . . maybe I can kiss her one last time.

Finally, a ruddy glow appeared through the mists. As he drew closer, he saw it was the fiery sphere around the *Sanguis* pillar. He stumbled out of the worst of the mists and hurried forward—only to find that sphere empty.

She was gone.

He leaned on the sword and searched around, realizing he was not entirely alone.

The lion cub waited at the edge of the lake, his gaze fixed on the ice. Jordan limped over to him, following that intent stare.

Two figures moved out there.

Rhun . . . *and Erin.*

She marched alongside the Sanguinist, clutching the Blood Gospel in her arms. The glow of the book cast them both in a golden light.

He wanted to cry with joy, to run to her side, but all he could do was fall to his knees at the edge of the lake, knowing he could not cross this outer plane of the fiery pyramid. He struggled to understand how she still lived, how she got through that barrier.

Had the book healed her, had its glow allowed her to pierce that fiery veil?

"Erin!" he shouted, wanting if nothing else to see her face again.

She heard him and turned.

The lower half of her face was covered in black blood. She spotted him, but there was no joy in her eyes, only sorrow. Rhun glanced back, exposing the wound on his own throat.

Jordan knew the truth. It was not the book that had healed her; it was not the glow that had let her pass the barrier unharmed.

I've lost her.

Rhun touched Erin's arm, and with one last desolate look, she turned away.

"She is gone," a voice spoke behind him. It was Elizabeth, soaked in blood, most of it her own.

Jordan glanced toward the fiery blue pillar on that side, where Elizabeth had been guarding the *Aqua* stone. It still blazed strongly.

"I was driven away," Elizabeth explained. "Some massive beast, churning with tentacles . . ."

Jordan didn't care. He returned his attention to Erin.

Elizabeth confirmed his worst fear. "I hear no heartbeat."

A tired sadness filled the woman's words—mourning not his loss, but her own.

Elizabeth sank to her knees beside him. As a *strigoi*, she could have crossed that barrier, gone out onto the ice. But she plainly had no reason.

Rhun was lost to her, too.

43

Erin wanted to turn around, to go running back to Jordan.

Rhun must have read her desire—not because they were blood-bonded, but simply because he knew her heart, even this new silenced one.

"You must go to Lucifer," Rhun said. "That is your destiny now."

She knew he was right, so she continued across the ice, clutching the Blood Gospel to her chest, taking strength from it to keep going. With each step, the book cast out its glow more brightly, pushing back against the darkness, burning through the heavier mists.

A scatter of twisted beasts came charging toward them, breaking away from the siege around Christian and Sophia. Something black shot out of the mists overhead and dove at them. Erin barely got a look at the featherless, reptilian shape before it struck that golden light around her and burst into flames.

Rhun tugged her aside as its body crashed to the ice.

Upon seeing this, the other beasts split away, fleeing that glow, slithering back into the darkness, wanting nothing more to do with that golden light.

She and Rhun hurried on, careful of the cracks in the ice, winding their way toward Christian and Sophia. The pair was not doing well. They were an island in a roiling mass of demons.

Christian had removed the sacred chain from the chest and slung the heavy links around his neck, even though the silver must burn him. He whipped the loose end of the chain like some sacred bola, lashing and striking out at the demons. It ripped through the horde as if those links were made of molten steel.

Still, Christian's face streamed blood, and his robes hung in tatters around him.

Next to him, Sophia was even worse off. The small woman noted their approach and perhaps that was all she had been waiting for—holding out only this long by sheer force of will.

Erin saw it in her eyes.

Don't . . .

Sophia gave one last valiant effort, swinging around and spearing a beast in the back before it could attack Christian. But to do so, it forced her to let her own guard down. The horde was upon her, swarming over her, bearing her down.

Christian tried to fight to Sophia's side, but there were too many.

Erin finally reached them, bringing her golden light, scattering the beasts. Something dark and spiny leaped away, leaving behind a broken body on the ice.

Erin skidded to a stop and covered her mouth.

No.

Sophia, earnest and kind, was gone.

Erin trembled, but Rhun steadied her.

"Only the book matters," he said. "It must reach Lucifer."

She nodded. *Or Sophia's sacrifice would be in vain.*

Still, it took a small push from Rhun to get her moving. Soon, though, she was running, flying across the ice, her limbs powered with preternatural strength, aiming for that cone of light. Demons gave way before that glow, but they no longer fled. They hissed and snarled in her wake, as if they knew that they would claim her soon.

And they might yet get that chance.

Even the Blood Gospel could not withstand such palpable evil for long. The golden light had begun to tatter, torn by those mists, shredded by the malevolence found here. The deeper she went, the worse the damage.

Rhun and Christian did their best to compensate, flanking her, keeping away anything that dared to approach. Christian lashed out with the chain and struck a loping hairless ape. The hiss of burning flesh accompanied the creature's agonized shriek as it rolled clear of their path.

Erin concentrated on their goal: Lucifer continued to strain from his throne, shattering new links. His wings, feathered by black flames, battered against the brilliance that imprisoned him. Each strike dimmed that light, streaking it with darkness.

She rushed to close the distance, but her strength faded with that golden light. Her legs ached, her arms felt too heavy even to hold the gospel, and her body began to scream again with bloodlust.

Ahead of her Lucifer thrashed, tearing at the silver chains that bound him.

Finally, she and the others reached the edge of that shining cone.

Erin slowed, stumbling the last of the way. Christian outpaced her and reached a hand toward that white light. He screamed and yanked his arm back, pulling back a smoking stump, ending at his wrist. The light had burned away his hand.

Christian swung to Rhun. Through the man's agony, an even greater pain shone forth: the knowledge that even the Sanguinists could not pass this last barrier.

Erin moved to join them, but as her golden light touched that barrier, it snuffed out, taking away her shield. Before the Sanguinists could react, a chitinous black beast leaped out of the mists behind her and landed on her back, latching jointed legs to her and sinking fangs into her shoulder.

She screamed.

12:25 P.M.

Rhun whirled, striking out with his silver *karambit*, severing two of the creature's six legs. It was enough for Christian to rip the beast from Erin's back and fling the monster toward that cone of light. Its body struck that barrier—and blew away into a cloud of fiery embers.

Rhun tugged Erin behind him, as he and Christian faced the gathering mass of beasts shadowing the heavier mists. Rhun bared his blade, while Christian slowly swung the end of the chain, back and forth, letting it scrape the ice menacingly.

"Rhun . . ." Erin moaned.

He turned, seeing a poisonous darkness creeping up from her neckline, boiling away her skin as it rose. She swooned on her legs. The Blood Gospel fell from her trembling hands.

Whatever had bit her must have been venomous.

He had turned to help her when something fell out of the fog overhead and knocked him hard to the ice. It appeared to be a leathery bat, grown to tremendous size. Needle-sharp teeth snapped at his face. With only one arm, he had to drop his blade and snatch the beast by the neck, keeping those jaws from his throat.

Off to the side, Erin began to topple over, falling toward that white light, but Christian rushed forward and caught her around the waist with his bad arm. He hauled her to safety, while grabbing the gospel from the ice and tucking the book into his coat.

As Christian retreated, Erin struggled in his grip, her head lolling, turning her face toward the light, toward Lucifer.

Even now she seemed determined to complete her mission.

Christian dragged her away, coming to Rhun's aid. He slashed with his chain, knocking the bat creature away, burning a swath through its thick hide. It hissed and flopped back into the darkness.

From those mists, darker shadows closed in on them.

"What now?" Christian asked.

12:26 P.M.

Erin's cold body ran with a poisonous fire. She felt the flesh melting around the bite wound in her shoulder. Her blood flowed heavily there, as if trying to put out that fire. The same venom ate at her face and ran down her arm on that side.

Again.

She had a hard time focusing through the pain, the nausea, but she knew that word was important. A moment ago, she had begun to fall. To brace herself, she had thrust out her arm, already flowing with toxins—only to have her hand and forearm pierce that blazing barrier. The purity of that light cooled her arm and vanquished that dark poison.

Then Christian had caught her and pulled her away.

The toxin was again flowing into her arm.

Too weak even to stand, she hung in Christian's arm. She found it hard to speak as her cheek blistered, but she had to get them to understand.

"The light . . ." she gasped out. "I can pass through it."

"She's delirious," Christian said.

"I can . . ." She rolled her head to face Rhun, letting him see the truth there, to trust in their blood bond, in their mutual understanding of each other.

"She speaks the truth," Rhun said, glancing toward that cone and the dark angel thrashing within that prison.

Before a plan could be made, the dark shadows of the mists fell upon them. Rhun was quickly separated from them. Compromised by his missing arm, he could barely keep the beasts from his throat, let alone return to their side. He soon vanished into the fog, but he still fought out there, revealing himself in flashes of silver.

Christian never let her go. He kept up a valiant fight, swinging his chain, clearing a space around them, holding the demonic horde at bay. But his strength began to ebb, as he reached the bottom of his reserves after battling so long beside Sophia.

His bad arm tightened around her, glancing toward that brilliance that imprisoned Lucifer. He swung the chain once more, striking a giant snake so hard that blood whipped from its body and spattered against the cone of light, burning away with a hiss.

Christian then shrugged off the heavy links from his shoulder.

Erin frowned. "What are you—?"

"It appears this can't get done without sacrificing a Christian." A smile flashed across his features. "I will miss you, Dr. Erin Granger."

She understood.

No . . .

Christian wrapped his arms around her—and leaped high, using the last of his strength to hurtle over the nearest beasts. Together, they struck the barrier. His body burst to fiery ash around her as she fell through. She crashed safely inside, skidding on her hip, a sob trapped in her throat. The Blood Gospel slid up against her, as unharmed as she was.

She sat up, feeling strength returning to her, the black poison vanquished from her body by the passage through the light.

She stared beyond the barrier, watching all that was left of her funny, irreverent, and brave friend drift down in a rain of fiery embers.

Christian deserved better. He had sacrificed himself to get her into this cone of light. She intended to make sure that debt was paid in full.

She picked up the Blood Gospel and turned to face the prisoner.

Lucifer sat upon his throne, no longer fighting, staring down at her, plainly curious and possibly surprised at her presence.

She did not shrink from that black gaze. She had given her soul and her life to stand before him. And now she only had one thing left to give.

She lifted the book in her palms.

Only Eve could pick the fruit of the Tree of Knowledge, and only the daughter of Eve could bring that knowledge back to the serpent.

Lucifer's lips moved, but no words came forth, only a sound like the peal of a great bell. Still, such a metaphor paled from the true beauty of that sound, the voice of an angel, the music of the spheres. The bell pealed again, bright and questioning.

He was speaking, but she could not understand him.

She raised the book higher, hoping he would understand, if not her words, then at least her actions.

"Here is the Gospel of Christ, written in His blood and hidden for many long years. My task is to bring it to you, to fulfill the covenant that you made with Eve long ago."

That head cocked to the side, those flawless features unreadable.

Erin splayed open the book between her palms to show him. As the cover broke open, golden light washed forth. Even without looking, she knew those pages were full of glowing script, all written in Enochian.

Lucifer leaned down, then reached a massive hand toward her.

Erin wanted to run, but she held her ground.

Once those fingers were low enough, she closed the book and gently slipped the gospel into his blackened hands. He sat back again, taking the book with him. With one ebony finger he opened the cover, and that golden light shone even brighter, flaring with such majesty that it burned Erin's eyes.

She had to look away, its glare more fearsome than a thousand eclipsing suns. Still, she felt that light burning through her skull, through her closed eyelids. For a moment, she felt shreds of understanding caught inside her mind: of the secrets of creation, of the movement of stars, of the hidden code of life. But those scraps fluttered through her, whirling away like leaves in a whirlwind. She tried to mentally grasp after them, to hold them, even though she knew such knowledge might destroy her.

So she weathered that storm, waiting for it to finally fade, which at last it did, accompanied by a heavy clanging that drew her gaze back up.

Lucifer still sat in his throne, but his chains lay at his feet.

He was free.

Still, that was not what drove her to her knees. His body was no longer black, but as white as polished marble, aglow with an inner fire that shone from his eyes as he stared upward, the gospel closed in his lap. The black of his sins had been cleansed from his body as surely as the poison had been from her flesh.

Lucifer had been redeemed.

His beauty and glory shone so brightly that the rest of the world seemed shadowy and insubstantial. The cone of light, the flaming pieces of the broken pyramid of fire had all vanished, consumed by the sacred brilliance.

Farther out, Erin could make out the dark lake, the gray mountains, and the blue sky. Even the bright wintry day was returning as the eclipse ended. Still, it all seemed distant, a dream of another world.

For a breath, that view shifted, filling in with a warmer light, melting winter into a summer of green grass, blue waters, and a blazing red sun. Off by the cliffs, two trees stood guard, their bowers thick with leaves, their branches heavy with ripened fruit.

Could this be the Garden of—?

Bells rang out again, impossible to ignore, pulling Erin's gaze back to Lucifer. But these joyous peals rose not from the redeemed angel, but from the heavens above. The chorus was one of elation and welcome, inviting Lucifer to return. After all these years, they wanted him to come home.

Lucifer rose up, expanding his wings, feathered now with white flames.

With his gaze never leaving the promise of Heaven, he reached down to her and rested a finger atop her head. From that touch, a warmth suffused through her, filling her body from head to toe. Joy bubbled up inside her like a spring.

Then a drum thumped once in her ears—then again, quieter.

She recognized that rhythm, having heard it all her life.

It was her heartbeat.

She covered her face, a sob of happiness escaping her. Lucifer had brought her back. She had sacrificed her life for him, and he had returned it.

The bells pealed louder now, with a touch of insistency, a new urgency.

It was time for this bright angel to return to his rightful place.

Answering that call, Lucifer beat his great wings together and rose into the air, climbing to hover over the valley. He hung for a long instant, holding the book against his chest.

Then he looked *down*, perhaps for one last time.

His gaze swept the lake, its surface frozen solid again. Atop the lake and out across the valley floor, inky shapes crawled, slithered, and lurched, their very movements foreign to this world. They fled and scrambled, mewled and howled, knowing their way home had been closed forever.

Lucifer stared down, not with loathing, nor with pity. Instead, love shone from his body. He opened his mouth, and a dark note pealed out. The nearest creatures stopped in their tracks. Again that head cocked, staring below, perhaps pondering the great evil that such demons could unleash upon this world.

If Lucifer left, the earthly realm might yet be damned.

As if seeking the right answer, Lucifer opened the gospel once more, allowing that golden light to shine across the planes of his face. After a moment, a shine of certainty grew in his eyes, maybe even a trace of regret.

Lucifer glanced Heavenward one last time, then drifted on wings of fire back to the frozen lake, touching lightly down on the ice. Sensing what was coming, Erin retreated until she felt cold hands grasping her warm skin.

Rhun . . .

As another dark peal rang out from Lucifer, Rhun gathered her to his side. Relief was writ large on his face. He knew that she was human again. Still, now was not the time for a reunion. Instead, he took her hand, and together they ran across the ice toward shore.

Demons and abominations of every ilk streamed past them, responding to the siren call of their master, rushing back to Lucifer's side.

Erin spotted Jordan standing with Elizabeth at the shoreline. The lion came loping out onto the ice, gamboling around their legs, his every movement one of joy, urging them all together.

Erin needed no such urging.

She broke free of Rhun and ran toward Jordan.

He hobbled forward to meet her, one arm wrapped around his belly. "Careful there, lady," he warned, but his smile was one of warm invitation.

She struck him without slowing and wrapped tightly to him, intending never to let him go.

But Rhun herded them off the lake. "Keep going," he ordered. "As far from this lake as possible."

They obeyed, climbing up to the shelter of those two ancient trees. Only then did they stop and turn around. Under that icy bower, Erin kept close to Jordan.

By now, the demons had gathered around Lucifer, shadowing the brightness of that angel.

Lucifer looked in her direction. Silver light beamed from his face, shining with peace and acceptance, clearly knowing what he was sacrificing by his next action. He lifted his wings high and batted them down. A blaze of light flared, blinding the eye—but not before Erin saw a dark hole open below the gathered horde and watched those shadows fall away—taking that shining star with them.

When the brilliance faded, the lake was empty, frozen over.

Tears streamed down Erin's face.

"He chose to go back," she said. "He could have ascended, but he went back to guard the demons, to keep everything safe."

"Because you redeemed him." Rhun touched his pectoral cross. "In the face of such glory, he chose to serve in Hell instead of Heaven."

44

March 22, 10:42 A.M. CET
Vatican City

Two days after the events in Nepal, Elizabeth sat beside Tommy's bed.

A Sanguinist guard had led her here and waited outside the door. It was a small concession in order to be allowed to see Tommy, to learn where the boy was being housed in Vatican City. She had intended to evaluate Tommy's health and make her plans. And in the worst of cases, she knew she could easily overpower the lone guard and whisk Tommy away before anyone was the wiser.

Once here, she had found Tommy asleep, looking much sicker than she had ever imagined. His heart told a story of disease and weakness. His pale skin was only a few shades darker than the pillow on which he rested his head. And his arms, folded atop his blanket, were riddled with dark lesions.

I must do something quickly.

As if sensing her presence, the boy's brown eyes opened, reminding her of a doe—round and innocent. He blinked, then rubbed his knuckles against his eyelids.

"Elizabeth? It's really you?"

"Of course it is I!" Her words came out harsher than she had intended.

"I heard you were back."

He struggled to sit, but she offered him no help, knowing how he prized his independence. Still, to hide her shock at his profound weakness, she reached behind him and adjusted his pillows to make sure he was well supported.

"I also heard you guys saved the world . . . *again*," he said with a tired grin. "That you're a hero among the Sanguinists."

"I have never wanted to be considered a hero by the Sanguinists," she answered.

He frowned. "But I thought you were one of them now."

"I have taken their vows, yes."

"Good."

She stiffened. "Why is this good?"

"I don't know," he answered with a shrug. "You can make friends with other Sanguinists. You won't have to be alone all the time. You won't even have to hunt."

His concern for her touched her heart. "I have found another way."

She told him what she had discovered in France— that there was another way to live outside the bounds of the Church, without falling prey to one's own feral nature.

"But won't the Sanguinists hunt you down if you try to leave?" he asked.

"They have been hunting me for many long years, but I am still here."

He grew quiet, his hands fiddled with his quilt, and he would not meet her eyes.

"What is it?" she asked.

"When are you leaving?"

She had not finalized such plans and said so. "I've not decided as of yet."

"Then will you at least stay . . . until I go?" He looked at the crucifix on the wall, the door, the window, everywhere but at her. "It won't take long, I don't think."

"I will stay with you," she promised. "Not to watch you die. But to help you to live."

Tommy covered his neck with his hand, plainly knowing what she meant. "No."

"No?"

"I don't want to become a monster."

"But you need not be a monster." Apparently she had not made herself clear enough. "I told you about France, about the Himalayas, about another way."

He shook his head violently. "I'm ready to die. I should have died in Masada with my parents."

"There is always time to die," she said. "It must not be so soon."

"No," he repeated, collapsing against the pillows. The effort of disagreeing with her had cost him much. "I don't want to be immortal. I don't want to live on blood or wine. I've seen that life, and I don't want it."

She touched his hand. It was warmer than hers, but colder than it should have been. She could take him. It would be easy. She was stronger. She had killed and changed more humans than she could count. Hundreds. But he would be the first that she killed out of love.

Tommy squeezed her hand. "Please, let me go."

"You do not know of what you speak."

"I do," he said. "I watched Rasputin and Bernard and Rhun and the others. I know how they live. They're not happy, and I wouldn't be either."

What did he know of happiness or of life? He was fourteen years old, and he'd spent two of those years dying of this disease. She could turn him. With time, he might forgive her, and even if he did not, he would still be alive. She could not bear the thought of him dying.

Those brown eyes stared into hers. They had seen much in their few short years, and yet they still reflected innocence and kindness. They were dark, like Rhun's, but she had never seen simple happiness or innocence in Rhun's eyes. Immortality had been thrust upon Rhun, too, and it had not suited him. He was not a killer. He had truly been meant to be a priest—someone who served others. Becoming a *strigoi* was a perversion of his nature.

Just as it would be a perversion of Tommy's.

How can I force my will on him and pervert that innocence?

It would be a selfish act. She would be taking his soul to spare herself the grief of losing another child. She could not hurt him to spare herself. Not ever.

Tommy must have seen the change in her eyes, because he relaxed and smiled at her. "Thank you," he whispered.

She looked away and blinked back tears. He would suffer, and he would die, and she would not save him. She rose from the chair, walked to the window, and faced the shutters so that he would not see her cry. She would bear up silently and stay with him until the end. She took a deep breath and reached inside herself for strength.

"Perhaps we should go outside, for a walk in the sunshine?" she suggested. She would help him enjoy the time he had left.

Before he could answer, a sharp rap sounded on the door. Without waiting for permission, Rhun burst inside, with the lion cub close on his heels.

"Forgive the intrusion." He looked between Elizabeth and Tommy. "I heard that you were here, Sister Elizabeth, and I . . ."

She scowled at him, knowing what had drawn him here so brusquely. Rhun had feared she would turn the boy.

"I'm fine," Tommy said.

She smiled down at his pale face. "This is the truth."

The lion bounded past Rhun and jumped up onto the bed. His golden eyes locked on to Tommy's, and the two stared at each other with rapt attention.

"Meet Rhun's lion," she said by way of introduction.

Tommy seemed deaf to her, lost in the beast's gaze, as if they knew each other.

Rhun watched and whispered quietly, "The cub reacted in such a manner when he first met Jordan. I think it's because of the angelic blood they once shared.

All three of them carried the angelic essence of the Archangel Michael at one time or another."

The cub leaned forward and rubbed his head against the boy's cheek, breaking the spell and raising a bright laugh.

Her heart ached at the sound, knowing how much she would miss it.

Rhun crossed to the window and opened the shutters. Sunlight flooded the room, but it did not bother her as much as it had even a few days before.

The lion basked under that morning sun, stretching out next to Tommy. A low purr rumbled from that furry chest. The sound was full of love, contentment, and simple pleasures.

As she listened, Elizabeth felt a strange warmth pass through her and away, leaving her slightly swooning. She leaned against a bedpost until it passed.

Maybe I'm not as accustomed to sunlight as I imagined.

Tommy lifted a pale hand and stroked the cub's snowy fur, a wistful smile on his lips.

If nothing else, it was good to see the boy happy. Even his heartbeat sounded stronger, his blood flowing more richly through his veins.

Then she stepped back in shock, staring at Tommy's pale skin. "Your arm," she said.

Tommy looked down, confused, then wearing a matching expression of surprise. "My lesions . . ."

"They're gone," Elizabeth said.

The lion raised his head at the commotion and drowsily opened his eyes. The snowy cub's eyes were no longer golden. They were a simple brown, like Tommy's own.

"Rhun . . ." She turned to him for some explanation.

He lowered to a knee, touched his silver pectoral cross, then gently examined both the lion and Tommy's skin.

"I feel better," Tommy said, his eyes large, as if surprised to be speaking those words.

Elizabeth smiled. She tried to stop it, but hope crept into her long-cold heart. "Is he cured?"

Rhun stood. "I do not know. But it appears the cub's angelic essence is gone. Jordan returned from Nepal with no evidence of that spirit in his blood. Perhaps this trace that persisted in the cat needed to perform this one last miracle."

Elizabeth remembered the strange warmth rising with the cat's purring. Was that what had happened? Ultimately, she cared little for the mechanism of the cure, only that it was so.

"We'll have the doctors look at him," Rhun promised. "But I think he's just an ordinary boy, one cured of his disease, but still a boy."

Tommy's smile broadened.

Elizabeth reached over and tousled his warm, thick hair. That was what he had always wanted—to be an ordinary boy.

After a few pleasantries and promises, Elizabeth followed Rhun out into the hall, trailed by the cub.

"I am glad that you did not turn him," Rhun said, once they were out of earshot.

"You thought that I would?" Elizabeth widened her eyes in a show of innocence that she knew he did not believe.

"I feared that you might," he answered.

"I am stronger than you think," she said.

"What will become of the boy?"

"He must be returned to his aunt and uncle, and I will see that done," Elizabeth said. "One such as I will not be fit to mother him."

"Can you simply give him up, then?"

"It will not be *simple*." She lifted her chin. "And I shall not give him up entirely. I shall watch over him, come when he needs me, and leave him alone when he does not."

"I doubt the order will allow you to have further contact with him."

Elizabeth laughed. "I am not their chattel. I will come and go as I like."

"You would leave the order, then?" He swallowed. "And me?"

"I cannot stay bound to the Church. You must know this better than any other. So long as you remain here, we can never be together."

"Then we should say our good-byes soon," Rhun said, touching her on the arm, drawing her to a stop. She turned to him. "I've been given permission to enter Solitude, to begin a period of seclusion and reflection within the order's Sanctuary."

She wanted to scoff at him, deride him for turning his back upon the world, but upon hearing the true joy in his voice, she could only look sadly upon him.

"Go then, Rhun, find your peace."

5:06 P.M.

Rhun descended through the halls of the Sanctuary with a quiet sense of joy, ready at last to forsake his earthly cares. He walked alone, his footsteps echoing through the vast chambers and passageways. With his sharp ears, he could hear whispers of distant prayers, marking the beginning of vespers.

He continued deeper, to levels where even such whispers would fade.

The bright world above had nothing more to offer him. Before Cardinal Bernard had sent him to Masada to search for the Blood Gospel, Rhun had been ready to live a cloistered life in the Sanctuary. He was even wearier now.

It is time.

From this moment on, the soaring ceilings of the Sanctuary would be his sky. Lost in meditation, Sanguinist priests would bring him wine, as he had once brought wine to others. He could rest here, in the bosom of the Church that had saved him so many years before. His role as the Knight of Christ was finished, and he did not need to serve the Church again. He was free of those responsibilities now.

Rhun bowed his head as he passed into the domain of the Cloistered Ones. Here his brothers and sisters rested in peace, standing in niches or lying on cold stone, forgoing matters of the flesh for eternal contemplation and reflection. He had been assigned a cell down here, where for an entire year he would not speak, where his prayers would be his own.

But first he stopped and lit a candle before a frieze of a patron saint, one of hundreds of such small moments of worship to be found throughout the Sanctuary. He knelt as the glow of the taper flickered over the features of a robed figure standing under a tree, with birds perched both on the branches and on the saint's shoulder—St. Francis of Assisi. He bowed his head, remembering Hugh de Payens and the sacrifice he committed to save them and so many others.

Rhun had said his good-byes to Jordan and Erin at the airport this morning, before their flight back to the States, heading to happy lives. They still lived because such heroes had died. Though the hermit had turned his back on the order, Rhun intended that he be honored, if only in this small way.

Thank you, my friend.

He closed his eyes and moved his lips in prayers. After a time, long past the end of vespers, a hand touched his shoulder, as light as the wing of a butterfly.

Rhun turned to a tall, robed figure standing behind him.

Surprised by the visitation, Rhun bowed his head even farther. "You honor me," he whispered before the Risen One, the first of their order.

"Stand," Lazarus said, his voice hoarse with age.

Rhun obeyed, but he kept his gaze lowered.

"Why are you here, my son?" Lazarus asked.

Rhun gestured to the silent figures nearby, covered in dust, unmoving as statues. "I have come to share the peace of the Sanctuary."

"You have given everything to the order," said Lazarus. "Your life, your soul, and your service. Would you now give the sum of your days?"

"I would. I gave these things willingly to a higher cause. I exist only to serve Him with a simple, honest heart."

"Yet you came into this life through a lie. You were not meant to serve so. You might have walked a different path, and you might still."

Rhun lifted his head, hearing not accusation, but only sorrow in the other's voice. He did not understand. Lazarus turned from him and walked away, drawing Rhun after him.

Lazarus shuffled past the motionless forms of nuns and priests who had come here to seek respite.

"Have I not paid enough for my sins?" Rhun asked, fearing he would be denied such peace.

"You have not sinned," Lazarus answered. "You have been sinned against."

Rhun continued after the somber figure, his mind whirling, numbering the sins he had committed in his long life and those that had been committed against him. Yet, he found no enlightenment.

Lazarus led him deeper, to darker halls, where forms were clad in ancient robes, with heads downcast or raised to the ceiling. Rhun had heard of this region, where those who came sought not just eternal reflection but also absolution, reflecting upon the meaning of sin—both their own and those of others.

Rhun looked around, staring at these faces shadowed by mortification.

Why was I brought here?

At last, Lazarus stopped in front of a priest who stood with his face downcast. He wore the simple brown robes that Rhun had donned long ago in his mortal life. Even though he could not see that face, Rhun sensed a familiarity.

It must be one of my brothers from long ago, also retired to a life of contemplation.

Lazarus leaned at the man's cheek, his breath disturbing the dust atop the figure's ear.

Finally, the man raised his head—revealing a visage that had haunted Rhun's nightmares for over four hundred years. Rhun staggered back, as if struck a hard blow.

It cannot be . . .

Rhun studied the long dark hair, the high pale brow, those full lips. He remembered those lips upon his throat, those teeth in his flesh. He could still taste the man's blood on his tongue. Even now, his body remembered that bliss. Even now, they were still connected.

Here was the *strigoi* who had attacked him by his sister's gravesite, who ripped his soul from his body, ending his life as a mortal. Rhun had thought the beast had been killed. He remembered seeing the creature being dragged away by Sanguinist guards loyal to Bernard.

But now that monster wore the robes of the order.

The man opened his eyes and looked on Rhun with great tenderness. He touched the side of Rhun's neck, where his teeth had pierced Rhun's flesh. His fingers lingered there. "I thought I served when I committed this sin upon you."

"Served? Served whom?"

That arm dropped away, and those eyes drifted closed again, awareness fading. "Forgive me, my son," the man said, his voice whispering away. "I knew not what I did."

Rhun waited for more, some words that would make sense of this impossibility.

"He is the symbol for a lie," Lazarus explained. "The lie that turned you from your pious path of service to a long road of servitude within our order."

"I don't understand," Rhun said. "What is this lie?"

"You must ask Bernard," Lazarus said, taking Rhun's elbow and leading him back toward the entrance to the Sanctuary. At the gate, Lazarus ushered him out.

Rhun faltered at the threshold, fearful of leaving the shelter of the Sanctuary, suddenly not wanting to know these last secrets.

But Lazarus blocked the way back, leaving him no choice. "Understand your past, my son, to know your future. Learn who you truly are. Then make your choice of where to spend your days."

Rhun left. He could not say how his feet found their way up the tunnels to St. Peter's Basilica, but as he climbed, a picture formed of that night when he was turned, how he had been found by Sanguinists before he could sin, how he was brought before Bernard, and how the cardinal convinced him to forsake his evil nature and lead the life of the Sanguinists.

All paths led back to Bernard.

The words of the man below echoed over and over in Rhun's head.

I thought I served when I committed this sin upon you.

Rhun knew the meaning behind those words.

Bernard had known of Rhun's nocturnal visits to his sister's grave. He had known that Rhun would be out in the night, alone and vulnerable. It was Bernard who had sent one of the order—masquerading as a *strigoi*—to the graveyard to turn him, to recruit Rhun, to force prophecy into existence, to create the Chosen One, a Sanguinist who had never tasted human blood. Bernard knew from centuries-old prophecies that only a Chosen One of the order could find the lost Blood Gospel.

So Bernard created one.

As understanding grew in him, rage burned through Rhun like a cleansing fire. Bernard had stolen his soul, and Rhun had thanked him for it, a thousand times over.

My whole existence has been a lie.

As if in a dream, Rhun found himself stalking through the Apostolic Palace, toward Bernard's offices, where the cardinal was still allowed to work while awaiting his trial for his blood sin against Elizabeth. Rhun did not knock when he reached that door. He barged inside like a storm.

Bernard looked up from a desk strewn with papers, his face wide with surprise. The man wore his scarlet cassock, his red gloves, all the trappings of his office.

"Rhun, what has happened?"

Rhun could barely speak, his rage strangling him. "You gave the order that robbed me of my soul."

Bernard stood. "What are you saying?"

"You commanded the monster who turned me into an abomination. You drove me into Elizabeth's arms and took her soul. My life, my death, all of this, was engineered by you, to force the will of God. To bend prophecy to your will."

Rhun watched as Bernard sifted his words carefully, searching how to best answer these accusations.

Finally, Bernard settled on the truth. "Then you know that I was right."

"*Right?*" the word burst from Rhun's lips, ripe with bitterness and pain.

"Now that all of the prophecies have come to pass, would you have had matters go otherwise? You know the price the world would have paid had we failed."

Rhun shook with fury. Bernard had stripped Rhun from his family, condemned him to an eternity of bloodlust, led him to believe that his only path was service to the Church, and turned the woman he loved from a healer into a killer.

All to save the world on Bernard's own terms. To fulfill a prophecy that might never have come to pass without his meddling. To keep all the Sanguinists in darkness about their choices beyond the Church, and beyond his control.

To Bernard's eyes, any sacrifice was worth that end. What was the suffering of one man when the world hung in the balance? One countess? A few hundred Sanguinists?

Disgusted and betrayed, Rhun turned on his heel and left Bernard's office.

Bernard called after him. "Act not in haste, my son!"

But it was not in haste. His betrayal had been centuries in the making.

Rhun fled into the papal gardens, needing fresh air, the open sky above him. With the night fallen, the air was crisp and cold. Stars swept the skies. A large moon loomed high.

Lazarus had sent him aboveground to learn the truth so that he could freely choose his fate, a choice that Bernard had denied him. Denied him and all other Sanguinists. The truth about Hugh and the Buddhist *strigoi* had already spread within the order, and others were facing the choice Rhun faced tonight—how and where to spend eternity.

He ran far into the gardens—until a familiar scent reached him.

The lion came bounding over the grounds, a piece of silvery moonlight running over the dark grass, chased by an irritated caretaker.

"Get back here, Nebuchadnezzar!"

The cub raced up to Rhun and hit him hard in the shins, then rubbed furiously at his legs. The lion was scheduled to be taken to Castel Gandolfo tomorrow, to be looked after by Friar Patrick, but it seemed someone had decided she owed the lion at least a final romp in the gardens after saving Tommy's life.

Elizabeth ran up to him, wearing black jeans, white sneakers, and a crimson sweater under a light jacket. Her hair was loose, curls blowing about her face as a gust wafted through the garden. She had never looked so beautiful.

She swore in Hungarian. "Cursed beast won't listen."

"Yet, you gave him a name," Rhun said. "Nebuchadnezzar."

"The King of Babylon," Elizabeth said, combing her hair back, challenging him to make fun of her. "It was Erin's suggestion. I thought it fitting. And just so you know, I'm taking him with me when I leave."

"Are you?"

"He shouldn't be cooped up in some horse stable. He needs open fields, wide skies. He needs the world."

Rhun stared at her, loving her with all his heart. As he stepped forward and took her hand, her strong fingers intertwined with his. She tilted her face and looked harder at him, perhaps sensing how much he had changed since this morning.

"Show me," he whispered.

She leaned closer, beginning to understand.

"Show me the world."

He bent down and kissed her, deeply and fully with no uncertainty. It was not the chaste kiss of a priest.

For he was a priest no longer.

And Then . . .

Late Spring
Des Moines, Iowa

Peace, at last . . .

As the sun rested low on the horizon, Erin stepped into the redwood gazebo and breathed in the delicate scent of the cottage roses that climbed the surrounding trellises. She sat on a bench and leaned back.

Nearby, children's laughter drifted across the lawn. They were playing a complicated game of tag in their rented tuxedos and fancy dresses, and more than one of them sported grass stains and scraped knees. Adults stood behind them in their own formal dress, sipping champagne and making small talk.

She liked them all, even loved some of them, but mingling among them was overwhelming. She only wanted to mingle with one person right now.

As if he had read her thoughts, a familiar figure slipped through the gazebo's entrance. He had followed her, as she had hoped he would.

"Room for one more?" Jordan asked.

"Always," she answered.

His wheat-blond hair had grown out in the past months from its military buzz. The longer locks gave him a more relaxed, less militaristic air, especially in his current uniform of a charcoal-gray tuxedo. His eyes hadn't changed—still bright blue with a darker ring around the iris. He leaned against the post at the threshold and smiled at her. Love and contentment shone from him.

She answered with a smile of her own.

"You are looking mighty fine, Mrs. Granger-Stone," he said.

"You, too, Mr. Granger-Stone," she told him.

Only an hour ago, she had taken on his name, and he hers, in front of his family and her friends, making vows under the blue sky.

Till death do us part.

After everything that had happened to them, those words held extra meaning. Jordan had proposed to her after they returned to Rome, and she had accepted instantly.

Time was too precious to lose even another second.

She touched the healing wound on her neck. She'd chosen a high-necked wedding dress to cover the pink scar, but it still peeked out the top. Her wound barely hurt now, but every day when she looked in the mirror she saw it, and remembered that she had died and come back to life, knowing how close she had come to losing her future with Jordan.

Jordan gently took her hand away from her neck and held it between his palms. His skin felt warm and natural. Even his tattoo had shrunk back to its original size. He was every bit the handsome and kind man she had met in the desert of Masada, before the Sanguinists had taken over their lives.

They had their own lives now.

Together.

Jordan took a deep breath and sat down next to her. "Big changes coming up. You and me working in the jungle—you digging up artifacts, me in glasses studying to be a forensic anthropologist. No battles, no monsters. Think you'll be happy with that?"

"More than happy. *Ecstatic.*"

Through contacts at the Vatican, she had landed a plum job leading a dig in South America, where she would fight to reclaim history from the jungle, to tease out its secrets, and preserve it for future generations. It would be tough work, but one that had nothing to do with saints and angels. Her life was her own now—her own to share with her new husband.

Jordan had received an honorable discharge from the military and had applied for a program to study forensic anthropology alongside her. He was ready to investigate ancient crimes instead of modern ones. He wanted to come in after the blood was long gone, when mysteries were intellectual puzzles and not emotional ones.

Such a life offered them a future together.

And not just for the *two* of them.

Jordan kissed her palm, his lips lingering there, sending a warm tingle up her arm. She buried her hands in his blond hair and pulled his lips up to hers, wanting to kiss him, to taste him, to lose herself in him. His hands slid down her back to settle on her silk-clad hips. One palm shifted to her belly.

She stared down, wondering if she was showing yet.

"Do you think your mother knows?" Erin asked.

"How could she? We didn't even know until after we got back to the States. It's just our secret for now." He gently rubbed her stomach. "But I think my mom is going to figure it out in about seven months. Especially with twins."

Erin placed her hand next to his on her belly.

Twins . . . a boy and a girl.

Erin relaxed in his arms, imagining a little blond boy with Jordan's blue eyes and daredevil attitude . . . and an amber-eyed girl who would read everything she could get her hands on.

"I was thinking," Jordan said. "How about the name Sophia for the girl?"

She smiled up at Jordan and kissed his lips softly. "That's perfect."

She happily rested in his arms, but a worry still rose in her.

Once back in the States, she had a battery of tests performed. Everything had come back normal. She had conceived when Jordan was carrying angelic blood, which raised a concern about what he might have passed on to the babies.

Or what I might have?

While pregnant, she had briefly died and carried *strigoi* blood.

Jordan sensed her fears and kissed her again. "Everything will be fine."

Erin drew strength from the certainty of his voice, trusting him.

A small, insistent voice shouted from across the lawn. "It's time to cut the cake!" That would be

Olivia, Jordan's niece, whose sweet tooth was notorious. "Hurry up, guys!"

Jordan grinned, his lips lingering over hers. "And for the boy—"

"Let me guess. You were thinking of naming him Christian."

"No, I was actually thinking *Thor*. It's very manly."

"Thor?" Erin pushed him back and stood. "Let's get some cake in you. See if sugar will bring you back to your senses."

She took his hand and led him out onto the sunlight grass. They passed through the scent of spring roses and toward the sweet promise of cake—and a life together.

Acknowledgments

James would like to thank his writing group, who have stood steadfast on this journey from the deserts of Egypt to the gates of Hell. I could not want a better team at my side: Sally Anne Barnes, Chris Crowe, Lee Garrett, Jane O'Riva, Denny Grayson, Leonard Little, Scott Smith, Steve and Judy Prey, Caroline Williams, Christian Riley, Tod Todd, Chris Smith, and Amy Rogers. And of course, both David Sylvian and Carolyn McCray, who have been my right and left hand, from the first step to this last leap. A special acknowledgment must also be extended to the people instrumental to all levels of production: my editor, Lyssa Keusch, and her colleague Rebecca Lucash; and my agents, Russ Galen and Danny Baror (along with his daughter Heather Baror).

Rebecca would also like to thank her writing group, including Kathryn Wadsworth, David Deardorff, Judith Heath, Karen Hollinger, and Ben Haggard for their numerous reads and for all the times they caught mistakes and put the book back on track. Also, a special thanks to writers, friends, and agents who helped me along the writer's journey with this book: Andrew Peterson, Joshua Corin, Shane Gericke, Sean Black, JF Penn, Alexandra Beusterien, Mary Alice Kier, and Anna Cottle. I appreciate greatly having friends like you. Finally, and most important of all, a giant debt of gratitude to her husband and son for their patience while she went off to battle monsters both real and imagined. The cat, Twinkle, gets no thanks as she is never helpful.

About the Authors

James Rollins is the *New York Times* bestselling author of thrillers that have been translated into forty languages. His Sigma series has been lauded as one of the "top crowd pleasers" (*New York Times*) and one of the "hottest summer reads" (*People* magazine). Acclaimed for his originality, Rollins unveils unseen worlds, scientific breakthroughs, and historical secrets at breakneck speed.

New York Times bestselling thriller author Rebecca Cantrell's novels include the award-winning Hannah Vogel mystery series, the critically acclaimed YA novel *iDrakula*, which was nominated for the APPY award and listed on Booklist's Top 10 Horror Fiction for Youth, and *The World Beneath*, the first book in an exciting new series and the winner of an International Thriller Writer award. She, her husband, and son currently live in Berlin.

HARPER LUXE

THE NEW LUXURY IN READING

We hope you enjoyed reading
our new, comfortable print size and found it
an experience you would like to repeat.

Well – you're in luck!

HarperLuxe offers the finest in fiction and
nonfiction books in this same larger print size and
paperback format. Light and easy to read, HarperLuxe
paperbacks are for book lovers who want to see
what they are reading without the strain.

For a full listing of titles and
new releases to come, please visit our website:

www.HarperLuxe.com